ANDREA LOCHEN

Versions

of

Her

Versions of Her
Red Adept Publishing, LLC
104 Bugenfield Court
Garner, NC 27529
http://RedAdeptPublishing.com/

First Print Edition: July 2019

Cover Art by Streetlight Graphics

This is a work of fiction. Names, characters, places, and incidents either are the product of the author's imagination or are used fictitiously, and any resemblance to locales, events, business establishments, or actual persons—living or dead—is entirely coincidental.

For K and J, my very own miracles

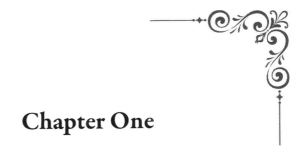

Chapter One

Kelsey was running late, of course. She had planned on making the trip to their family summer home the previous week, as her sister had requested, to air it out and take stock of everything, but the seventy-five-minute drive to Lake Indigo had seemed excruciatingly long and unnecessary at the time, especially when she would be making the same trip the following week and could simply come early and kill two birds with one stone. But Kelsey didn't *do* early, particularly because she worked at Green Valley Pet Lodge, the most unpredictable and chaotic place on the planet. She'd spent the morning wrangling the meanest little Chihuahua and hadn't realized how late it was until Josh had called across the room, "Hey, K. K. Didn't you need to leave at eleven?"

Now it was twelve forty-five. The realtor was meeting her at one, and Kelsey was still at least thirty minutes away—even with her lead foot. At a stoplight, she peeked at her reflection in the rearview mirror, looking for any stray clumps of dog fur clinging to her—an occupational hazard. Finger-combing her long blond hair, she dislodged a wiry gray-and-black curl that looked like it belonged to a Kerry blue terrier. She pinched the errant fur between her fingers and let the breeze sweep it out the window.

Kelsey remembered what Melanie had said on the phone. "She's one of the premier agents in lakefront property, very sought after, very booked up, so if you don't think you can find the time to meet with her..." Melanie had drifted off as her true meaning became apparent. If Kelsey didn't think she could *handle it* was what her sister meant and clearly thought. "I could try to get an earlier flight," Melanie had continued, "but I really need to submit these final grades soon, and I'd rather not bring student work with me..."

Kelsey had insisted she could "find the time" to take care of everything and was perfectly capable of opening up the house and showing a realtor around and that Melanie didn't need to worry and could wrap up her semester in peace. It had simultaneously irritated and saddened her that Melanie still viewed her as the flaky, flighty little sister, yet there Kelsey was, proving her right, as usual. She cursed as, up ahead, railway crossing lights started flashing and a gate lowered across the road. It seemed like the perfect metaphor for how her life was going.

The realtor wasn't answering her cell phone, so Kelsey left a message. "Hi, Charlene. This is your one o'clock appointment at Lake Indigo, Kelsey Kingstad." She paused a moment, hoping the agent would hear the clattering of the train in the background. "I'm just calling to say I'm running a tad late, but I will be there. Very soon. So sorry for the inconvenience. If you want to, in the meantime, there's a dock behind the house. You're welcome to check it out."

Is the dock still structurally sound? It had been a very long time since she'd been to the house, and she didn't know if the Holloways had maintained the property as well as her father had. She imagined Charlene, whom she'd never met before, in a bouclé dress suit and high heels, breaking through the rickety, rotting dock and plummeting into the brisk May waters. "Or maybe not," she amended. "Either way, I'll see you soon."

It had been fifteen years since the Kingstads had inhabited their summer home, four years since their mom had passed away, and over a year since the Holloways had given their notice that they were moving out and discontinuing their long-term lease, and *now*, for whatever reason, Melanie had a fire under her butt to sell the place. When she'd called Kelsey two weeks earlier, out of the blue, she'd launched into her plan as if it were something that they had been discussing and ruminating on for years instead of a topic never broached before. Melanie had rambled on and on about how the housing market was finally improving, and Lake Indigo had recently been named one of the best summer vacation spots by *Midwest Living*, and since she had the summer off and could easily come visit, it would be the perfect time to prepare the house to put on the market. But Kelsey didn't have the summer off, and she couldn't imagine weeks or maybe even months of her perfectionist older sister breathing down her neck and scrutinizing every dusty corner of her life.

She turned onto the county road that led to the lake, densely thicketed by trees on both sides, and immediately felt a small stirring of nostalgia. It was twenty years ago. She was eight again, ensconced in the back seat of her parents' station wagon, dreamily watching the lacy patterns of the tree-branch shadows dance on the pavement. The prospect of the summer ahead—staying up past her regular bedtime, living in her bathing suit, skipping showers, picking raspberries, and playing with the Fletcher kids—glittered before her eyes like a yellow brick road. Now she rolled all the car windows down, letting in the crisp smell of lake water.

It was 1:20, but her urgency to meet Charlene had dissipated. It was a stunning house on a stunning lake. *Why* wouldn't *it sell?* And Kelsey suspected Charlene would stand to make a hefty commission off it. Kelsey should be the one with the upper hand, not the "premier agent of lakefront properties." And if Melanie were there, *she* wouldn't be all frazzled, apologetic, and kowtowing. She would tuck her already perfectly smooth, perfectly tidy hazelnut hair behind her ears before striding across the lawn to shake the realtor's hand. *Melanie Kingstad-Keyes*, she would say. *Thank you for meeting with me.*

The road curved sharply, and suddenly Kelsey could see it—the gravel driveway snaking through the trees, down toward Lake Indigo and their family summer home. She let out a small sigh as the smudge of violet blue came into view. The lake had been named factually instead of romantically. At certain times of the day, typically around dusk, the water turned the majestic shade of irises. Next appeared the peaked roof of the two-story gray-and-white Victorian. It was impressive even from that angle, though Kelsey knew the front with its turret and wraparound porch that faced the lake was considered the prettier approach. She could just make out the Fletchers' red-roofed bungalow next door then the shiny white sedan parked at the end of the driveway.

Her feeling of empowerment waned as the realtor got out of her car. Charlene wasn't the fussy, petite, gray-haired lady Kelsey had been expecting. Instead she was tall, thin, and young, maybe even only Kelsey's age. But her pulled-together aura, her manicured fingernails and huge diamond solitaire ring, and her expensive-looking car, which Kelsey could see up close was a BMW, made her instantly feel inferior. Maybe Melanie's inclination had been right—Kelsey wasn't up to handling the meeting.

"I just got your message." Charlene's smile was as polished as the rest of her. "I'm sorry I didn't answer. My cell phone reception has been spotty out here. But I've been enjoying the view." She picked her way across the gravel to warmly squeeze Kelsey's hand. "Lake Indigo is one of my favorite lakes," she said, as if confiding some great trade secret. Kelsey was sure she said this to all of her clients.

"Thanks so much for coming out," she said, dropping Charlene's hand. "I'm sorry to have kept you waiting." She fumbled with her key ring to find the set of keys her dad had mailed her over a year ago. She hadn't thought to dab them with a different shade of nail polish like she did for most of her other important keys, so she hoped they wouldn't be too hard to pick out. "Why don't I show you the house?"

"That would be wonderful. It's been in your family for quite some time, hasn't it?" Charlene pulled a sheaf of papers from her sleek tote bag. "I wasn't able to find any past sales information on it, so I printed some comparables that I think we'll find useful."

Kelsey snagged a bronze key that seemed about right in size and shape. At least she hoped it was right, because she didn't want to test out a bunch of keys like a dolt in front of the realtor. "My great-great-grandparents built it in 1900, I think. It's been in my mom's family ever since."

Charlene was on Kelsey's heels as they mounted the porch steps. From up close, Kelsey noticed the house was in desperate need of a fresh coat of paint. "But we've been renting it to some tenants, who lived here year-round for the last fifteen years," she added. "An older couple." Her palms felt slippery as she guided the key into the lock. *What else in the house is run-down and neglected?* She wished she hadn't been so lazy last week and had inspected the house, like Melanie had asked. At least that way she wouldn't be walking into the situation totally blind.

Fortunately, the key turned, and the door creaked open, revealing a foyer, a living room, and a twisting oak staircase that had all once been elegantly understated and gleaming but now looked deadened and ordinary in the dim light, under a thick layer of dust, with a few leftover pieces of the Holloways' kitschy hunting-lodge-inspired décor. Kelsey hurried inside to start pulling back the curtains and opening the windows. As the stuffy air assaulted her nose, she suppressed a sneeze.

"Sorry," she muttered as she hid an ugly longhorn cow skull behind a drape. "It hasn't been aired out recently."

But Charlene's expression was unreadable as she methodically made her way around the first floor. She drifted from the living room to the dining room to the kitchen, jotting down notes on a legal pad and occasionally asking Kelsey questions to which she didn't know the answers. Charlene opened up closets and kitchen cupboards. She flicked light switches on and off. At one point, she stood gazing up at the ceiling and crown molding for so long, Kelsey thought she might have fallen catatonic.

The afternoon started to take on a surreal quality for Kelsey. It was the house she'd spent many of her childhood summers in, the house of her imagination, and therefore, so many years later, at twenty-eight, everything felt slightly off to her. The lake house seemed somehow both a little smaller and a little bigger than she remembered it. The touches the Holloways had left behind—the tribal-pattern kitchen curtains instead of her great-grandmother Montclare's hand-tatted lace valances; the succulents in the window boxes instead of her mom's petunias and impatiens; and the beige-and-brown walls, which had always been a clean, bright white—were off-putting and disorienting. In addition, she was trying to see it through Charlene's appraising eyes—*would it be a good property for the realtor to take on?*—as well as Melanie's. *I would've taken down that hideous antler chandelier,* Kelsey could practically hear Melanie grumbling. *At the very least, you could've used some glass cleaner on those windows. They're filthy!*

Upstairs, the Holloways had done little to modify the three bedrooms, the two bathrooms, and the turret reading room, and Charlene became a little more vocal. She delighted in the built-in bookcases and the window seats in the turret room and adored the art deco subway tile and claw-foot tub in the master bath. But most of all, she loved the spectacular views of Lake Indigo that almost every upstairs window afforded.

In the bedroom that had been Melanie's, and their mother's when she was a girl—Charlene asked about the furniture. "Would you be selling the house partially furnished?" She tipped her legal pad toward the antique bedroom set and the colorful tapestry hanging on the wall. "Some of these pieces might be quite valuable. You should probably have them appraised. But if the right buyer for the house came along, you might consider including them. For a price."

Though relieved by Charlene's increasing enthusiasm, Kelsey was also starting to feel a little possessive and a teensy bit resentful. She studied the tapestry, which she'd always coveted. Her bedroom had had no tapestry and only the slimmest view of the lake—as well as the slimmest chance of a night breeze.

The wall hanging was a rich blue and depicted an elaborately branching tree with multicolored flowers budding all over it and had a garland of similar flowers as a border. Four different birds were roosted on opposing limbs, some with golden plumage, others with crimson breasts. Melanie had once said it was supposed to be the Garden of Eden, but Kelsey had doubted her sister's knowledge. *If it's the Garden of Eden, where are Adam and Eve? Where is the apple? The serpent?*

"No, we'd be keeping the furniture," she heard herself saying to Charlene. "We want to keep at least that much in the family." She glanced down at her feet then and noticed a clump of black dog hair stuck to the shin of her jeans. She attempted to brush it off without Charlene noticing, but Kelsey suspected the immaculately put-together woman had observed it from the get-go.

The realtor recorded something on her legal pad. "Well, it looks to me like this house has some really good bones and one-of-a-kind features. And though it hasn't been updated, that might be appealing to some buyers who want to do their own renovations or prefer an authentic Victorian. At this point, I would say all it would need to show well is a really thorough top-to-bottom cleaning."

Kelsey felt her cheeks flush at the implication—she hadn't bothered to clean the place *at all*.

"Let's check out the basement, the exterior, and the lake access then sit down for a chat, shall we? Fingers crossed we don't run into any major problems out there."

"SO HOW DID THINGS GO with Charlotte today?" Melanie asked that night.

"Who?" Kelsey replied, intentionally misunderstanding her. She tucked her phone between her chin and shoulder as she scrutinized the contents of her nearly empty refrigerator. Since she'd left the lake house, she'd been craving raspberries, her mom's zucchini bread, and freshly squeezed lemonade. But no raspberries, zucchini, or lemons popped into view, let alone anything that bore a semblance to dinner. She'd have to squeeze in a trip to the grocery store soon, or she'd be sharing kibble with her schnauzer mix, Sprocket.

"The realtor, Charlotte Hallbeck?"

"Oh, you mean *Charlene*." Kelsey bit her lip as she shut the fridge.

A few hours ago, she would've given almost anything to have Melanie by her side as the realtor had dropped the unexpected bombshell on her. Her older sister wasn't fazed by anything. But now that she had Melanie on the phone, Kelsey was worried she would somehow think the bad news was Kelsey's fault. Because Melanie was so capable, she tended to expect everyone else to operate on the same superhuman level as her. She thought strings could always be pulled or old-fashioned elbow grease could be applied to any conundrum. Other people tended to let her down, especially Kelsey, it seemed.

"Yes, Charlene. Whoever." Melanie sighed in a huffy, teenage way, probably rolling her eyes on the other end of the line. They always seemed to bring out the immaturity in each other. It came with the territory of being sisters who were only two years apart, Kelsey guessed.

"So how did it go?" Melanie pressed. "Is she interested in representing us? Does she think the house is market ready?"

"Well..." She flopped onto the couch, and Sprocket jumped up and sat beside her in solidarity. "She said the house has 'really good bones,' and she was impressed with all of the original features and lake views. She said that since that article you were telling me about came out, Lake Indigo homes have been in high demand, and there aren't many of them for sale since it's such an old family community."

"That's great," Melanie said excitedly.

Sprocket dropped his head onto her knee, and Kelsey scratched his ears. She was about to employ the old "good news-bad news sandwich," as Beth, her boss, called it. "But then we went into the basement," she started, which sounded like a good opening for a horror story. "And apparently some serious water damage occurred—some flooding, probably—while the Holloways were living there, and they appear to have done nothing about it. I'm not sure why—maybe they didn't go in the basement much and didn't know it was there, or maybe they thought it would be too costly to fix. But whatever the case, Charlene says the damage is really bad. Rotted plaster and lathes and a terrible mold problem, and what's worse, the source of the flooding was never properly remedied—no new sump pump or drain tiles or whatever—so it could happen again."

Melanie was quiet for a few seconds. "Well, that sucks, but it's hardly a deal breaker, right? I'm sure a lot of old lake homes have atrocious basements and water damage. But if a buyer loved the house, they could just fix that before moving in, right? No big deal."

Kelsey nodded, reassured that she and her sister had shared the same faulty line of reasoning. "Not quite, I guess. According to Charlene, most lakefront-property buyers are going to be really put off by that amount of work, no matter how much they adore the place. Or they'll write us a really lowball offer, factoring in the costs. Either way, she says it would never pass inspection because it's a health risk. So we'd probably be ordered to do the repairs, regardless."

Again, Melanie was quiet, and Kelsey thought she could hear her sister's husband, Ben, talking in the background. "I'm on the phone,"

Melanie hissed, her hand not quite blocking out the speaker. "*Yes. My sister. No.*" She sounded short-tempered and cross, which was not how Kelsey was used to hearing lovebirds Melanie and Ben speak to one another. Melanie uncovered the mouthpiece. "So how much are the repairs?"

"Charlene wasn't sure. She recommended a guy who could come out and do an estimate for us. But she implied it would be *a lot* of money."

At another long pause, a breathy one, Kelsey wondered if her older sister was crying. But that was a stupid thought. *Crying about mold and a basement renovation?* Their dad had called her Melanie the General, joking that at the first sign of the apocalypse, he wanted his older daughter in his camp.

"If we're smart about this sale, we can recoup our initial investment, I'm sure," Melanie said without a hint of breathiness or tears, and Kelsey felt reassured. The problem of the basement had seemed so formidable, so out of her depth, that transferring it to Melanie's shoulders made Kelsey instantly feel ten pounds lighter. "We just need to factor in Charlene's commission and the other fees and hope we get our asking price. So have you called Charlene's guy? When can he come out?"

Kelsey stood up from the couch and stretched her lower back. "I haven't called him yet," she admitted.

"You could probably still catch him tonight. These contractor types tend to answer their cell phones at all hours. Maybe he still has an opening for tomorrow."

"I work tomorrow, Melanie."

"All day?"

"All day." Sometimes Kelsey got the sense that her sister thought her job was no more than a glorified dog-walker position for a couple of hours a day, or whenever she felt like it, perhaps.

"Well, Saturday, then."

"I work Saturday too."

"But you can still pick me up from the airport, right? My flight's supposed to land at three forty-five."

"Yes, of course." Kelsey tried to sound indignant, but she had completely forgotten Melanie's flight was coming in Saturday afternoon. She would have to ask to leave a few hours early again and maybe see if Josh could cover for her. If she kept that up, Beth was bound to get annoyed. The approaching summer, with families going away on vacation, was their busiest time of year, and everyone needed to pitch in. "Delta, right?"

"American Airlines, actually," Melanie corrected her. "They were the only ones with a direct flight from Cleveland. Well, I would call him, anyway, and see if you can set something up for Monday. *I'll* meet him then. We need to get the ball rolling here. It's almost the end of May already, and the sooner we can get this house on the market, the better. I doubt a lot of buyers are looking for a lake house in the fall."

"Fine. I'll call him." Kelsey hated how defensive she sounded. She had gone out of her way to meet with the realtor, and it still wasn't enough for Melanie. She made Kelsey feel like a juvenile delinquent shirking her duties or a track runner who could never quite gain the lead.

"Great. Thank you."

"You're welcome." She wanted to get off the phone so she could order a pizza or some other takeout for dinner. Her stomach was audibly growling. Sprocket cocked his head at the sound. Then she'd have to try to get ahold of that stupid mold mitigation guy. Kelsey didn't even know what she was supposed to say to him. She didn't want to come across like a dumb blonde who didn't know the first thing about fixing the aftermath of a basement flood—even though she *was* a blonde who didn't know the first thing about fixing the aftermath of a basement flood.

"You know I'm really looking forward to seeing you," Melanie said. "Spending some quality time together." Her voice had taken on that hopeful, maternal quality that Kelsey sometimes found comforting and sweet and other times downright patronizing.

"Me too," she lied, bending down to rest her forehead against the back of the sofa. Her sister was still in a different time zone, and Kelsey already had a headache.

Chapter Two

Though Melanie had flown over three hundred miles with the express purpose of escaping what she had lost and what she now knew she would never have, it already seemed like her plan had been in vain. On the plane, a young mother with a six-month-old and a toddler had been seated behind her, and when Melanie had asked to be moved, the stewardess looked at her like she was a monster. But the elderly woman she'd been situated next to instead had wanted nothing more than to pass the hour-long flight by showing Melanie photos of her three beautiful grandkids, ages five, two and a half, and eight months.

And even while waiting in arrivals for Kelsey—who was late, as Melanie had known she would be—she found herself sitting across from a pregnant woman. The woman wore a stretchy orange dress pulled so taut across her hugely round belly that it resembled a ripe peach. She had to be at least thirty-three or thirty-four weeks along, close to that turning point when doctors recommended no longer using air travel. Melanie couldn't help sneaking peeks at her even though every glimpse felt like a stab to her chest and belly. When the woman's husband approached with their luggage, an adoring grin on his face, Melanie forced herself to look away—it simply hurt too much.

She trained her eyes on her issue of *Scientific American*, willing herself to focus. She'd optimistically brought it along with several scholarly journals she'd been meaning to catch up on. When Ben had seen her packing them, he'd laughed as he browsed through the stack. "Want me to pick up *People* and *Us Weekly* before you go?" On their honeymoon, he'd been delighted to discover her habit of "using decoy magazines," as he called it. While lying on the beaches of Grenada, he'd read paperback thrillers, and she'd perused celebrity magazines tucked artfully inside the pages of *The Journal of Biology*. She wished she'd said yes and allowed him to buy her the silly magazines, anything to hold her interest and distract her from the thought of Ben and his sadness, his hurt looks, and his confusion about her desire to go away on her own for a few weeks.

The happy parents-to-be walked away, and suddenly it seemed easier to breathe. Melanie rolled her neck back and forth a few times then returned *Scientific American* to her bag. She glanced at her cell phone—still no text updates from Kelsey even though it was four o'clock—and pulled out *Midwest Living* instead. It was the issue her friend Rose had given her a couple of weeks ago with a particular page dog-eared—"This is the lake you grew up on, right?" The humble glossy magazine had somehow reached her in the blackness of her despair.

She flipped to the dog-eared page. *Lake Indigo, Wisconsin: Small-Town Charm Combined with Dazzling Beauty*, the heading read. The accompanying photo didn't do the lake justice. It was taken from the south end, where the water was notoriously deeper and rockier and didn't reflect the sky as well. Still, the image conjured a flood of memories, some as dazzling as the magazine promised, some as dark as the south end of the lake, but all of them having to do with her mom, who had passed away four years ago. Melanie missed her. Her mom had been more of a practical, private person than a touchy-feely type, but she had always supported Melanie, and she had always seemed to know just what to say. *What now, Mom?* Melanie sometimes wanted to ask her. *What do you have to say about all of this?*

Their house on Lake Indigo had been standing empty since Ned and Lucinda Holloway had decided not to renew their lease last January. Apparently, the two-story Victorian and Wisconsin winters were getting to be too much for them in their old age, and they wanted to retire closer to their kids and grandkids in North Carolina. Melanie's dad, who was a lawyer, living in Arizona with his second wife and stepchildren, had told her he hadn't been able to find a new tenant for the place, living so far away, and he suspected it would need some maintenance and a local landlord if they wanted to continue renting it. He had advised that selling might be the more practical thing to do, but he wouldn't have time to make the trip to Wisconsin for quite a while because of his busy law practice. Besides, the decision was up to Melanie and Kelsey, he reasoned, since the lake house was part of their inheritance.

Melanie had realized that it was the perfect project for her when Rose gave her that fateful issue of *Midwest Living*. It was something that would temporarily take her away from Ohio and the dreary prospect of facing the long summer ahead with no teaching at Kinsley College to preoccupy her thoughts. It would also grant her a reprieve from too-considerate Ben and his offers of romantic weekend getaways and his constant stream of unhelpful suggestions: culinary classes, dinner parties with friends, bike trips, and learning to reupholster chairs. He had recently taken up training for the Philadelphia Marathon with a zeal she once would have mocked but now found downright heartbreaking.

Preparing the lake house for the market was also something challenging that she could throw herself into, really drawing on her strong organization and financial skills. It was something that could be broken down into easily completed steps and, best of all, a concrete end goal that she felt sure, unlike that other hopeless goal of her heart, she could actually accomplish. Though it would be bittersweet to sell the house, which had been in the Montclare family for almost a century, Melanie couldn't help feeling like it would set her mom free, in a way. It would give both her and Kelsey closure that, years later, Melanie still hadn't been able to achieve.

Of course, seeing her little sister, working side by side on the house together, and strengthening their bond was an added bonus. Melanie hadn't seen Kelsey since last Christmas, when they'd flown to Tucson to celebrate with their dad and his new family. But Melanie had been so obsessed with ovulation tests at the time that she hadn't spent much of the week trimming the tree or baking cookies with Kelsey and their significantly younger stepsiblings. They spoke on the phone about once a month, but Kelsey was often the one to end the call, usually because of some dog-related excuse. Sometimes Melanie got the feeling her sister found her tedious.

Her cell phone chirped and lit up with a new text message.

Just getting off highway. Be there in five.

Arrivals, American Airlines, Melanie typed back. *I'll meet you outside. By the way, you really shouldn't be texting and driving.*

She slipped her magazine and cell phone back into her carry-on bag and hoisted it over her shoulder. After popping up the handle on her suitcase, she started rolling it toward the exit. As promised, five minutes later—though it was a full thirty minutes later than the time Melanie had told Kelsey to pick her up, and truly forty minutes later since Melanie's flight had landed early, though Melanie wouldn't hold her accountable for that—Kelsey's light-blue little beater of a car pulled up in front of the loading area.

Kelsey hopped out of the front seat, slammed the door, and dashed around the car to embrace Melanie. They were the same exact height, five foot five, so Melanie's face was buried in Kelsey's wild blond mane, which smelled faintly of oatmeal. It would be easy to hate a girl for that kind of hair, which was long, wavy, and naturally the color of ash wood—mermaid hair, Melanie had always thought of it as—if Kelsey had been the least bit vain about it. But as it was, she hardly bothered to run a brush through it or have it trimmed regularly, and she treated it as though it were a friendly but often troublesome pet that couldn't be tamed instead of the spectacular, head-turning hair it truly was.

"Welcome home," Kelsey said. "Oh crap! I hope I didn't just lock my keys in the car with it running." She stepped backward out of their hug and widened her eyes in panic.

"Don't worry. The windows are rolled down," Melanie pointed out. "Should I put my bags in the trunk?"

"We'd better. The back seat is Sprocket's territory, and I'm sorry to say I haven't had a chance to vacuum it out in a while." She took the suitcase from Melanie and wheeled it over to the car. "Standard schnauzers aren't supposed to shed much, but Sprocket sheds like a fiend, so I guess it's the 'other' in his bloodline that makes him lose so much of his fur year-round. I try to clip him every other month, but he's so scared of the clippers that it just hardly seems worth it sometimes..." She drifted off suddenly then looked up with a bright smile. "Hey. How was your flight?"

"It was fine," Melanie said, settling into the passenger seat. The gray fabric roof lining was drooping down, brushing the crown of her head and making her feel a little claustrophobic. She ordered herself not to say anything about it. *Doesn't the lining need to be intact to properly house all the side and curtain airbags?* But she doubted the old car had airbags in the steering wheel and dashboard, much less side and curtain airbags. She was lucky it had functional seat belts. She held her arm protectively against her abdomen for a second before remembering there was no longer anything there to protect.

"It was nothing like that miserable ten-hour, two-stop flight to Tucson," she abruptly added. "Maybe we can persuade Dad to let you host Christmas this year. Do you think he and Laila would come? It's kind of a nice midpoint between Arizona and Ohio, and I don't know about you, but to me, Christmas just isn't Christmas without the snow."

"Ummm..." Kelsey struggled to shift the car into gear. She jerked back into the flow of traffic without signaling or even looking over her shoulder. "My apartment is kind of small to host five people. Seven with you and Ben."

"I'm sure they'd insist on staying in a hotel. Something to think about, anyway." Melanie watched the airport getting smaller in the distance, the planes taking off and landing, all the cars driving away to their separate, chosen destinations. "How far is it to the lake house from here?"

"Two hours, at least. But it's only an hour to my place in Bartlett."

Melanie gave her a puzzled look. "But we're going to the lake house, right? I'm dying to see it after all these years. And I really want to check out the basement situation and maybe get started cleaning and sorting through stuff right away."

"Melanie..." Kelsey said, her voice strained. "It's almost four thirty already"—*Believe me, I know*, Melanie thought—"and by the time we get out to Lake Indigo, it will be close to six thirty, and we won't be able to stay for very long, anyway, because I'll need to get home to feed and walk Sprocket. Why don't we just go there tomorrow? I have the whole day off, and we can leave bright and early. I promise. That way, tonight we can just grab some dinner and catch up, and you can just relax."

Relaxing was the absolute last thing she wanted to do. If Ben or her doctor told her to "just relax" one more time, she thought she might scream. She wanted to dig into the soil and plant purple-and-white annuals like her mom had shown her. She wanted to paint a room or dust baseboards or just do something, *anything* useful toward reaching her goal.

"Oh, I think you misunderstood," she said. "While I'm here, I really want to stay at the lake house. Like the old days."

Kelsey nodded. "That's fine, but just not for tonight. Believe me—everything is covered by at least an inch of dust, there's no food, and God knows what shape the plumbing is in after the basement problems. Besides, you won't have a car, so if you need to go somewhere for any reason, you'll be stranded until I come back."

"I'll be okay." Melanie forced herself to chuckle. "I've gone camping hundreds of times. How different can it be? And if I need to go to town to pick anything up, I can just walk or row there like we did as kids."

Kelsey turned to gape at her. Her blue eyes were spaced a little too far apart, and her nose was a little too beaky, like their father's, which tempered the effect of those gorgeous locks, but still, Melanie thought her little sister was far prettier than she knew—even in her standard uniform of jeans and a T-shirt and with a light dusting of dog hair all over her. She had a straightforwardness about her, a kind of purity.

"I just don't think it's a good idea," Kelsey said. "Not until we're sure everything's totally livable and safe. There's not even good cell phone reception out there if you had an emergency. What would Ben think about it?"

"Whoa. You're starting to sound like me," Melanie teased. She was touched by her sister's concern, but the more reasons Kelsey listed off as to why she shouldn't stay in Lake Indigo that night, the more determined Melanie became. She couldn't explain it, but she felt like the house was calling to her, drawing her into the past and the years when her family had been a solid four-person unit instead of the limping creature it had become. Standing in the lake house's foyer felt like a physical craving at that point. "Tomorrow, you can help me pick up a rental car, okay? Then I won't be such a stranded damsel in distress."

Kelsey rolled up the windows and turned on the windshield wipers as a light drizzle started to fall. "Are you sure you don't want to just spend the night with me? I made up the guest bed and everything. And you've never even met Sprocket."

"Aw, thanks, Kels-Bels. I would love that. But maybe next weekend once we've made some progress on the house? You know me. I'm just too anxious to enjoy myself until I've at least gotten my feet wet." She ducked her head under the feathery weight of the saggy ceiling lining and thought, *Almost there now*.

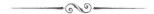

IT HAD STARTED RAINING in earnest twenty minutes after Kelsey left, so any plans Melanie had entertained about walking the path around the lake or taking the rowboat across to Dern's Market to pick up some food and cleaning supplies were quickly quashed. The rain's steady patter against the windows made the lake house feel somehow both sheltered and cozy as well as achingly desolate. She turned on every light as she walked from room to room until the Victorian was all lit up like it had been on the nights her parents threw their boisterous parties. She traced her fingers in the dust—Kelsey really hadn't been exaggerating—drawing curlicues, and observed the tacky changes Ned and Lucinda had made, thinking of how best to undo them. Melanie had already made a mental list of about fifteen different tasks she needed to do before she reached the second floor.

Her old bedroom, she was pleased to see, had mostly been untouched. Even the *Tree of Life* tapestry was still in place, hanging directly across the room from her black walnut headboard. The sight of it, with its brilliantly feathered birds, as familiar and dear to her as old friends, was almost enough to make her cry. The bird-bejeweled tree had been the last thing she'd seen before sleep every night and the first thing she'd laid eyes on every morning in her childhood summers there. Her mom must have also memorized every detail of the tapestry from sleeping in the same bed as a girl and wanted it to serve as a connection between her and her first-born daughter across the years. Melanie knew that because her father had once proposed having the wall hanging professionally cleaned and packed away in storage, saying it was too valuable to risk getting soiled or torn. But her mom had been adamant that the tapestry wouldn't be moved as long as they lived in the house.

Melanie finished her inspection of the house, saving the basement for last, which was unfortunately just as bad as Charlene and Kelsey had made it out to be—maybe worse. Particularly distressing to her were the washer and dryer—she'd been hoping to use them that night to freshen up the musty quilt and sheets she'd found in the linen closet before she went to bed—which seemed rusted to their electric sockets. She was worried she might burn down the house if she tried to run them, and she suspected both appliances would need to be replaced as well as all the electrical wiring in the basement. *Did the Holloways have flood insurance?* Even so, there had to be a statute of limitations on that kind of thing, and she had no way of knowing when the damage had occurred. The thought of sending a strongly worded letter of reproach to them in North Carolina made her feel slightly better as she mounted the creaky basement stairs.

She found a forgotten, dusty bottle of Malbec on the top shelf of the kitchen pantry, wiped the bottle off, and opened it with a twisted wire coat hanger, a trick a friend had shown her that made her feel a bit like MacGyver. No reason to abstain from alcohol anymore. When she found no glasses, she sipped it straight from the bottle. Thank goodness Ben couldn't see how pathetic she was acting. She hadn't heard her phone ring but found a voicemail from him, already a few hours old.

"Hey, Mel. Hope you had a good flight. Can you just call me to let me know you got there safely? I miss you already. Hope you and

Kelsey are having some nice 'sisterly bonding' time tonight. I know I've expressed my doubts about this whole plan of yours, but I want you to know that I support you and whatever you need to do right now to get through this. I just can't help wishing that we could get through this together, side by side. So if you change your mind or need some help, remember I still have a couple weeks of vacation coming my way, and I'd love to see your family's old summer home. Just say the word. Okay? I love you, Mel. So much. No matter what."

Her heart clenched in a way that she had come to understand wasn't a physical heart attack but an equally unbearable emotional pain that differed only because it meant she wasn't dying. She would somehow live through it. It wasn't much of a consolation.

Since her cell phone had only one reception bar, just enough to maybe sneak him a text message, she had the perfect excuse for not calling. Feeling guilty, she typed, *Got here safe and sound. Lots to do and not great cell reception. Try to call you tomorrow night? Miss and love you so much too! XOXO.*

She carried the Malbec and the in-flight package of pretzels up to her bedroom. In between bites and swigs, she tried to think of innovative ways to use the items she'd packed in her suitcase to tidy up her bedroom and the small bathroom she had shared with Kelsey when they were kids. The plastic canister of wet wipes worked great on the sink, the toilet seat, and the bathroom's dingy tile floor. The microfiber cloth she ordinarily used to wipe off her laptop screen took care of most of the dust on the headboard and nightstand, and the clean-linen-scented room-freshening spray provided a temporary fix to the mustiness of the bedding she'd have to sleep on—if she ever felt like going to sleep. The more she cleaned—and the more wine she drank—the more renewed and energized she felt.

"What do you think, Mom?" she asked, knowing she was being a tad theatrical but not minding since she was all alone and she'd drunk half a bottle of wine by then. "Not bad considering I don't even have Lysol and a sponge, right?"

Melanie walked toward the midnight-blue tapestry, wondering how someone even went about cleaning something so old and treasured. She could probably look up a how-to blog or video as soon as she had the Internet connected. It was most likely a time-consuming process involving a soft-bristled toothbrush and diluted baby shampoo or something. Or maybe she should simply whack it with a carpet beater. Up close, the fibers were even more densely woven together than she had imagined, but a graying fuzziness rested over the otherwise vibrant colors. She doubted it had been cleaned in the last few decades, not since Grandma Dot, maybe.

She reached out one timid finger to lift the edge of the tapestry away from the wall. Her parents had forbidden her to touch the tapestry as a child, and it had been impressed upon her, over and over again, how the oils on her hands could harm it, how she was not to lay one finger on it, not even to stroke her beloved birds, which looked so soft and realistic in certain lights—no, not even once. So she felt a little guilty when her nail and the pad of her finger came into contact with the scratchy backing of the tapestry and she gave a slight forward tug. It was heavy and would be more difficult to remove than she had thought. She slid her whole hand behind the tapestry and gently pulled again. Yes, she would definitely need Kelsey's help to take it down for a proper cleaning.

As it fell back against the wall, faintly disturbing the still air, Melanie noticed something that had been hidden behind it—a long, thin crack that ran from floor to ceiling. It was too straight and uniform to be a flaw in the wall. She drew the edge of the tapestry toward her again, pressing her face against the wall so she could better see behind the *Tree of Life*.

It was a narrow crevice, all right, like the edge of a door, and right beside it, at elbow height, was a small metal plate, perhaps some kind of hinge. With her entire arm hoisting the tapestry away from the wall, and her head almost completely behind the rug, she strained to make out what she was seeing in the dimness, and she saw that it *was* in fact a door—a frameless door that blended right into the wall, flush and undetectable, with a tarnished silver flat handle. A door that had been hidden behind the tapestry for all those years. *But why?*

She stumbled backward, and the tapestry dropped back into place, concealing its secret. Crossing her arms over her chest, she took a deep breath. A particularly strong torrent of rain rattled the windows, and she scurried to the bed and sat down. Hopefully, the basement wasn't flooding anew with all the rain.

She brought the bottle of Malbec to her mouth, though it was starting to taste bland to her increasingly numb lips and tongue. She wished Kelsey were with her. Kelsey had always been the braver, more adventurous of the two girls, and Melanie knew her sister wouldn't be cowering on the bed, as she was. Kelsey would be prying open the secret door with a screwdriver or by any means necessary. But instead of striving to uncover things that had been intentionally hidden from her, Melanie felt it was wiser and safer to simply let them be.

Her cell phone chirped, and Melanie nearly jumped off the bed. But it was only a text message from Kelsey: *Hope you're holding up in this storm! The place isn't haunted, is it? Let me know if you get too scared and you want me to come get you! :P But not really... I'm going to bed.* It was almost like she could read Melanie's mind. Or maybe it was a sign that she shouldn't be such a baby and she should just peek inside the tapestry's hidden door, like any normal human being with even a modicum of curiosity. Then in the morning, in the bright light of day, she could show the door to Kelsey, and they could laugh about how Melanie had been nervous to open up the former maid's quarters or defunct bathroom or whatever mundane thing it was that lay behind the *Tree of Life*.

She stood up and crossed the room before she could lose her nerve and lifted the bottom right corner of the tapestry to duck under it. It felt warm and itchy resting on her shoulders. She studied the door's handle, a silver square no bigger than a credit card with a half-circle latch. That would be her fail-safe, her excuse for not going any farther. No doubt it was locked or overly complicated, and she wouldn't have the tools necessary to open it. But at least she could say she tried.

But when she hooked her finger around the half-circle latch, it twisted easily, and she was able to pull the door open. Melanie's pulse raced, and her eyes strained to adjust to the darkness of the mysterious room within.

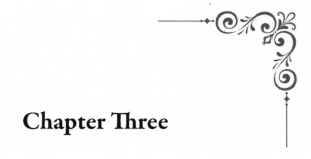

Chapter Three

S omething tickled Melanie's cheek, and she yelped, imagining it was a spiderweb or something worse. Her instinct was to swat it away, but when her fingers brushed the offending thing, she realized it was nothing more than a long piece of string, a pull cord to a light fixture. She gave it a good yank, and a single light bulb suddenly illuminated the space behind the tapestry.

With equal parts relief and disappointment, she saw it was only a small, mostly bare room about four feet by four feet: a closet, really. It had a lower ceiling than the bedroom, dirty white walls, and a built-in wooden bench along one wall. A small stack of items rested on the bench, and Melanie stepped into the room to see what they were—a cream-colored cardigan that she suspected had been her mom's, two books with titles she didn't recognize, and a pack of cigarettes. *But whose cigarettes?* Nobody in her immediate family smoked. She bent down to examine the books more carefully, when a loud gust of wind shook the house and slammed the closet door shut.

She told herself not to panic, but her hysterical brain was already calculating how long she could survive without food and water and ways she could alert Kelsey to her presence behind the hidden door. *Does the tapestry have a sound-dampening effect?* she wondered with absolute dread. She should've followed her wussy instincts and left the daring exploration to her sister. She was going to die there all alone, and Ben would never know what had happened to her.

Don't be such an idiot, she reproached herself. All she had to do was push the door back open. In fact, there was even a regular silver knob on this side of the door. Melanie stepped forward and gingerly rested her palm over the doorknob before attempting to rotate it. She had to turn it and push at the same time, as the tapestry was heavy and blocking the door's outward path. Once she had gotten it open a few inches, she squeezed her arm through to nudge the tapestry out of the way. And to think, years and years of never even so much as tapping the antique wall hanging with her pinkie, and there she was, practically manhandling it.

The rain had stopped in the few minutes she'd been trapped in the closet, and the first hints of dawn were brightening the bedroom. *What time is it, anyway? Have I really stayed up cleaning the whole night?* The room looked different in the kinder, gentler light—the seashell-pink bedspread, the fluffy white rug, the lamp with the fringed shade, the dolls and teddy bears propped against the pillows.

Dolls and teddy bears? What the hell? Where is my suitcase? The blue-and-white quilt I spread across the bed? My cell phone? The Malbec? She rubbed at her eyes. She was overtired, drunk, and nostalgic—a terrible combination. Obviously she was imagining the room as it had been when she was a little girl. Although that wasn't true. It looked like a little girl's room but certainly not hers. Her bedspread had been a yellow-and-red starburst quilt, and only one stuffed animal had ever graced her bed: a plush dolphin named Marvelous.

I'm dreaming, she thought. *I must have finally fallen asleep.* Of course, that made the discovery of the secret door behind the tapestry make much more sense. But it annoyed her that she was having one of those stressful dreams again, the kind that made it feel like she was working all night, figuring out problems, instead of resting and renewing her tired brain. *Change dreams. Go somewhere peaceful like the beach. Try to imagine Ben lying beside you.*

But of course, that tactic never worked. She lay down on the pink comforter, closed her eyes, and drummed her fingertips against her forehead. A loud *thump* came from downstairs. Her eyelids shot open. The *thump* sounded again.

Is someone in the house? What if this isn't *a dream?*

She swung her legs over the edge of the bed and cautiously stood up. There had to be a logical explanation. Maybe Kelsey had come to check on her, or maybe the rainstorm had knocked a tree branch loose, and it was banging against the side of the house. But perhaps some squatter who was used to the house being abandoned had broken in. Melanie shivered at the thought of a total stranger lurking downstairs. She wondered why she hadn't listened to her sister and waited just a day or two until she knew the lake house was "totally livable and safe." Because there she was, a sitting duck without a car and without cell phone reception—not that she could find her cell phone in this strange pink room anyway.

If an intruder were downstairs, she decided, she would sneak out the back door and run to the Fletchers' house, or whoever lived there now, and ask to use their phone to call the police. With that plan in mind, she felt a little less afraid, enough so to force herself to tiptoe out of the bedroom and creep down the flight of stairs. She froze halfway at the sound of female voices coming from the kitchen—at least two of them, and neither of them sounded like Kelsey. Melanie strained to make out what they were saying with no luck. *What are strange women doing in the kitchen? Did Charlene Hallbeck schedule a showing already without telling us?*

Melanie continued down the stairs, feeling like a ghost in her own family's house. Everything looked different, just slightly off-kilter. The walls were back to their original white instead of the drab brown Ned and Lucinda had painted them, and the antique grandfather clock was back in its proper place in the foyer. But framed pencil sketches and photographs that she had never seen before were hanging on the walls, and a lime-green velour couch was standing squarely in the living room like a bad hallucination.

She paused on the bottom step and massaged her temples. *This is just a weird dream.* The female voices were still chatting pleasantly, and she heard cooking sounds and smelled the delicious scent of cinnamon, brown sugar, and apples. Slinking down the hall to the kitchen doorway, she nearly tripped over a shag throw rug and felt like the world's worst spy. She poked her head around the corner. A tall, broad-shouldered lady with curly brown hair was standing at the stove. Melanie's heart stopped. It was her mom.

She stepped into the kitchen. Her voice broke. "Mom?"

But her mom didn't turn around. She continued stirring something in a saucepan, one hand on her apron-covered hip.

Melanie moved closer. She tried again, raising her voice. "Mom?"

But her mom still didn't respond or even acknowledge Melanie's presence. Instead she bent down and opened the oven door to look inside. From that angle, Melanie was startled to see that though the woman looked very much like her mom, she wasn't. This woman's eyes were a dark brown instead of sky blue, and her forehead was high and rounded. She was also wearing red lipstick and large pearl earrings, things Melanie's mom would never have been caught dead in.

"Finish your oatmeal, Christine," the woman said. "Bobby's about to come downstairs any minute, and I need you two to run to Dern's for me to pick up some more milk."

Melanie's attention abruptly shifted to the kitchen table, where a little girl in a yellow plaid short set was seated. She had curly brown hair tied into two pigtails and clear blue eyes, and she looked to be about seven or eight. And her name was Christine—Melanie's mom's name. In a kitchen that looked suspiciously like it was from the sixties. With a woman who looked suspiciously like a much younger version of Grandma Dot.

Melanie reached out for the counter to steady herself and almost bumped into her grandma, who was hurrying to the fridge. "Oops, sorry," Melanie said instinctively, but young Grandma Dot rushed by, acting like someone hadn't almost run her over. Melanie had never had a dream like this before. Normally, she was free to speak and engage with the other people in her dreams, but she felt like she wasn't even present. The sensation of being a ghost in her own house returned.

"Hi, Christine," she tried again, seating herself directly across the table from the little-girl version of her mother. But her mom didn't look up. She only spooned more oatmeal into her mouth.

She was impossibly cute, and while Melanie could see how the child's soft, angelic features would mold into her mom's sharper, shrewder face one day, she could also see hints of both Kelsey and herself in that little girl, and it made her feel a little teary. She wished she could reach out and touch her mother. She felt so nostalgic that she would even accept a hug from Grandma Dot, who had been a bit of a crank later in her life. But her earlier almost-brush with her grandma told her that the dream wouldn't allow physical contact. Even sitting in the kitchen chair, Melanie felt detached from the environment, like she was floating a centimeter above the seat. It was disconcerting, and despite the pleasantness and novelty of glimpsing her mom as a kid, she wished she would wake up.

"Do I really have to go? Can't Bobby go without me?" her mom whined, drumming her fingers on the tabletop. "I want to go swimming and play with the Birdwells."

"Christine..." Grandma Dot said in a warning tone, and that was the end of that, Melanie guessed. She had never been able to talk back to Grandma Dot either.

She couldn't decide if it was highly inventive or just plain cruel of her subconscious that it had created this dream for her. Just when Melanie was missing her mom, there she was again, yet not as the sage, calming force she had been in Melanie's life but as a small, beautiful child.

And the sixties décor, her grandma's unlined face and brown hair, the mention of Dern's Market, the very same market she had frequented as a girl—it all felt emblematic of something Melanie couldn't put her finger on. She was, quite frankly, impressed with her mind's ability to concoct those era-appropriate details, but her brain's possible ulterior motives troubled her. Yes, this house had a history far longer and more expansive than she could fathom, but that didn't mean that she couldn't fix it up and give it a new life with some other family who would enjoy it as much as theirs had.

Sitting in the early-morning light of her grandma's kitchen, across from her eight-year-old mom, Melanie felt overwhelmingly tired. She wished she could switch scenes and go to that beach to take a nap in the sand next to Ben. How unusual to be so exhausted when she knew she was already sleeping. But she hadn't slept well for the past few weeks. Every time she closed her eyes, she saw the horrible stain in her underwear, the blood in the toilet, and her hopes and dreams slipping away.

Maybe she would just go back up to that pink bedroom—her mother's, she realized—and lie down for a while. Hopefully when she awoke, everything would be back to normal, and she would feel well rested and ready to take on the day. She had so much to do.

She wearily pulled herself to an upright position. "I love you, Mom," she whispered and kissed the crown of her mom's head, the place where her pigtails were expertly parted by a steady comb. She wished the girl would somehow sense her ghostly kiss, but if she did, her mom gave no indication. "I hope you get to go swimming today. And every day."

WHEN KELSEY FINALLY arrived at Lake Indigo Sunday morning, it was much later than she had hoped, nearly eleven o'clock. But between Sprocket's terror of the thunderstorm and her drunk-dialing ex, Tristan, she'd gotten a lousy night's sleep. Then she'd tried to be a thoughtful sister by stopping at her favorite café in Bartlett for doughnuts and travel mugs of coffee—though by that point, Melanie's was lukewarm at best. Kelsey was worried she'd be walking into a grizzly bear's den. After a stormy night in a dirty environment, Melanie was probably not in one of her finer moods. Kelsey hoped the sugar and caffeine would help deescalate the situation.

But when she walked up the porch steps—balancing the bakery box under her chin and juggling one coffee cup in each hand—and let herself into the foyer, she was totally unprepared for what she saw. It was like someone had filled a bucket with pure sunshine and spilled it all over the foyer and living room. All the curtains had been taken down from the windows, letting in the bright daylight, and the wood floors were positively gleaming. Kelsey smelled lemon floor cleaner and impossibly... cinnamon. *Is Melanie* baking? After only sixteen hours in the place, Melanie had already transformed it into something out of a Pottery Barn catalog. Even the mantel held a vase of orange tulips.

"Hello? Is anyone home? I brought reinforcements," Kelsey called as she set the bakery box down on the spotless table in the entryway. "Doughnuts and coffee."

"How sweet of you," Melanie called back. "We both had the same idea, I guess. Brunch together."

Kelsey made her way to the kitchen, which she was kind of pleased to see was a total disaster area. Brown paper bags were clustered everywhere—the table, the chairs, and the floor. A sprinkling of oats and a streak of orange juice trailed the countertop. A still-wet mop leaned against the wall, and an assortment of disposable dishes and cutlery wrapped in plastic lay near the sink.

"Pardon my mess." Melanie looked up from the fragrant substance she was stirring on the stove. "I made a trip to Dern's Market this morning when it opened at seven. Although sadly, it's not called Dern's anymore. Now it's owned by the Lamson family, so we'll have to learn to call it that, I guess. They have basically the same stuff with just a few more departments. Like flowers and greeting cards." That explained the tulips.

"You walked there?" Kelsey asked in disbelief, staring down at all the bags Melanie had somehow lugged back on her own.

"No, I rowed." Melanie held up her palms as if she'd been caught guilty of something. "It's a lot harder than I remembered. I think I'm going to have blisters."

"You're crazy." Kelsey swept the dry oats into her cupped hand and brushed them into the sink. "Did you sleep okay?"

Melanie got a funny look on her face. "Yes and no. I think I slept through most of the storm, but I still feel kind of exhausted today." *Hmm... maybe because you got up at the crack of dawn to row half a mile then clean and cook.* "Was the storm bad in Bartlett?" Melanie asked. "How did you sleep?"

Kelsey considered telling her about Tristan's three a.m. call but decided against it. Melanie used to be fun to talk to about guys, wanting to hear everything about Kelsey's life of singledom—living vicariously through her, she said—but lately, whenever Kelsey relayed her "misadventures in dating," as she liked to think of them because it made her life seem more humorous and less depressing, Melanie got really serious sounding. "Aren't you starting to see a pattern here?" she'd asked Kelsey once. "There are nice guys out there, you know. Guys who are faithful and will adore everything about you, every quirk, every freckle. You deserve that, Kels." And when Kelsey had protested that Melanie didn't know, that she'd been out of the dating game for so long and things had changed, and that not everyone was as lucky as she was to find their Ben at only age twenty-two, Melanie had simply said in the most infuriatingly superior tone imaginable, "Maybe you're not looking in the right places." Right. Like Kelsey could simply pick up the perfect boyfriend if she just knew which floor of Ikea to shop at. If only it were that easy.

"We had some real boomers," Kelsey said, "and poor Sprocket is terrified of thunder, so he was huddled up against me, shaking and whining all night, and pretty much hogging the bed. My boss, Beth, says I should look into buying him a ThunderShirt. Have you heard of those before? It's this little pressure vest that the dog wears that's supposed to help relieve their anxiety. I guess it's kind of like the equivalent of swaddling a baby, you know, to soothe them—" She glanced up to catch a distracted frown on Melanie's face. Bored again, of course. Her sister never seemed interested in anything work or dog related, which was pretty much the same thing in Kelsey's case.

"What are you making?" she asked to change the subject. "It smells really good."

"Thanks. Apple cinnamon oatmeal. I had a craving." Melanie turned off the burner and carried the pot to the counter, where she had two bowls waiting. "Grandma Dot used to make it for Mom when she was a little girl."

"I didn't know that. Where did you get the recipe?"

Melanie furrowed her brow in concentration as she poured out two even amounts of the thick golden oatmeal. "I didn't. I just kind of made it up, so I hope it tastes okay. Should we eat on the porch?"

"Sure. I'll grab the doughnuts."

The wraparound porch was the best feature of the lake house. Kelsey had spent many hours rocking on the porch swing, reading books: Ann M. Martin's *The Baby-Sitters Club* series, R. L. Stine's spooky thrillers, and her personal favorite, C. S. Lewis's *The Chronicles of Narnia*. Shaded by the roof and with a direct breeze from the lake, the porch was one of the coolest places to be on a hot day.

Almost every weekend morning, their parents had been found out there, drinking coffee, admiring the lake, and reading in quiet companionship—their dad read newspapers, and their mom read thick nonfiction books that never looked very compelling to Kelsey.

"This is really nice," Kelsey said with a sigh. She took a drink of orange juice and contemplated the gorgeous view before them. The deep-blue water was so still that there was hardly a ripple. Their old dock and rowboat looked sweet, simple, and picturesque. The grass and trees glistened with the previous night's rainfall. She thought she could probably sit there staring all day in complete contentment.

"I agree." Melanie smiled at her and took a bite of her oatmeal. "A change of scenery was just what I needed." She dabbed her lips with a paper towel.

"It brings back so many good memories, doesn't it?" Kelsey leaned back in her chair. "Do you remember the time Mom and Dad let us sleep out here because it was about a hundred degrees upstairs? But we only lasted a few hours until we were covered from head to toe in mosquito bites."

Melanie laughed. "My favorite is the time they let me drive the pontoon boat, and for the first half hour, I pretty much took us in circles. Then on the way home, we were crawling, probably at less than one mile per hour—turtles were paddling by faster than us—and you and Dad were complaining that we needed to get home for dinner, and Dad wanted to take over for me, but Mom insisted I stick with it and said that I was piloting the boat just fine, and if one mile per hour was the speed I felt comfortable going at, that was fine by her. She could enjoy seeing the dragonflies better that way."

"Or the times the Fletchers took us on their speedboat?" Kelsey offered. "Man, that was fun. I haven't been tubing or waterskiing in ages. I wonder if there's somewhere around here we could rent a boat. Just for a day." Their parents had sold their pontoon to a neighbor when they'd rented out the house.

"Or the times when it would rain," she continued, "and Mom would bring out those old ridiculous board games from when she was a kid? Go For Broke and Creature Castle and Manhunt. She'd pop a big bowl of popcorn, and it would almost be even better than if it was sunny outside and we could go swimming. I remember sometimes she'd laugh so hard, she would start crying."

Melanie nodded, a small smile fixed on her face as she looked out at the water. A pontoon boat with about six people aboard cruised past, leaving a frothy wake behind it. They all waved, and Kelsey and Melanie waved back.

"It just makes me wonder..." Kelsey hesitated, not sure how to frame the thought to Melanie without upsetting her. "Since we had so many good memories here, especially with Mom..." She gripped her bowl of oatmeal with both hands. "If we should really be thinking about selling this place." She risked a glance at Melanie, who was still gazing at the lake, so Kelsey rushed on. "Being back here makes me wish we could somehow keep it in the family. I mean, don't you think it would be awesome to have your children come here one day and sleep in the very same bedroom as you did? And they could learn to swim in Lake Indigo and pick raspberries and row to Harris Beach. I feel like keeping on with our family traditions would make Mom really happy and proud."

Melanie abruptly stood up, her back turned to Kelsey. She was silent for a long time. "You were only twelve the last summer we came here," she said at last. "And I'm glad you mostly remember all the happy times we had, but I don't think you have a very complete picture of what life was really like for us at Lake Indigo. For Mom." She spun to face Kelsey. Her eyes were shiny—with tears or indignation, Kelsey didn't know.

"This lake haunted her, in a way," Melanie said, pacing along the porch railing. "Something from her childhood that she never talked about. Remember how she never went swimming, even though

Grandma Dot said she was a champion swimmer as a teenager? And yes, she laughed a lot and could be a ton of fun to be around, but other times, she was so sad and distracted, it was like we were hardly there. Dad was working constantly, so the weekends were the only time he could come up, and even some of those weekends, he was too busy to sneak away and had to stay in the city. Mom was so lonely. They argued about it all the time. Then that last summer, when Jilly Fletcher almost drowned, and Mom and Mrs. Fletcher had that huge falling out... I really think that was the straw that broke the camel's back—the reason Mom and Dad decided to rent out the house and never return."

Kelsey shifted uncomfortably in her chair. Though she knew all those things were true—their mom's sadness, their parents' disagreements, and that terrible day when Jilly had almost died—she didn't believe them to be the damning evidence that Melanie did. It was just the gray, slightly out-of-focus background of her otherwise happy childhood. Her mom had seemed sad and distracted at times in their home in Elm Grove as well. Certainly the lake house hadn't been the cause of her sadness. It was just a natural state for her on occasion, as it was for many people, unfortunately.

"I'm not as naïve as you think I am," Kelsey said. "I know we had unhappy times here too. Just like we had in Elm Grove. I guess I just feel particularly close to Mom right now. And it makes me miss her even more than I have in a while."

Melanie walked back across the porch. In the sharp lighting, she looked a little more careworn than she had inside the house. "I miss Mom, too, Kels. But holding on to this money pit of a house isn't going to bring her back. We need to look ahead and make smart decisions for our family now. She would want that."

Stooping to peer inside the bakery box, she changed the subject. "We're not going to let these beauties go to waste, now, are we?" She selected a vanilla-iced Long John for herself and handed a chocolate cake doughnut to Kelsey. "We have a long day ahead of us and need all the energy we can get. First I thought we could swing by the Target in Arbor Creek to pick up some of the things I wasn't able to get at Dern's. Then I was hoping we could go to the Laundromat to wash some bedding and all of the curtains I took down. And finally I thought we could stop at the car rental place to see if they have anything cheap on the lot for me. Then once we get back, we can get started on the kitchen and dining room..."

Kelsey bit into her doughnut. The entire state of Wisconsin probably didn't have enough chocolate doughnuts to get her through a day dictated by Melanie the General.

Chapter Four

It was still much too cool for swimming, but Kelsey kicked off her shoes, rolled up her jeans, and waded out into Lake Indigo up to her shins anyway. The ground under her bare feet felt cold and silty, like some kind of exotic spa treatment. She curled her big toes into the sand, stirring up a bloom of sediment and tiny fish.

She wished she had brought Sprocket along. Dog-paddling for tennis balls was one of his favorite pastimes. But instead he was home alone again despite it being her regular day to take him to the dog park. All because Melanie had called a few hours ago, pleading with Kelsey to meet with the second basement guy because Melanie had a conflicting appointment at the only time he was available. She hadn't offered up the details of her "appointment," and Kelsey hadn't pressed her, even though it was baffling how someone who didn't live in the area and was supposed to be on vacation already had an appointment to keep after being there for less than three days.

"The first guy that came out this morning, Bill from Basement Restoration—he was the one the realtor recommended—seems great, like he really knows his stuff," Melanie had said. "But his quote was a little high for my liking, so I want to see if we can do any better. I found this other guy in the *Yellow Pages*. So all you have to do is unlock the door and show him to the basement and get a detailed estimate for us to compare. Okay?"

And it would have been okay if Kelsey hadn't already driven out to Lake Indigo three times in the past four days and if she hadn't

needed so badly to go grocery shopping and if she hadn't been looking forward to a blissful afternoon at the dog park and watching
a marathon of cooking shows after the previous day's physical and
mental exertions running errands with Melanie. But Kelsey had
agreed because she'd known she'd be working for the next five days
straight and wouldn't be able to help out, and preemptive guilt
gnawed at her. Apparently her sister had trained her well.

Kelsey's feet were starting to go numb, so she splashed toward
the shore. Over the sound of her splashing, she thought she heard a
vehicle pulling into the driveway—the basement guy, only ten minutes late. *Ha! So I'm not the only one with tardiness problems!* She
stopped and listened but couldn't make out any other noises except
the gentle lapping of the lake. Maybe she'd heard someone visiting
the neighbors. Either way, she thought she should check it out. But
as she plodded toward the shore, she lost her footing in a small underwater divot and went down on one knee.

"Ah!" Her jeans were instantly soaked, and the ends of her hair
were sopping wet. She hurriedly stood up and trudged the rest of
the way in, feeling soggy and klutzy but, most of all, really chilled.
She hoped she could change into a pair of Melanie's pants before the
basement specialist arrived. She pounded up the steps of the wraparound porch, unlocked the back door, and dashed inside, dripping
water all over the hardwood floors. Someone was knocking on the
front door.

She debated answering. Maybe she could keep him waiting another minute or two until she had dry clothes on. But his knock
sounded a little pushy, like the knock of a total know-it-all. Maybe
she could just ignore him altogether and pretend the meeting hadn't
gone well, the estimate was even higher, the guy a total asshole, and
that they should give their business to Bill from Basement Restoration. But she had come all the way out there, for Pete's sake, and she
hadn't been too impressed with Bill's phone skills when she'd called

to set up the meeting. He'd treated her brusquely at first, as if he weren't sure he could squeeze her into his busy schedule, then condescendingly when she couldn't answer some of his questions. *Why not give someone else the chance to edge him out?*

She flung the door open. "Hi! Sorry! I was in the—" Her breathless tumble of words hit a wall. The man standing on her doorstep was a total hunk, not the middle-aged pudge she'd been expecting. With his tousled black hair, boyishly handsome face, and athletic build, he looked like a movie star she would've plastered on her bedroom walls back in high school, or like a perfect combination of Coach Larez, the dreamy Venezuelan transplant who'd coached the boys' varsity swim team her senior year, and her ex-boyfriend from tech school, Neil—the hottie who sadly hadn't had much going on beneath his beautiful exterior.

"The basement?" he supplied for her, crooking one shapely black eyebrow in concern. "Is it still actively flooding?" He leaned forward slightly, as if ready to spring inside, carry her to safety, and secure the dangerous area.

"No." She laughed. "I was in the lake. The basement's fine except for the extensive water damage and major mold problems—all old, though. Would you like to come in and see it? I'm Kelsey, by the way."

He grinned at her to reveal honest-to-God dimples, her one surefire weakness in men. "Thanks, Kelsey. I'm Everett." He handed her his card, which read Floor Repair Pros. It looked kind of chintzy with its watery-blue background, like those business cards she could order online for free, but for all she cared, his contact info could have been scrawled on the back of a rumpled napkin. *Those dimples! Ay yi yi.*

She led him through the main level of the house to the basement door, hoping he wasn't studying her wet backside and wondering if she'd peed her pants. *I was in the lake.* She couldn't believe she had really said that out loud, without any further explanation. Although admitting to stumbling and falling in wouldn't have been very smooth either. She opened the basement door and flicked on the switch, and they descended into the buzzing, fluorescent-lit space, which smelled like a cross between a boys' locker room and a fisherman's wharf.

Though the realtor had recoiled from the sight and the smell, Everett didn't seem fazed in the slightest. He probably saw basements in more atrocious states all the time. After snapping on a pair of latex gloves and a blue face mask, he set to work, prodding the concrete walls and ceiling beams, crouching to examine the rust-stained drain in the floor, scraping mold samples, and taking notes on his clipboard. Kelsey wondered if it would be a good time to slip away and change into some dry pants. Maybe Melanie had a cute pair of yoga pants or leggings that would accentuate her butt. Her damp hair and clothes, in the perpetually damp basement, were starting to make her shiver.

"When did this happen?" Everett asked. The elastic strings of his mask were pushing his ears forward in a dopey, completely adorable way. Kelsey couldn't see his mouth or dimples, just the straight bridge of his nose and his sparkling hazel eyes.

"I'm not exactly sure," she admitted. "My family has been renting this house out for a long time. We think probably within the last two years."

"I bet it was last April," he said. "This area had record rainfall then, and a lot of the houses, especially on the north end, experienced flooding. You should have seen the lake. Some of the docks were completely underwater, and Harris Beach was covered by at least three feet of water." She must have been staring at him in wonder because he shrugged and explained, "My uncle has a fishing cabin nearby, so I spend a lot of time here in the spring and summer."

"Really?" she asked, unable to rein in her enthusiasm. "Where's his cabin? How long have you been coming here?"

The dimple in Everett's left cheek escaped his mask as he grinned. "It's about two blocks south of the lake, on Clover Trail, but we have lake rights and a boat slip. My uncle's been coming here for decades, and I've been joining him for, oh, probably about ten years now."

So their paths hadn't crossed when they were young adolescents. Kelsey was fairly certain she would've noticed a boy like Everett if they had. She wondered if Melanie would be impressed to have a contractor who was so knowledgeable about the area. She doubted Bill from Basement Restoration was a Lake Indigo local. A loose strand of her wet hair slithered over her shoulder, tickling her arm, and she shuddered from the cold contact.

"We can finish talking upstairs." Everett peeled off his gloves with the efficiency of a surgeon, but his mask stayed on. "You must be absolutely freezing. What were you doing in the lake so early in the season, anyway?"

She liked that question, which demonstrated that he'd been listening and seemed like something a concerned date would ask, not a basement repair guy. She just knew he had a flirtatious curve to his lips as he asked it—if only she could see them. "I had only planned on wading in a ways," she said, leading him back up the stairs. "But a hidden drop-off had other plans for me."

"Oh, I've been there." Everett laughed, an unexpected, breathy explosion, almost like a series of high-pitched sneezes.

Kelsey had to turn around to make sure he was indeed laughing. She didn't want to embarrass him—or herself—by saying, "Bless you." The laugh didn't fit him at all, but she decided it made him even more likeable. It was the guys without the immediately obvious flaws a girl needed to worry about, like nearly perfect Tristan, with his hidden penchant for sleeping with other blondes.

They stood side by side in the foyer, Everett's gorgeous smile finally liberated from the mask.

"So," he said, leaning forward.

Kelsey leaned forward instinctively too. He had a tiny vertical line on his smooth, tanned cheek where the edge of his mask had put pressure on it, almost like a crease from a pillow. He tilted the clipboard so she could see his notes. *Oh right. The basement estimate.* He began rattling off his three-step plan for renovations—removing and treating the mold, drying out the basement and replacing the rotted plaster and lathes with new drywall, and installing a waterproofing system to prevent future flooding. It sounded legit, and his quote was a few hundred dollars less than Bill's.

"We're kind of in a hurry to get the house on the market," she said. "When do you think you could have it done by?"

"Two weeks, tops." He paged through the sheets on his clipboard. "I'm free to start next Monday."

Basement Restoration hadn't been available to start until the next Thursday, a fact that had bothered her antsy sister. Everett was offering a cheaper price and an earlier start date with a Lake Indigo native who really *knew* and respected the area. It certainly didn't hurt that he was easy on the eyes, either, although she certainly wouldn't mention that to Melanie as a selling point for fear of losing all credibility. *All signs point to yes,* she thought, remembering the Magic 8-Ball that had determined a majority of her life decisions when she was a thirteen-year-old.

"That sounds perfect," she said, giddiness warming her limbs. "Why don't you pencil me in?"

MELANIE HAD SPENT THE better part of the past two years waiting: waiting to ovulate; waiting for Ben to get home from work so they could try again; waiting to get her period, as she always, inevitably, did; waiting in doctors' offices; waiting to find out test results; waiting for the other shoe to drop. She had read a whole lot of issues of *People* magazine and *Us Weekly* while she'd waited. And there she was, waiting again, this time to have her blood drawn since Ben had persuaded her the night before over the phone to follow her doctor's orders. He'd even found a nearby lab for her that accepted their insurance.

She shifted her weight on the boxy, low-backed loveseat and wondered how Kelsey was faring with the guy from Flood Repair Pros. She was pretty sure they should go with Basement Restoration—Bill's thirty-year-old company had all five-star reviews, and their work came with a lifetime guarantee—but she knew it never hurt to get more than one estimate. That was something her dad had taught her. He'd called that morning to see how she and Kelsey were managing, and when she told him about the extensive water damage in the basement, he'd been as disgruntled with the Holloways as she was.

"Mrs. Kingstad-Keyes?"

Melanie leaped up from the loveseat, impatient to get the blood draw over with. But it wasn't the phlebotomist who had called her. It was one of the receptionists at the front desk, the one with the hairsprayed helmet of silvery-blond hair who had checked her in. The receptionist waved her over.

"Mrs. Kingstad-Keyes, I'm not seeing the order your doctor put in." Her nasally voice sounded almost accusatory. "What was her name again?"

"Sarah Maroney." Melanie stared down at her purse as the receptionist tapped away on the computer keyboard.

"I see all your past lab work but no new orders. I can try calling Dr. Maroney's office again, but it might take a while for us to hear back, if you don't mind waiting. Was today supposed to be a progesterone or HCG screen? I see you've had both."

The receptionist's voice was so loud that Melanie almost winced. She couldn't help glancing over her shoulder to see who in the crowded waiting room had overheard. *Hasn't this woman ever heard of HIPAA?* But before Melanie could answer the question in a hushed tone, the receptionist continued at maximum volume, "Progesterone levels are usually to measure if you've ovulated. HCG levels are to determine if you're pregnant or to confirm a miscarriage. Have you had a miscarriage recently?" She said the word *miscarriage* as if it were something ordinary, routine—a haircut, a manicure, a miscarriage.

Melanie could feel the blood draining from her face. "Yes," she hissed under her breath. "I had a miscarriage. I'm here for an HCG panel." Dr. Maroney had directed Melanie to come in once every two weeks so they could make sure her pregnancy hormones were dropping appropriately over time and a D&C wouldn't be required. She had added that Melanie and Ben shouldn't try again until her hormones were significantly reduced.

Back on the loveseat, Melanie felt hot and lightheaded. The elderly woman in the chair across from her gazed at her sympathetically, and Melanie looked away. She wished that Ben were with her, as he had been for so many of her other appointments. God, she'd had a whole slew, and he'd been by her side at almost all of them, asking off of work so he could be there, holding her hand and making jokes to lighten the mood. But his optimistic brand of comfort had stopped working on her not too long ago. Sometimes she wanted to physically shake the hope out of him until he was as empty and barren as she was.

The year she'd finally completed her grueling PhD program in Biology and secured a tenure-track position at Kinsley College, she'd gone off birth control. She and Ben had joked about her getting pregnant too quickly and how that would look to her coworkers and students if she had to take maternity leave her first year. They had sex all the time—in the shower, on the stairs, on the rug in the living room, and once even in Melanie's small campus office at the end of the Biology Department hallway, with the door locked and their paranoid hearts racing the whole time. "Never again," Ben had sworn afterward, tucking his shirt back into his pants. "Unless you want me to die of a heart attack." They were like newlyweds again, unable to keep their hands off each other.

After about seven months of passionate sex with no results, Melanie started to get worried. She knew the statistics: that about half of all healthy couples got pregnant after only three months, and over two-thirds got pregnant by six months. She started recording her basal body temperature every morning to try to determine when she was ovulating and to pinpoint her peak days to conceive. Sex became a little less spontaneous and a lot more scheduled. She bought ovulation kits to pee on, praying for a smiley face to indicate her egg was in position and ready to go. Many months, she didn't get a single smiley face, then some months, she got a string of smiley faces, and she texted Ben eagerly to come home. *Yes, ma'am*, he texted back. *I am your willing slave. Have your way with me.* Despite his jokes, Ben was starting to worry, too, she knew. She saw it in the new fine lines around his mouth and his subtle, careful way of asking how she was feeling, usually around the time they were waiting to see if her period would arrive—and it always did.

At fourteen months, Melanie finally broke down and made an appointment with Dr. Maroney, the highly recommended ob-gyn she had hoped would monitor her pregnancy and deliver her baby one day. Dr. Maroney diagnosed her with *infertility*, the term like a cold, hard rock settling in Melanie's gut. It was the fear that had been plaguing both her and Ben since the fun, lighthearted early phases of their trying had ended. "It's just a clinical label," Dr. Maroney had tried to reassure her, "mostly used for billing purposes. It doesn't mean that there isn't hope. There are still plenty of things we can try."

We, she'd said, as if making a baby suddenly involved three people: Melanie, Ben, and Melanie's ob-gyn.

But first they had a month-long battery of tests to undergo: blood tests, a painful procedure to check the function of Melanie's ovaries, and a semen analysis for Ben, which he found humiliating. The good news was Melanie's ovaries worked and Ben's sperm count was just fine. The bad news was Melanie wasn't ovulating regularly, sometimes at all, and Dr. Maroney didn't know why. But she thought fertility drugs might help. So they spent the next five months tinkering with the dosage to get it just right, and for the next six months, Melanie took the drugs on designated days, and they had sex on designated days, which was about as exciting as mowing the lawn or unloading the dishwasher. Sex had become a chore—no, worse than a chore because they felt so much pressure in the act. The stakes were so high, and it was so easy to fail.

Ben kept saying he thought they needed to take a break, go on a tropical getaway, and just forget about it all for a while. He thought things might happen naturally for them if they stopped trying so hard. He'd heard several stories of couples who had become pregnant, almost as if by accident, when they threw out their diligent schedules and just relaxed. He thought Melanie was too wound up by her full-time teaching schedule, academic committees, and research project, and the added stress of trying to get pregnant was just too much for her. But his well-intentioned advice only made Melanie feel doubly responsible for their infertility. Not only was it her fault she couldn't get pregnant because of her anovulation, it was also her fault because her job was too intense and her normal temperament too high-strung. She stopped sharing her day-to-day worries and stressors with Ben as much. The intimacy in their marriage started to erode, little by little, and she didn't know what to do about it. A baby was the one thing that could restore their happiness, but it was also the one thing that was tearing them apart. Then in early

March—the only miracle that had ever happened to her, seemingly so small but really so colossal it had overflowed her heart—she had gotten a positive pregnancy test. She'd taken four of them just to be sure.

"Melanie Kingstad?" a woman called from the doorway to the lab. It wasn't the nasally receptionist's voice but a younger, kinder voice. "Keyes?" she tacked on uncertainly.

The phlebotomist led her to a back room with a blue pleather recliner. Though Melanie didn't feel like making small talk, the young woman, Erin, seemed nervous and eager to chat. Melanie quickly ascertained that Erin was a newbie, only two weeks out of tech school, and though Melanie didn't relish the thought of being a practice pin cushion, she also didn't think she could bear to wait any longer for a more experienced technician. She gritted her teeth and looked away as the phlebotomist dug in her veins repeatedly and unsuccessfully. Finally the girl had to try her other arm, and Melanie knew her right inner elbow would be black-and-blue. A few seconds after Erin announced she was about to give up and ask for help, the tech finally found a vein and was able to fill the necessary vials. Melanie leaned back in the chair and closed her eyes.

When she had told Ben the good news, he had actually dropped to his knees on the carpet and wept. She had crouched beside him and draped her arms around his shoulders, and they had stayed like that for a long time. They decided not to make the announcement to their families and friends until Melanie was safely into her second trimester, so the rapidly multiplying ball of cells remained a shimmering secret between them—something miraculous and tender and alive and just for them. Every time they looked at each other, they couldn't help breaking into ear-to-ear grins. Melanie scheduled her first prenatal appointment with Dr. Maroney, who was thrilled and wanted to see her at the eight-week mark.

But the day before her doctor's appointment, Melanie started experiencing slight cramping. At first, she attributed it to a bad egg salad sandwich she'd had for lunch, but when she went to the ladies' room in Cornelius Hall between her afternoon classes, she saw a dark, ominous streak in her underwear. Bright-red blood perfused the toilet-bowl water when she sat down.

She stuffed her fist into her mouth to muffle her sobs. Her baby was gone. She knew it with the same cold, rock-solid certainty she had experienced when Dr. Maroney had first diagnosed her with infertility. It wasn't the normal, occasional spotting that some pregnant women experienced. There was way too much blood. It was a spontaneous abortion—a miscarriage.

Melanie texted her colleague Aimee to contact the department secretary to put up a sign on her three thirty class's door, announcing that it was canceled. A few women came in and out of the bathroom, flushed the toilets, and washed their hands. But finally the bathroom emptied out, and Melanie was all alone. She wrapped her arms around herself to stop the shaking and let the tears slide freely down her face. She stared down into the bloody water, both desperate and afraid to see anything that resembled the tiny, beloved fetus.

One particular clot of blood, larger than the others, drifting on the surface, reminded her, strangely, of the red Betta splenden she'd had as a girl. The fish had been breathtaking, so beautiful it sometimes made her ache to look at it as its delicate fins had waved and fanned in an act of violence whenever she had held a mirror up to its bowl. It had died after only a few months in her possession, and she had flushed it, too, down the toilet, its small body no longer as vibrant, its fins closed around it, still. Her baby had transformed into a fish.

Melanie didn't know how she would go on, how she would be able to affix a pad to her underwear, button her pants, wash her hands, and leave the restroom as though her world hadn't been dashed into pieces. She didn't know how she would be able to walk calmly to her office, turn off her computer, say goodbye to her colleagues, and sit in rush-hour traffic. She didn't know how she would face Ben.

She couldn't fathom how women who had carried a baby for months and months only to miscarry could endure it, how mothers who birthed stillborn babies or had babies born with health problems and died shortly thereafter didn't just stop breathing from the tremendous pain. It had been only eight weeks, and she had been head over heels in love—eight weeks, and now her heart didn't want to keep pumping blood if it was only for her, if it wasn't for both of them. The glowing candle inside of her had been extinguished.

If she hadn't been in a campus bathroom, where anyone could come upon her, she would have lain down on the dirty tile floor at that moment and prayed for it all to end. Because even worse than her pain was the pain of having to tell Ben. She couldn't bear the thought of her husband falling to his knees again—only that time not out of joy but out of grief.

Chapter Five

A note from Kelsey was on the entryway table when Melanie got back to the lake house. *Flood Repair Pros are great, very knowledgeable and* reasonably priced! *Will start next Mon.* Underneath was a barebones, sloppily written estimate for the job on a flimsy yellow carbon copy, nothing like the tidy, line-by-line description of services and prices from Basement Restoration. *What does Kelsey mean by "Will start next Mon"? She didn't offer the guy the job without consulting me first, did she?* Melanie tried calling her sister immediately, but Kelsey's phone went straight to voicemail. She left a message.

Melanie knew she should dive into one of her many projects—painting the living room, cleaning out the fireplace, or walking around outdoors and drawing up plans for what flowers to plant where—before her heart could sink too far down into her chest, like an anchor, making her heavy and immobile. Not succumbing to the inertia of grief was a daily battle for her, and the only solution she had found was to keep her mind and body constantly occupied. But the insensitive receptionist and painful blood draw had stirred up some of her darkest memories, and she doubted the simple act of cleaning or painting would be enough to distract her.

She needed something totally immersive and exhausting, like a swim or another row across the lake—though her blistered hands were still pretty sore. Or maybe she should confront something disconcerting that she had been avoiding for the past twenty-four hours: the *Tree of Life* tapestry and what it might or might not be concealing.

When she'd woken up on Sunday morning after having the dream of her mom as a little girl, Melanie had been bizarrely still *inside* the dream. As she lay motionless in bed, she took stock of the satiny pale-pink comforter and the white teddy bear with the gold heart embroidered on his chest. Through the open window, she could hear the delighted cries and splashes of children playing in the lake. No two ways about it: she was in a dream within a dream, and no matter how hard she pinched herself or how tightly she squeezed her eyes shut then reopened them, she was still in the 1960s, in her mother's childhood bedroom at the lake house.

That was when she had had the idea to try to walk through the door behind the tapestry again. It was how the peculiar *Alice in Wonderland* dream had started. Maybe it was how the dream was supposed to end too. So she'd slipped behind the wall hanging, yanked open the silver latch, and stepped inside the secret room. She sat down for a moment, counted to ten, and thought about clicking her heels like Dorothy but then dismissed the thought as childish—and anyway, she was barefoot, and she was pretty sure the ruby slippers were an important ingredient in *that* magical formula.

When she'd opened the door and pushed the tapestry away, she was relieved to see the room was dimly lit, the windowpanes glazed with rain, and the bed covered by the musty patchwork quilt she'd pulled from the linen closet earlier. She nearly stumbled over her suitcase, which was spread wide-open in the middle of the floor. She reached for her cell phone on the nightstand: six o'clock on the proper date. Thank God. She was so grateful to be back in the correct era that she didn't question why she hadn't woken up in her own bed and why she'd needed to go through a closet to get there.

But that night, she had lain awake, unable to fall asleep, consumed by speculations about her strange dream. As she stared at the tapestry, the scarlet-and-gold-embroidered birds almost seemed to glow in the moonlight. All it would have taken to dismiss her belief in the secret door as pure imagination would have been one little peek, one little lift of the wall hanging. But something had stopped her—fear, most likely, but also reluctance to unravel an enigma. So she'd rolled over onto her side, facing the other direction, and repressed the thought of the hidden room, thereby keeping it a fantastic, far-off possibility but a possibility nonetheless.

Melanie took the steps two at a time to her old bedroom. The afternoon sunlight washed out the midnight-blue tapestry, fading it to a dusky blue gray. She sat cross-legged on the hardwood floor in front of it, poring over the complex woven pattern as if for clues. She leaned closer and traced her pointer finger lightly over the chain of flowers—scarlet, violet, yellow, and turquoise, with frilly, curvaceous petals like those of hibiscus. The four birds roosting on different branches seemed to be two pairs of mates, the males more vividly colorful, with longer tail feathers, and the females smaller and more monochromatic.

She was stalling. Her pulse quickened as she reached out to draw the bottom right-hand corner of the tapestry away from the wall. The long, thin crack was still there—the edge of the door. She stood up, still holding on to the heavy woven fabric. Her hands were shaking. Just because the hidden door existed as it had in her dream didn't mean it was somehow supernatural, she chided herself. It was just an unused closet, nothing special about it. She was wide-awake and not under the influence of any alcohol. Nothing extraordinary was about to take place. She would be disappointed by her ordinary discovery.

The flat, square door handle was right where it had been in her dream, at waist height. It turned easily with a click. That time, she knew to reach up for the dangling piece of string to turn on the light. Her mom's cream-colored sweater was still on the bench as well as the cigarettes and books. She pulled the door closed gently behind her and waited. For what, she didn't know.

When what felt like a sufficient amount of time had passed, she opened the door. She nudged the tapestry an inch or two outward and froze. *People* were in the bedroom—two girls, to be exact. Melanie resisted the urge to slam the door shut. She began trembling from head to toe as she leaned forward, trying to make out what the girls were saying. *Oh, why didn't I decide to paint the living room this afternoon instead?* Melanie wasn't the daring type. She didn't think her wimpy nerves could handle it.

"I'm pretty sure he's making it up," one of the girls said. "Why would there be a sunken ship in the middle of the lake? How would it even get there?"

Melanie couldn't tell if it was her mother's voice. The girl sounded older than the eight-year-old version of her that she had seen.

"That's part of the mystery," the other girl said with a mouth full of bubble gum, which she was chewing ferociously. "I heard that it was a merchant vessel carrying all kinds of exotic fabrics, spices, and jewels. And the captain of the ship had just gotten married, and he had his beautiful bride on board. But the ship capsized in a terrible storm and everyone drowned. The captain and his bride never got to celebrate their wedding night. Some people say that she's still down there, mourning her husband and the life she didn't get to have. They say she comes out and haunts the lake every year on the anniversary of her death."

"Why was the ship carrying jewels and spices? Where was it carrying them *to*? Where had it carried them *from*? The Mediterranean all the way to Wisconsin? Via the Great Lakes, perhaps?" the first girl scoffed. "My dad says this is a spring-fed lake. That means it gets its water supply from groundwater beneath the lake. It's not like there's a river connected to it, and even if there was, it wouldn't be big enough for a ship to—"

"Gosh, Christine! Why do you have to be so *scientific* about everything? It's a ghost ship we're talking about, and the thing you have a problem with is how it got here? Maybe it floated down from the sky. Happy now?"

They paused, then suddenly both the girls broke into a fit of giggles.

Melanie used that opportunity to press the door open another few inches. The weight of the tapestry made it difficult, but she had a clearer view of the girls. One of them, definitely her mom—she could tell even from the back, with her mom's characteristic curly light-brown hair and erect posture—was sitting at a small desk that hadn't been there before. The other—a pretty redhead who looked somehow familiar—was sprawled across the pink-comforter-clad bed, all long, loose limbs and shiny hair. The dolls and stuffed animals were gone. The girls looked to be about twelve or thirteen. *What year is it now? The late sixties, maybe early seventies?* She struggled to remember what year her mom had been born and quickly do the math, but her frazzled brain flat-out refused. Neither of the girls seemed to notice that the hidden closet door was cracked open and a woman was spying on them.

"One day, I'd love to explore a real shipwreck," her mom said with a wistful sigh. "Go diving in the Great Lakes or the ocean and recover all kinds of lost artifacts." She turned around in her desk chair to face the other girl, and all at once, her youthful beauty overcame Melanie again—the softness of her face and her creamy, unmarked complexion, as if life hadn't stamped its hardships and sorrows on her yet, and the way she was somehow both Melanie's mom and not her mom at the same time. The effect was uncanny.

"You will! You'll be the great Rachel Carson of our generation. Maybe you'll even write a book about it one day," the redhead said. She was hanging upside down off the bed, her sheet of coppery hair nearly touching the floor.

"You're sweet, even if you don't know what you're talking about!" Melanie's mom said, standing up. She lay down beside her friend and hung her head over the edge too. Her fat curls hung like sausage links, and her face turned pink. "Rachel Carson was a marine biologist and conservationist. I want to be a marine *archeologist* and *limnologist* studying lakes. You should know that by now, Vinnie."

Vinnie? The redhead was Mrs. Lavinia Fletcher, or Vinnie, as all her friends called her, their old next-door neighbor—Jilly, Beau, and Stephen's mom. Melanie had thought the girl looked familiar. She'd known that Mrs. Fletcher and her mom had been old friends, but she hadn't realized quite how old, just like she'd never realized her mom had been such a science enthusiast as an adolescent. She wanted to know more about that brave, funny girl with aspirations of diving and exploring sunken ships—that girl who grew up to be an elementary school reading specialist who refused to swim.

"I really don't need another lesson on the subject, please. Now, are we going to go diving or not? Shipwreck or no shipwreck, I bet there are still some neat things at the bottom of the lake."

"Yeah, like probably your brother's swim trunks from last week. That was so gross!"

"Actually, I think those would float."

"Double gross!" Melanie's mom jostled her shoulder against Vinnie's. "You know I have to ask my mom first. It's getting close to dinner, and she'll need my help."

Vinnie sighed, and the girls exchanged a significant look. Then without another word, they righted themselves and hopped off the bed. Their faces were cheerful and flushed as they scurried out of Melanie's view, and she could hear footsteps pounding down the stairs in unison.

She took a deep breath—the first, it seemed, since she'd touched the secret door's handle. Her body had stopped trembling, but she still felt unsteady, like a boat passenger who first touched land again.

She wanted to sit down but was too scared to step farther into the room and rest on the bed the girls had just occupied in case they came back. But if she stepped back into the closet behind the tapestry and perched on the bench, who knew where it would take her next? *Will it take me back to my bedroom in the present? Or elsewhere?* She was pretty sure she had just discovered a portal into the past.

KELSEY CLIPPED LEASHES to the two corgis' collars. "Come on, Duchess. Let's go, Zeus. Do you want to go outside?" The dogs' nails scrabbled on the tiled hallway floor as she led them to the back door.

It was a beautiful day, the warmth and strong sunshine heralding that summer was not far away. Josh was already outside with two labs, one yellow, one chocolate, and a border collie mix. He raised his hand in greeting and lobbed a tennis ball across the fenced-in play area for the dogs to retrieve.

"How's it going?" she called, bending down to unfasten the corgis' leashes. Zeus immediately darted away to join the three bigger dogs. Duchess stayed where she was and squatted to pee.

"Can't complain. On days like these, I can't believe I actually get paid to do this." Josh pried the ball from the chocolate lab's slobbery mouth and tossed it again. "But I guess it all evens out because, most of the time, I feel like I'm not getting paid nearly enough to put up with this crap. Literal crap, as you know." He gave her a slightly lopsided grin.

"Aha. Yes."

"How are you doing, K. K.? Any progress on your parents' house?"

The breeze ruffled her hair, and she brushed it out of her eyes. "Kind of. Melanie and I have been cleaning it nonstop, which makes a big difference, and we just hired a contractor to fix the water damage in the basement." She tried not to blush at the thought of Everett. Already, she was planning what to wear on Monday—her short green jersey-knit dress and gladiator sandals—and trying to come up with excuses for hanging around him in the basement so he'd pick up the hint and ask her out.

"Expensive?" Josh asked.

"Not too bad." She set the leashes down on the picnic table and walked toward him. "Melanie thinks we'll be able to get our initial investment back once we sell the house."

"And you two haven't killed each other yet?"

She laughed. "I'm still here, right?"

Before her sister's arrival, she'd confided in Josh about Melanie's demanding nature. As the youngest of four boys—his three older brothers were all smart, athletic overachievers, as he told it—he'd been sympathetic. But she was reluctant to tell him about their latest spat, if she could even call it that since Kelsey had simply been refusing to engage. Melanie's first voicemail had clearly shown her irritation that Kelsey had hired someone without her permission. But Kelsey—immaturely, she knew—hoped that the more time that passed, the harder it would be for Melanie to cancel their work order with Everett and give the job to Bill instead. It wouldn't be good etiquette. So she didn't pick up the phone whenever her sister's name flashed across her screen, and she replied only once to Melanie's frequent text requests to call her. *Can't talk now. Busy at work.*

Josh leaned against the fence. His black-framed glasses winked in the sun. "I'm glad. Hopefully you can work together just long enough to get the house on the market and find a buyer for it."

"Me too," Kelsey said, although she wasn't sure that selling it was what she really wanted. The thought of the old Victorian still standing there on the banks of Lake Indigo but no longer accessible to them, owned by some other family, made her stomach ache.

After returning Duchess and Zeus to their cages, she dashed to the front desk, where the phone was ringing off the hook. She wondered where the heck Taylor, the receptionist, was. Kelsey answered a few phone calls, booking appointments, jotting down special instructions for one of their current high-maintenance guests in residence, and quoting prices on their various services. She needed to get back to the kennels to finish taking out the Pooch Place dogs, but she still saw no sign of Taylor, and she couldn't leave the front desk unattended.

A tall girl with short black hair streaked through with green plunked a red plaid handbag on the desk in front of Kelsey. The purse had about a hundred zippers and a diamond-studded skull decal. The girl was Leona, Beth's teenage daughter.

"Is my mom here?" she demanded.

"Nope. Not until five, I think." Kelsey consulted the schedule on the bulletin board. "Yep, her shift starts at five."

"Bitch," Leona murmured.

"Excuse me?"

"Not you." The girl glared at her, her unnatural lavender contacts making her expression eerie. "My mom. She's such a bitch, always forgetting about me."

Kelsey had a hard time believing that her boss, who was even more responsible and organized than Melanie, for Pete's sake, had forgotten about a meeting with Leona. It was more likely that Leona had misunderstood her mom or just decided to show up because the time suited her. Beth was constantly worrying about her sixteen-year-old daughter, fretting that she wouldn't finish high school, that she was getting involved with drugs, and that she was dating a boy much too old for her. She had even cried a few times in Kelsey's presence, lamenting all the ways she had tried to make Leona feel like opening up to her—a weekly mother-daughter breakfast at a restaurant of Leona's choosing, trips to the mall, and dropping everything to answer her texts and phone calls no matter how busy Beth was. And still, Leona had the gall to refer to her mom as a bitch.

Kelsey bit her lip. "Why don't you call her? Maybe you can meet her at home."

Leona snatched up her handbag. "Right. And play into her trap? I don't think so. If you see her, tell her I'm hanging out at Dave's, okay?"

Dave was the much-too-old boyfriend—twenty, if Kelsey remembered correctly. Sympathy for her boss overwhelmed her as well as jealousy for the selfish girl who didn't realize how good she had it: a loving mother who would do just about anything for her.

"Leona!" she called after the teenager, who already had one hand on the door. "Just call your mom first, okay? She loves you so much. I don't know if you know this, but you're her whole world. She talks about you all the time." *And she might not always be there. Like my mom. Gone so early, too young. Gone before I could even truly appreciate all that she was.*

"I bet she does." Leona made a face and yanked the door open.

As if on cue, Taylor suddenly reappeared, carrying a half-eaten sub sandwich. Kelsey reprimanded her for leaving the desk unattended without telling anyone and hurried back to the kennels to finish her earlier task. As she took care of the other ten dogs, walking and playing with them, refilling their water bowls, and cleaning out their cages, she couldn't help remembering how selfish and ungrateful she had acted as a teenager and young adult, even after her parents had taken her back in to live with them at the age of twenty-four—right before her mom passed away.

Unlike Melanie, who had graduated as class valedictorian and immediately started at the University of Wisconsin as a declared biology major, her whole life reading like the perfect curriculum vitae, Kelsey had been a lot more aimless post-high school. She loved animals, but she knew she wasn't smart enough—or tough enough emotionally—to become a veterinarian. She loved talking to people and reading novels and baking cookies, but she didn't see how any of those skills could translate into a career that could support her. So she'd stayed on at her high school job, working at a grocery store bakery, getting up at an ungodly hour five mornings a week to bake bread, buns, and croissants. And she'd continued to live with her parents until her dad had asked her to either chip in more with the household chores or start paying rent, at which point she'd decided to move in with her then boyfriend, Eamon, a college student and aspiring filmmaker. Kelsey had quit her job at the bakery and started waiting tables at a steakhouse so she could have more compatible hours with his nocturnal lifestyle. She'd been so in love with him and his adorable Irish accent that she'd actually picked out names for their future children: Patrick and Cassidy. But their relationship had lasted less than a year.

Next she'd moved in with a high school friend, Ingrid, but struggled to pay the rent and her share of the food and utilities with her measly tips—she was an atrocious waitress, always forgetting who had ordered what and neglecting to stop by to ask if anyone needed refills or more ketchup, sometimes even failing to bring the bill. Eventually she'd asked her mom if she could come live at home for a while and help out around the house as her dad had previously suggested. They agreed. For a while, it was a tremendous relief to be back at home, sleeping in her cozy bedroom and eating her mom's meals, which always included healthy side dishes and were eaten on china plates. But after only a month of that, Kelsey grew mopey and thankless again, waiting to be asked to do her chores, annoyed when her parents treated her like a child. She was especially bitter when Melanie, the golden child and perfect daughter, came home from graduate school with her fiancé, Ben. Her sister's life was clipping along at an impressive pace, while Kelsey's remained stagnant.

It was shortly after one of these visits, in early May, that Kelsey and her mom had had a fight. Her mom had been vexed that Kelsey hadn't loaded the dishwasher the night before, as she'd been asked to, after their celebratory going-away dinner for Melanie. Melanie had won some kind of biology award or fellowship, a regular occurrence for her. The dishes were still stacked in the sink, where her dad had left them, crusted over, and would need to be soaked and washed by hand.

"I don't know why you asked me to do it instead of Melanie," Kelsey said. "She was here all weekend and hardly lifted a finger, but I had to wash her bedding and dust her room *and* do the dishes." She stopped herself from adding, "That's so unfair," because she knew it sounded juvenile.

"Melanie was only here for two days," her mom said, putting the drain stopper in place and turning the faucet on. She tested the water temperature with her fingertips. "We hardly see her, and she runs herself ragged during the semester. It's nice for her to get a little break every once in a while. Besides, she did help out. She made us those delicious pancakes yesterday morning."

"But she didn't do the dishes," Kelsey grumbled before remembering that Ben had rinsed off the plates and cutlery. "I'm sorry I forgot last night. But you know, I could use a little break every once in a while too."

"Couldn't we all?" Her mom squirted some dish soap into the water and looked up. Her face was pink from the rising steam, and she had slight frown lines around her mouth and eyes. She was dressed in the pale-blue sweater set and tan slacks she would wear later to her job at the elementary school.

Kelsey knew she should offer to take over and do the dishes, but something stopped her. Perhaps it was those frown lines and the exasperated look in her mom's eyes. She hadn't seen that look on her face all weekend when Melanie was around. But since it was just the two of them, it was back. Kelsey wished her mom would look at her the way she looked at Melanie, with delight and anticipation, as if she couldn't wait to see what amazing act her older daughter would perform next—honors, awards, recognition for her research, soon marriage, and eventually grandchildren. Meanwhile, her younger daughter was too lazy and incompetent to even load the dishwasher.

"You wish I were more like Melanie," Kelsey stated. It was a sore spot in their relationship, a debate they'd had many times in her twenty-four years of life and one that never got any better, no matter how much her mom denied it, because Kelsey knew it was true. "You wish I'd gone to college. You wish I'd get a real job and find a nice guy like Ben to date. You wish I didn't leave old take-out containers in the fridge and toothpaste spatter on the mirrors."

Her mom smiled tiredly at that last accusation. She pushed a curl out of her eyes with the back of her hand. "Kels-Bels, all I wish is that you'd be happy. Because it's very clear to me that you're not right now. So you need to find what makes you happy, no matter what that is." She started dropping silverware into the hot, soapy water. "Believe me. I would be the last person on this earth to force you to be something you're not."

It was the same worn-out advice Kelsey had heard from her mom since her adolescent years. *Find what makes you happy, no matter what that is.* So she'd devoured good books and swum on the varsity team and volunteered at the animal shelter and learned to knit and dated cute boys and went dancing and baked banana nut muffins, and it was a lot of fun, but none of it seemed like a *calling*, like what her sister had: a clear purpose and vocation. So instead of taking her mom's advice to heart and seeing all the love and kindness wrapped up in it, she dismissed it as avoidance of the true issue, that things would be a lot easier for her parents if she were more like Melanie. They wouldn't have to worry so much, and they wouldn't have an adult daughter living with them, failing to do the tiniest tasks asked of her.

"You know what would make me happy?" she asked, swinging her purse over her shoulder. "If Melanie didn't visit every single month to rub my nose in her perfect life."

Her mom's face fell, the subtle lines becoming deeper, more pronounced wrinkles. She looked like she was going to say something but thought better of it. Instead, she shook her head and continued stacking plates in the sink. So Kelsey hurried out of the house to go to her hair appointment without even saying goodbye.

When she'd gotten back two hours later, her mom's car was still parked in the garage, which was unusual because her mom typically would've left for her afternoon sessions with her reading students by then. The dishes were arranged neatly in the rack next to the sink, and everything in the house was tidy and quiet—too quiet. An ominous feeling settled over Kelsey like a stormy sky.

"Mom?" she called, walking toward the living room. Her mom was *never* late for work. She rarely called in sick, and she'd seemed fine that morning. Maybe it was a half day for teacher conferences. But her mom had been dressed in work attire that morning. "Mom?" She expected to hear a reply from the bathroom or somewhere upstairs, but the quiet was intense and oppressive.

The door to her dad's office was ajar. Everyone called it "Dad's office," although it was supposedly a shared workspace. Both her mom and dad's books were in there, and they each had a desk and file cabinet. But while her dad spent most of his nights and weekends poring over notes and preparing cases at his desk, her mom only flitted in and out to grab student worksheets and stickers occasionally, so it became "Dad's office."

"Mom?"

Her mom's desk had a couple of brightly colored readers stacked on top of it, but her school bag was tipped over on the floor near the desk. A few pens and a roll of tape had fallen out. And something else was there on the Oriental rug too.

Kelsey choked back a sob. "Mom!"

She stumbled forward and fell to her knees. Her mom was lying curled on her side in the fetal position, with her brown curls covering her face. Kelsey frantically swept the hair aside. Her mom's forehead was cool to the touch. Her lips were a blue gray. "Oh God, Mom. What happened?" She tried to remember what to do next. *Check for a pulse? Give her breaths? Call 911?*

She settled for yanking her dad's phone to the floor to call for an ambulance while she pressed her fingers against the side of her mom's neck—no pulse—and listened to her chest—no heartbeat. *How long has she been out? Did she have a heart attack? A stroke?* The paramedics would know a way to revive her. But even as she gave her address to the emergency operator and described the situation, she knew it was too late. Her mom's arms and legs looked splotchy, like they were covered in a red rash. Her skin was abnormally cool, as if all her warmth and life had fled. She called her dad at work and Melanie, who had just returned to Madison. She didn't know what she said to them, if she was coherent at all, just that something was very wrong with Mom and they needed to come quickly.

Then Kelsey lay down beside her mom, cradling her cold body. She stroked her mom's hair and told her that everything would be all right, that she was sorry she wasn't Melanie, because with all her scientific training and her take-charge attitude, Melanie certainly would've known what to do. But at least she, Kelsey, was there with her now and wouldn't leave her side. She was sorry she had left at all. *Why did I go to that stupid hair appointment, anyway?* She was sorry she hadn't been there to do CPR and call 911 immediately when her mom fell, sorry she hadn't hugged her mom goodbye and said, "Don't worry about me. I'll find a way to be happy. You and Dad make me happy. I love you both so much."

"Kelsey?" Taylor's voice broke into her sorrowful recollection. The receptionist was standing at the end of the kennel hallway.

"What?" Kelsey blotted hastily at her eyes with her sleeve.

"You have a phone call." Taylor danced anxiously from foot to foot, like she might dart off at any second. "I didn't want to leave the desk unattended, but I wanted to let you know..."

"Thanks," Kelsey said sharply. "You can go back up front. I'll pick up the extension back here. Line one?" She tried to smile, but her lips and cheeks felt numb. Even though it had been four years since her mom had died of an unexpected pulmonary embolism, the memory of her awful discovery that day was still enough to dredge up all her feelings of horror, guilt, and an unbearable, engulfing loss that still had the power to suck her under like a riptide.

"Line two," Taylor clarified and scurried away.

Kelsey took a few deep, cleansing, yoga-style breaths—*in through the nose, out through the mouth*—before picking up the phone. "Green Valley Pet Lodge. This is Kelsey." She hoped it wasn't Pepsi's owner, who had been calling all week with ridiculous instructions about the dog's diet, exercise regimen, and bowel schedule.

But it wasn't a client. It was Melanie. "I'm so sorry to bug you at work, but you weren't answering your cell phone!" she exclaimed in mock chastisement. "Kelsey, you are not going to believe it! I found something amazing in the house! Something you absolutely need to see and right away. It has to do with Mom. When's the soonest you can come out?"

Chapter Six

When Kelsey arrived at the lake house on Sunday afternoon, with Sprocket in tow—it was her one stipulation since Melanie wanted her to spend the night—her sister was sitting on the porch steps, waiting for her. Melanie dropped the magazine she'd been reading and stood up, following Kelsey's car's progression down the driveway with her eyes. Kelsey had hardly freed herself from her seat belt when Melanie poked her head through the passenger-side window.

"Do you need any help carrying your stuff in?" she asked, her face half-hidden by the car's sagging roof lining. "Is this Sprocket? Oh, he's so darling and scruffy! He reminds me of Toto from *The Wizard of Oz.*"

In the back seat, Sprocket started his frantic wiggling dance, pawing at the doors and whining to be let out. "Thanks," Kelsey said. "I'll take care of him if you wouldn't mind getting my bag out of the trunk." She wondered if one week alone at Lake Indigo had driven her sister stir-crazy and made her desperate for companionship. She opened one of the back-seat doors, and Sprocket launched himself into his new territory. He raced around the yard, lifting his leg and marking every tree in sight until coming to a rest at Melanie's feet, eager for admiration.

"Hello, Sprocket. Aren't you a cutie? Do you shake?" She stooped down to his level but redirected her question to Kelsey. "Does he shake?"

"We're working on it." As a rescue dog with a rough past, Sprocket hadn't learned the usual repertoire of tricks that most puppies picked up. In fact, Kelsey was mostly just impressed—and grateful—when he didn't have accidents inside the house or attack her throw pillows. He was also a champion at fetch if someone didn't mind tossing a slimy ball until their arm cramped up.

Melanie strode toward the house, Kelsey's duffel bouncing on her shoulder and Sprocket hot on her heels. "Just wait until you see what a difference the new paint job made in the living room. It's so much lighter and airier, just like the old days. Remind me—do you like salmon? The fish, not the color. Dern's—I mean Lamson's—had it on sale, so I picked up a couple of filets I thought we could grill for dinner. But if not, I also have chicken breast."

Kelsey had to trot, both physically and mentally, to keep up with her sister. "Salmon sounds good. Damn! I just realized I left the chocolate chip cookies I made this morning on my kitchen counter."

"Oh, too bad." Melanie nudged the front door open with her hip, and Sprocket skittered inside ahead of her. "Well, that's okay because I have fresh strawberry shortcake for dessert. Dad's favorite, remember?" She unceremoniously dumped Kelsey's bag on the couch and whirled around. "So. About this thing I discovered. I don't know how to explain it, so I thought it would probably be best just to show you—"

"Sounds good. Can I just use the bathroom first and get my stuff stashed in my room?" Kelsey stepped around her to retrieve the duffel. She wanted to hang up the green dress before it got too wrinkled. The car ride had made her sore, tired, and kind of cranky, and she couldn't fathom what had gotten Melanie so fired up. On the phone, she'd described it as something of their mom's, something astonishing and almost inconceivable. Embarrassingly, Kelsey's mind had leapt to something sex related: lingerie, a sex tape, or old love notes or photos, all things she *really* didn't want to connect to her mom. But she figured prudish Melanie would've acted more aghast, were that the case.

"Fine. Just let me know when you're ready. You're really not going to believe this..." Melanie called after her.

Kelsey reached the top of the steps and stopped outside her old room, Sprocket colliding with her legs. The afternoon sunlight was beating down through the open window—the only one upstairs without a lake view—and already, the room felt hot and stuffy. Melanie had pulled out a pink-and-purple quilt for the rickety twin-size bed, and a vase of bluish-purple hydrangeas sat on the nightstand. *Pretty*, Kelsey thought. But otherwise the room looked like a prison cell, with bare floors and walls and no other furniture. She drifted next door to her sister's room, where another, larger bouquet of hydrangeas graced the desk. The sunlight was less glaring in there, and a refreshing breeze was drifting in off the lake. Melanie had somehow maneuvered an upholstered wingback chair from downstairs into one corner of the room. But best of all was the *Tree of Life* tapestry, which gave the room depth, warmth, and character.

Kelsey frowned and continued down the hallway to what had been her parents' bedroom. It was the largest of the three rooms, with a triple bank of windows that directly overlooked the lake and a luxurious four-poster queen-size bed. She remembered her mom lying alone in that bed, wearing her favorite gray nightgown and reading glasses, her forehead wrinkled in deep concentration as she read. When Kelsey had come in to hug her good night, it always took her mom a few minutes to extract herself from the world of her book and realize Kelsey was there. But then she would smile, give Kelsey a quick squeeze, and murmur, "Love you, honey. Sweet dreams." Her focus would be back on the book, her thoughts private and inaccessible again, before Kelsey had even left the room.

She dropped her overnight bag on the four-poster bed. *Who says I have to stay in my old tiny bedroom when this one's available?* It didn't make sense for her to sweat and toss and turn when she could be sprawled out coolly and peacefully. She doubted her mom would have minded, and her dad wasn't there and probably wouldn't ever be there again before the sale of the house. Only Melanie would care, but her sister could deal with it. She hung up the dress in her parents' closet then used the bathroom.

Melanie was leaning in the master bedroom's doorway when Kelsey came out. "You're going to stay in here?" she asked casually, but Kelsey could see her hands were clenched in tight balls.

"Yeah. Why not?" Kelsey responded equally as casually. "No one else is using it, and I'll be much more comfortable. Besides, I don't think Mom and Dad would mind, do you?"

Melanie shook her head stiffly. Maybe she was kicking herself for not staking a claim on the room first. It probably hadn't occurred to her because her room was so much nicer than Kelsey's. If she had, Kelsey would've been happy to stay in the bedroom with the tapestry. "I'll have to take one of the queen-size quilts to the Laundromat," she said.

"I could do it," Kelsey offered. "Or I could sleep with the twin-size quilt tonight. I really don't care." She bent down to scratch behind Sprocket's ears and saw his tongue was hanging out in a doggy grin. She would need to set out a bowl of water for him soon. "So what is this thing of Mom's you wanted to show me?" She tried to sound appropriately enthusiastic.

But Melanie's eagerness seemed to have lessened somewhat. She was still staring into their parents' bedroom as if Kelsey had desecrated it somehow. "Right." Melanie slowly returned her attention to her sister, and Kelsey got the distinct impression she was being appraised. "It's in my room," she finally said and ducked into the doorway of the middle bedroom. "But we should probably sit down first."

Kelsey sat in the wingback chair. Melanie sat on the bed, and Sprocket stretched out on the hardwood floor on his side.

"The first night I got here, I was cleaning the place, and it occurred to me that the *Tree of Life* tapestry probably hadn't been taken down and cleaned in decades," Melanie started. "So I was trying to figure out how best to get it off the wall, but it was really awkward and heavy, so I decided I'd better leave it for the time being. While I was doing that, though, I noticed something hidden behind it—a door."

"A door?" Kelsey scooted forward in her chair, her curiosity piqued. "A door to what?"

Melanie sucked in a deep breath. "I thought at first it was just a closet. A really weird closet because it doesn't have any clothes bars, hooks, or shelves, just a bench. And some of Mom's things were in there. But then I pushed the door open again, and when I came out, well, everything was... different."

Kelsey stood up and crossed the room to the wall hanging. She lightly gripped its edge with her right hand and drew it toward her. Sure enough, she saw the outline of a door with some kind of metal handle level with the wall. Her whole body tingled as she deliciously lived out her childhood fantasy of discovering something so secret, so mysterious that it had to be hidden away from the rest of the world: the overgrown, walled-off garden in *The Secret Garden*; the wardrobe leading to Narnia; or the clues Nancy Drew stumbled upon to help her solve her mysteries. She imagined stepping into the room to discover whatever belongings of their mom's Melanie had unearthed—probably photo albums, journals, or maybe childhood keepsakes, nothing quite so magical as the classics of her childhood. But still, the thought was thrilling. She released the tapestry's edge, and it fell back against the door with a soft slap.

"Be gentle with that," Melanie said.

Kelsey rested her palm over one of the red birds. If it were real, it would have fit neatly into her cupped hand. "What do you mean, 'everything was different' when you came back out?"

"It's so crazy that I can't decide if I should just show you or if I should try to prepare you. I guess I would've appreciated being prepared, but I seriously doubt I would've believed anyone who tried to warn me." Melanie pressed downward on the bed, as though she couldn't decide if she should stand up or plant herself more firmly in place.

"Stop being so melodramatic and just let me look," Kelsey teased. She pulled the tapestry away from the wall again and set to work on twisting the silver handle. But before she could turn it, Melanie's hand stopped hers.

"Okay," Melanie said. "But on one condition. We always go together. Never alone."

Go where *together? Inside the closet? Can't we just haul the stuff out and pore over it at our leisure? Especially if it's a cramped space.* That seemed like a weird demand, but the suspense was killing Kelsey, so she nodded. Melanie released her hand, and Kelsey swiveled the circular latch the rest of the way. They squeezed inside.

Melanie reached overhead to turn on the light, and Kelsey was disheartened to see it was, in fact, just a closet, as Melanie had said, and not a particularly big one at that. And it had no boxes of long-lost keepsakes. The room was basically empty except for a wood-plank bench with a small pile of items stacked on one end.

Kelsey held up the cigarette pack. "Is *this* what you wanted to show me? Do you think Mom smoked without us knowing?" She sat down on the bench, feeling deflated.

"I don't know," Melanie said dismissively. "Maybe. Or it could be someone else's. But that's not what I wanted you to see. Come on. Let's go back in the bedroom."

"Already? But I thought you wanted to show me something in here."

Melanie pursed her lips. "Kelsey, bear with me, okay? I'm *trying* to show you."

Kelsey rolled her eyes but stood up and followed her sister back through the hidden door. Immediately, her gaze landed on the spot where Sprocket had been lying on the floor, but the little gray dog was gone. Maybe he'd gotten anxious when they'd disappeared into the closet and gone looking for her. She hoped he wasn't off destroying furniture.

"Sprocket?" she called then noticed that the hardwood floor wasn't bare anymore. It was covered by a shaggy white circular rug. *Where the heck did Melanie get that from, and why didn't it make an impression on me before?* But everywhere her gaze landed, she found something different about the room. The vase of hydrangeas was missing, and in its place was a lamp with tassels dangling from its shade. The quilt was a solid pink instead of a patchwork blue and white. Notebooks and what looked like hardcover textbooks were stacked on the desk, and a red one-piece swimsuit and a beach towel were draped over the desk chair.

"Sprocket?" she called again.

"He's not here," Melanie said, stepping toward her. "But don't worry. He's just fine, I'm sure."

Suddenly dizzy, Kelsey grabbed the back of the desk chair to steady herself. The swimsuit hanging there was damp, and she drew her hand away. "Where is he?"

"He's in my bedroom, probably still fast asleep on the floor. But a better question would be: Where are *we*?" She gestured to the rug, the bedspread, and all the details Kelsey had only just cataloged. "This is going to sound incredible, but we're in the past, Kelsey. Probably somewhere in the seventies. This is Mom's bedroom when she was a girl. That's her swimsuit. Those are her notebooks."

Kelsey could only gape at her sister. "How do you know?"

"I've seen her. And Grandma Dot. And even Mrs. Fletcher as a girl. As far as I can figure it, the closet is some kind of time portal."

"You've seen Mom? Where is she? Can we talk to her?" It was better than her childhood fantasies, better than *The Secret Garden* and *The Chronicles of Narnia* and Nancy Drew all wrapped up into one. It was a direct channel to her mom's past, a way to speak to her mom one more time from beyond the grave. "Mom?" she shouted. She started toward the door, but Melanie grabbed her elbow.

"They can't see or hear us," she said. "And I don't think we can move things or affect them in other ways. We're basically like ghosts. All we can do is observe."

"I still want to see her," Kelsey said.

Just then, the sound of heavy footfalls came up the stairs. She froze in place.

"Dorothy?" a man called.

"In here," a woman trilled back from what sounded like the turret room.

"Do you want to see Grandma and Grandpa first?" Melanie whispered, peeking out into the hallway.

"I thought you said they couldn't hear us," Kelsey whispered back.

"They can't. But it's still kind of unnerving, isn't it?"

It *was* deeply and truly unnerving. Kelsey's hands were clammy as she followed her sister to the end of the hallway, where Grandma Dot—who had passed away two years earlier, after her daughter—was watering hanging plants, and Grandpa Jack—who had been deceased for at least twenty years—was sitting on the window seat in a pair of white shorts and boat shoes, one tanned, hairy leg crossed over the other. They looked so young, healthy, and *alive*.

Melanie stepped into the room and hovered on the periphery, but their grandparents didn't bat an eyelash at her intrusion. Kelsey hung back, watching and listening from the doorway.

"I don't like this," Grandpa Jack said. "I think we should tell her she can't accept the position."

"Oh, Jack, don't be silly." Grandma Dot tipped the yellow plastic watering can into a plant with tiny white blooms. "She's a good swimmer, and it will give some structure to her days. Plus she can tuck away some of the money to help pay for college. You always say you don't want her loafing around the house all summer. This will be good for her."

Grandpa Jack frowned at the sole of his boat shoe. "You're right. I don't like her loafing around the house, frittering her summer away with the Birdwells and the other yahoos around here. But from what I can tell, that's just what the lifeguards at Harris Beach do, except in skimpy bathing suits, and I won't have my daughter being ogled on some lifeguard stand by all of Lake Indigo. Why can't she spend more time studying like Bobby? Or if she has to get a summer job, why not a proper one like Keith, who bags the groceries at Dern's?"

"You would really want your daughter bagging groceries?" Grandma Dot raised her eyebrow, and for the first time, Kelsey realized how much her mother favored her. Old age and ill humor had weathered her grandma's features, but in the middle-aged version of Grandma Dot, Kelsey could see that their thick brown hair, thin lips, and slightly upturned noses were exactly the same.

"Well, no." He flicked an invisible piece of lint off his crisp white shorts. "But I don't like the message this sends to our neighbors—that we're permissive parents who approve of girls parading themselves around in bathing suits. I just wish Christine were more modest. And maybe more focused like Bobby. Here my brother went to all this trouble to get her those limnology textbooks, and has she cracked them just once since we got here?"

Grandma Dot set the watering can down and wiped her hands on her apron front. "Jack, she's only sixteen, and it's summer vacation. You know she was grateful to Jim for those books. But I think she also feels conflicted because of how you reacted to her wanting to study lakes and shipwrecks. You all but told her the only respectable majors women could choose were education or clerical studies."

"Well, they are." Grandpa Jack stood up to look out the window. "I think it's pretty generous of us to plan to send her to college at all when she's probably going to stop working once she's married and settled down with a family anyway. God knows she'll never want for money with the trust fund we've set up for her." His spine suddenly went rigid, and he bent forward, his nose practically digging into the window screen. "Who's that boy with Christine and Lavinia? I don't think I recognize him."

"It's not Bruce Birdwell?" Grandma Dot asked with disinterest.

"No. I think I'd recognize our next-door neighbor, the king of the yahoos."

"Mom's out there?" Kelsey whispered to Melanie. She wanted to look out the window and catch a glimpse of her mom but was nervous about bumping into her grandparents and somehow alerting them to her presence.

Melanie edged carefully around Grandma Dot to get a better view. "Yes," she said. "She's a teenager!"

"Well, let's go and see her up close," Kelsey said, raising the volume of her voice a hair. She turned away from her grandparents and started to head for the stairs.

"What? You mean—go outside?"

"Sure. Why not?" She thumped down the stairs, trying to imagine her mom at sixteen. She had seen pictures, of course—posed photos of her next to Uncle Bob, the two of them bored and unsmiling, and pictures of her at Christmas, on her birthday, or in her polyester high school cap and gown. But to see her in the flesh, talking, smiling, walking, and swimming... Kelsey hardly processed the rest of the seventies décor in the house as she sped to the porch door. But once again, Melanie caught her first.

"Wait! Maybe we shouldn't go outside," she said, positioning herself between Kelsey and the door.

Kelsey could hear shouts and laughter coming from outside. One of those voices was her mom's.

"We don't know the rules of this time travel," Melanie continued. "What if it just applies to the house, and if we leave it, we can't come back?"

"Good point. You stay here, then, so you can let me back in." She yanked at the door handle, but it wouldn't budge. Oh no. Maybe Melanie was right, and the boundaries of the weird reality only extended to the edges of the house. *How long will I have to wait for Mom to come back inside?* She gave the door another forceful yank, and though it still didn't open, her arm slipped through it, as if the solid wood were actually made of tissue paper. She turned back to widen her eyes at Melanie, who looked even more bug-eyed at the development. "Wish me luck," Kelsey said as she disappeared through the paper-thin door out into a sunny summer day from her mom's adolescence.

Everything looked eerily bright: the lime-green grass, the bright-blue sky, and the deep-purple lake. A vintage-looking speedboat was tied up at the end of the fresh and sturdy dock, which looked as if it had just been built. It probably *had* been. Three teenagers were standing in the shade of a tree, talking and laughing. She recognized her mother immediately.

Almost as tall and broad-shouldered as the boy, her mom was wearing a striped halter top, tiny navy-blue shorts, and platform sandals. Her curly brown hair was wet and fell down her otherwise-exposed back. She was gorgeous, and Kelsey didn't want to look away, not even long enough to examine her mom's two companions.

"We're having a bonfire tomorrow night," the teenage boy said. "You should both come."

"That sounds like fun. Doesn't it, Vinnie?" Kelsey's mom asked in a lilting, musical tone she had never heard her use before—flirting.

"It does," the other girl said. That was Mrs. Fletcher—Vinnie, Lavinia—from next door. "But I don't know if we can make it, Christine. Remember we told Bruce we'd go to that thing?"

As Kelsey's mom turned her head away from the teenage boy and toward Vinnie, so did Kelsey. Though her mom was vibrant and youthful and at her very prettiest, Kelsey could see that Vinnie was clearly the more striking of the two girls. Petite-featured, petite-bodied, fair-skinned, and with silky, coppery hair parted in the middle, she was like a porcelain doll Kelsey had once coveted in a gift shop. But at that moment, her features looked stormy. *What is her problem?*

"Oh," her mom said, her face falling a little. "That's right. I forgot. Well, maybe next time?"

"Sure. Next time," the boy said. He had shaggy, feathered dark-brown hair and blue eyes. He was wearing a white polo shirt and too-short shorts and was handsome in a seventies-heartthrob kind of way, if a person was into that kind of thing.

Kelsey did a double take. His blue eyes looked familiar. *Is that Dad? Am I witnessing the moment when my parents first met?* She tried to reimagine the teenager with graying, shorter hair and about forty extra pounds on his lean frame.

"Well, I'd better go," he said. "I'll be seeing you at the beach, I guess."

"I hope so!" her mom called after him. "Goodbye!"

Kelsey willed her mom or Vinnie to say his name. *Goodbye, Charlie! Charles Kingstad? Is that really Dad?* But neither of them voiced his name, and the boy was slinking across the lawn before Kelsey could study him in any further detail. She watched her mom's blue eyes follow him longingly and Vinnie's almond eyes flash contemptuously at him.

"What *thing* are you talking about?" her mom hissed.

But before Kelsey could hear Vinnie's reply, Melanie was standing beside her. "You broke my one condition. You left me behind," she said. She sounded half-furious, half on the verge of tears.

"Whoa," Kelsey said. "You were the one who thought it would be safer to stay in the house. I would've been happy for us to stick together." She tried to tune back in to their mom and Vinnie's conversation, but Melanie was still talking.

"Well, we need to go now. That's *if* we can travel back to our time. I tried to test the porch door, but it's hard to know if we'll be able to get back through or be stuck out here. All I know is we have to go into the secret closet again to have a hope of making it back at all. And who knows how much time has passed in our world?"

The idea that time would travel more quickly out there hadn't occurred to Kelsey. *Poor Sprocket—is he anxious and hungry, chewing on everything in sight?* Kelsey took one last look at her mom. She wished her mom would look back at her and acknowledge her presence, maybe even reach out and hug her. But she was just as separate and unknowable to Kelsey as she had been throughout much of her life. Maybe that was about to change.

Chapter Seven

"That couldn't have been Dad," Melanie said, setting salad plates on the rough, faded surface of the wraparound porch's outdoor table. She wondered if she'd have time to squeeze in sanding and staining it before the professional photographer came the next week. "Mom and Dad didn't meet until she was eighteen, remember? At that Harvest Festival mixer? I don't think Dad visited Lake Indigo until the following summer."

"Oh, boo, I bet you're right." Kelsey poured a generous measure of Sauvignon Blanc into each of their glasses. She looked disappointed for only a second before leaning forward on her elbows mischievously. "So who do you think he was, then? A first love? Mom never mentioned dating anyone before Dad."

Melanie sank into her chair. She'd been eagerly looking forward to having a frank conversation with someone about the surreal world behind the tapestry, but since it was finally happening, she felt wrong-footed and caught off guard. She knew that it partially had to do with the sting of hurt feelings she was still recovering from—Kelsey abandoning her inside the house to eavesdrop on their mom and her friends as well as disregarding their mom's memory by simply taking over the master bedroom—but also because Melanie was no longer the sole person in possession of the secret. She was no longer the only one in control of how things would unfold and at what pace, and her sister's "act first, ask questions later" approach seemed reckless. Clearly they were on the edge of something huge, something potentially dangerous and of cosmic significance, maybe, and definitely world-as-we-know-it changing. Some ground rules were in order.

"Probably a neighbor boy," she said, trying to hide her irritation behind a bite of salmon since she hadn't even been able to get a good look at the guy in question, while Kelsey had.

"He was pretty cute, and Mom was definitely crushing on him, but Mrs. Fletcher, not so much. I think she made up an excuse so they wouldn't have to go to the bonfire, but you could tell Mom was disappointed." Kelsey speared a spinach leaf on her fork. "Oh my gosh! That halter top and those platforms! Who knew she had such adorable clothes? I wonder what she did with them. I would've loved to wear them as a teenager."

Melanie took a long swallow of her wine. *Is that really the most pressing question Kelsey has? What happened to Mom's seventies wardrobe? And who's the cute mystery boy?* Her head was spinning with more substantial questions: How did the closet work? What were its boundaries and limitations, and *why* did it work? She wondered if there was a danger of getting stuck in the past, a possibility of affecting the outcome of bygone events, and if so, if it could negatively—or positively—impact the future. *What if we accidentally mess something up and make it so we were never born? Are the benefits of glimpsing Mom worth the risks of tampering with fate?*

"I wish we could talk to her," Kelsey said wistfully. "Find out all the things she never would have told us later in her life. Her sixteen-year-old self just seems so *open*. And happy."

Melanie adjusted her chair to get out of the direct glare of the slowly setting sun. "Even if we could talk to her... how would that conversation go? 'Hi, we're your adult daughters from the future'? Like that wouldn't freak her out at all."

"Of course not. We'd have to pretend to be new neighbors or something, befriend her over time," her sister said as though it was something she had already seriously considered. "But it's a moot point, right? Because you're absolutely positive we can't interact? That they can't see or hear us?"

"Kels, I'm not positive about *anything*. We're both operating on the same limited information. But you saw the way they stared right through us and didn't react. The conclusion there seems pretty self-evident." She paused to swat at a mosquito, mentally tacking 'Buy citronella candles' on her to-do list. "And even though, admittedly, it would be really fun to talk to a young version of Mom, it's probably a lot safer this way."

"You mean so we can't interfere in the past and screw something up. Like in *Back to the Future*."

"Right." At least, Melanie *hoped* that not being able to physically affect the alternate world would protect their mom and them. *How much harm can passive observation do?* But all of her scientific training felt monumentally useless in the face of a hidden closet capable of time travel. She sliced off the burnt edge of her salmon filet and dropped it discreetly from her plate. Sprocket, camped out between them under the table, gobbled it up within seconds.

"Yes, but what's the point of being able to view the past if we're not able to somehow change—did you just feed my dog table scraps?" Instead of the disapproval Melanie had expected, Kelsey looked amused.

"Maybe." Melanie grinned sheepishly as Sprocket sat down close to her heels, licking his chops, her new faithful friend. "Hey, I've got an idea. Why don't we catalog everything we know so far about the closet and how it works? I've been in there three times now."

"I know! Lucky duck. You don't need to rub it in," Kelsey interjected sourly. Melanie had just filled her in on her two previous trips into the past.

"And each time I went in, Mom was a different age. The first time, she was about eight, the second time, thirteen, and just now,

sixteen. So that means that either the time travel is moving in a rela-
tively chronological fashion through Mom's life, or it just randomly
happened that way, and we could go in tomorrow and witness her as
either a baby or a forty-year-old."

"Holy crap." Kelsey's face paled a shade. "You think it's not just
her childhood and teenage years? You think it goes up until her
death? You think *we're* in there? That we could see ourselves as children?"

"I honestly don't know if it's just Mom's life." Melanie gripped
her wine glass. "Maybe it's the entire life of the house. For all I know,
it could go back to a hundred years ago when the house was first built
and Great-Grandma Jane and Great-Grandpa Montclare were dancing the Lindy Hop. But I do think we can count on one thing for
certain: the closet can only show us events that happened *at* the lake
house. Mom was here only during the summers, so it can't show us
what happened to her the rest of the year. And she stopped coming
fifteen years ago. Our last summer here." She set the glass down without taking a drink.

Kelsey pulled her hair to one side and twisted it into a rope. She
contemplated the lake, where the sun had spilled a thousand glitter-
ing gold coins across its surface. "I wouldn't want to revisit *that* summer again." She gave a small shiver.

Melanie agreed. She could still see the flash of Jilly's hot-pink
two-piece swimsuit as she jumped from the raft, the small girl's rust-
colored hair, then how one minute she simply wasn't there. Beau
had splashed and shouted to the shore, calling out to their moms,
who had also been there one minute and gone the next. Finally,
Mr. Fletcher had come outside because of the racket, and when he'd
heard what had happened, he yelled at Stephen to call 911 and tore
through the water as though it were a field of tall grass he couldn't
cut through fast enough. At last, Jilly's body had emerged in his arms,
but flimsy and as pale as a stone at the bottom of the lake. Her temple

had been swollen and bruised. Melanie had never felt so helpless and afraid before in her fourteen years of life. She'd looked up to see her mom reappear then, tall and rooted to her spot on the sand, pressing her fist against her mouth in horror. Mrs. Fletcher was behind her, but Melanie couldn't make out her face.

"Thank God Mr. Fletcher was there," Kelsey murmured as she stood to collect her silverware and plate.

"Thank God he knew CPR," Melanie added.

They carried bowls of strawberry shortcake to the dock, where they sat side by side on the bench. It was a tradition their dad had started, dessert on the dock. Usually, the three of them had eaten their bowls of ice cream or slices of zucchini bread out there while Mom had cleaned up and done the dishes inside. Their dad had tried to cajole her into joining them on several occasions, but she had always insisted that washing the dishes was better for her figure. Melanie remembered their dad's abysmal imitation of the loon's call—he'd sounded more like a cartoon ghost than the bird's other-worldly, plaintive song. She listened for it, but the lake was silent except for the gentle lapping of waves. Sunday nights were the quietest nights at Lake Indigo.

"So what else do we know about the closet?" Kelsey asked around a mouthful of strawberry shortcake. "It doesn't sound like much. Time may or may not move chronologically inside it. It probably just shows events at the lake house, although we can't know for sure unless we try to leave the area once we've gone through the door, right? Like by hopping in someone's car or something?"

The thought made Melanie's abdomen clench. It wasn't an experiment she thought she would be brave enough to try. She had hardly been able to muster the courage to step outside on the grass, let alone leave Lake Indigo for another part of Wisconsin. *What if we hitched a ride then couldn't return to the lake house and it turned out to be our one portal back to the present day? Would we be stuck in the past as voiceless shadows forever? Would I never be able to return to my life with Ben?*

"I think there's plenty to explore here without hopping in someone's car." She scratched her wrist. A mosquito had gotten to her after all.

Kelsey grabbed Melanie's hand. "Hey. What happened here?" She turned Melanie's arm over so the purplish bruises from the inexperienced phlebotomist's pokes were just visible in the waning light—a chain of violets.

"Nothing," Melanie said, tugging her hand away. "I just had to have some blood drawn, and the tech treated me like a pincushion." She could see the concern written plainly across Kelsey's face, and it made her chest ache in that familiar way. She knew if her sister prodded her even just a bit more, she'd be tempted to unload it all—the months of trying, the infertility treatments, the miscarriage, the distance that had grown between her and Ben. *How would Kelsey react? Would she be hurt that I kept her in the dark for so long?* Though they had never been the type of sisters who shared every detail of their lives, that seemed like a particularly big lie of omission for all those times when Kelsey had asked her during their monthly phone calls, "So what's going on?"

Would Kelsey expect me to relive the experience detail by awful detail? Or even worse, would she try to minimize my suffering as Rose, the one friend I confided in, did? "Oh, Melanie, I'm so sorry, sweetie. But thank goodness you were only in your first trimester," Rose had said then gone on to share a heartbreaking story about a friend of a friend who had lost her baby boy at thirty-seven weeks, which had only made Melanie feel guilty for her comparably smaller loss and weak for the tremendous grief she was still feeling.

For as long as she could remember, Melanie had always been what Kelsey had expected her to be—no, *required* her to be: strong and capable. She was the one who pried a bee off the palm of Kelsey's hand when the stinger got stuck, the one who helped her with her middle school global studies projects when their dad was too busy with a case, the person who drove to her aid at midnight when Kelsey got into a fender bender. And later, she was the one who helped Dad with the funeral arrangements, the daughter who acted as the family spokesperson at the wake and burial, and the one who saw to it that the donations made on their mom's behalf got to the proper charities. Never mind that Melanie was also a devastated wreck.

So what would Kelsey think if she found out that my strength is all an act? That I am in fact powerless and a failure on the most basic level? She couldn't bear the thought of being demoted in her sister's eyes and becoming an object of pity instead of a source of strength. Kelsey would never look to her sister for help or advice again, and at the moment, Melanie needed that.

No, she couldn't bring herself to tell her sister, not yet, at least. They had enough to deal with as it was—first the repairs on the house then the unimaginable portal into the past where the shimmering memory of their mom still lived and breathed. The house was most important. That was why Melanie had flown to Wisconsin in the first place, not to wallow in her troubles.

"Melanie, is something wrong?" Kelsey asked. She set her bowl down on the bench with a clatter.

Melanie took a deep breath. "No, I'm okay." With twilight closing in on them, the lake turning a rich shade of plum, and three hundred miles separating her from the grief she was trying to shake free of, she could almost believe it. "I do have something else I think we should add to our list of what we know about the closet, though," she said as a new thought occurred to her. "I think Mom knew about it."

She tried to explain to Kelsey what she had remembered earlier—their mom's insistence that their dad not take down the *Tree of Life* tapestry to have it cleaned and stored away. As a child, she'd thought that meant their mom wanted Melanie to have the beloved tapestry in her bedroom, but now she suspected it had more to do with what the wall hanging was hiding. "She must have known the hidden door was behind it," Melanie concluded. "And if she thought it was just an ordinary closet, she wouldn't have cared if anyone found out about it. So she must have known you could travel back in time in it."

Kelsey cocked her head to one side. It was getting so dark that she was nothing more than a silhouette and a voice. "That would explain why her cardigan was in the closet. Not the cigarettes, though. It's weird enough to think of Mom sneaking around behind our backs, smoking, let alone time traveling into the past." She inhaled sharply. "Hey! If Mom was using the closet, too, do you think we could somehow communicate with her? Like leave her little notes on the bench? Maybe she could write us back."

Melanie's abdomen gave another tighter clench. She had seen enough science fiction movies to know that changing just one small detail in the past—a sixteen-year-old reading a letter written by her future daughters, for example—could massively alter the present in unexpected, detrimental ways. Quantum physicists called it the butterfly effect. Though the thought of what Kelsey was suggesting terrified her, it also tugged at something she'd buried deep down years ago: a daughter's wish to talk to her mother just one last time. *But at what cost?*

"Maybe," she said slowly. "But I think we need to be smart about this and not rush into anything we can't take back."

Kelsey paused thoughtfully, and a bullfrog croaked its bass-drum belch. "You're probably right. At this point, I don't even know what I'd want to say to Mom, anyway. It's just so strange to think about her—good old regular Mom—keeping this bombshell of a secret from everyone. I mean, would she tuck us into bed then sneak back into your room for a jaunt into the 1970s to see her old high school flame? It just makes me wonder: Did we know anything about her at all?"

For once, they were on the same wavelength because Melanie had been wondering the same thing. She thought back to the eulogy she'd given at her mom's funeral and the portrait she had painted of Christine Montclare Kingstad—the supportive mother, the thoughtful wife, the caring reading specialist, and the avid reader. Several people had complimented her on the "lovely tribute" she'd made to her mom, but now she had doubts about whether she'd truly done her mom justice. *Isn't a daughter's perspective on her mother's life always a little myopic?*

"I think," she said, "that this is finally our chance to find out."

MELANIE'S PHONE RANG in her back pocket as she spread a ten-pound bag of potting soil in the window box the next morning. She peeled off her dirt-stained gardening gloves to answer it, knowing who it was without even consulting the screen: Ben. They'd mostly been communicating by texts because of the spotty reception for over a week. It was the longest they'd ever gone without a proper phone conversation to catch up. Even when Ben was on his annual camping trips with his brothers, they tended to talk once or twice if the guys stopped at a convenience store to pick up supplies.

"Hey," he greeted her, a smile in his voice. "Good morning, babe."

"Good morning," she said with a grin. Though Ben was one hour ahead in Ohio, of course he knew she was an early riser. She suspected he was probably calling her on his drive to work at the Edgewater Pharmacy. "Stuck in traffic?"

"Oh, can't complain. We're clipping along at a pretty steady pace of five miles per hour. I've had the same view of that gentleman's club billboard you hate for the last ten minutes now."

"The Rhinestone Rhino?" she said with a groan. "Do you want me to describe *my* view?" She stepped carefully around the black plastic flats of impatiens on the grass and turned to face the lake. "The sky is gorgeous and completely cloudless, almost like someone hung out a baby-blue sheet on the line too long and it got a little sun bleached. The lake's a grayish silver and very calm, only a few ripples from the waves and a passing kayaker. The trees still have that springy 'new leaf' look, so fresh and green that you can't help already feeling a little sad for the coming fall."

Ben let out a long, appreciative sigh. "I wish I were there with you." But before she could acknowledge that comment, he added, "Your reception sounds a little better. Do you have full bars?"

She pulled her phone away from her ear and glanced at it. "I do. I guess the side of the house is where we need to have our conversations from now on. I'm planting flowers in my mom's window boxes. Pink-and-white impatiens, her favorite."

"That sounds great. You should snap a picture and send it to me when you're done. You know, our front walkway is looking a little lonely with our tulips and daffodils wilting. Maybe when you get back, we can plant a border of impatiens along it and get some hanging baskets for the front porch."

"Sure," Melanie said and squatted down to examine the flowers. She picked a dead bloom off one of them. As much as she loved him for his continued cheerfulness and his ability to take an interest in anything she showed an enthusiasm for, sometimes she wished he would stop trying so hard and say what he really felt. It would almost be refreshing to hear him tell her off for once for abandoning him or that he was exasperated with her for her failure to scrape herself up off the floor and move on, as he had done. Because surely he was thinking those things, and she didn't blame him.

"The basement contractor is coming today." Melanie described the flood damage to him and how she and Kelsey had had differing opinions about which company to hire. She filled him in on the projects she'd been undertaking—painting and cleaning the house from top to bottom—and how their realtor, Charlene, wanted to list the Victorian as soon as the basement was finished and hold a big open house. Then she told him about Kelsey's overnight stay and how cute Sprocket was and how they'd eaten their meals out on the porch and their dessert on the dock. She told him everything, basically, except for the preposterous news about the hidden closet capable of time travel and how she'd been wandering around her mom's childhood in her free time.

Without a doubt, she knew that there was no way he would ever believe her without visible, tangible proof. It was way too outlandish a story, and Melanie would never have believed it had it not happened to her. They were both science-minded people, and mentioning it would only cause him to question whether she'd finally gone off the deep end. She didn't want him to worry about her even more than he already was. So she held her tongue and said nothing, only that she felt really close to her mom at the lake house and was especially missing her right then. Even though her reasons for not confiding in him were perfectly sensible, she still hated withholding that from him. It felt like their marriage was becoming a kind of Venn diagram: things she kept to herself, things he kept to himself, and only a shared sliver between them.

Ben finished telling her about the punishing ten-mile run he'd gone on the day before, tackling the hilly terrain of Churchill Park, then shifted gears. "So how did things go with your bloodwork?" he asked nonchalantly, as if it had only just occurred to him, but Melanie knew he'd been dying to know if she'd gone to the lab or blown it off.

"Fine." She toyed with the plastic handle of the garden trowel. "Dr. Maroney said my HCG levels are dropping appropriately. She still wants me to go in for tests every two weeks, though, until my levels are back at zero. She said we can't start on another course of Letrozole until then."

"Well, that's good, right?" He paused for a few beats too long. "Look, Mel, I've been thinking. Why don't we take a little break from the fertility drugs? Five months, six months tops. Just some time to let your body recover, to let *us* recover. We'll just throw the schedule out the window and make love whenever we feel like it, not because some ovulation timetable tells us to. I was just talking to our pharmacy tech, Avani, the other day—"

"You didn't tell her about us, did you?" Melanie interrupted, affronted.

"No, no, of course not. But she and her husband struggled for *five* years to have their son, and they did everything, Mel, absolutely everything. They had just finished their fourth unsuccessful round of IVF and had decided they were done trying. They were finally going to look into adoption. So they stopped everything, then two months later, she found out she was pregnant. It seems like sometimes the harder you try, the harder it becomes."

Tears blurred Melanie's view of the impatiens, turning them into a blood-tinged smudge. Ben had advocated for breaks and told her those "miracle baby" stories before, and it dismayed her. "Have you forgotten the year of 'not trying' we did?" she asked, her volume rising despite her best efforts to keep it level. "Why do you think a break would be any different this time? We were so close, Ben. So close—" Her lips trembled, and she suppressed a sob.

"I know, sweetie," he said softly. "But I think we need this." She imagined him in his parked car outside of the pharmacy, needing to go inside but not wanting to hang up just yet, his hand cradling his cheek. "*I* need this." His voice was gentle yet firm.

He had supported her every step of the way, done everything she asked of him, and never asked for anything in return except for a half-year break without the Letrozole her body needed for her to have even a slim chance of getting pregnant. The one thing she didn't want to give him.

She wiped her eyes with the back of her hand. "I've got to go," she said, ignoring his plea, avoiding giving him a response. "The contractor just pulled up, and I need to show him to the basement." A blatant lie but a plausible one. It was supposed to be the guy's first day of work, and he was already fifteen minutes late.

"I understand. Let's continue this talk tonight, though, okay?"

"Okay."

"And don't forget to send me a picture of your impatiens when you're done, all right? And why don't you throw in one of the house and lake while you're at it too?"

"Will do."

"I love you, Mel."

"Love you too." She dropped the cell phone to the ground and crouched beside the flowers, wrapping her arms around her knees. Her body felt brittle and hollow, a cracked-open seed. Becoming a mother had never been further away. Even Ben was giving up on her.

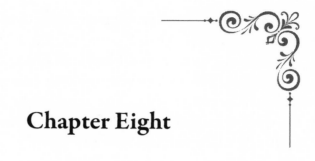

Chapter Eight

Kelsey had overslept. Her plan had been to wake up early, take Sprocket for a quick walk, shower, slip into her flirty green dress, harass Melanie into another exploration of their mom's past, and have a couple of loaves of banana bread baking in the oven, the sweet scent wafting through the house, all before Everett arrived so she could greet him at the door. But when the doorbell rang at 8:25, she was just pouring a bowl of kibble for Sprocket and a bowl of cereal for herself. She froze, unsure what to do. She hadn't showered and had some serious bedhead—not the gently-tousled-yet-kind-of-sexy bedhead most women complained of but tornado-tangled, sticking-up-straight-in-a-faux-hawk-on-one-side bedhead. She frantically tried to pat it down and dove behind the refrigerator door.

"Hi." Melanie's voice floated from the foyer. "Everett from Flood Repair Pros?" Kelsey couldn't make out his reply, but Melanie let out a forced-sounding laugh. Maybe he had offered a lame excuse for his lateness. "It's okay," she said. "I'm Melanie. Come on in."

Sprocket licked his bowl clean and chose that moment to burp loudly. He heard the unfamiliar voice in the foyer and ran to the front door, his claws scratching the wood floor, his bark low and tentative. Kelsey shut the fridge and crept toward the doorway, still out of sight but within better earshot. It was the moment of truth. Though Sprocket didn't know how to roll over or play dead, his true talent lay in his impeccable judgment of character. Kelsey took his first impressions very seriously. He had hidden behind her legs when he'd met Tristan, and look how that relationship had turned out.

"Well, hello there, buddy!" Everett exclaimed.

"Sorry," Melanie said. "That's my sister's dog, Sprocket. He can be a little overexuberant sometimes. But he'll love you for life if you play fetch with him. Or feed him salmon, apparently."

"You like fetch, huh, Sprocket? So do my goldens, Bailey and Bella. They love diving off the pier and going for a swim."

Kelsey risked a quick peek around the corner to see that Everett had dropped to a squat and was scratching behind Sprocket's scraggly ears. She ducked back into the kitchen, a wide smile spreading across her face. *He's a dog person. Yay!* And Sprocket approved and was even letting him pet him on their first meeting. *Double yay! So what if Bailey and Bella are some of the most common, uninspired dog names he could have picked?* That didn't mean that Everett was an unimaginative guy. Maybe the names had come with the dogs, like Sprocket's had from the *Fraggle Rock* fan at the animal shelter where Kelsey had adopted him. Although she definitely thought the name suited him and his offbeat personality.

"So what's the plan for today?" Melanie asked.

Kelsey cringed. Her sister was all business. Kelsey could have kicked herself for hitting the snooze on her alarm. If only *she* had been the one to answer the door. She would have asked Everett follow-up questions about Bailey and Bella, but no, no, Melanie couldn't be bothered to make small talk about pets—yawn.

"Mold remediation," Everett said cheerfully. "I'm going to seal off the vents and doors, get an exhaust fan going in one of the windows for negative pressure, then get to work removing it."

"Sounds good," Melanie said. "We're on a pretty tight schedule to get this place on the market. You quoted us two weeks for the whole restoration, right? Was that two weeks of eight-hour week days?" Her voice drifted off as they descended into the basement.

Kelsey left her untouched cereal on the counter and tiptoed upstairs to the master bathroom to shower, with Sprocket in noisy pursuit.

She stood under the pulsating spray, thinking about Everett and his golden retrievers and his irresistible dimpled grin. She imagined the two of them on the dock with their three dogs, tossing tennis balls into the water for them to retrieve as the sun slowly sank below the horizon. It was a pathetic fantasy, she realized, a sure sign she was rapidly approaching her thirties, but one that gave her a warm, relaxed feeling.

Dear Mom, she composed in her head. *At what point did you know that Dad was the one?* She imagined stepping behind the *Tree of Life* and witnessing her parents' first kiss, their first earnest exchange of I love yous, or maybe even her dad's marriage proposal, but if she remembered correctly, that had happened in Madison, not at Lake Indigo.

The life of singledom was getting to her. Most of her friends were married or in committed relationships, and she was tired of going out for drinks and having them ask eagerly about her love life, as if they, too, hadn't just climbed out of the trenches and already had amnesia about how awful it could be. Though she loved cooking and baking, she rarely did either anymore because it seemed like too much effort for just one person, and she hated doing the dishes afterward. She worked constantly, and what little time she had left over, she spent trying to assuage her guilt for leaving Sprocket home alone by chucking balls for him at the dog park—which she had once thought would be a good place to meet single guys but recently seemed only populated by happy couples. So she spent the majority of her free time on the couch with Sprocket, eating frozen pizza from a paper plate and watching the cooking network, as lonely as the orphan she sometimes felt like—no mom and a dad with another family in Arizona.

So dog lover Everett with his fishing cabin, business cards advertising a *real* business—even one as unglamorous as mold remediation—and not to mention gorgeous body was an appealing fantasy. She decided that by the end of the day, she would ask him over to her apartment for dinner if he hadn't already proposed a date on his own by then. The thought of them eating rosemary lemon chicken by candlelight at her little kitchen table gave her tingles.

But when she opened the basement door, she was greeted by a sheet of clear plastic taped up halfway down the steps. Behind the taut plastic wrap, she could see Everett—at least she assumed it was Everett—wearing a white suit, mask, gloves, and goggles like some kind of spaceman.

"Hello?" she called over the loud whooshing of a fan and the whirring of some tools, but Everett didn't hear her. "Hello?" Already, she felt ridiculous in her jersey-knit dress and eyeliner and was just about to turn around and head back upstairs in defeat when he noticed her.

"Hey!" he shouted, turning off one of the whirring tools. "I'm sorry. You can't come down here right now because of the mold spores in the air. It's not safe. Did you need something?"

"No," she said, ducking her head so he could see her face, or at least what little he could make out of her face through the thick plastic. "Just came down to say hi."

"Oh, hi." He waved at her with the spray bottle he was holding in one hand. "Kelsey, right? You haven't fallen in the lake lately, have you?"

She blushed with a mix of pleasure and embarrassment. *He remembered!* Oh God, but he remembered what a klutz she was. She struggled to come up with a witty comeback and failed. "No. But it's almost warm enough for a swim now."

"Yeah. I heard they're forecasting eighties by this weekend. My favorite kind of weather." He tapped his goggles with one gloved finger and leaned his muscular white-cotton-clad body against the stepladder he was standing on.

The basement looked even worse than before he had started, which hardly seemed possible—chunks of plaster were missing, and a fine layer of white powder covered every surface. The exhaust fan continued to hum, and somewhere overhead, Kelsey could hear Melanie's footsteps. She was probably looking for Kelsey to put her to work dusting baseboards or cleaning windows and would be irritated if she knew Kelsey was distracting the contractor.

"Mine too! But I'd better let you get back to work," she said, trying not to sound as disappointed as she felt. "It looks like you're pretty busy." The goal she had set for herself—to ask him out by the day's end—was clearly not going to happen unless she sprang it on him like a total novice. *Outlook not so good*, her Magic 8-Ball would say. *Ask again later.* And since she had to go back to Bartlett that night for five straight days of work at the pet lodge, she wouldn't have another opportunity to see him again until the next week. Lucky Melanie would get to be there with both Everett and the time portal all week, and she would probably choose to spend the time spreading mulch and pulling weeds or something equally as dull. The thought made Kelsey wish she could call in sick and stay in Lake Indigo, but she knew she couldn't leave Beth short-staffed during one of their highest-volume times of the year.

"Yeah, this first step is a pain in the ass," Everett agreed with one of those rapid-fire, high-pitched laughs. It was a little endearing how weird sounding his laugh was. *Is he self-conscious of it or totally unaware of how different it is?* "It's really easy to screw up and miss something."

KELSEY FOLLOWED HER sister into the kitchen and put her hands on her hips. "But if we don't go now, the next time I'll be able to go is Sunday! And you'd better not break your own rules. Do you hear me? You said we should always go together—never alone. I don't want to miss a single glimpse of Mom's life."

Melanie opened cabinet after cabinet in search of something. The cupboards were mostly empty except for a few cheap dishes they had bought at Target. "We can't go in there right now," she protested. "What if the basement guy has a question or needs us for something? He can't come upstairs to find an empty house."

"He won't," Kelsey said. "I was just down there, and believe me—he's tucked behind plastic and won't be done for *hours*."

"Aha!" Melanie pulled down a green margarita pitcher. "This might do the trick."

Kelsey raised her eyebrows. "It's only ten o'clock. I'm not really in the mood."

Melanie laughed. "It's not for us, dummy. I need to water the flowers, and I thought to buy all the gardening supplies I needed *except* for a watering can. And the Holloways took their hose with them." She said the last bit as if it were the stingiest thing imaginable. "Can you just wait until he leaves? I doubt he'll work past four or five. We'll go then, okay?"

"I can't, Melanie. That's way too late. I work tomorrow, remember? And I have mountains of laundry waiting for me when I get home. You know it's over an hour's drive back to Bartlett, and I really need to get to bed at a decent time tonight because I have to get up so early tomorrow."

"Like you did this morning?" Melanie rolled her eyes and turned to leave the kitchen, the plastic pitcher dangling between her fingers.

"Come on! Aren't you dying to know if Mom went to that cute boy's bonfire? Tell me you're not the least bit curious! Don't you want to know if Grandpa Jack let Mom be a lifeguard? If we wait too long, who knows? She might be in her twenties the next time we visit. We might miss her entire teenage years!"

Melanie paused in the doorway. Kelsey almost had her. She could sense Melanie's resolve crumbling.

"I'll set my watch for one hour," Kelsey promised. "That way, we can be back before Everett even thinks to take a lunch break."

Melanie set the pitcher on the kitchen counter, and before Kelsey could process what was happening, she sprinted into the hallway. Kelsey darted after her, trying to catch the fluttering tie on Melanie's short-sleeved blouse and pull her backward. They giggled like little girls as they raced each other, their bare feet pounding on the wood steps. With her head start, Melanie got to the top of the stairs and her bedroom first, where she gleefully slammed the door in Kelsey's face.

"Butthead!" Kelsey cried as she yanked it open. She almost expected to hear their mom's voice admonishing them from the master bedroom. *No running indoors, girls! Someone is going to hurt themselves.* Before the thought could make her sad, she focused on the fact that they were going to see her right then.

Melanie already had the tapestry pulled back and the door revealed when Kelsey entered the room. "Do you want to do the honors?" she asked.

Kelsey grinned as she turned the latch with a flourish. She felt like Lucy Pevensie climbing inside the wardrobe, but instead of fur coats, pine branches, and snow, the door opened only on the low-ceilinged, claustrophobic room. Two packs of cigarettes lay discarded on the bench next to a tarnished gold lighter. She picked the lighter up. "Do you really think Mom smoked? Maybe we're wrong and this stuff belonged to someone else."

Melanie shrugged. "If she did smoke, talk about being a hypocrite. All those lectures she gave us about lung cancer and COPD and wrinkly skin and yellow teeth. Oh God." She suddenly sounded anguished. "But her PE would make more sense. You know that smoking increases your risk of blood clots, right?"

A chill went down Kelsey's spine as she tried to push away the thought of her mom curled up on the Oriental rug with her blue lips and cold, mottled skin. *Fifty-five years old.* She angrily snatched up the cigarettes but then didn't know what to do with them since she was still wearing a dress. She thrust the packs at Melanie. "We're taking them. Put them in your pockets."

Melanie looked like she was going to object.

"Should we leave a note?" Kelsey asked. "Maybe one of Mom's gems? 'Smoking is a disgusting habit'? 'Smoking causes one in five deaths every year'?"

"No," Melanie said quickly, squishing the cigarettes into the front pockets of her khaki shorts. "No note."

Kelsey didn't bother arguing. She opened the closet door once more. It was late afternoon, and they couldn't find their mom anywhere, not in her bedroom, not in the living room or kitchen, not in the yard, and not sunning herself on the dock. In fact, the only one home at all was a gawky teenage version of Uncle Bob, who was sitting on the porch swing, reading a zombie comic tucked inside a human anatomy textbook. Apparently using decoy reading material was an inherited family trait.

"Well, I guess this was a waste of time. Let's come back later," Melanie said.

"I already told you I won't have time later," Kelsey pouted. She sat down next to Bobby and felt a pleasant floating sensation as he pushed the swing back and forth with his long, thin legs. "Hey, Uncle Bob, where's your sister?"

He ignored her and continued to read his comic.

"Why don't we go next door? Maybe Mom is hanging out with Vinnie."

Melanie looked pained. Through the trees, she studied the Fletchers' cream-colored bungalow as if it were a maximum-security prison filled with murderers and rapists instead of the neighbors' house, where they had spent many a summer day playing. "I don't know. Doesn't it seem kind of nosy? I mean it's one thing to snoop around our family's house, but to go over there and intrude? What if Vinnie's parents are having sex?"

Kelsey laughed and leaped off the swing. "I just want to see if Mom is over there. Tell you what: we won't poke around their bedroom, and if for some reason we come across Mr. and Mrs. Birdwell doing it in the kitchen in broad daylight, we'll leave."

It turned out they didn't have to venture very far into the house. Vinnie and her brother, Bruce, were in the kitchen, packing a Coleman cooler with cans of Pepsi and Tab, but they saw no sign of their mom. Melanie was already turning on her heel to leave when Kelsey stopped her.

She pointed at a straw bag propped open on one of the kitchen chairs. "Beach towels and baby oil," she said. "I bet they're headed to Harris Beach. Maybe Mom is there! Maybe she's lifeguarding."

"Or maybe not." Melanie backed out of Vinnie's way as the teenager flitted around the kitchen. Vinnie looked as sexy as a Bond girl in her gold bikini with a twisted-bandeau top under a peekaboo crocheted cover-up. "You promised we'd stay for only one hour, Kelsey. And if we somehow manage to follow them out to Harris Beach, there's no way we're going to make it back in time."

"Will you hurry up?" Vinnie snapped at her brother. "Christine's going to think we're not coming."

"See? She's there! Come on, Melanie. How can we pass up the opportunity to see Mom in action? We'll just hitch a ride with these guys then come back with Mom when her shift is over."

Kelsey was on a roll with her powers of persuasion. Usually Melanie was the one with the plan and had very specific ideas about how things would unfold, but in the past, Kelsey seemed unsure of herself, and she was all too happy to take charge for once.

The Birdwells had a family canoe rather than a rowboat, and Kelsey and Melanie had to squish together and balance precariously in the middle, Kelsey with her butt perched on top of the cooler, while the siblings, oblivious to their stowaways, paddled it across the lake. Kelsey wondered what would happen if she or Melanie fell out. *Would we make a splash? Would we get wet?* She didn't particularly care to find out, so she focused her attention on maintaining her equilibrium. But when the strip of sandy beach came into view, she suddenly felt cold despite the warm sunshine.

Vinnie jumped out and tied the canoe to the dock while Bruce grabbed ahold of the cooler. Kelsey scrambled to a standing position and would have fallen out had Melanie not reached for her with a steadying hand. The beach and roped-in swimming area were more crowded than she had ever seen them before. During the summers she and Melanie had spent at the beach, mostly young families had occupied the space—kids building sandcastles and riding boogie boards, and middle-aged moms congregating together to gossip on checkered blankets. But in the 1970s, there were teens as far as the eye could see. All of the girls had long, straight hair parted down the middle, and all of the guys wore swim trunks that were colorful and well above the knee. KC and the Sunshine Band's "That's the Way (I Like It)" blared through the speakers of someone's radio, and the smell of grilling hotdogs and coconut tanning lotion scented the air. With a pang, Kelsey wished that *that* had been the Harris Beach of her childhood.

Melanie spotted their mom before Kelsey did and pointed her out. Two lifeguard stands were on opposite ends of the beach, and their mom was in the one the farthest from them. Kelsey could just make out her red swimsuit and the tangled waves of her brown hair. It was disorienting to see her characteristically modest mom, the nonswimmer, in such a position of power. With her athletic shoulders squared and a bullhorn in her lap, she continuously scanned the water as though she might dive off the stand at any moment.

"How badass is Mom?" she quipped as they trudged through the sand, careful not to trip over any of the teens sprawled out on towels and blankets.

"She's amazing," Melanie said, her hand cupped over her eyes to shield them from the sun. "She kind of reminds me of you back in the day, on the starting blocks at your swim meets. So fearless."

It was the nicest thing her sister had said to her in a long time, and Kelsey didn't know how to respond. She thought about downplaying it with a joke but decided against it. "Thanks," she said simply.

A teenage boy wearing orange swim trunks was approaching the lifeguard tower too. *The heartthrob with the feathered haircut!* Definitely not their dad—Kelsey could see that clearly now, with his shorter height and angular jaw. But something that she couldn't quite put her finger on was still familiar about him.

"Hey, Christine," he called, as if she were Rapunzel in her tower or Juliet on her balcony. In just those two words, Kelsey could tell that the young man had it bad for her mom. He saw the same beauty and strength in Kelsey's mom that she was seeing.

Only she wasn't Kelsey's mom yet. She was *Christine*, a confident young woman with her own hopes and dreams, separate from her daughters, and it was embarrassing, really, that it had taken Kelsey so long and under such extraordinary circumstances to realize it. Her mom was her own person and the main character in her own story. She mentally tested calling her mom by her name. *Christine*, Kelsey thought. *Christine.*

"Hi, Lance," Christine called down to him, her smile a flash of white against her bronzed complexion.

"Lance?" Kelsey mouthed at her sister, but Melanie wasn't paying attention. His name, too, was familiar. *Why? Did Mom mention him once upon a time?*

"I wanted to say thanks for lending me your album," Lance continued. "I can't believe I hadn't given The Guess Who a chance before. They're far out!"

"Far out?" Kelsey and Melanie repeated at the same time with matching smirks.

"Christine!" someone else called. Vinnie. She and Bruce had caught up to them and were setting up shop only a few feet from the lifeguard stand. Bruce was spreading two towels out on the sand, and Vinnie was peeling off her crocheted cover-up to expose her pert, perfect body. The sight of them, for some reason, gave Kelsey a sinking feeling in the pit of her stomach.

She didn't know much about Mrs. Fletcher—just that as a teenager, she was gorgeous and self-confident and apparently didn't want their mom hanging out with Lance. *Did she think he wasn't cool enough? Or did she simply want him for herself?* As a middle-aged mother of three, Mrs. Fletcher had still been a great beauty with a penchant for sundresses and chunky jewelry—turquoise rings, amber-beaded necklaces, cowrie shells, and coral bracelets. Despite being petite, she had a large presence, and Kelsey had always been a little intimidated by her. She could never anticipate if Mrs. Fletcher was going to be extravagantly friendly and generous or cold and quick to find fault. Sometimes she pulled Kelsey onto her lap—even if she was getting to be much too big for that kind of thing—rested her chin on the top of her head, and offered her a sip of her sangria. Other times she was distracted and impatient, as if she didn't even remember Kelsey was her neighbor but thought perhaps she was another child from across the lake.

"Fletch, man! What's happening?" Bruce called. He dug into the cooler and extended a can of Pepsi to Lance.

At the same time, Vinnie said to Christine, "It looks busy today! Must be because the Crofts are having that sweet sixteen party for Mary Ann this weekend. Did you get an invitation? I heard they're going to be serving champagne spritzers."

Kelsey was having a hard time keeping up. The three teenagers were crowding her view of her mom. She had to take a step back as two little boys holding black inner tubes around their waists raced past. *Lance is "Fletch?" Of course! He's Lance Fletcher, a.k.a. Mr. Fletcher, a.k.a. Vinnie's future husband.*

Kelsey whipped around to face Melanie at this revelation, but Vinnie was in the way, her sun-bright hair a mesmerizing veil between them. With the dual conversations going on, the steady roar of the beachgoers, and the sun beating down on her, Kelsey couldn't focus. Maybe it was for that reason that it took her several seconds to recognize a sound that should've been unmistakable—cries for help, desperate and panicked.

"My brother!" a girl screamed. "He was just here a second ago!"

Christine clambered down from her tower, pushing Lance and Vinnie out of the way. But Kelsey could see that the mustached lifeguard, stationed all the way on the opposite end of the beach, was already closer to the knot of terrified tweens. *How did he get there so quickly?* Already he was interrogating a black-haired girl, then he plunged into the water, and Christine was still making her way through the maze of spread-out blankets and sunbathers, seemingly in slow motion, though sand was flying everywhere. Kelsey squeezed her arms around her ribcage so tightly that it hurt. It was like one of those bad dreams in which she was late for her destination but could never quite reach it.

Christine finally made it into the water, thigh deep, and she was helping the male lifeguard carry a small boy with dark hair, probably only three or four years old, back to the shore. He was as flimsy and pale as Jilly's body had been the summer she had almost drowned. Flimsier. Paler.

Kelsey gasped as something cold pressed against her arm. Melanie was tugging on her. "Come on," she mouthed, pulling Kelsey toward the action.

They didn't need to skirt around the teens that time. The blankets and towels were vacant as everyone stood in a loose circle around the tragic scene unfolding at the water's edge. Kelsey and Melanie ghosted right through the onlookers.

Christine and the male lifeguard crouched beside the tiny lifeless body. She gave breaths while he pounded rhythmically on the child's chest. But Kelsey could tell in an instant that it was already too late. She understood it in the same way she had immediately understood her mom had been long gone when she found her curled up on the office floor. His lips were the color of the lake at twilight, and his limbs and chest were deathly still and gave off the impression of someone not just asleep but no longer of this world. His young, fragile soul no longer inhabited his little body.

"Kevin," someone sobbed. "Kevin."

Kelsey knelt down in the sand behind her mom, who was still forcing useless air into the boy's lungs, and wished she could feel the gritty sand scratch against her knees. She wished she could rest her hand on her mom's shoulder and tell her that it was time to stop, that she had done her best but it was over. The male lifeguard abruptly ended his compressions, checked for a pulse one last time, then sat back on his heels.

"I'm sorry," he said to the black-haired girl standing a few feet away. Sweat and what might have been tears were pouring down his dark-red face. "I'm so sorry. He's not coming back."

"No!" the little boy's big sister said. "You're wrong. He's not dead. You can't give up! *She's* not giving up!" She pointed at Christine, who was doubled over as if protecting the small body with hers, blowing into the child's purple lips.

"Christine," the male lifeguard said gently. He touched her wrist. "There's no pulse. No breath. We don't know how long he was under, and we've been at this for twenty minutes. We need to face the fact that he's gone."

She gave the dead boy one long last breath then drew back and glanced up for the first time, as though dazed to find others around her. The black-haired girl shouted at her, "No, please! Please don't give up!" but she hardly seemed to notice. Instead she brushed a wet curl off the boy's forehead with shaking fingers then turned to look into the distance, except Kelsey and Melanie were standing right there.

It was like she was looking straight at her daughters. Kelsey couldn't bear to see the expression on her young mom's face—the flat eyes, the pained grimace, the ashen complexion, the snarled hair. It was almost as if she were the one who had drowned, and Kelsey was looking at her mom still trapped under the water. It was a look of utter anguish. And as Kelsey instinctively twisted around to drape her arm over her sister's shoulder and pull her close, she saw it was on Melanie's face too. In the distance, the ambulance from neighboring Arbor Creek, woefully belated, sped up the road.

Chapter Nine

Though Melanie had been nothing but impressed with Charlene in their short time working together—her level of professionalism, her punctuality, even her immaculate wardrobe—quite frankly the realtor was getting on her last nerve. Charlene had arrived at 7:58 in the morning with a photographer in tow, and the two women had been meticulously moving from room to room, staging and snapping pictures for the last two hours. Melanie appreciated thoroughness as much as the next homeowner, but *two hours...* they hadn't even moved outside yet.

She had managed only three hours of sleep the previous night. Melanie didn't know exactly how much time she and Kelsey had spent—an hour and a half, maybe two hours tops—watching on helplessly as the emergency responders loaded up the child's body then walking back home when they realized the Birdwells wouldn't be canoeing back anytime soon, but when they'd gotten back to the house and through the closet, Everett was long gone, and a note was on the kitchen counter—*Phase one complete see you tomorrow!* The sun had already started the descent into its watery bed, and Sprocket was whining for his dinner. While time in the present had apparently clipped along at its regular rate, that tragic day in the 1970s had dripped by like honey. Nothing else explained the stretch of eight hours that they had lost. The time discrepancy gnawed at Melanie, but she had other things to worry about.

Kelsey had stayed until eleven o'clock, and they had rehashed every detail of the child's drowning, wondering if it was why their mom had stopped swimming, why she had never mentioned life-guarding at Lake Indigo, and why Jilly's near drowning that last summer had sent their family packing, never to return to the lake house. And they couldn't stop themselves from asking if she would have noticed the commotion in the water sooner if she hadn't been distracted by her friends. Maybe she could have saved the little boy's life. *Kevin*, Kelsey kept calling him, and each time, it felt like a blow to Melanie's chest. She could still hear his older sister's shrill cries and could only imagine how his mother had reacted when she learned of his death. She hoped their mom hadn't been present at the time.

Once Kelsey had packed up Sprocket and left for her apartment, Melanie had gotten ready for bed and tried to fall asleep to no avail. Eventually she gave up, slipped a purple afghan around her shoulders, and walked out to the moonlit dock. She wanted to talk to her mom so badly right then that she would have given almost anything. She wanted to know how her mom had managed to heal after the tragedy, how she had moved forward with her life. But the answer scared her because, in some ways, like her mom's refusal to go in the water, it seemed like she had never recovered.

"Why didn't you ever tell us?" Melanie asked softly. The May night air was chilly, and she pulled Grandma Dot's afghan more tightly around her. "Did you think we would think less of you?" She tried to imagine her mom sitting them down one afternoon, probably in their teenage years, and revealing the story of the three-year-old drowning on her watch. She could imagine Kelsey bursting into sympathetic tears and hugging their mom, but her own fictional reaction was harder to pin down.

Shock, she realized. She would've been in pure and utter shock, not to find out that her mom had something so sad and troubling in her past—Melanie had intuited that long ago with her mom's many blue days—but that she would actually make herself so bare and vulnerable before them. Christine Kingstad never drank too much and never took sick days. She rarely cried, not even when they watched *Titanic* together as a family and their dad was blowing his nose into his hanky. She pasted on a smile when they asked her, "What's wrong, Mom?" and replied, "Oh, nothing. I just miss your dad," or "This weather's just getting me a little down. Good thing I've got my sunshine in you girls!"

That vulnerability would have shocked Melanie at the time, maybe even frightened her. Her mom was so sturdy, so ordinary, so mom-like, and easy to take for granted. But right then she wanted to curl up inside her mom's vulnerability, like an old blanket or sweater. Melanie wished she could lean on her mom's shoulder and listen to her pour out her sorrow about the drowned boy. She wished she could tell her mom about the baby she had lost, her fear that there would never be another and that she and Ben were drifting apart. *But I can't. Or can I?* Kelsey's suggestion of trying to communicate with their mom through the time portal flitted treacherously across her mind.

Once Charlene and the photographer were outside, Melanie made a beeline for the basement to check on Everett. The plastic sheet was still up, but he wasn't wearing the white jumpsuit, just the mask, gloves, and goggles. In his ripped jeans and tight paint-spattered T-shirt, he looked like one of her college students—the kind who was always ten minutes late for her lecture.

"Hey," she called. "The photographer is gone, so you're welcome to come upstairs if you need to."

"Thanks," Everett said. "I'm just about done wiping everything down with the solution. It will take at least forty-eight hours for it to dry out, though, so I won't be here tomorrow. Just wanted to let you know."

Melanie pursed her lips. It hadn't escaped her notice that Kelsey had chosen Everett over the other contractor simply because he was cute. Her sister was a sucker for dimples. Once, Melanie had explained to her how dimples were actually a genetic deformity of the cheek muscles, and Kelsey had slugged her. But cute only went so far in Melanie's book.

"Was the forty-eight hours of drying time included in your two-week estimate?" she asked.

"You bet." He stood up from his squatting position, his eyes crinkling at the edges as if he were laughing at her, and scratched the bridge of his nose. "You're really eager to sell this place, huh?"

"Kind of." She craved the sense of accomplishment she would feel once the lake house was in the hands of some other happier family. The nice sum of money that would be deposited in Kelsey's and her bank accounts wouldn't hurt either. It would give her a backup plan, a last resort, that she didn't even really want to verbalize to her subconscious mind—IVF treatments and adoption fees. The fact that their dad wouldn't have to lift a finger to help out made her proud too. Then she could go home to Ben, renewed and more herself than she'd been in over a year, and they could try again.

But the discovery of the time portal made the sale of the house feel like she was literally selling off pieces of her mom. She couldn't go through with the sale until she had seen more of her mom's life and learned all she could, all that the door behind the tapestry had in store for them. At that point, she and Kelsey could seal up the closet or figure out a way to divest it of its magic so that its new owners couldn't accidentally trespass on their mom's memories. It would be like a second funeral, one that would finally give her closure.

"But not your sister?" Everett asked.

It took Melanie a few seconds to realize what he was asking. She crouched down on the step so they could see each other better through the transparent tarp. "You're right. If it was up to Kelsey, she'd probably love to keep this house in the family forever."

"But it's not?" he said, his inflection halfway between a statement and a question. "Up to her, I mean."

"No," she agreed, feeling like a bitch. But someone had to make the prudent decision. Maybe Kelsey couldn't see it, but selling their summer home would be best for everyone in the long run. "It's not up to her."

IT WAS ONLY SEVEN O'CLOCK, the sun still high in the sky, but Melanie was already in her pajamas, with her teeth brushed and her face washed. She sat in the twin-size bed with the blue-and-white quilt pulled up to her armpits, staring at the *Tree of Life* tapestry. Though she was physically, mentally, and emotionally exhausted and should just go to sleep, all she wanted to do was step into the closet.

You'd be breaking your own rules, she scolded herself. It would be hypocritical if she asked Kelsey never to go into the time portal without her then did that exact thing behind Kelsey's back. But Kelsey was working at Green Valley Pet Lodge all week and wouldn't be back to Lake Indigo until at least Sunday. That was five whole days Melanie would have to wait to glimpse their mom again. Years seemed to pass so quickly inside the portal that she could be in her twenties or even older by then. Melanie would never know how their mom had borne up under the devastating accident at Harris Beach. She would never know how Lance had gone from being their mom's crush to Vinnie's husband. She would miss the remaining high school years and the entrance of her dad in her mom's life. All of that could be happening at that very minute on the other side of the door only a few feet away from her.

She climbed out of bed. *Why can't Kelsey just take a few days off from her job?* She took care of pampered pets, not animals with life-threatening injuries and illnesses. And it wasn't every day that a person discovered a direct gateway to their mom's past. Surely exploring it warranted a few personal days away from work.

She rested her palm on one of the turquoise flowers on the tapestry's border. Maybe she could check on her mom without cheating Kelsey out of anything. She could just sneak behind the tapestry for five minutes, survey the bedroom to make sure her mom was okay, then leave an anonymous note of sympathy on the bench. An unsigned note couldn't hurt anything. One small gesture of compassion wasn't going to make the future spin wildly off course, and more importantly, if her mom did find it and read it, perhaps it would help her feel less alone. And if the note didn't make it into her hands—if the time portal didn't allow for that kind of contact—then no harm, no foul. At least Melanie had tried. After what she and Kelsey had just witnessed, she felt like she owed her mom that much. Then tomorrow, she resolved, she would call Kelsey and ask if her sister could come any sooner than Sunday for another visit.

Melanie snatched up a pen and the pocket notebook that she used for grocery and to-do lists. Then she lifted the tapestry out of the way, unfastened the door, and hurried inside before she could second-guess herself.

Peering into her mother's bedroom, she knew immediately she had made the right decision. It was like she and her young mom were identical versions of each other separated only by decades. Her mom sat in the antique bed with the comforter pulled up high, just as Melanie had only moments before. Her brown curls were wet and glossy, her cheeks flushed and her eyes teary. She was all alone in her misery. It was like the encounter was meant to be, like Melanie had arrived at just the right moment to comfort her. If only her mom could sense her presence.

"Hi, Mom," Melanie whispered, pushing the door open another inch wider. She wondered how much time had passed since the boy's drowning—hours, days, maybe weeks. "How are you holding up?"

It was the same thing Ben had asked her the day after the miscarriage, one of those well-meaning yet insufferable questions it was impossible to answer without a tinge of venom in her voice. She was suddenly glad her mom couldn't hear her.

Her mom wiped her eyes and stared up at the ceiling.

"I'm so sorry you're going through this right now," Melanie murmured. "I know you can't hear me, but I wish you could know that things are going to get better for you. It's not always going to be so bleak. Somehow you're going to endure this, and you're going to be stronger for it. And you're going to grow up to marry the love of your life and have two daughters who adore you."

She held up the notebook in her left hand, trying to keep the door propped open with her right elbow so she could scrawl her message. *Dear Mom*—the door gave way against her weight, skidding open, propelling her forward. Her handwriting looked atrocious. It was impossible. *I'm sorry, Kelsey*, she thought as she gave up the ruse of that one last technicality and stepped into the bedroom.

Her note was all wrong, anyway. She couldn't address her as "Mom." Melanie sat on the desk chair, no red swimsuit hanging from it now. *Christine,* she started again on a new piece of paper, then words failed her. *What exactly can I say to my teenage mother who's grieving the fatal drowning of a child on her watch?* She studied her mom, whose blank gaze was still fixed on the ceiling. It was no one's fault. It was simply a terrible, terrible accident. But Melanie knew that just like her mom, if the tables had been turned, she, too, would have blamed herself.

You did the best you could, she jotted down before she could overthink it, *but sometimes tragedy simply has your number and even your best isn't enough. You are a* good *person, and it's not your fault that he died. Be gentle with yourself, okay? There are several people—*

The bedroom door suddenly creaked open. Melanie swiveled in her chair to see Vinnie carrying a glass of water. She strode past Melanie and squeezed herself into a tiny space on the bed near Christine's hip. "Drink this," Vinnie ordered, and childlike, Christine obeyed.

Melanie's first reaction was one of resentment. Vinnie was intruding on their mother-daughter moment, which Melanie quickly recognized made no sense: her mom couldn't see or hear her and, in fact, had no idea she even *had* a daughter. Still, Melanie couldn't help the ill will she felt toward the redhead who had distracted Christine from her lifeguard duties in the first place. But of course, Melanie was being unfair. The child would have been submerged by the waves even if the Birdwells and Lance Fletcher hadn't shown up. Vinnie had done nothing wrong by chatting with Christine on the lifeguard tower.

Melanie realized with a jolt that, just as Kelsey had confided the other night, she too had started thinking of their mom inside the time portal as "Christine." It was a weird, blurry distinction, but it somehow helped Melanie reconcile the different versions of her mom. "Mom" was a finite, knowable identity, or so Melanie had thought, but they were just starting to plumb the depths of Christine.

"Are you wearing flannel pajamas under there?" Vinnie asked, tugging the comforter down. "You do realize it's eighty degrees outside, right? Not to mention only eight o'clock on a Saturday night. Even my granny is still out and about right now."

Christine handed Vinnie the empty glass and sullenly rolled away to face the wall.

There are several people—who love you more than you know, Melanie had been poised to write, but she watched, distracted, her unfinished note on the desk.

Vinnie set the glass on the floor. "Move over." She gave Christine a gentle shove and lay down beside her on top of the covers, and suddenly, Melanie's dislike of Vinnie evaporated. She was being the kind of support that Melanie wished she could be for her mom, the kind of friend Christine needed right then, and for that, Melanie was grateful.

"You do realize I'm missing the Birdwell Family Sheepshead Tournament to be here, right? And you know how much I love card games. And my dipshit family." Vinnie stroked the back of Christine's damp head. "God, I could use a cigarette. Do you want one? Your mom won't know. We'll blow the smoke out the window."

Christine turned over halfway and accepted a cigarette from Vinnie's pack of Virginia Slims. She let Vinnie light it for her then propped herself up against the headboard, exhaling deeply as if she'd done it many times before. Melanie couldn't take her eyes off the sight of her health-conscious mother puffing away. She had no doubt as to whose packs of cigarettes she and Kelsey had stolen from the closet bench.

Vinnie jumped up from the bed to grab a ceramic dish off the dresser to use as a makeshift ashtray, then she curled back up next to Christine and lit her own cigarette. The two friends smoked in silence for so long that Melanie was sure her five-minute pledge to herself had expired and she should leave.

"You can't keep beating yourself up," Vinnie said at last, extinguishing her cigarette in the dish.

"Sure I can. I'm quite good at it. Just watch me." Christine stubbed out her cigarette and reached for Vinnie's pack, but Vinnie pulled it away. She caught Christine's hand in hers.

"Look, you can tell me to get bent if you want to, and I'll leave you alone, but you need to stop blaming yourself. No one blames you. In fact, just yesterday, Mrs. Granger was saying how strong of a swimmer you are, and how if you couldn't save him—"

"Get bent," Christine said. Her blue eyes were light and playful, but her tone was dead serious.

Vinnie was still holding the hand that had been reaching for the cigarette pack. She leaned in so that her forehead was lightly touching Christine's, then their noses brushed, and finally their lips met. And before Melanie could process what was happening, Vinnie was kissing Christine, and Christine was kissing back.

Melanie stood up from her chair and took a step back, clutching the small notepad to her chest. She felt warm and light-headed, embarrassed by the intensely private, intimate moment she was witnessing. She was an interloper, a Peeping Tom. She took another step back, crashing noiselessly into the desk but thankfully not feeling it as the solid wood passed right through her time-traveling leg.

Still, she couldn't look away. As the girls continued to kiss, Vinnie wrapped her arms around Christine's narrow waist, and Christine tangled her fingers through a hank of Vinnie's long coppery hair. One of them, Melanie wasn't sure who, let out a breathless sigh. She stumbled to the closet and fumbled to lift the tapestry.

"Vinnie," Christine said. "Stop. We can't do this."

Melanie was tempted to pause and listen to what followed, but her desire to get away was even more pressing. In the sixteen square feet of space behind the door, she collapsed onto the bench, not even bothering to turn on the overhead light. She hastily ripped the note out, laid it on top of the cardigan, took a deep breath, then let her eyes adjust to the dark. Unbidden, the kiss replayed in her mind again and again—Vinnie leaning in and tenderly bringing her face closer and closer to Christine's, the graceful meeting of their lips, their tongues. *Was it their first kiss or something that happened frequently throughout their teens?*

Oh, why did I break my own rules and go through the time portal tonight? It was like walking in on her parents having sex—which neither Melanie nor Kelsey had ever done, thank God—except ten times worse. Parents were supposed to have sex. Melanie's mother, whom she had always thought was straight, was not supposed to be making out in bed with her best friend, the neighbor girl.

Melanie returned to her twenty-first-century bedroom, crawled under the covers, and tried to imagine what Kelsey would say if she knew: "You're overreacting. You're being a prude. Plenty of people experiment in their teens. It doesn't mean Mom was a closeted lesbian." The imagined sentiments were so reassuring that Melanie was tempted to call the real Kelsey and spill all, and only the thought of how pissed off her sister would be stopped her. Just like the initial revelation of the door behind the tapestry, the new one wasn't something that could easily be explained over the phone.

Melanie tried to remember her first kiss—with a boy named Duke Randolph at a post-homecoming party her freshman year of high school. It had been wet and sloppy and tasted like Dr. Pepper. He hadn't even been her date that night, but they'd both chosen to stay upstairs in the family room, watching a horror movie, while everyone else had disappeared into the basement to smoke pot. Duke had slid over on the plaid couch until their thighs were touching, draped his arm heavily over her shoulders, and gone in for the kill.

Where the heck is Duke Randolph now? Probably married with two kids, a mortgage, and a flabby stomach. But it didn't matter. What mattered was Melanie had once kissed him as a fifteen-year-old but had gone on to fall in love with and marry Ben. The same was true for her mom and Vinnie, she consoled herself. Maybe it was their shared traumatic experience. Maybe it was just experimentation, adolescent hormones, the seventies, young love, whatever. It had passed as they'd both matured into happily married women with their own children. *How else were they able to continue to be such good friends living right next door, summer after summer?* Until that final summer when Jilly nearly drowned, of course.

What troubled Melanie as she drifted off to sleep that night was the thought of her parents kissing. Surely they'd had more passionate kisses behind closed doors, but all Melanie could recall right then were stiff pecks on the cheek as her dad left for work. Chaste, closed-mouth kisses when he got home, her mom turning away immediately to tend to whatever was cooking on the stove—nothing half as sensual as the kiss between her mom and Lavinia Fletcher.

Chapter Ten

"Have you tried a pill pocket?" Josh asked, leaning against the Siberian husky's kennel door. "Peanut butter?"

"I've tried everything!" Kelsey insisted. "Peanut butter, pill pockets, his food, a chunk of cheese. He's too smart. He finds it and eats around it or spits it out. His owner warned us. He said we'd basically have to force him to swallow it." She glanced down at the small green bottle in her hand. "Great. Three times a day. This is definitely a two-person job. Can you help me out? I'm not in the mood to get bitten."

"Sure." Josh rolled up the sleeves of his navy-blue hoodie and stepped inside. "Hi, Koda. Gosh, you're handsome. Has anyone ever told you that you look like a doggy Frank Sinatra with those blue, blue eyes?" He reached out his hand to let the husky sniff him.

Kelsey handed him the pill bottle. "A doggy Frank Sinatra?"

"Don't tell me you can't see the resemblance."

She carefully opened Koda's jaws, squeezing his lips against his teeth. "Oh, definitely. I guess I was more surprised by your use of the word 'doggy.' What are you—three years old?"

He laughed and deposited the pill in the back of the dog's throat.

Kelsey gently closed Koda's mouth, holding it shut until she heard him swallow. "Good boy." She stroked his chest. "Good doggy," she added for Josh's benefit. After giving Koda the rest of the cheese slice she'd unsuccessfully tried to wrap the pill in, she stood up. "Thanks. It's been such a crazy morning that I've had to pee for over an hour and still haven't gone. The grass out back was actually looking kind of tempting when I was last out there."

"Sheesh! Please go relieve yourself. I'll cover for you." He grabbed Koda's water bowl to refill it. "It's only going to get busier, you know!" he called after her. "Beth told me we're getting at least ten more dogs this afternoon and two cats. It's a sign of the apocalypse. And Memorial Day weekend, I guess."

Beth intercepted Kelsey on her way back from the bathroom. "Can I talk to you in my office for just a second?" she asked.

A list of scenarios whirled through Kelsey's mind, all of them ending in Beth asking her to pick up more hours. "You bet," she said, trying to hide the reluctance she felt. She snitched a miniature Milky Way from the candy dish on Beth's desk as she sat down across from her.

Beth let out a tearful sigh, and it quickly became apparent that the talk was a Leona-related one not a work-related one. Kelsey relaxed a little, still sympathetic to her boss's parenting struggles but relieved that she wouldn't have to spend any more time at the pet lodge and away from Sprocket and the lake house.

As Beth went on about Leona's latest act of defiance, wanting to drop out of high school and move in with twenty-year-old Dave, Kelsey let her thoughts drift elsewhere—to her mom and the drowned boy, Kevin; to Melanie all alone at the lake house, probably obsessing in that uniquely Melanie way she had; to the alternate reality of the lake house in the 1970s, with her mom's teenage years unfurling, hour by hour, day by day, and slipping away into the ether, unobserved; and to Everett and his hazel eyes and cute butt. She was missing it, all of it, and she couldn't help feeling both resentful and slightly desperate.

"So what do you think?" Beth asked with a worried look on her face.

"Umm..." Kelsey chewed the bite-size Milky Way to buy herself time. She had no idea what her boss was asking her. She vaguely recalled hearing Beth say something about her parents' house in Tennessee. *Is she planning to send Leona to stay with them, hoping that their influence will reform her wild ways?* "I think that could work..." she said in as noncommittal of a voice as she could muster.

"You do?" Beth leaped up from her chair and squashed her in a hug. "Oh, Kelsey! You have no idea how much this means to me! I know it's going to be the busiest weekend ever, but there's no one I trust more to take care of things around here than you. And I'm just so hopeful that a visit to my parents will do both Leona and me some good. And I promise you, I promise you, I will make this up to you. How does a nice, long paid one-week vacation sound? As soon as we're not so busy..."

She rattled on, but Kelsey was too distressed to listen. Oh crap. She'd just agreed to work that Sunday and Monday—her only two days off, the light at the end of her tunnel, the days that she had promised Melanie she would return to Lake Indigo and they would dive back into the time portal with a vengeance. It was a holiday weekend, no less, when so many families boarded their dogs, and it was bound to be pure chaos.

"Just to clarify," she ventured, "Josh isn't available this Sunday and Monday?"

"He's already working," Beth said distractedly, scrolling through her cell phone. "I'm going to text Leona right away. She loves her grandpa. If anyone can get her to see reason, it's him."

"What about Alan?"

"He asked off ages ago. He and his family always go to their cabin up north for Memorial Day."

Lucky him, Kelsey thought. "Have you considered asking Taylor to help out?" she asked, her last resort, even though she knew she was grasping at straws. Their receptionist was a sweet girl who loved dogs and was always offering to get more involved in the animal-care side of things, but she wasn't a quick learner. She did best following basic directions, which was tedious for whoever else was working with her.

Beth made a face. "In a real pinch, maybe. But not over Memorial Day weekend. I know you and Josh can handle it, though. You guys make such a great team." She stood up, cell phone still in hand, and started walking toward the door. It was clear Kelsey was being dismissed.

How am I going to break the news to Melanie? Her sister already thought she wasn't pulling her weight and was even more frantic to have her around since the discovery of the door. And it would be weeks until Kelsey could drive out there again for a visit, weeks until she could glimpse her teenage mom—if she was still a teenager by that time—weeks until she could enjoy sitting out on the twilit dock, eating strawberry shortcake, and weeks until she could flirt with Everett again, if he was even still working on the basement at that point.

Beth opened the door, and Kelsey nearly collided with Josh, who was standing right outside. Behind him, astonishingly, was Melanie, dressed in a crisp white blouse and a denim skirt. Seeing her sister in her place of employment was like seeing a minor celebrity on the street, like spotting the Channel 4 news anchor in the restaurant booth next to hers. Kelsey did a double take. Her first thought was that Melanie somehow already knew about Beth's request to have her work more days, and she was there to take Beth to task. No, Melanie was shrewd, but she wasn't clairvoyant.

"Wow," Kelsey said, stepping forward to embrace her sister and give Melanie's hazelnut braid an emphatic tug. "What a nice surprise! What are you doing here?"

"I realized I couldn't come all the way from Ohio and not see the place where you spend so much of your time," Melanie said. She was smiling broadly, but her gaze was directed somewhere over Kelsey's left shoulder. "I wanted to meet the people and dogs you speak so fondly of." Her eyes flicked guiltily toward Kelsey, and Kelsey's initial wariness slunk off into a corner.

Is Melanie finally making an effort? Is she really here to meet my coworkers and get a tour of the place, in the same way I flew out to Cleveland to tour the campus when she got her tenure-track gig? Her stomach gave a cautious little leap. Melanie was taking her seriously for once and showing an interest in her work. It dropped back into place within seconds, and she began wondering what Melanie would think of Green Valley Pet Lodge and if her suspicions would be confirmed that Kelsey really was a glorified pet sitter. Maybe she would wrinkle her nose at the funky smells back in Pooch Place. And afterward, she might try to give Kelsey another pep talk about returning to college and making something worthwhile of herself. Kelsey's hackles rose at the thought. *Slow down, girl*, she warned herself, *and don't assume the worst of Melanie.* She hadn't said or done anything wrong—yet.

"Is this your sister?" Beth asked, grabbing both of Melanie's hands and squeezing them. "The doctor?"

"Not that kind of doctor," Melanie corrected with a charming, self-deprecating smile. "I teach college biology. You must be Beth. I've heard so many good things about you."

So Melanie did listen to her, at least some of the time. Kelsey rocked back on her heels and watched the two women interact. Nearby, Josh was trying to catch her eye. He wiggled both eyebrows upward in a meaningful way, and she remembered all the less-than-flattering things she'd confided to him about Melanie. She wiggled her eyebrows back at him.

He hooked his thumb in the direction of Pooch Place. "I'll take care of the dogs, K. K.," he mouthed. "You take your time."

"Thanks," she mouthed back to him. "I won't be long."

tragedy that had happened the summer she was sixteen, but there she was, sitting with Melanie, and they were acting like *real* sisters, or at least the kind of sisters Kelsey had always wanted to be. *I wish Mom could see us like this.* Maybe it would somehow erase the mean comments Kelsey had made about Melanie right before her mom's pulmonary embolism. It saddened her that her mom had died thinking her daughters didn't get along.

Their lunch arrived, and Melanie leaned forward on her elbows. "I need to confess something," she said, and Kelsey was tempted to stop her. Whatever Melanie was going to confess was probably going to ruin their pleasant moment, and she wanted to linger in it as long as possible. She studied her sister's face and read the guilt there she had noticed earlier—not guilt that she had never shown an interest in Kelsey's job before but guilt over something else.

"Last night, I went inside the closet," Melanie said.

Kelsey almost laughed. It sounded ridiculous spoken in such a melodramatic hush. She stared down at her pomegranate-and-millet salad and tried not to embarrass herself by shouting. *Is this why Melanie wanted to treat me to lunch? So we would have an audience and things would have to remain civil?* Leave it to Melanie to try to orchestrate even Kelsey's reaction. She always, always, *always* had to have the upper hand. She had been the one to dictate their time-traveling rules, but since they were *her* rules and meant to suit only her, she didn't mind flouting them.

"Why am I not surprised?" Kelsey scowled at her sister.

"I'm so sorry," Melanie rushed on. "I know I'm the one who suggested we always go in there together, and I know there's no excuse. But I was just so worried about how Mom was doing after we left her, and I couldn't sleep, and I thought just peeking in on her for five minutes would put my mind at ease." She fingered the paper-napkin-wrapped bundle of silverware, avoiding Kelsey's disapproving gaze. "But it didn't. I saw something that made things worse."

Kelsey considered not taking the bait—for about two seconds. She imagined her mom getting fired from her lifeguarding job and the small lake community shunning her and wondered if her mom had been clinically depressed or maybe even suicidal. "What did you see?"

"Mom was in bed, clearly grieving," Melanie said. "And Vinnie was there, trying to cheer her up. They were talking and smoking cigarettes"—she widened her eyes momentarily at the mention of the cigarettes but gave no other comment and sped right on—"then Vinnie kissed Mom. And Mom kissed her back. Like a *real* kiss. Not a friendly peck on the cheek but serious making out." She exhaled heavily, winded, as though she had just sprinted one hundred meters.

Kelsey sat back in her chair. "Mom was making out with Vinnie? You mean Lance, right?" Melanie had the names confused. It was an easy mistake since Vinnie was a boy's name.

But Melanie shook her head back and forth slowly. "Not Lance. Vinnie. La-vin-ia." Then, as though Kelsey might be dumb and needed it spelled out further, she added, "Mrs. Fletcher."

In her mind's eye, Kelsey saw her mom and Mrs. Fletcher standing at the kitchen counter, elbow to elbow, making sandwiches for the kids. Her mom slathered the mayonnaise on the bread. Mrs. Fletcher slapped on the slice of bologna and cut the sandwich into two halves. Her mom poured everyone glasses of cherry Kool-Aid while Mrs. Fletcher swatted Stephen's hand away as he tried to steal more pickles. Those were the two people Melanie had seen kissing in bed—it was unfathomable.

"Are you sure you didn't somehow misinterpret what was going on? Catch it out of context?" she asked, scooping spinach, radicchio, millet, and avocado onto her fork. "I mean Mom was grieving. She wasn't in a good place. You said Vinnie was comforting her."

"That's true," Melanie conceded, frown lines settling around her lips like parentheses. "But what I saw was pretty hard to misinterpret.

They were wrapped around each other, in bed, kissing. Fully clothed, though. At least they were when I left."

"Thank God for small favors," Kelsey murmured around a mouthful of salad.

"I hadn't thought of that, but I suppose you're right," Melanie said, and a snorting laugh escaped.

Melanie rarely snorted when she laughed, but when she did, it usually indicated the onset of a case of the giggles, which tended to set Kelsey off on her own laughing fit, too, then they fed off each other's laughter like an explosive chain reaction. The more inappropriate the situation, the more hilarious and difficult it was to stop laughing. Once, at a funeral for their great aunt, the elderly man behind them had farted, and they had been tearfully breathless from their silent giggles until their dad had sternly ushered them outside and told them to calm down and rejoin them when they had themselves under control. They hadn't gone back inside for twenty minutes, ten of which they'd spent laughing, and the other ten they'd spent just talking and hanging out because the funeral was boring.

Now Kelsey was laughing so hard she was worried she was going to choke. She tried to wash her food down with a swig of herbal tea, but her shaking hands caused it to dribble all over her T-shirt. "Stop it. Stop it. It's not funny," she wheezed, half scolding herself, half scolding Melanie.

Tears were streaming down Melanie's face, and the couple at the table next to them was staring at them as though they'd just escaped from the looney bin.

"She started it," Kelsey addressed them, pointing at her sister. "I swear, I can't take her anywhere."

This caused Melanie to laugh even harder. The couple smiled tolerantly and looked away.

Eventually, they managed to contain themselves, mostly by taking deep breaths and pointedly not looking at each other. But Kelsey could feel the giddiness just below the surface, threatening to bubble up at the slightest smirk or chuckle from Melanie. The laughing fit and the news about her mom had left her feeling hollow and muddled, like she'd just woken up from a strange but very realistic dream.

"Do you think it was their first kiss?" she asked soberly. "Like a one-time thing?"

"I honestly don't know," Melanie said, picking up and nibbling on her untouched croissant sandwich. "When I was leaving, I heard Mom say, 'Stop. We can't do this.' So maybe it was their first time and they just got swept up in the moment. Maybe they laughed about it afterward. Or maybe Mom meant, 'Stop, we can't *keep* doing this,' like it had been going on for a while, and it was something she wanted to put an end to. I really have no idea."

Do you think Mom loved her? Kelsey wanted to ask next but knew it was an impossible question and one that Melanie would probably scoff at. But it was what she most wanted to know. Like a wife who had found out her husband had cheated on her: *Do you love her, the other woman?* Because the emotional betrayal was somehow worse than the physical one. Although that analogy didn't work because Kelsey wasn't the betrayed spouse in the situation, and her mom hadn't cheated on anyone. Vinnie had come well before her mom had even met her dad. *So why do I feel so betrayed?*

She had always considered herself to be an open-minded person. Her best friend in high school, Ingrid, had come out as a lesbian their junior year, and Kelsey had done her best to support her, even helping her break the news to her less open-minded parents. But it was somehow very different to discover that her mom might be gay or bisexual. For starters, it was hard acknowledging her mom had a sexuality at all—the woman who wore large, shapeless nightshirts and seemed to use her bed primarily as a cozy reading place—but to imagine it as something separate from the bonds of her marriage and the birth of her children was even more problematic. Kelsey had been willing to believe that her mom had had crushes and first loves—had been tickled even by her flirtations with Lance Fletcher—but realizing Vinnie was the object of her mom's affection somehow changed that. *Why? Am I not as progressive as I thought I was?*

No, she thought adamantly. It wasn't that her mom had kissed another girl. It was that certain bedrock beliefs she had held were being shaken to the core, tiny things she'd taken for granted—for example, when Mom called cigarettes a "disgusting habit," she meant smoking was something she had never done—and larger things she had counted on as indisputable facts—that Mom was heterosexual, she only had eyes for Dad, and she had a perfectly ordinary friendship with the neighbor lady at their summer lake house. Kelsey had anticipated—even relished—the possibility that the time portal would reveal some surprises about her mom. But she hadn't anticipated such a big revelation. She couldn't have when her mom had always been such a closed book.

"Well, we obviously need to figure out what their relationship was," she said, scooting her chair closer to the table. "As soon as I finish this block of shifts, we'll go back into the portal—together. And we'll observe Mom and Vinnie as much as possible."

Melanie fiddled with her braid, her eyes cast down. "But don't you see? That's the thing. I don't think we should go in there anymore. It feels like a huge invasion of Mom's privacy. Initially, it was just observing her childhood memories, like paging through pictures in a scrapbook. But now, it's really big, personal stuff that Mom chose not to share with us. It's like snooping in her diary but even more intrusive. I mean, would you want someone digging around in your teenage years without your permission? Viewing your stupid mistakes? Your first sexual encounters?"

Kelsey's face felt warm. "Are you being serious? You act like we're doing it maliciously, but we're doing it with the best of intentions—to be close to Mom and better understand her. She never had a chance to tell us these things because she died unexpectedly. How do you know that the magic of the time portal isn't in some way connected to her? That she isn't showing us all the important moments that made her who she was?"

The parenthetical frown lines were back, and Melanie's forehead was creased too. "If she was so eager for us to find the time portal, Kelsey, then why did she keep it hidden behind the tapestry? And why did she stop taking us to the lake house and rent it out to the Holloways instead?"

"But she left the house to us in her will. She must have known that one day, when the time was right—"

"No," Melanie interjected. "I'm pretty sure about this. *She doesn't want us there.*" She bent down, rooted around in her purse, and pushed a folded rectangle of yellow paper into Kelsey's hands. "That's Mom. In her own words."

Kelsey couldn't open the note quickly enough. One of the edges ripped as she unfolded it.

Who is this? the note read in the loopy, precise cursive of a teenage girl. *I don't know how you found this room, but it is OFF LIMITS and very private. Please respect that and keep out of my business. You clearly don't know the first thing about me or what happened last month. Let's keep it that way. C. A. M.*

Kelsey flinched as if she'd been personally scolded. She glanced up at Melanie, who was studiously looking away, then back down at the note, scouring it for clues in an effort to understand. The words were written so deeply in the paper, she could trace the raised ridges on the other side with her fingertips. C. A. M., Christine Ann Montclare, had clearly been very angry when she'd written them.

"What the hell?" Kelsey half whispered, half shouted at her sister, vaguely mindful of the couple at the table next to them, who were packing up to go. "Why did she write this? What did you *do*?"

"I was trying to catch you around your lunch break," Melanie said, glancing over her shoulder as Josh departed. "I know you guys are swamped this week, but I was hoping to steal Kelsey away for a quick bite to eat."

"I don't know—" Kelsey started, thinking about all of her unfinished duties piling up and all of the new pets arriving that afternoon, but Beth interrupted her.

"Of course! You two go! Enjoy yourself. Josh and I can take care of things. It's the least I can do." Beth was clearly delighted that she was able to do a good turn for Kelsey so quickly. But Kelsey hoped Beth didn't consider it paying her back completely and that a week of paid vacation was still on the table. The two things were hardly equivalent.

"Great," Melanie said. "Thanks so much. Where should we go, Kels-Bels?"

"I know just the place."

THEY SETTLED INTO A cozy corner table at Kelsey's favorite café in Bartlett: Soup, Sandwiches and Such. On the drive, Melanie had filled her in on the photo shoot and Everett's day off while the basement was drying out. Kelsey had broached the subject of the Sunday and Monday shifts she had accidentally agreed to pick up, but instead of seeming pissed off, Melanie had seemed only slightly disappointed and even sympathetic. She had only nice things to say about the pet lodge—how friendly Beth and Josh were and how they clearly both thought the world of Kelsey, how clean the kennels were, and how cool the playground equipment in the fenced-in yard was.

As Kelsey sat across from her sister and sipped her herbal tea, a sense of well-being settled over her. Yes, she still had to work for ten days straight, and yes, she and Melanie were still at odds about selling the house, and yes, her heart still hurt for her mom and the

"I didn't *do* anything," Melanie insisted. "Like I told you, I went into the portal for five minutes last night, saw Mom and Vinnie kissing, and left. But I couldn't help wanting to reach out to her in her grief. I wanted her to know that someone else understood her and wasn't judging her, so I... I left a brief note. Then this morning, I stepped back inside and found this reply on the bench."

Kelsey leaned forward, tensing the muscles in her back. "And what did this 'brief note' say?"

"Just that it wasn't her fault that the boy drowned and to not be so hard on herself." Melanie jutted her chin out defensively. "It was only a few sentences, and I didn't sign my name."

"Obviously." Kelsey rattled the thin paper in her hand for effect. "And you didn't think that would freak her out? Getting a note from some creepy, anonymous Big Brother? In a secret place she thinks no one else knows about? A place that travels to her most intimate memories?"

"Writing her a letter was *your* idea!" Melanie said. "And yes, clearly, it was a misguided one. But when you put it like that, can't you understand why we need to stop this thing *right now*?"

Kelsey wanted to say so much, but she didn't trust herself to thoughtfully articulate it to her sister when she was so furious. How dare Melanie impose rules on the time portal and say they needed to be "smart about it and not rush into anything we can't take back" then disregard her own advice and potentially muck everything up.

"Listen, I really need to get back to work, but this conversation is far from over. So I have a proposition for you." Kelsey gritted her teeth and tried to sound more welcoming than threatening. "If you don't have anything pressing to do today, why don't you stick around Bartlett? You can hang out at my apartment with Sprocket until I get home and just relax for once, and when I get off work, I can make us dinner, and we can finish this discussion. You could even stay overnight if you want. I still have the guest bed made up."

Melanie was going to turn her down, Kelsey knew, rattling off some excuse about needing to re-grout the bathroom tiles or be there to meet Everett early in the morning. She didn't even know what had made her offer except that, for better or for worse, she and Melanie were embroiled in the hot mess together, and they had no one else to confide in without sounding like crazy people. But Melanie had probably had enough "sisterly bonding time." She probably wanted to return to her delusional place of moral high ground back at the lake house, where no one was around to contradict her.

But Melanie surprised her. "Sure. Thanks." She stood up from the table, grabbing her to-go coffee cup. "But just so you know, there's no way you're changing my mind. I am officially done with the time portal, and I would strongly advise you to do the same."

Chapter Eleven

K elsey's apartment was tiny and rather messy—not dirty, just cluttered with open cookbooks on the kitchen counters, brightly colored dog toys littering the carpet, and so many take-out menus stuck to the fridge with magnets that Melanie couldn't see the cream-colored surface beneath. If it were Melanie's house, it would have driven her crazy, but since it was someone else's place, it felt artistic and kind of homey that way. It was a temporary refuge from her real life—both her old troubles back in Ohio and the new ones brewing at the lake house. She and Sprocket went for a long walk around the neighborhood, as Kelsey had suggested, since the weather was so beautiful. She snapped a picture with her phone of Sprocket grinning and texted it to Ben with the caption, *Hard not to become a dog person when I'm in the company of this cutie.*

He replied almost immediately, even though she knew he was probably still at work. *Great! Does that mean we're getting the St. Bernard I've always wanted?*

Sitting down on a bench near the apartment complex's man-made pond, she let out more of the retractable leash so Sprocket could explore. *There's no emoji to reflect my facial expression right now, so let's just say no.*

He texted her a string of frowny faces. *What about a dog that weighs less than me? Something like a border collie? Or even a Yorkie. I'm not picky.*

She laughed, surprising herself by how carefree she felt despite the past twenty-four hours, and Sprocket shot her his droopy-tongued smile again. She texted his picture to Kelsey with the simple caption, *Look who misses you.*

Give me a little more time to warm up to dogs in general, she replied to Ben. *Right now I love only one, and I doubt that Kelsey would ever give him up.*

She didn't want to get Ben's hopes up, but she had been more seriously considering his proposition of getting a dog, which was among the hundreds of other propositions he'd made, like ballroom dancing lessons, learning to rock climb together, and hosting a monthly board game night with their friends. Not having grown up with pets, she had never been an animal person, and it mystified her how Kelsey could have turned out so differently. She wondered if Kelsey had learned to love dogs or if her love was just somehow innate. While Melanie thought some cats and dogs were beautiful creatures, they just didn't seem worth all the effort—cleaning up the fur, the slobber, and the poop, having to commit to a rigid feeding and walking schedule, and needing to find someone to take care of them whenever she traveled. It was like having kids without the benefit of having kids, which of course was her main problem.

She watched Sprocket rolling in the grass on his back with joyful abandon. That was why people loved dogs. Dogs embraced life and savored every second of it, no matter if it meant looking like a total dork. When she bent forward to scratch his belly, he licked her wrist in appreciation. She liked how she was out there in the middle of the day, sitting on a bench unselfconsciously, something she would not have ordinarily done, and all because she was walking a dog. Not only was Sprocket a good companion, he was also like a permission slip to be more present in the world.

They headed back to Kelsey's apartment at a leisurely pace, Melanie allowing Sprocket to mark his territory every ten feet or so.

Either he was an overzealous little guy, or he had a bladder problem. It was nearing the time Kelsey had said she would be home from work, but there was still no sign of her, so Melanie curled up on one end of Kelsey's couch. It took her a second to realize it was her parents' old sectional—silvery gray with navy-striped pillows. When their dad had sold their house in Elm Grove and moved to Tucson, he had asked both of them if they wanted any of the furniture because his second wife, Laila, wanted to pick out new things. Melanie had asked only for the dining room table, which had been Grandpa Jack and Grandma Dot's wedding gift to her parents. But Kelsey had apparently snagged the couch, the coffee table, some end tables, and even an ottoman. No wonder the place felt so homey to Melanie.

She pulled one of her mom's old throw pillows onto her lap and balanced her phone on top of it. *I learned something pretty shocking about my mom*, she texted Ben.

Five minutes later, his reply came. *Do tell.*

It's not something I can really explain over text, she said.

I'm leaving soon. I'll call you.

I can't really talk tonight. I'm staying over at Kelsey's, and she'll be home any minute.

Okay, he texted. *Tomorrow, then. Keep me in suspense.*

She ran her fingers over the row of buttons on the pillow's slipcover. *Just one hypothetical question for you before I go. If you found one of your parents' diaries, would you read it?*

You found your mom's DIARY?

Melanie couldn't help smiling. If he only knew the truth of what she had *really* found. *I said this was a HYPOTHETICAL question!*

There's no way my mom would have ever kept a diary, and if my dad had ever kept one, it probably would've just detailed every fish he ever caught, so no. Too boring.

While she agreed with Ben's assessment of his straightforward, salt-of-the-earth parents, she had once thought the same thing about her mom, so it wasn't too much of a stretch to imagine that Jim and Barb Keyes also had surprising secrets in their pasts. Maybe Jim's adolescent journal, if it existed, was a rip-roaring, adventurous page-turner complete with his own homosexual encounters. But probably not.

Thanks, that's very helpful, she texted. *Not.*

Oh, so this was more of an ethical scenario than a hypothetical scenario?

You could say that.

Several minutes passed without a response, and she figured he was busy helping a customer. There was more to her resolution to quit using the time portal than she had told Kelsey earlier. Invading her mom's privacy and the handwritten warning she'd found were about seventy-five percent of her reasoning. The other twenty-five percent was fear, plain and simple. The kiss between her mom and Vinnie was like a stray thread on a sweater, a thread that her sister was eager to pull. But Melanie was afraid that if they dove any deeper into their mom's past, the whole sweater would unravel right before their eyes. They would continue to find out more things about their mom that they wished they didn't know. The memory of her mom was the only thing Melanie had left of her, and she couldn't bear the thought of it being tarnished, not when her mom wasn't there to answer their questions and contextualize her past for them.

Her phone dinged as Ben's response arrived. *If one of my parents was dead, and it was my last connection to him or her, I think I would want to read it.*

Even if you found out something shocking?

Yes.

She sank back into the couch. It was one of the things she loved most about her husband—his sense of assurance. At his core was an abiding belief that he and the people he loved deserved good things, so good things would happen to them. Most of the time, they did.

And when they didn't, he had faith that things would turn out all right in the end. It seemed like such a naïve, childlike way of viewing the world, yet it had been one of the qualities that had initially drawn her to him. He was such a happy person with that worldview, and she was happier in his company. If she could only adopt his same upbeat strategy, it seemed like she could let go of so much of the stress that plagued her on a daily basis. But it was a lot harder to do than it seemed.

Even if the front cover said, 'Warning! Keep out! Do not read! This means you, Ben!'? she wanted to ask but didn't. Her mom's outraged rebuff of her well-meaning note still smarted.

"Hi-ho, Kelsey the Frog here," Kelsey called from the front door in the Kermit impression she had perfected in childhood. She was carrying a paper grocery bag and shoved over a cookbook on the counter to set the bag down as Sprocket sprang from the couch to greet her.

"Hey," Melanie said, slipping her cell phone into her pocket. She stood up to stretch and gauge her sister's mood.

"Are you hungry? I thought I'd make us some comfort food. Dad's famous artery-clogging bacon macaroni and cheese and double-fudge brownies." Apparently, most of the pissed-off energy that had been crackling off of Kelsey earlier had dissipated. She bent down to Sprocket's level. "Yes, I know *you're* hungry. You're always hungry. Would you like some *dinner*? Some *food*? Is that what you're trying to tell me?" The schnauzer spun more and more frantic circles around Kelsey after each emphasized word, until she finally filled his dish. "Gosh, I can't tell you what a relief it is to come home and know that this poor dog isn't holding his bladder and bowels. Thanks so much for walking him earlier."

"It was my pleasure," Melanie said, and she genuinely meant it. "And yes, I'm starved. I think we deserve some comfort food after today."

THE BROWNIES WERE IN the oven, and Melanie and Kelsey had played a quick game of rock-paper-scissors to see who would get the mixing bowl and who would get the wooden spoon. Melanie had won, and she was standing against the counter, lazily licking the rich, chocolatey batter from her index finger. It was probably salmonella laced from the raw eggs, as her mom had always warned them, but at least she would die a happy death. For the two months she had carried her baby, she had religiously steered clear of all the common foods to avoid during pregnancy—raw cookie dough, sushi, deli meats—but it hadn't mattered.

"I've been thinking more about what you said," Kelsey started, "about respecting Mom's privacy. And I totally get it, especially since Mom could be such a private person. But you have to understand where she was coming from with that note, right? Here she is, only sixteen years old and at a crazy low point in her life, and she finds this random message from God knows who in her special hiding place. It would be like finding a stranger's commentary at the end of your diary entry. Of course she was upset. I know I would be! But that doesn't mean that the woman she grew up to be wouldn't be open to letting her daughters view her memories, right?"

"That's awfully convenient logic, though, isn't it?" Melanie asked. "Since we can't really ask her older self how she would feel about us time traveling through her life." The shameful memory of her voyeurism washed over her. Spying on her mom and Vinnie wasn't fair to Melanie's sixteen-year-old mom, so vulnerable in her grief, so new and fumbling in her sexuality, and it also wasn't fair to her deceased, middle-aged mom, who had never hinted at the fact that she and Lavinia Fletcher had ever been anything more than friends. If her mom hadn't been cremated, Melanie suspected that she would be rolling in her grave at the thought of her adult daughters ogling her teenage exploits.

"But we *can* ask her." Kelsey had stopped licking the wooden spoon and was staring at her. "We might have to wait a few weeks until she's a little older, of course, but then we can write her another a note. A clearer note, identifying ourselves and explaining everything—"

Melanie reeled backward as if her sister had struck her. "Identifying ourselves?" She set the bowl in the sink so she could steady her hands against the counter. "You mean you want to tell her our names, who we are, and what year we're traveling from?" She closed her eyes and tried to imagine the shockwave that could set both in backward and forward motion. Their mom would know ahead of time what gender her children would be and what names she was going to give them, for starters. She would know that they were watching her and could access any moment she lived through at the lake house, which could alter any of her major life decisions. It might make her want to destroy the tapestry or board up the closet. If it changed the past, she might try to talk to them, approach them one afternoon when they are adolescents, and say somewhat mysteriously, "I know what you're going to find in the lake house one day." A chilling thought suddenly swept across Melanie's mind. "You're not going to tell her about her death, are you?"

Kelsey blinked her wide-set blue eyes very slowly. "No, of course not. Well, maybe. God, I don't know." She flailed her hands between them as if trying to erase the last minute of their conversation. "I'm not trying to open up Pandora's box here. I'm really not," she repeated when Melanie sucked in a breath in preparation to protest. "I don't want to botch up our lives, and I certainly don't want to botch up Mom's. I just miss her so much, and I want to know her better, and I can't help feeling like she or maybe even some higher force is guiding us, like we were meant to discover that closet and we were meant to see those particular glimpses of Mom's life. I don't know the reason yet, but I'm confident there is one. We can't just walk away right now. We have to keep exploring."

Melanie made her way back to the couch, feeling like she might otherwise collapse. Kelsey had always been fearless, but the line between fearlessness and reckless stupidity was sometimes razor thin. "Maybe you're right. But I just don't think I can go inside the time portal in good conscience anymore. Though I understand if you still want to," she added hastily. "Mom and the time portal belong just as much to you as they do to me, so I can't tell you what to do." She wasn't exactly trying for reverse psychology, but if it worked, then all the better. But her big -sister instinct told her that Kelsey's enthusiasm for dredging up her mom's early love life would wane once she witnessed her mom in as compromising a position as Melanie had. "I just ask that you exercise *extreme* caution in your interactions, and if you do decide to write Mom a letter, would you please just let me read it ahead of time, just to make sure..."

"Just to make sure I don't reveal that bell-bottoms go out of style, spiral perms briefly make Mom's naturally curly hair the envy of all her friends, and that Y2K is really no big deal? Don't worry. I won't."

Melanie frowned at Kelsey's joke. Part of her suddenly wished the thought of taking the tapestry down for a cleaning had never occurred to her and she'd never looked behind it or, at the very least, that she'd kept her temporary insanity to herself and not shared the discovery with her sister, because it seemed Kelsey wouldn't be satisfied until she'd let all of the evils escape from the jar.

"So you're just fine with me continuing to go into the closet?" Kelsey squirted some dish soap in the sink and turned the faucet on.

"Not really, but I'll try to be." Melanie toyed with her phone on her lap, wondering if she should offer to do the dishes since Kelsey had cooked but making no motion to stand back up.

"And you're not going to be even a little bit curious?" Kelsey asked loudly to make herself heard over the running water.

"Of course I'll be curious. But you know what they say about curiosity."

Kelsey looked skeptical. "You're not just saying this because you know I won't be able to come to the lake house for the next week, then all of a sudden you'll change your mind?"

"No." Although she had to wonder what age Mom would next be by the time Kelsey dropped in again—in her early or midtwenties, maybe. It was hard to predict how quickly the days passed inside the parallel reality.

Her phone buzzed, and she glanced down to see that Charlene had e-mailed the link to the photos of the lake house. *Thank God, a distraction.* "Hey, I just got the pictures of the house. Do you want to see them?"

Kelsey turned off the water and grabbed her laptop so they could view the images on a bigger screen. They sat next to each other on the couch, clicking through them. Charlene's staging skills and the photographer's talent had done wonders, and Melanie liked to think that her careful cleaning and repainting had helped too. Each photo was more gorgeous than the next. Even the tiny third bedroom upstairs looked bright and airy. It was like looking at pictures of herself on her wedding day, wondering who that vaguely familiar but positively radiant creature was. The house was truly showing its best self, and Melanie had no doubt once the listing became live, Charlene's phone would be ringing off the hook for showings.

"This is really going to happen, isn't it?" Kelsey asked in a small, quavery voice, and Melanie turned to see that her sister was on the verge of tears. "The pictures make it seem more real. You're going to sell the house that's been in our family for over a century."

"Kelsey..." Melanie gently shut the laptop and set it on the coffee table. "I thought we'd agreed that—"

"No, *we* didn't agree. You called me one day and *told* me we were going to sell the lake house. You told me about that magazine article and the real estate agent you'd found, and everything was already set in motion before you even stopped to consider what *I* might want."

"Yes, I did," Melanie said, pushing the memory of Everett and his astute question from her mind. *"But it's not up to your sister?"* *"No, it's not up to her."* "I considered what you wanted and what would be best for both of us. Do you have any idea how much the property taxes alone on the place cost? Not to mention the maintenance. Is that how you want to spend your inheritance? Having it gradually eaten away on a vacant house? Because it *would* be vacant. There's no way we could have found new tenants for it without having those basement repairs done, and Everett didn't come cheap. The only way we can afford him is because we're going to recoup the cost of the repairs on the sale."

The oven timer went off, and Kelsey stormed into the kitchen to check on the brownies. "Don't pretend like this is all about the money. I don't care about the money. I'd be happy to pay for the taxes and repairs out of my inheritance. I'll even buy out your half of the house if it would make you happy." She banged the brownie pan down on the stovetop.

That proved again that Kelsey had no idea how much the house was worth. Their mom had left each of them a generous sum in her will, money passed down from a trust the wealthy Montclares had established, but it wasn't enough to buy the lake house at fair market value, or even half of the value, for that matter. Melanie tried to remember the wording of her mom's will about the sale of the Lake Indigo property so she could recite it for Kelsey as evidence, but four years had passed, and Melanie hadn't exactly been at her best when her mom's lawyer had rattled off the specifics. Maybe she could have Ben scan the codicil and e-mail it to her, and she could prove to her sister that selling was what Mom had wanted, that it had never been her intention for them to somehow try to keep and maintain the old place.

"In the part of her will where Mom left us the house, she specified that we should sell it one day if we chose to no longer lease it as a rental property."

"If we chose. Stop using Mom as an excuse. If she truly wanted to sell it, why did she rent it to the Holloways in the first place? Why didn't she put it on the market then? She kept it in the family so that we could make the decision one day, Melanie. Why does it have to be now? What's the rush? Maybe once you and Ben have kids, you'll feel differently. Maybe if *I* ever get married and have kids, I'll want to live there year-round."

Melanie covered her face with her hands. All the burdens she'd been struggling to hold aloft for so long were multiplying and compounding. The weight was grinding her down. In the cupped space of her palms, she breathed deeply. "I won't..." she murmured. She dropped her hands to her lap, resigned. "I can't have kids. We've tried. For two years now. Something is wrong with me. I don't ovulate regularly, I guess. And even when I do, with the help of fertility drugs, my body still can't..." Her matter-of-fact approach wavered as she thought of her baby, forever arrested at eight weeks old. Tears tightened her throat and made her voice unnaturally high and shaky. "I had a miscarriage three weeks ago."

Kelsey's arms were around her the next second, and Melanie let herself be embraced. She tucked her head against her little sister's collarbone and wept harder than she had since she'd broken the news to Ben. Between breathless gasps, she told her everything—how they'd waited to try until she finished her doctorate; the over-the-counter ovulation kits she'd brought with her to Tucson last Christmas; Dr. Maroney's diagnoses; the tests, tests, tests, then finally, their miracle, followed by her spontaneous abortion in the women's bathroom of Cornelius Hall; how Ben wanted to take a break; and how it felt like he was giving up.

Kelsey didn't interrupt her. She didn't ask questions or offer advice but rubbed Melanie's back in the same soothing way their mom had when they were sick. After handing her tissues, she whispered, "I'm so sorry, Melanie. I had no idea. I'm so, so sorry."

Melanie eventually pulled herself upright, embarrassed by the wet patch her tears had left on Kelsey's T-shirt. Her eyes felt hot and gritty, and her nose was runny, but she felt strangely weightless sitting on her parents' old couch with her sister and her sister's dog beside her. It reminded her of the time Ben had persuaded her to go zip-lining, even though she wasn't a huge fan of heights. For hours before the trip, her stomach had twisted in knots, but they had prepaid, and she didn't want to let Ben down, so she'd seen it through. She had kept her eyes scrunched shut the majority of the time, but afterward, she had been buoyant with relief that it was over.

Kelsey brought the pan of warm brownies and two forks into the living room. "I know it's a small consolation, but doesn't this show that at least you're capable of getting pregnant? That it could happen again with a better outcome?" She handed one of the forks to Melanie and sat back down.

It was the same thing that Dr. Maroney had said immediately after she had confirmed that Melanie had miscarried, but it had been cold comfort for Melanie when she'd already fallen desperately in love with the baby inside of her. And it still felt like cold comfort because Dr. Maroney wouldn't let her continue with the fertility drugs until her hormones were back to normal, which ultimately didn't matter since Ben wanted them to take a six-month break regardless. Even when that time had passed, and they started to try once more, Melanie didn't know if she could ever trust her body again. It kept betraying her, and she didn't believe that it was capable of doing such an important job as growing and safely carrying a baby. Even if she was able to conceive again, which seemed like such an insurmountable *if,* she would live every day of the nine months in absolute terror that her body would fail her and her baby.

"You're right." She tried to nod, but her neck felt stiff, her head stuffy and leaden. "I don't have a lot of hope, but I suppose there is still *some.*" She leaned against Kelsey to reach for the brownies. "Hey! Are you literally just eating the middle? Stop it! Save some for me!"

Chapter Twelve

Kelsey knew it was a bad idea. Beth was counting on her—had explicitly put the business in her hands, dismissing everyone else's competence—and Kelsey had only about sixty percent confidence in Taylor's abilities despite the girl's eagerness to pitch in. And who knew what poor Josh would think when Taylor showed up Sunday morning. But life was too short not to succumb to bad ideas every now and then. Kelsey was champing at the bit to slip back inside the time portal, and besides, an afternoon with Everett and Melanie at the Harris Beach Memorial Day cookout was just what she needed after her week of drudgery.

When Melanie had offhandedly relayed the information to Kelsey—that Everett had asked Melanie if they were going to the neighborhood cookout on Sunday and Melanie had replied with indifference—Kelsey had clenched her teeth and tried to have patience with her sister. "You're really not interested in going?"

"No, I don't think so, not by myself, at least. If you were here, I might consider it. But it's not like I'm going to know anyone there except for Everett. It's been ages since we were summer regulars. We don't even know our next-door neighbors anymore! I haven't seen any signs of life at the Fletchers' house since I arrived."

That antisocial comment made Kelsey worry more about her sister than she would have a week ago. Ever since Melanie had confided in her about the miscarriage, Kelsey had been grieving—for Melanie and Ben, for the loss of her little niece or nephew, and for the fact that she hadn't known sooner and hadn't been there for her sister. But it was awfully hard to be there for someone who refused to let you in ninety-nine percent of the time. She couldn't tell if Melanie's offhand mention of the Memorial Day cookout was a subtle plea for Kelsey's company. Either way, the idea of the festivities on Harris Beach and the opportunity to see her mom again had consumed her imagination until finally she'd broken down and called Taylor to see if the receptionist was interested and willing to work for her on Sunday. Taylor had been.

So Kelsey was driving on a country road in her little blue car, green farm fields all around her, when she should have been at the pet lodge. She had that giddy feeling that came only from narrowly escaping a tedious commitment, yet it was dampened by the memory of Melanie's body-wracking sobs, the most grief-stricken Kelsey had seen her sister since she learned the news about their mom's pulmonary embolism. Every time she thought of Melanie and Ben's struggles, it was like stepping on a jagged rock trapped inside her shoe—a painful reminder that could be temporarily forgotten but wouldn't go away. Everything had always come so easily for Melanie that it was almost unfathomable that any area of her life, especially one she desired so badly, could be out of her reach. Despite her sister's fussy tendencies, Kelsey knew Melanie would make a terrific mother—if it could only somehow happen for her and Ben.

All the windows were rolled down, and the loose fabric ceiling was flapping against the top of Kelsey's head but not unpleasantly. Sprocket was sitting in the passenger seat beside her, his tongue lolling out halfway to his chest. She'd had a doggy harness installed in the back seat for safety, but he cried whenever she put him in it, so she often gave in and let him ride shotgun.

Her phone beeped with an incoming text message, but she refused to look at it while she was driving. It was probably Melanie, asking her to reconsider skipping out on work. Though Melanie had been initially glad to hear Kelsey would be joining her for the cook-out, she had been none too pleased to find out why Kelsey was suddenly available. Her preachy recitation of all the reasons Kelsey was being unprofessional echoed Kelsey's misgivings, and she was still working hard to tamp them down. But deep down, Kelsey suspected that Melanie's protesting just a little too much was because she was secretly happy she wouldn't have to spend the holiday weekend alone.

Or maybe the text was from her dad, who was still pretty new to the world of text messaging and had recently started sending out garbled strings of words that he'd dictated into the voice-activated software on his phone and failed to proofread. They'd been playing phone tag for the last couple of days with their conflicting work schedules. He wanted to know how she was faring with Melanie the General and the basement repairs, or at least that was what she'd pieced together from his latest nonsense text: *Hey tell sells how are you and Megan is a fennel getting along at the like house question mark. Give the contractor me a morrow number of no wrong in trouble I will try games. Love common dad.*

At the only stop sign in town, right after the LAKE INDIGO, UNINCORPORATED sign and just before Lamson's Market, Kelsey dropped her eyes to her phone to read her text message. It was from Josh, not Melanie or her dad. It said only three words—three letters, actually: *WTF?*

She winced. Her "playing hooky" feeling dissipated. She could imagine him standing in the narrow, artificially lit corridor of Pooch Place, surrounded by barking dogs, annoyedly punching the message into his phone. She knew the *F* stood for "fudge," because Josh had been raised in a big Catholic family with a swear jar—a dollar per naughty word—and the clean habit had stuck into adulthood. Josh's alternative curse words were one of the things Beth and Kelsey teased him about regularly, but in private, Kelsey found them adorable.

What the fudge? Good gravy! Holy cats! Only never before had they been directed at her. She knew that if their roles had been reversed, she would have been pretty pissed at him for ditching her too. Working with him was often the best part of her day, and it was the only thing that would have made her shift today tolerable. She suspected he felt the same way.

Kelsey pulled into the lake house's driveway and was surprised to see a large, expensive-looking truck and a shiny silver SUV parked in front of the Fletchers' bungalow. So maybe Melanie's theory that the house was abandoned was wrong. Maybe they just didn't open the place up until Memorial Day weekend like a lot of the summer families. She parked her car next to Melanie's sleek black rental and hurried to reply to Josh's message.

So sorry! she typed. *I owe you big, I know! Tony's on me, next week. Any toppings you want.* But the text wouldn't send because she had almost no reception. Sprocket was scrabbling in the front seat, eager to get outside and pee on everything, so she didn't have time to worry about the failed message right then. She would have to try again later.

Melanie was standing on the back porch in a cute turquoise sundress. "Sprocket!" she called out to him, and he bounded toward her, his stubby tail wagging furiously.

"Hello to you too," Kelsey called back, slinging her duffel bag over her shoulder. She wasn't really mad. It actually delighted her that Melanie had fallen as thoroughly in love with her dog as she had and made her feel like she had done one good thing in her life. Taking Sprocket home from the animal shelter the previous November was probably the best decision she had ever made—perhaps the *only* good decision she had ever made, she chastised herself, mentally crossing her fingers that her boss wouldn't fire her when Beth got back from Tennessee.

"Hello, Sprocket's owner." Melanie stood up and smiled wryly. Her hair was wet and combed neatly behind her ears. Something about Melanie right then—Kelsey couldn't quite place it—reminded her of Mom. *Her perfect posture? Her commanding presence? The thin-lipped smile that reveals so little?*

Kelsey wanted to hug Melanie but worried her sister would think of it as coddling. Instead she climbed up the stairs and jerked her head in the direction of the neighbors' house. "When did they arrive? Have you met them?"

Melanie pressed her finger to her lips. "Shhh." She made a sour face as they stepped inside. "They're not very friendly."

"Is it the Fletchers?"

"No. A dark-haired guy about my age. I thought it might be Beau or Stephen, all grown up, so I went over there with a loaf of zucchini bread—don't worry, there's more—to say hi. His name's Nicholas, and when I asked if he knew the Fletchers and mentioned we had been friends with them growing up, he acted really annoyed and said the house was still in the family. Almost like I was challenging their right to live there. Which I wasn't," she added huffily. "I'm just curious. He's probably some distant cousin twice removed."

Kelsey was already cutting herself a slab of zucchini bread, which was still warm. She didn't bother putting it on a plate but ate it over the sink. It was even better than her memory of her mom's bread. "Maybe he's Jilly's husband."

"No, I saw the wife. She's a blonde."

"Maybe Mr. and Mrs. Fletcher divorced and remarried and he's a step-kid or the product of a second marriage." A divorce didn't seem too wildly out of the cards for the Fletchers, considering Lavinia was most likely gay. However, Kelsey didn't know what that said about her parents' marriage. They had stayed together for twenty-nine years, up until her mom's untimely death. Her dad had waited two years to start dating and a third before marrying Laila. Her parents had seemed committed, companionable, and if not wildly or passionately in love after all that time together, at least affectionate.

Melanie shrugged. "I don't know, and I doubt Dad would either." She brushed some bread crumbs Kelsey had left on the wooden cutting board into her palm. "I asked Nicholas if he knew about the cookout on Harris Beach today, and he acted like I was inviting them to a hillbilly hoedown. But the worst part is, as I was leaving, I could hear him say to someone, maybe his wife, 'Now I see what you mean about this being a very prying community.' *Prying?* Just what the heck is that supposed to mean? Well, excuse me for bringing them zucchini bread and trying to make them feel welcome. I'll just take my *prying* hospitality somewhere else, I guess." Her cheeks were turning red, and Kelsey could tell her sister was deeply offended.

"What a jerk!" Kelsey said, helping herself to another slice. "Do you think we could get it back? It seems kind of tragic to waste good zucchini bread on ungrateful neighbors."

Melanie laughed, which was a good thing because Kelsey knew her sister wasn't going to like the next thing she said. She wanted to hop into the closet and her mom's past for an hour or two before they had to leave for the beach party. Kelsey could only imagine what was going on just on the other side of the tapestry right then. *Were Mom and Vinnie really romantically involved, as Melanie claims? Is Mom still in high school, or have her teenage years zipped by as I worked this past week?* But even more intense than her curiosity about her mom's life before kids was her longing simply to *see* her mom—to hear her voice and be in her presence again.

IT WAS LATE MORNING in Kelsey's world but nighttime in her mom's. As she crept out of the closet into the dark bedroom, careful not to trip over anything, she wondered if everyone was sleeping. She was going to be irked if one of her only chances to see her mom was wasted on the wee hours of the morning when nothing was happening. Her eyes slowly adjusted to the dark. The bed was empty. That was good. The window was open, and a gentle lake breeze was fluttering the curtains.

Kelsey could hear the low murmur of voices outside. She peered out the window and saw the orange flames of a bonfire in the Fletchers' backyard. The fire reflected off the inky lake, making two twin blazes that seemed to blur toward one another. Several silhouettes congregated around the bonfire, and Kelsey just knew that her mom would be one of them. She hurried to join the group.

"Where did Bruce go?" a boy asked.

"He snuck off with Mary Ann," a girl said. "They've been gone for a while now," she added meaningfully, setting off a round of laughter.

"I heard he's got some primo weed," another boy said, and Kelsey was amused to see it was her uncle Bob. He looked incredibly out of place at the "cool kids" bonfire, with his knobby knees, bowl haircut, and huge seventies glasses. She suspected he'd only gotten an invite because they were neighbors. Or maybe Christine had had something to do with it.

"Don't be stupid, Bobby," someone with a familiar voice snapped from across the circle of lawn chairs. The fire flickered and illuminated Vinnie. Her long hair had been cut into a pageboy bob since Kelsey had last seen her, but it somehow made her face even prettier. "You can't smoke it here. My parents' window is right over there, and they'll smell it." Her tone softened a little, as if she were placating a small child. "When Bruce gets back, you can go down to the boathouse."

Kelsey tried to make out the other faces in the circle. Feather-haired Lance was sitting next to Vinnie, and on his other side was an apple-cheeked blond girl Kelsey didn't recognize. Next to the blonde was her mom, wearing a white peasant blouse with her flat midriff exposed. She turned to look at the person next to Christine.

Holy crap! Is that Dad? Her teenage father was tall and broad shouldered and had a lot of thick brown hair—not a dreamboat like Lance but somehow both wholesome and powerful looking, like he might need to step into a phone booth and morph into Superman at any moment. He was wearing a short-sleeved button-down shirt and what her mom would have called "slacks," which made him look a little older and more important than the other teens around the fire. Probably because he was, Kelsey remembered. He had been twenty, two years older than her mom, when they first met.

"Christine said you're going to be a sophomore at UW-Madison," the blond girl said, turning toward him. "What are you studying?"

"Prelaw," her dad said. Even the way he was holding his bottle of beer made him look more mature. "I want to practice environmental law. Specifically protecting the wetlands."

Ha, Kelsey thought. No wonder her Rachel Carson–idolizing mom had fallen for him. She suddenly remembered a photo she'd seen of them together at an antinuclear power protest at the capitol square. But her dad had hastily parted with his ideals midway through law school in favor of corporate law, which, coincidentally, made a lot more money.

"Righteous," the blonde breathed, appropriately impressed. "That's where you're going in the fall, too, right, Christine? I wish my dad weren't so set on sending me to Concordia."

Kelsey was transfixed by her parents. They were so young—younger than her, even—and in the first bloom of love. They reminded her a little of Melanie and Ben, how whenever they sat side by side, they always found a way to subtly touch each other. Kelsey aspired to that kind of nauseatingly sweet love one day. Her mom's elbow was draped on her dad's thigh, and he was absentmind-edly playing with her curls.

Oh, why isn't Melanie here to see this? So maybe their mom and Vinnie had kissed. Maybe they had even had a romantic relationship. But that had been before their mom had met their dad, the person she was meant to spend her life with. And now that they *had* met, things were clicking along rapidly, like pieces fitting into an already half-finished puzzle. Kelsey lowered herself into one of the vacant lawn chairs. She had the satisfied feeling of rereading one of her favorite novels, recognizing the important plot points that would lead to the inevitable conclusion.

"I can't believe Mr. and Mrs. Prim and Proper are letting him stay," Vinnie said to no one in particular. She had wiggled herself into Lance's lap, and his stunned expression revealed that he couldn't believe the turn of events. They looked good together, Kelsey thought, like a Hollywood power couple. Lance wrapped his arms around Vinnie's waist, another piece of the puzzle snapping into place.

"I'm bunking with Bobby for the week," her dad clarified, as if worried Christine's reputation was at stake.

Vinnie whispered something to Lance that Kelsey couldn't hear. He laughed and touched her cheek.

"When Mary Ann's boyfriend came from New York last month, her parents made him stay in the guest house," the blonde volunteered. "Lot of good that did, though."

"Why don't you mind your own potatoes, Patricia?" A curvy brunette, presumably Mary Ann, retorted as she and Bruce rejoined the group, holding hands. Kelsey had to jump up from her chair to avoid being sat on by the girl.

"Yeah, Patricia," Bruce said, a swagger in his step. He dropped Mary Ann's hand and peered into the cooler. "Who drank all the Schlitz?"

"There's more in the basement," Vinnie said. "I'll go get some." She untangled herself from Lance and flirtatiously pushed him back down when he attempted to follow her. *I'll be right back*, she mouthed.

"I'll help you," Christine said, standing up too. It was the first time she had spoken since Kelsey arrived. Vinnie didn't acknowledge that she had heard her friend. She was halfway across the lawn to the red-roofed house by the time Christine had squeezed Charlie's hand and set off after her.

Kelsey lingered undecidedly behind Mary Ann's chair. Melanie's words reverberated through her head. "*An invasion of Mom's privacy… like snooping in her diary but even more intrusive. I mean, would you want someone digging around in your teenage years without your permission?*" She watched Christine get smaller and smaller. Soon her mom would disappear into the house behind Vinnie. Kelsey looked back at the gray-and-white Victorian, imagining simply going back through the portal.

But it was what she had gone there to find out—the extent of her mom's relationship with Vinnie. And if she left, if she didn't tail them, she might never put her suspicion to rest. But if she headed down to the Birdwells' basement and watched them chatting with each other and carrying beer, she could go back to Melanie and confidently tell her that she had been wrong, that Vinnie had been only a blip on the radar, and that their parents had fallen in love and everything was back on course.

Kelsey sprinted after her mom. Christine was paused on the front porch, her hand frozen on the doorknob, almost like she was waiting for her daughter to catch up with her.

Kelsey was meant to be there. She felt the conviction deep in her gut. Out of the countless moments she could have stumbled in on—her mom sleeping, her mom reading a book on the porch, the family playing Parcheesi or eating a meal—she had been transported into that one, the first week her dad had come to Lake Indigo, when a bonfire where all the key players in the love quadrangle were present. It seemed too significant to be a mere coincidence.

Her mom let out a deep breath and opened the door. Kelsey crept behind her into the silent, sleeping house.

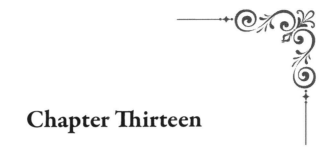

Chapter Thirteen

"Real mature, Vinnie." Christine stood with her arms folded across her bare midriff. "Do you even like him, or are you just trying to get back at me?"

Vinnie glanced up from her crouched position in front of the open fridge. "Who? Fletch? He's a hunk. Anyone with eyes can see that. And the last time I checked, you were unavailable." She continued sorting through the cans of Tab and Pepsi. It appeared the beer was hidden in the back.

"You used to call him The Pretty Boy. You said he has no personality. You compared him to plankton."

Vinnie looked up with a smirk. "Did I?" She grabbed a couple of cans of Schlitz and Pabst Blue Ribbon and set them on the concrete floor. "Well, I don't know what to tell you, Christine. People change. I change. You change. Maybe even Pretty Boy Fletcher can change."

It was an unfinished basement, and Kelsey felt chilled in her T-shirt and shorts. She was sure, in their skimpy outfits and bare feet, the girls were even colder. Across from the fridge were a vintage brown-floral couch with a wood frame, a round rag rug, and a few shelves of board games. It looked like the ideal hangout for teenagers, the perfect place to smoke pot and make out.

Christine watched Vinnie without comment, her fists balled up at her sides. "I'm not trying to hurt you," she said at last. "Bringing him here wasn't my idea."

Vinnie tossed a disinterested look over her shoulder.

"I just wanted you to know that I'm not deliberately... *parading* him in front of you. My parents asked him to be our guest. My dad loves him more than me and Bobby combined, I think."

A deep and turbulent current was flowing just beneath the surface of their words, an unspoken shared past. Kelsey curled herself up on the bottom step. It somehow felt less like blatant spying that way and more like watching the events of a drive-in movie unfold—or so she tried to convince herself.

"Of course Jack loves him," Vinnie said. "He couldn't have custom ordered a better future son-in-law—polite, prelaw, and Protestant. The question is..." She closed the refrigerator door with a metallic click. "Do you?"

"Here, let me help you." Christine took a few steps toward Vinnie and bent down to cradle the beer cans in her arms. "They're going to be wondering where we are."

"I don't care. I asked you a question, Christine."

Christine bit her lip and tilted her head. "And I told you I didn't want to hurt you."

They stared at each other for an uncomfortably long time, so long that Kelsey had to lower her eyes. "*I just don't think I can go inside the time portal in good conscience anymore,*" Melanie had told her. Kelsey had thought Melanie was being melodramatic at the time, but now she had to admit that Melanie kind of had a point. Watching her mom in this private moment with her first love made Kelsey feel confused and abandoned and misled and heartsick all at once. She knew she should probably climb back up the stairs and go, but she needed to hear what her mom had to say about her dad first. She wanted her to defend him, to list off all the reasons she had fallen in love with him, to use his name at the very least.

"He can't know you better than I know you," Vinnie said softly. Her almond-shaped eyes were glistening.

"Maybe not yet," Christine conceded. "But Charlie and I haven't known each other as long."

"He'll never know the real you. Not like I do."

Christine laughed mirthlessly. The first hint of frown lines appeared on her otherwise-smooth cheeks. "How can you say that, Vin? *I* don't even know the real me."

Vinnie reached her thin arms tentatively across the space between them, as though worried Christine would slip away. She didn't, though, and Vinnie gripped her shoulders. "She's right here," she said. "Looking at me. How can you not know?"

"If your parents wake up..." Christine started then drifted off, touching a turned-under lock of Vinnie's sleek new haircut. "The beer, and oh God, if your mom finds us down here together again..." Her face blushed bright red, and Kelsey wondered what exactly Mrs. Birdwell had seen on another occasion.

"They won't. My mom drank about four brandy old fashioneds before bed tonight."

"We should go back anyway." Christine gently shook herself free from Vinnie's grip. "I want to go back. Help me with the beer, okay?"

"Fine." Vinnie stooped to collect the remaining cans. "Just answer one more question for me."

Christine shook her head but turned to follow Vinnie anyway. Kelsey stood up as the girls headed for the basement stairs. She clung to the railing to steady her balance. Her hands were freezing.

"Why him and not—"

"It's just easier, Vinnie," Christine cut her off. Her voice was suddenly tired. She sounded the same way she had during the last argument she and Kelsey had had before her death—resigned. "It's just easier to be with him."

KELSEY HAD NO IDEA how much time had elapsed since she'd stepped into the time portal. It could have been twenty minutes, an hour or two, or even ten hours. Melanie had warned her about the erratic disconnect in time that existed between the two parallel worlds. For all she knew, she had missed the Memorial Day cookout, and Melanie was probably freaking out, imagining the havoc she was wreaking in the past, but she couldn't work up the energy to care about that right now.

It's just easier to be with him. Her mom's words rang in her ears—a confession, an indictment. *Was my parents' marriage only one of convenience?*

Kelsey was sitting on the bench in the closet, trying to compose a letter on a sheet of butterfly stationery she had brought along expressly for this purpose but now felt stupid for using. *Butterflies? What am I? Ten years old?* She kind of felt ten years old, filled with the righteous indignation of a preteen daughter whose mother had done her a serious wrong. Incensing her further was a new pack of cigarettes on the bench.

Easier, like that was a quality poets touted in their sonnets. "The Road More Easily Traveled." Like her dad was her mom's second choice—because he was.

Didn't you ever love Dad? she wanted to ask. The furious force of her pen would rival the deep impressions her mom's note had left. *Or not even in the very beginning? Was Vinnie the one who always had your heart? Why did you marry him if she was the one who understood you so well? Why did you choose to have two children with him and grow old with him if he was only ever second best? Was it the societal restrictions of the time? You thought that your life would be easier if you chose to be with a man? Or was there something more to it?*

But she didn't write any of that because she knew it would never pass Melanie's censorious inspection, and more importantly, she suspected it was what she would recognize as a selfish, unfair tirade once she had a clearer head in the morning. *That* was not the way she wanted to introduce herself to her young mom. Accusatory and meddling was definitely not the first impression she was hoping to make, especially after the false start Melanie had already accomplished. Kelsey wanted to come across as warm and generous in spirit, but the struggle to do that with her mom had never been harder. *Just who the hell were you, Mom?* was all she really wanted to say in the letter.

Then she had an idea, a different way to introduce themselves, no letter needed. She ducked out of the closet—thank goodness Melanie wasn't waiting on the other side for her—and dashed into the master bedroom, where her duffel bag was sitting on the queen-size bed. She dug inside for the red Moleskine journal she brought with her everywhere. It had been a Christmas gift from her mom the year she passed away, though Kelsey had never written in it. Instead, she had tucked a few photographs between its pages as well as her mom's funeral program.

"Kelsey?" Melanie's voice floated from downstairs, and Kelsey hurriedly flipped through the blank pages until she found the particular three-by-five color photograph she was looking for.

"Kelsey?" Melanie called again. "Are you back already?" Her voice sounded closer. The stairs creaked as she started to climb them, and Kelsey darted back to her sister's bedroom and the door behind the tapestry. Before Melanie could interfere, Kelsey slipped into the closet and dropped the photograph on the bench for her mom to discover. Then for good measure, she stole the cigarettes for a second time.

HARRIS BEACH WAS BUSTLING. Tables and chairs were set up in the paved apron adjacent to the sand, and two men were manning a giant black barbecue grill that looked like a locomotive. Games of horseshoe and bean bag toss were being played on opposite ends of the beach, and some generous neighbors had tied their colorful kayaks and paddleboats to the dock for anyone who wanted to take them out for a spin. Only a few brave souls—mostly kids—were swimming in the still-seventy-something-degree water. Lake Indigo wouldn't properly warm up for at least another week or two, at least in Melanie's opinion. She preferred bathwater temperatures.

"There's Everett!" Kelsey exclaimed.

Melanie caught sight of him making his way through the crowd to them. He looked even more like a college kid in his cargo shorts, sleeveless T-shirt, and flip-flops. Kelsey definitely had a type. She liked her guys to be clean-cut and dark haired with a swimmer's build, and if they had dimples or a British, Irish, or Australian accent, so much the better. She also tended to gravitate toward guys who were cocky and self-absorbed, Melanie thought glumly. She hadn't met the last one, Tristan, but he sounded like a real douche canoe.

Kelsey smiled for the first time since she had come out of the time portal. She had been quiet and distant ever since, but Melanie was reluctant to ask her what she had seen. Since Melanie had sworn that she would no longer go into her mom's past herself, it seemed like it would be compromising her resolution or even encouraging her sister's actions, so she tried to keep quiet. The only question she had allowed herself was inquiring how long Kelsey had been inside the time portal because, to Melanie, it had been only five minutes. Kelsey had confusedly replied that she couldn't be sure, but it had definitely been longer—an hour or more—which confirmed Melanie's theory. The correlation of time between the two worlds was totally unpredictable, which made the closet seem even more volatile to her. *What if Kelsey goes inside again and disappears for days? What if she never comes back?*

"Hi!" Kelsey greeted Everett. "It's weird seeing you outside of our basement."

Everett laughed. It sounded nasally, like someone with a severe upper respiratory infection. "I do feel like I spend about eighty percent of my life in basements," he agreed. "Thankfully they let me out sometimes so I can work on my tan." He cupped his hand around his mouth and stage-whispered to Kelsey, "But I bet your sister wishes I weren't taking the holiday off tomorrow and would finish the job for her already."

Melanie had been thinking something along those very lines only a moment ago. She rolled her eyes at him in mock exasperation. "As long as you have it finished by next Monday." She had meant to sound pseudostern, but she worried she had come across as real stern instead. "Is your uncle here? You said he has a fishing cabin nearby, right?"

"Yeah, over on Clover Trail. But it's my cousin's graduation party this weekend, so I've got the place to myself. All three hundred square feet of it. He's been letting me stay there while I work on your basement so I don't have to drive back and forth to Arbor Creek."

They got in line for the brats and hamburgers, and Everett regaled them with stories of Bailey and Bella, his golden retrievers who were from the same litter. The dogs had been a Christmas present for him and his younger sister from his parents, but they were so inseparable that when Everett left home and took Bailey, Bella insisted on coming along too. As Everett told it, the pair was a tag team of mischief-makers, devouring a whole pound of raw bacon off the kitchen counter one time and pulling all the stuffing from a futon mattress another. Kelsey countered with a story about Sprocket eating her phone charger and barfing it up on her bed. Melanie had to grudgingly admit to herself that Everett and Kelsey had at least one thing in common, but she wasn't too keen on how he kept checking out any young woman who walked by in a pair of short shorts.

"You can just barely see your house from here," Everett said, squinting across the lake.

Melanie followed his gaze, and sure enough, she saw the century-old Montclare family Victorian. Its white façade glowed golden in the setting sun. From their vantage point, it looked like an idyllic little dollhouse. "There it is," she said softly.

"There's some really good fishing over on your side of the lake," he said, gesturing to the northeast end. "Uncle Mick and I catch northern pike as big as my arm, a ton of white bass, and some of the best walleye pike you've ever tasted." He bit into his hamburger, chewed briefly, and continued talking. "Nothing like the bullheads over on this side. Filthy bottom-feeders."

Kelsey caught Melanie's eye, and her look was heavy with meaning, but Melanie wasn't sure what meaning. *Is Kelsey trying to draw my attention to the house's beauty and alluding to the fact that she doesn't want to sell it? Is she as bored with Everett's recitation of fish as I am? Or is she trying to convey that she's falling for him?* Melanie wondered if Kelsey wanted her to make an excuse and leave the two of them alone.

As she finished eating her corn on the cob, she wished Ben were there with them. They had talked earlier in the week, and he had offered to fly to Wisconsin to spend the holiday weekend with her, but something had made her turn him down. She was aching to see him: his messy blond hair that was always in need of a trim, his puppy-dog brown eyes, the dorky T-shirts he wore on the weekends that had things like "All those years in school, and now I'm a drug dealer" printed on them. He was probably sporting a beard since she had been gone for two weeks. She preferred him clean-shaven, but he hated shaving, so he always let it go whenever they were apart.

She knew that as soon as she saw him, as soon as they embraced, everything would come rushing back, and she wasn't quite ready to pick up that yoke just yet. Maybe a few more weeks apart, and she would be strong enough to shoulder it again. Focusing on the lake house and her mom and Kelsey seemed like the more manageable dilemma for the time being.

"That lady keeps staring at us," Kelsey said. "On your right. With the stroller."

Melanie tried to turn casually. Two women stood near a stroller—two blondes, one probably in her midthirties, the other in her sixties, so mother and daughter, maybe. The older woman was holding the hand of a little boy wearing blue-and-white-striped swim trunks and a T-shirt with a red star on it.

"I bet that's our new neighbor," Melanie said. "The wife."

"The zucchini-bread hater?" Kelsey asked scornfully. "I thought they wouldn't deign to come to the cookout." She bent forward to fill Everett in.

"Hush up. They're coming over here."

"Hi! It's Melanie, right?" The younger woman parked the stroller in front of their table. It was one of those fancy ones with the click-in infant carrier, a detachable canvas sunshade, and large, rubbery all-terrain wheels. "You dropped off that zucchini bread earlier today, right? I just wanted to tell you thanks again. It was delicious! We really enjoyed it, didn't we, Noah?"

The little boy took a step back and hugged his grandma's leg. He looked about two or three years old and was round-eyed and chubby cheeked—a Raphael cherub.

"You're very welcome," Melanie said, shooting Kelsey and Everett a dirty look as they stifled laughter. She considered asking if the woman and her family were just there for the weekend or were planning to stay the summer, but Nicholas's comment about "prying" neighbors still stung, so she pursed her lips and let an awkward silence ensue.

"Sorry, I should introduce myself. I'm Jess, and this is my mother-in-law, Marie. You've already met Noah, and this..." She paused to flip back the stroller sunshade and reveal a tiny sleeping baby. "Is Gracie."

"Nice to meet you," Melanie breathed, hardly able to take her eyes off the baby girl. She still had the wrinkled, pinkish face of a newborn, and her rosebud lips were puckered in a pout. Melanie just knew that if she picked the baby up and held her against her chest, Gracie would be warm and sweet smelling, like a fresh loaf of bread. "How old?"

"Noah's two and a half, and Gracie just turned five weeks old. Nicholas thinks I'm crazy that I wanted to bring her here—he's a total germophobe—but Gracie and I didn't want to miss the fun, did we, peanut?" She cast an adoring glance at her infant daughter then flipped the sunshade back down.

"I'm Kelsey, Melanie's sister," Kelsey thrust in. "And this is our friend Everett." They seemed to have scooted closer together on the bench. Kelsey's bare shoulder touched Everett's tan arm.

The neighbors exchanged friendly pleasantries about where they were from and what they did for a living. They lived in Middleton. Jess was a web designer, and Marie was an art therapist. Nicholas, ironically, was also a pharmacist like Ben. Noah gradually became less shy and detached himself from his grandmother's leg. He started to make a little game of running to the edge of the pavement, scooping up a handful of sand, letting it rain down, then darting back to the adults.

"Ha!" he laughed like a little maniac. "Ha-ha!"

"Your house has been in your family for a long time, hasn't it?" Marie, who had the husky voice of a long-time smoker, asked. "I wonder if Lavinia would remember your family. She grew up here, you know. Her family came every summer."

Melanie and Kelsey turned to stare at each other.

"Lavinia Fletcher?" Melanie asked. She wanted to ask how they knew her, if she still owned the house, and if she was staying there with them. *Prying, prying, prying*, Nicholas's voice rebuked her.

Marie smiled, delighted. "That's the one. Not a very common name, is it?"

Noah dashed toward them with a fistful of sand and deposited it on his mother's sandal.

"Noah! That's not very nice," Jess admonished him. "Now Mommy's foot is all dirty."

"She was friends with our mom, Christine Kingstad," Melanie said loudly over the little boy's whining.

"Hmm... I'll have to ask her," Marie said, but she looked distracted as she crouched down to hold her grandson's hand. "What do you think, Jess? Time to feed the troops? Is the brat stand just over that way? It was so nice meeting you all. I'm sure we'll be seeing you around."

Disappointed, Melanie gave them a little wave and sat back down. She wished that Everett would leave so that she and her sister could discuss the new development in private. *Is Mrs. Fletcher still living right next door?* Perhaps they could talk to her. And ask her what exactly, Melanie wasn't quite sure, but the opportunity felt momentous.

Kelsey, however, seemed unimpressed by the bombshell. She was smiling up at Everett as he pointed out something on the lake to her. And Melanie thought meanly, *Oh*. That was why Kelsey had risked blowing off work to come to Lake Indigo. Kelsey wasn't there for Melanie. She wasn't even there for their mom. She was there for a boy—another handsome, charming, stupidly superficial boy. Melanie tried not to let the splinter of hurt pierce her heart too deeply.

Chapter Fourteen

Kelsey followed Everett up the three short steps to his uncle's fishing cabin. He hadn't been lying when he said it wasn't much more than a glorified shed—brown-painted clapboard, green shingles, and a pair of what looked like moose antlers.

"Watch your step," he said, taking her gently by the wrist and guiding her inside. His hand on her skin felt like warm sunshine. She wanted to lean into him like a cat and nuzzle her face against his chest. "I apologize in advance for the smell. Uncle Mick is self-conscious about the place stinking like fish, so he goes a little overboard on the air freshener."

A wave of lilacs, roses, and lilies overwhelmed her when she stepped inside. Just beneath the flowery potpourri was a sour, fishy note.

"It's okay. Eau de fish bouquet just so happens to be my favorite scent."

Everett hesitated a beat before rasping out a laugh. "You're funny. Can I get you something to drink? I've got beer, water, orange juice, and more beer. A beer, perhaps?"

"I'd love a beer."

"Good choice."

He cracked open two cans and carried them over to where she was perched on a blue velour couch. The whole cabin appeared to be one room. It had a small kitchenette with a plastic tablecloth-covered table and two wooden chairs, a blue velour armchair that matched the couch, an old tube television, and two twin beds with plaid quilts. A faded print of a howling wolf was framed on the wall. Melanie would think the cabin was dingy and tacky, and it was, Kelsey had to admit, but it had something sweetly masculine about it, too, the stripped-down functionality of it. A broom and flyswatter hung from nails next to the door. A handwritten sign above the sink read, *Don't clean your fish here! Use table out back, please!*

"So you guys are putting your house on the market as soon as I'm finished?" Everett asked, arranging himself next to her in a way that made her pulse flutter and her cheeks feel hot.

Kelsey nodded. "It's a good time to sell, I guess. My mom left it to us in her will, and we can't really afford to keep it without renting it out or something."

"I'm sorry," he said and sipped his beer. "I didn't know your mom had passed away."

She tried to wave his sympathy away, as if her mom's death were something firmly planted in the past that she had come to terms with ages ago. "It's been four years," she said. It somehow felt like both no time at all and an eternity since that fateful afternoon.

"How did she die?"

God, she didn't want to talk about that. *Is he genuinely interested, or is he just trying to get into my pants?* She would let him into her pants with no demonstration of his empathetic, sensitive-guy listening skills required.

"It was a pulmonary embolism," she said, hoping to shut down that line of inquiry. "A blood clot in her lung."

"That's awful," he said, his sexy black hair flopping into his eye.

She reached out to brush it back. "It was," she agreed. Pieces of her mom's conversation with Vinnie were still ricocheting around her skull, making it hard to think straight. She wished Everett had offered her something a little stronger than beer.

He'll never know the real you. Not like I do.

How can you say that, Vin? I don't even know the real me.

Did Mom ever find peace with her "real" self? Or did she perform the version of herself she thought people liked best and expected of her until the day she died? The thought made Kelsey horribly depressed.

"You and your sister seem so different," Everett said, shifting his weight so that their thighs touched briefly.

That was another topic she decidedly did not want to talk about at the moment. He was on a roll. When Kelsey had asked Melanie if she could feed and walk Sprocket because she might not be coming home, Melanie had coolly replied in the affirmative and walked away. She didn't need to say anything else. The judgment was plain on her holier-than-thou face. Everything that Kelsey did—still going into the time portal to "spy" on their mom, going home with an almost stranger—was clearly beneath her.

"My dad calls her Melanie the General because she can be so bossy," she offered just to see Everett's dimples pop into view. They were slightly asymmetrical. The right one was deeper than the left, but Kelsey wanted to kiss them both all the same.

"My sister and I are really different too." He leaned back against the sofa. "Laura's at the University of Wisconsin, at the top of her class, studying molecules or microbiology or something."

"That's where Melanie went too. She's a biology professor now at this prestigious little liberal arts college in Ohio." She frowned. "Hey, where are your dogs? I was looking forward to meeting them."

"Back at my place in Arbor Creek. They're too high-energy to be here alone when I'm working." He tentatively touched one of her curls and gave it a little tug to watch it spring back upward. "I really like your hair."

"Thanks." The image of her dad toying with her mom's curls in front of the bonfire came back to her. They'd seemed so in love. But it was all a ruse, at least on her mom's part. She tried to focus on Everett's fingertips lightly brushing her hair, only centimeters away from the sensitive skin of her earlobe and neck, but something was niggling at her. "Someone's watching them?" she asked.

"Yeah, of course." His fingers traced an invisible trail down her brow and along her cheek to her jawline.

"Like coming in and walking them every day?" she persisted, not sure why. *Why can't I just shut up and let him kiss me?* It was clear he wanted to. His face was so close she could see the specks of black stubble above his lip.

He faltered for a second. "Yes. Please don't worry about Bailey and Bella. Trust me—they're in good hands." He put one palm on each of her cheeks and pulled her face to his.

He was a good kisser—slow and deliberate. But she couldn't enjoy herself and sink into the moment because she had a sudden premonition of how it would end. She was pretty sure he had a live-in girlfriend based on the way he had answered her questions about who was taking care of the dogs. She had seen the signs before—in Tristan, in Neil, in Eamon—but in the past, it had somehow seemed easier to ignore them.

"Give me one second," she said, nimbly extricating herself from his embrace. "Do you have a bathroom I can use?"

The bathroom was tiny and even more flowery smelling than the rest of the cabin. She practically gagged at the sickly-sweet stench. It had a grimy sink and toilet, a narrow shower stall, and no hand soap, and the only towel was damp, crumpled up, and lying on the floor. But that was fine because Kelsey didn't really need to use the bathroom. She shut the toilet seat and sat down.

She was freaking out that there were only flirtations and soft kisses and subterfuge, that real love didn't exist. It hadn't existed for her parents, and even Melanie and Ben's marriage seemed to be on shaky ground lately because of the miscarriage. She couldn't believe Ben hadn't visited once in the time that Melanie had been staying in Lake Indigo, when normally they were joined at the hip. A shared tragedy was supposed to bring people closer together, not render them apart. Those two couples were her models for loving, committed relationships, and if she didn't have those, she didn't have anything to cling to when her love life was a bleak, pathetic mess.

She remembered what her dad had said in his toast at Melanie's wedding. "No marriage is perfect because nobody is perfect. The closest you can get to a perfect marriage is by choosing your partner and choosing love over and over again. Every day." But presumably he hadn't known his wife hadn't felt the same way, that she had secretly chosen someone else over him.

Kelsey wiped her eyes furiously. It was stupid that she was even considering going back out to Everett and continuing their kiss. He was cute and sexy, but he wasn't very quick-witted, and his laugh was terrible, and there was a ninety-nine percent chance he already had a girlfriend. She didn't know if staying and rolling around with him on the blue velour couch would boost her spirits or depress her even further.

The sky had a rosy glow outside the frosted bathroom window—sunset. Kelsey checked the time on her phone and saw the text message that she had composed to Josh earlier. It seemed like a lifetime ago. She clicked send, and a second later, her phone beeped, signifying a successful delivery. Apparently the fishing cabin's reception was awesome. Go figure. She assumed her text was probably much too late, anyway—any damage to their friendship had already been done.

MELANIE PUSHED THE porch swing back and forth lazily with her heels. Sprocket was sprawled out a few feet away, snoring louder than any small dog had the right to. She had been reading an article in *Scientific American* about seawater desalination, but no daylight was left to read by, so she'd dropped it into her lap and kept rocking instead of going inside.

Lights were on in the Fletchers' house, and she could imagine Nicholas bathing Noah and reading him bedtime stories and Jess feeding Gracie and rocking her to sleep. They were probably frazzled and exhausted, rushing to get the children put to bed so that they could steal a few minutes of alone time together to eat a quick dinner and drink a glass of wine, but Melanie would have traded places with them in a heartbeat. She let her head loll back on the wooden swing. *Would my baby have been a boy or a girl?*

Sprocket suddenly shot up and sniffed at the darkness encircling the wraparound porch. Before Melanie's mind had time to jump to horror-movie scenarios, her sister called out, "It's just me," and the little gray dog bolted toward his master.

"You're home early. I didn't hear a car."

"He didn't drive me home. I wanted to walk."

Kelsey looked small and sad. Even her springy hair looked deflated. Melanie was reminded of her senior year of high school, when Kelsey, a sophomore at the time, had been invited to the prom by a popular junior, Wyatt Jameson. She had been so pleased with herself, getting to go to prom ahead of her time, since only juniors and seniors were allowed to go. Melanie had been unattached and had gone with a group of her other unattached friends, and that had seemed to sweeten the experience of going with a date for sixteen-year-old Kelsey—a date who bought her a red-rose corsage and drove a black Mustang convertible. But that night had ended early too. Melanie and her mom had patiently pulled bobby pins out of Kelsey's up-do—sixty-seven of them—and listened to her recounting the night's disasters. Food poisoning at dinner and one too many trips to the restroom had caused Wyatt's eye to turn to another girl. Kelsey had found them making out in the twinkly-lit courtyard while her favorite song, "Drops of Jupiter," played in the gymnasium.

"He's not worth the salt in your tears," their mom had said, handing her a tissue, then locked eyes with Melanie over Kelsey's head. Her frank gaze seemed to say, *We adults understand these things, don't we?* Melanie had felt great affection for both her mom and her sister at that moment.

But her mom wasn't there now, and Melanie didn't know what to say. She suspected anything she did say would be interpreted as sermonizing or one giant "I told you so." She sat quietly to see what Kelsey would do next, if she would go straight inside to her parents' bedroom or if she would sit down. She sat down.

Melanie started rocking them on the swing. "I have been racking my brain, trying to figure out who Everett's laugh reminds me of, and I think I finally have it."

Kelsey turned to her, enticed despite her studied indifference. Her eyes were red rimmed, like she had been crying.

"Ernie. You know from Ernie and Bert?" Melanie mimicked Everett's laugh. "He-he-he-he-he!"

"Oh God, you're right!" Kelsey burst out laughing. "He's totally Ernie." She imitated the laugh with more success. Her impressions had always been better than Melanie's. She did a spot-on one of their dad's wife, Laila, with her lilting cadences and oddly placed pauses.

"You sound like a hissing cat having a seizure!" Melanie picked up Sprocket and put him between them on the swing, but he jumped down after a few seconds. "Do you think something is wrong with him? Like maybe he has a deviated septum?"

"Maybe he just watched a lot of *Sesame Street* as a kid." Kelsey undid her sandals and tucked her feet under her. "A laugh like that is kind of a deal breaker, though. His girlfriend probably wants to murder him when they watch comedies together."

His girlfriend? Melanie had known he was a player—those dimples probably made him think he could get away with anything. *Did he voluntarily share this information with Kelsey, or did she find out some other way?* The red-rimmed eyes made her suspect the latter.

"I mean, if Ben laughed like that, you wouldn't have married him, right?"

"Of course not!" Melanie said, but in her heart, she thought, *Yes, yes, yes.* Of course she still would have married him. She would have married him if he sounded like Oscar the Grouch—*heh-heh-heh*—or Fozzie Bear—*waka waka!*—or a trumpeter swan honking. But that wasn't the case. He had a warm, pleasing, and quite infectious laugh.

"Don't worry. We parted on good terms," Kelsey said, an edge to her words. "In case you were worried he wouldn't be coming back on Tuesday."

"I wasn't worried about that," Melanie answered truthfully. The possibility that Everett would be so unprofessional as to terminate their contract because of a romantic mishap with Kelsey hadn't occurred to her. But she was grateful to be reassured nonetheless. "I'm worried about you, though. Are you okay?"

"No." Kelsey exhaled. "I saw Dad in the time portal today. His first time out to Lake Indigo, when he and Mom had just met."

Melanie scrambled to catch up. "Dad?" She had been expecting Kelsey to describe her evening with Everett and the revelation about his girlfriend, not what she had seen behind the tapestry. Though Melanie had promised herself that she wouldn't try to dredge up any more of her mom's private life, their parents meeting seemed like a piece of shared history, a moment that somehow also belonged to Melanie and Kelsey. It was where all their threads came together.

"Yes. Young and buff. But I know you don't want me to tell you any of this."

Melanie let her bare feet drag, slowing the porch swing down. It felt like Kelsey was intentionally tempting her, but she found she couldn't resist. She pictured the wedding photo of her parents hanging in her living room back in Ohio: her mom in a sheer, lacy bodice and puffy sleeves, her veil a frothy waterfall behind her, and her dad in a matching white suit, both of them with one-hundred-watt smiles, grinning like it was going out of style. She couldn't look at the photo without smiling as well. "Was Dad just as suave as he claims to be?"

"Kind of. He seemed very gentlemanly." Then Kelsey relayed, in detail, what she had seen and heard: the teenagers at the bonfire, especially their lovey-dovey parents, how Lance and Vinnie were flirting, how their mom had followed Vinnie when she went to get more beer, and their conversation in the basement. "Mom wouldn't answer Vinnie when she asked her if she loved him. She would only say that she didn't want to hurt her. Then Vinnie claimed to know Mom better than Dad, the real her, and she asked why Mom would choose him over her. And you know what Mom said? She said, 'It's just easier to be with him.'"

"Hey. Take a deep breath." Melanie patted her sister's hand. Just as she'd predicted, the sweater with its stray piece of yarn was unraveling. "It sounds like they were together, but they broke up. She chose Dad, didn't she?"

Kelsey unfolded her legs and began rocking the swing jerkily. "Did she do it for the right reasons, though? Or just because it was easier to pretend to be straight? To stay in the closet and make her parents happy?"

"You act like 'easy to be with' is damning someone with faint praise, Kels, but it's actually a pretty appealing quality in a mate. Maybe you misunderstood Mom. Maybe she meant that Dad was more enjoyable to be around, more relaxing, more comfortable. From what I know of Mrs. Fletcher, she could be pretty temperamental. Witty and charismatic, yes, but other times downright moody. Do you remember that time she threw her steak over the porch railing? She said Mr. Fletcher had overcooked it."

Kelsey didn't look convinced. "I don't know. The way she said it... I just feel like there's so much raw emotion between them. Like this crazy spark."

Like Catherine and Heathcliff from *Wuthering Heights*, all fiery passion and doom. Yes, Melanie had felt it, too, had witnessed it in that kiss. "So you're worried that Mom settled? That she and Vinnie maybe continued their relationship even after Mom and Dad got married?"

Kelsey folded her arms across her chest and rocked the swing so hard that Melanie's head bumped the back of the seat.

"Ouch. Watch it!"

"Sorry." Kelsey stopped her rocking abruptly. "I hadn't phrased it that way to myself, but yes, that's exactly what I'm scared of."

No loons were out, or if they were, Melanie couldn't hear them over the Memorial Day bonfires and get-togethers all around the lake. Snippets of laughter, rock music, and splashing carried across to them. Sprocket was sawing wood again.

"Well, the solution is obvious, isn't it?" Melanie said. "You need to stop going into the past. No good is coming from it, and it's making you upset. Mom and Dad loved each other, and they loved us. Was it a perfect marriage? No, but whose is? Fortunately, most couples' marriages don't have to withstand the scrutiny of their adult children time traveling to examine them from every which angle." She rubbed the back of her head. "What would be the outcome of you finding out for sure if Mom and Vinnie were having an affair? It would only taint things. I don't think that would be healthy."

"So ignorance is bliss?" Kelsey asked sarcastically. "Keep your head in the sand, and all that jazz?"

Melanie smoothed her sundress across her lap. "If that's how you want to think about it, fine. But I think that's a pretty immature viewpoint. It's really not about us. It's between Mom and Dad—"

"And Mom and Mrs. Fletcher."

"Right. I'm not saying you should ignore anything or pretend you haven't seen what you've already seen. I'm just suggesting you stop actively seeking it out. For your own peace of mind."

Kelsey pushed herself up and walked across the porch. Melanie thought she was going to go inside, but she paused by the railing. "I don't think I can stop quite yet," she said softly. "I did something to-day that you're not going to be very happy about. I left a picture in the closet for Mom."

"A picture?" Melanie's heart hammered against her ribcage. "Of whom?"

"Us." Kelsey turned around to face her. "Mom's favorite picture. The one she kept framed on her desk in Dad's office."

Kelsey didn't need to describe it any further. Melanie could im-mediately visualize it in her mind's eye. In it, Kelsey was five, and Melanie was seven, and they were lying on their backs on a quilt together, looking up at the twilit sky, waiting for some fireworks to start. Melanie's arm was draped protectively around Kelsey, and Kelsey's head was resting against Melanie's side, and though they weren't smiling, they looked as content as kittens. Melanie thought it might have been taken at Lake Indigo's Fourth of July fireworks display. She couldn't remember that moment or that night, even, but she wished she could. The photographer, her mom, perhaps, had seemed to capture on film the only sweet, sisterly moment that had ever occurred between them.

"Did you leave a note with it?" Melanie asked. The furious pace of her heart had slowed a little. At least it wasn't a more recent photo.

"No."

"Was anything written on the back?"

"Our names and the date, I think. Maybe our ages too." Kelsey hugged herself. Her bare shoulders glowed white in the moonlight, and Melanie suspected she was cold. "I know this is a weird thought, but I can't help wondering about it. I acted compulsively, and it was

such an automatic decision—like that photo was the obvious choice
to show her. So what I keep asking myself is, Did I put that picture
in the closet because it's Mom's favorite, or is that picture Mom's favorite because it was the one I put in the closet? The first picture she
ever saw of us? Do you get what I mean?"

"I do," Melanie said. It was a "butterfly effect" question—one of
those knotted situations she had been hoping to avoid. She tried to
envision what her eighteen-year-old mom's reaction would be when
she found the photo. It would be like looking at her future through
the wrong end of a telescope. She was still so far away from becoming their mother, yet Kelsey had seen to it that she knew about them.
"Why did you choose to leave that photo right then?"

"Hmm?" Kelsey cocked her head.

"I'm curious about your timing," Melanie said. "Why leave her a
photo of us after that intense interaction with Mom and Vinnie you
had just seen?"

"I don't know. I guess I had similar motives to yours for writing
that note. Mom was upset, and I wanted to leave her with something
to look forward to. I wanted to introduce her to the people she's
sharing the closet with in a kinder, gentler way," she added somewhat
defensively.

Melanie set the swing lightly rocking again. "So it didn't have
anything to do with wanting to influence Mom's choices? Wanting
to lay claim to her and make sure she chose the right horse, so to
speak?"

"That's ridiculous!" Kelsey snapped, pushing off from the railing.
"If you're suggesting that I planted that photo there just so Mom
would feel obligated to choose Dad over Vinnie, you're forgetting
a pretty important piece of the puzzle here. We already know that
Mom married Dad! Otherwise we wouldn't be here!"

"*I* know that. *You* know that. But eighteen-year-old Mom *doesn't* know that. I just want her to understand she made that choice of her own free will, not because she felt pressured by her future daughters."

"I do, too, of course. But that doesn't change the fact that I already left the picture there, and Mom has probably already found it by now."

They raised their eyebrows at each other as they mulled over that exhilarating yet alarming possibility.

"Come on, Sprocket." Kelsey whistled, and he wiggled himself into a sleepy, seated position. "I'd better get to bed. I've got to leave here at six tomorrow morning if I want to get to work on time, so I probably won't see you."

"Okay," Melanie said. "I think I'm going to sit out here for a little while longer." One of the lights had gone out on the near side of the Fletchers' house. She could imagine the little boy nestled in bed, a teddy bear tucked under his arm.

"Good night." Kelsey opened the screen door then hesitated. "Hey. How do you think our neighbors know Lavinia? Do you think they're renting from her?"

"I wondered the same thing," Melanie said. "Maybe she's their landlord. But it seemed like they knew her more personally, didn't it?"

Kelsey swatted a moth away from the open door. "I guess so. Do you think she knows that Mom died?"

"I don't know. She might have seen it in the paper. Or maybe they still had mutual friends." She tried to remember the long list of names she'd kept track of, the people who had sent their condolences and flowers or monetary donations. *Was Lavinia Fletcher's name among them?* If it had been, it certainly hadn't stood out to her at the time.

Kelsey batted away another moth and started to close the door. "Well, I was just wondering. Good night," she repeated.

"Good night. I love you, you know," she added as an after-thought. Maybe it was her mom guiding her. She had told both her daughters that she loved them every night before bed.

"I do know. And I love you too," Kelsey said before disappearing inside the house.

Chapter Fifteen

For the next week, Everett was especially polite to Melanie, and she made an effort to hold her tongue and stay out of his way. She went to the lab to have more blood drawn, raked leaves out from under the shrubs, polished the spindles on the oak staircase, and sanded and stained the outdoor table on the wraparound porch. She liked how the table turned out so much, she wondered if she could somehow get it back to Ohio. It would look much nicer on their deck than the cheap patio set she and Ben currently owned.

Charlene had stopped over on Wednesday to show her the final house description: *Gorgeous 4 bedroom, 3 bath Victorian mansion on stunning Lake Indigo! A must see...* The listing would officially become live on all the major real estate websites that Friday, and the open house was scheduled for next Sunday at one o'clock, and—Charlene was emphatic about it—they should have no private showings before then to generate lots of interest and competition on the big day. Melanie wondered what she would do with herself during those three hours when she needed to be out of the house. Maybe if Kelsey wasn't working, they could go to a movie together or go shopping.

On Friday afternoon, she sat at the kitchen table, refreshing the house listing on a web page that kept track of how many people had viewed the listing and saved it to their "favorites." *Days on the Market: 1. Views since Listing: 82. 29 Shoppers Favorited this Home.* Stalking the online listing was better than thinking about her mom's lack of reply. Kelsey had reported to Melanie that she'd checked the closet three times before she left for Bartlett, and she'd seen no note. But Melanie supposed something could have shown up since then. She hadn't permitted herself to check, but the thought of a letter from her mom sitting there, unread, was maddening. What if her mom, disappointed or insulted that it was still there, took it back and threw it away before Kelsey could get it?

Melanie got up to refill her glass of water, sat back down, and hit refresh again. *Views since Listing: 88. 31 Shoppers Favorited this Home.* She felt a small glow of pride. Some of the other houses listed in the area—she had scoped out the competition—had been on the market for sixty days or longer and still hadn't gotten that many views or favorites.

She took her cell phone with her outside to the window boxes, where she'd learned was the best place to make a call.

"Is Charles Kingstad available?"

"One moment, please. May I ask who's calling?"

"His daughter. Melanie."

As she waited to be transferred, she plucked out a few stubborn weeds and tossed them on the grass.

"Melanie! How are you doing, kiddo? It's so nice to hear from you," her dad said. He sounded genuinely delighted, even though she knew that on a Friday afternoon, he was probably swamped with last-minute preparations for a Monday trial.

"I'm good, Dad. I'm good. I just wanted to let you know the lake house is officially on the market. I emailed you a link to the listing a little while ago."

"Really? Wow, that was fast. Hang on. Let me see if I can find it." She heard some paper shuffling and computer clicking. "Oh, here it is. Wow. That's beautiful. Just beautiful." More clicking. "Simply lovely. And the asking price seems just right. You must have a real pro working for you. Well done. I couldn't be happier with this, Melanie.

You girls are doing a great job. I'm sure it will sell fast, then you can use the money to make some investments, build an addition on your home, buy plane tickets to come visit us, whatever." He laughed.

"Thanks, Dad. How are you?"

"Oh, you know, busy as usual. Catching up after the long weekend. Laila and I took the kids up to Phoenix to visit her parents and go to a water park. I've been digging out ever since. Hold on." A short muffled conversation that Melanie couldn't quite make out followed. "Sorry about that. Kelsey told me you girls were sticking around the lake for Memorial Day and crashing that barbecue over on Harris Beach. How was it? Do they still make those giant cream puffs? Man, I miss those. Even better than the ones at the state fair."

"Nope, no cream puffs anymore, but we still had a nice time. We met our new neighbors."

"Glad to hear it," her dad said amiably. "So the basement renovation is almost finished, then? Have you been happy with the quality of the guy's work? Remind me—it comes with a warranty, right? You should definitely include that in the property disclosure statement. Buyers will be looking for it."

"Okay, will do. Thanks. Yeah, I've been pretty happy so far with how it's turning out." Melanie fingered the satiny petals of a pink impatiens. The flowers were the prettiest she'd ever seen them, perhaps because she was out there talking on the phone and watering them so often. "About those neighbors. They're staying in the Fletchers' house, and I wondered..."

"Oh, did Fletch sell?" She heard clicking in the background, quiet, like he didn't want her to hear.

"I don't know. That's why I wondered if you knew anything about it."

"When we first started renting the place, they were still spending their summers there, but that was quite a while ago. I obviously haven't kept in touch."

His "obviously" sounded bitter, and for the millionth time, Melanie wondered what exactly had happened that last summer they had spent together at the lake house as a family—the summer that Jilly had almost drowned. It had something to do with Vinnie, Melanie was pretty damn sure.

"Do Mr. and Mrs. Fletcher know that Mom died?" she asked.

"Of course. They sent a flower arrangement, if I remember correctly. Something big and expensive, I'm sure. They didn't make it to the funeral, though." There it was again, that bitterness, like he was carefully spitting each word out as if it were a cold, hard seed. *Where is it coming from? Was there really an affair like Kelsey suspects? And if so, did Dad find out about it? Is that why we rented the place to the Holloways abruptly and never returned?* He had never let on to Melanie and Kelsey, but then again, their mom had never let on that she had once been in love with Mrs. Fletcher either. Perhaps both her parents were just awfully good at hiding the truth.

"Dad, that last summer at the lake..." Melanie started. *Why am I doing this?* She had warned Kelsey against digging into the past, and there she was, doing the same thing. She was just as hungry, just as driven to make sense of it all as her sister. During her life, their mom had been like a folded paper fan to them, and they were slowly starting to unfurl her, fold by fold, to see the delicate, ornate pattern painted on her skin. It was hard to let that go, to simply snap the fan shut once she knew what fascinating complexities were inside. "Why did you and Mom decide to stop spending our summers there?"

"A lot of things, really," her dad said, and the bitterness was gone. *So not the discovery of an affair? Or is he just a really good actor?* "I could only come out on the weekends to see you guys because I was still working in downtown Milwaukee. And the whole time I was there, I couldn't enjoy myself because I was doing little odd jobs around the house that had accumulated over the week. I couldn't ever sit still and relax—it drove your mom crazy. It was such a big house and required so much maintenance, and your mom could never be bothered with that kind of thing. You know her—always with her nose in a book. She thought I should hire someone, but that gets expensive.

"Anyway, we went round and round about it, until the day that neighbor girl hit her head on a rock and nearly drowned. Your mom was really shaken up about it. She was worried something like that might happen to you girls. So we decided it might be best to take a break, rent the house out for a while, and maybe do a few road trips to different parts of the country in the meantime. Remember our trip to Washington, DC? Wasn't that fun? We should plan another one of those, get the whole gang together—Kelsey, you and Ben, Laila and me, Ezra and Joni. I know the kids would love to see Mount Rushmore."

"Yeah, definitely, we should sometime," Melanie said as noncommittally as possible. A family road trip with Laila instead of Mom sounded awful. She plopped down in the grass. "But we were strong swimmers by then. Fourteen and twelve. And you guys didn't rent it out for just 'a while.' You rented it out for fifteen years."

"Ah, well. When your mom made her mind up about something..." He chuckled. Some high-pitched beeps emitted, and Melanie couldn't tell if it was her phone or something in her dad's office.

Does he honestly not know about the lifeguarding accident, the drowned boy? Where Mom's dread of the water came from? Or is he just not sharing the information with me because Mom asked him not to?

"Did she ever say anything about—"

"Sorry, kiddo. Just got another important call on the line here. I'm going to have to let you go. But thanks so much for calling, and good luck with the house sale. I'm so proud of you girls that I'm going to... I'm going to send you an enormous fruit basket. No grapefruit, though, because I know you can't stand them. Promise me we'll talk again soon, okay, kiddo?" And he was gone. Even before Melanie had time to say goodbye, the line was dead.

FOR PURELY SCIENTIFIC reasons, Melanie needed to know how the time portal worked, if the tapestry was the source of the magic or the closet or a combination of the two. Or maybe it was the house itself. She spent a good twenty minutes walking in and out of all of the closets—and crawling in and out of the cabinets that were big enough—and feeling downright silly. She was glad no one else was in the house to see how ridiculous she looked.

Next she needed to make sure the door behind the tapestry was in working order before she started tampering with it. She entered the tiny closet, feeling like the world's biggest hypocrite—*If only Kelsey knew!*—and immediately tossed the contents of the bench, looking for a note. The cardigan and the books were there but no cigarettes that time. She examined the books more carefully and saw that they were *The SS Edmund Fitzgerald Wreck* and Rachel Carson's *The Sea Around Us* and even shook them upside down to see if anything would flutter out but no such luck.

Maybe the photograph hadn't gotten to her mom. Maybe it was lost somewhere in time, sent back to the early 1900s. Perhaps her mom had gotten the photograph but was struggling with how to respond to them. Or maybe she was icing them out, plain and simple, ignoring their attempts to communicate in the hopes that they would just "keep out of her business," as she had demanded in her last missive.

Then Melanie saw a scrap of yellow paper peeking out between the buttons of the cardigan. Her blood roared in her ears as she reached for it. It wasn't a full sheet like last time—just a quarter sheet ripped cleanly along a folded edge, not a lot of space to write. She unfolded it slowly.

Thank you for the picture. The little girls are lovely. Are they mine? I assume so, because the blonde has my curls, and the brunette has my nose and mouth. I can't wait to meet them one day. –C. A. K. P.S. May I ask who this is?

Melanie almost laughed in relief. The note wasn't guarded and resentful, like she'd feared, but it also didn't display that her mom had figured everything out, either—who her mysterious pen pals were and every last detail of what the future held in store for her. It was, for the most part, utterly benign. She wondered how old her mom had been when she'd written it—definitely not a teenager anymore. *How much time whizzed by after Kelsey planted the photo the night of the bonfire?* It hadn't escaped Melanie's notice that her mom's initials were C. A. K.—Christine Ann Kingstad.

She pocketed the note and reemerged to find her room had changed, not to the pink twin-size bed this time, though. Instead, a queen-sized bed was piled high with pillows. A pair of men's white tennis shoes had been kicked off near the door, and a briefcase was on the desk.

She had found her mom's correspondence and established that the time portal was still working, so she should pop back out and move on to phase two. But it was clear that her parents were married, presumably in the early years of their marriage, if they were still staying in that room, and Grandpa Jack and Grandma Dot hadn't turned over the full run of the house to them yet. It would be so easy just to catch a glimpse of them.

No, Melanie told herself firmly. God knew what she would stumble across that time. She reemerged safely in the present and clicked the silver latch in place behind her, temptation averted.

Phase two consisted of her removing the *Tree of Life* tapestry from the wall and laying it across her bed. She studied the two pairs of birds for any clues she had initially missed, but they just perched placidly on their golden branches. She returned to the door, which was so exposed and naked looking without its protective covering. When she went into and came out of the closet, she was still in her own bedroom, laptop and cell phone on the desk, patchwork quilt on the bed.

That surprised her. She had been almost one hundred percent certain it was the closet itself that housed the magic. *Why else was it hidden behind the tapestry?* But apparently, the *Tree of Life* had something to do with the enchantment. Otherwise, Melanie had just somehow broken the time portal, and her sister was going to kill her.

She rushed through phase three, too worried that she had irreparably screwed up their one connection to her mom to try hanging the tapestry in several locations and instead chose just one. Her parents' bedroom had a hook above the closet door where her mom had hung party dresses, so Melanie hung the tapestry there. She waited one minute before opening the door and stepping inside then another minute before emerging—still in her parents' room in the present day. Kelsey had forgotten some of Sprocket's toys on the wooden floor.

So it wasn't just the tapestry either. She couldn't just slap it anywhere in the house and expect to create a tunnel to the past.

Melanie carried the midnight-blue wall hanging back to her bedroom to restore it to its rightful place. She flopped down on her bed and closed her eyes. She was too nervous to retry the closet again immediately. She didn't know what she would do, how she would explain things to Kelsey, if she had somehow damaged the "mystical seal," as she had embarrassingly come to call it in her head, between the tapestry and the hidden door.

She reviewed what she had just learned. Time traveling into her mom's past seemed to require two things—both the *Tree of Life* and the secret closet. One didn't work without the other. In some ways, that was a relief. When they sold the house and took the tapestry with them, some strange man, woman, or child couldn't go innocently stumbling into her mom's bedroom in the 1970s. In other ways, it was a crushing blow. She couldn't simply give the tapestry to Kelsey to hang in her apartment and pop in to see their mom whenever they particularly missed her. When the house was sold, their gateway to the past would be closed off for good.

But what puzzled Melanie was how the particular combination of the wall hanging and the door had come to be. It had made sense to her that someone, most likely her mom, had discovered the magical properties of the closet and attempted to cover it up. But with her new understanding, she saw how that thinking was backward. Instead, what had happened was someone wanted to hide an ordinary closet—*to hide some sort of contraband, maybe?*—concealed it with the tapestry, then voila. The mystical seal occurred, and a time portal was born. *Ha-ha. Take that, Stephen Hawking.*

But who did it? Grandpa Jack or Grandma Dot? Or maybe even one of the great-grandparents? While that was an interesting possibility to ponder, what was even more interesting to Melanie was *when* her mom had discovered it. *How old was she? How often did she time travel? What moments in the house's history did she see? Glimpses of her childhood and adolescence? Glimpses of her own mother's?*

Melanie wondered if she would ever be able to ask her mom—and while she was thinking of it, how she and Kelsey should reply to their mom's note. She might be less cordial if she knew her pen pals were in fact her grown-up daughters. With more information exchanged and more interactions came more risk of "butterfly effect" moments. Melanie could already foresee Kelsey and herself arguing about the most prudent way to respond.

Opening her eyes, she sat up in the bed. She needed to check out the time portal once more to make sure it still worked after her experimentation. Her heart galloped in her chest as she reached to open the doorknob from the inside of the closet. She hadn't known how much the portal meant to her until she realized how easily it could disappear. Melanie had meant all of her pleas to Kelsey not to use it, but still, she just wanted to know that it existed, that it was still there if she ever desperately needed to lay eyes on her mom or hear her voice.

She pushed the door open, and there it was again—the queen-size bed. She let out a deep breath. The white tennis shoes had been moved, but that was because a man was kneeling down to lace them up—her dad. She stepped into the room, just to get a better look at him, really. He was so thin, and his hair was so dark, and he had so much of it. But it was Charlie Kingstad, all right, just younger and dressed in eighties clothes—cutoff jean shorts, a tight polo shirt, and tube socks. She couldn't believe it was the same man who had just rushed her off the phone. He grabbed a plastic bottle of something off the desk, pills of some kind, and dashed out the door.

She had to follow him.

Just five minutes, she told herself as she chased him down the stairs. He made a beeline to the empty kitchen for a glass of water and headed for the wraparound porch. Muffin wrappers and half-finished glasses of orange juice were strewn on the outdoor table, and sitting on the porch swing, rocking, in the exact same spot that Melanie had been sitting the previous night, was her mom. She was wearing some kind of pale-blue smock, like a swimsuit cover-up. It had a white Peter Pan collar and wasn't particularly flattering. It was a maternity dress.

Melanie stood still, watching her dad hand her mom what she now saw were chewable antacid tablets. Her mom was having heart-burn—because she was pregnant. The grace of the moment took Melanie's breath away, and she suddenly understood Kelsey's claim that their mom *wanted* them to see these glimpses of her life, that she was somehow guiding them to particular flashes of the past, events she hoped would provide illumination for them.

"Thanks, honey," her mom said. "You can probably still catch them if you go now. The boat hasn't left yet."

Sure enough, down at the dock, a small knot of people was boarding the pontoon boat: Grandpa Jack in a sun visor and aviator shades, Grandma Dot in a flowery sarong, and two people in orange life vests Melanie didn't recognize.

"I'd rather stay here with my wife and baby," her dad said, sliding into place next to her mom. He reached for her hand, and their fingers interlocked.

Melanie's heart gave a happy squeeze. She was seeing where it all began. Melanie and Kelsey had been born to parents who wanted them, who loved them, and who loved each other. She didn't know there were tears in her eyes until she felt them drip off her chin.

"I'm afraid it might be a somewhat dull afternoon." Her mom closed her eyes, a smile on her lips. "A nap might be in order."

Her dad rested his head on her shoulder and whispered something in her ear.

"A real nap," she clarified, and they both laughed.

Time to go, Melanie thought. Surely, five minutes had passed, and the scene was the kind of luminous, perfect memory that could nourish her for weeks, months even. It could get her through the emotional difficulty of selling the house. Maybe it could even get her back to Ohio and back into Ben's arms, willing to patiently wait the requisite time to try again—because it was clearly worth it. The glow of her parents' faces... it was like they were sharing the world's greatest secret.

"I know it's kind of boring here, staying with your in-laws and a wife who won't swim," her mom said. "I would understand if you didn't want to come up again next summer. I think my parents would, too, since we'll have this little one by then."

"I'm not bored. Are you bored?" He took a sip of water. "I know how much this place means to you and your family, and I wouldn't want to get in the way of that. Plus, I think it's kind of wonderful that it's been in your family for so long. Your dad grew up here. You grew up here, and now our child will grow up here too. What a way to put down some roots."

Melanie couldn't tell because the porch swing faced that direction anyway, but she thought her mom was staring at the Fletchers' house. She wondered if Lavinia and Lance were married yet, if they were staying with Mr. and Mrs. Birdwell for the summer, and if Lavinia was already pregnant with Beau, who was only a little younger than Melanie. She wasn't sure how many months younger, but they had been in the same grade.

"Roots," her mom echoed. "What is that old quote about roots? The two things parents should give their children? 'One is roots. The other: wings.'"

"I don't know. I've never heard that before. But I like it."

As her young parents-to-be rocked on the porch swing, Melanie realized that her dad's interpretation of why they had left the lake house had been wrong. Leaving hadn't been a notion that had suddenly struck Christine that particular summer. It had been a prevailing idea that had been with her from the very start, probably once her mom and Vinnie had ended and her mom and her dad had begun.

"Remind me again why you don't like the name Kenneth?" he asked suddenly.

"There was a boy named Kenneth in my second-grade class who picked his nose and didn't even try to hide it. He sat in the front row."

"Ah. Right. Old Kenneth the Front-Row Nose Picker. And we've definitely vetoed Charles Junior? Chuck for short, of course."

Christine's lips were twitching with amusement. "If your heart is really set on Charles Junior, that's fine by me. But I keep telling you—we don't need to worry so much about boys' names, because this baby is a girl." She affectionately patted her swollen abdomen. "This baby is our Melanie Jane."

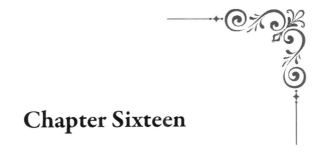

Chapter Sixteen

B eth wasn't exactly giving Kelsey the silent treatment, but she had made it abundantly clear that Kelsey's "day off" stunt had demoted her from her previous status of most trusted confidante. In fact, she hadn't even shared with Kelsey how the mother-daughter trip to Tennessee had gone, but Kelsey intuited that it had been a disaster by the way Beth kept sneaking out to "run errands" and taking private phone calls in her office with the door closed. Her grim, defeated expression spoke volumes.

According to Taylor, things had gone pretty smoothly on Sunday. They'd only had a few mishaps, such as when she had accidentally let a toy poodle in heat into the yard with two male dogs, a boxer and a beagle. "But Josh was really good about helping me separate them!" Taylor gushed. "He was so nice and patient with me all day!"

Kelsey had to take her word for it because Josh had several days off in a row, and he hadn't responded to her text. He worked Wednesday, but that was finally her much-needed day off, so she didn't get to see him then either. She would have to wait until Friday, when they both worked, to get his version of events and gauge just how irritated with her he was.

In the meantime, she enjoyed her day off with Sprocket. She didn't tell Melanie she wasn't working, because she badly needed a break from the lake house. It was hard to believe that only a few days ago, she had been so eager to get out there that she had skipped work for it. But things had changed. She hoped if she waited it out long enough, Everett would finish the basement restoration and she wouldn't have to see him again. And as for the house being formally listed, the impending open house the next weekend, the memory of her mom and Vinnie's conversation in the basement, the thought of her poor, young, unsuspecting dad sitting alone in front of the bonfire, and the fact that her mom had countered their childhood photograph with dead radio silence—well, Kelsey didn't want to think about any of it.

She spent hours at the dog park, Sprocket flitting from scent to scent like a happy hummingbird. A friendly guy with a dachshund approached them, but at the end of the exchange, he didn't ask for her number, and she didn't offer it. He was a bit too short for her liking, and his khakis had a perfect crease down the front of each leg. *Don't be so shallow*, she could practically hear Melanie scolding her. *True attraction is fifty percent looks and fifty percent personality.* Which was easy for Melanie to say because not only was Ben the nicest guy ever but he also looked like a model from a Land's End catalog.

She went to the grocery store and bought two hundred fifty dollars' worth of groceries—butterfly-cut pork chops and rib roast and shallots and spinach and rhubarb and ginger root and something that smelled spicy and heavenly. She didn't know what it was but intended to find out. Kelsey also bought dog food and enough rawhide bones to last Sprocket through the rest of the summer as well as two bottles of red wine, two bottles of white, and more flour, sugar, vanilla, and cocoa to replenish her baking supplies. That evening, she binge-watched four hours of cooking shows as she caramelized shallots on the stove, tied the pork chops with kitchen twine, and drank half a bottle of red wine.

When she arrived at work on Friday morning, she couldn't help feeling slightly nervous to see Josh. She wouldn't blame him if he gave her the cold shoulder like Beth. She had, after all, abandoned him on one of the busiest days of the year. But instead of Josh, with his black-framed glasses and crooked grin, Kelsey found lumberjack-bearded Alan in Pooch Place, mopping the floor. Apparently Josh had called him the night before to see if Alan could come in for him. Alan didn't know for sure, but he'd assumed Josh wasn't feeling well.

Is he giving me a taste of my own medicine? It seemed too timely to be a mere coincidence, but she wasn't so egotistical that she supposed he had called in sick simply to avoid her. *Or am I?* As she and Alan silently and efficiently took care of the dogs, Kelsey fretted that she had ruined her friendship with Josh. Besides Beth, he was her favorite person to work with. They joked around all day long, and the hours flew by. But without Josh's easy banter, and with Beth depressed and hardly speaking to her, Kelsey felt the drudgery of her job for the first time.

She clipped nails. She cleaned cages. She picked up poop. She measured out food. She ran in circles around the yard. She picked up more poop. *I'm approaching thirty, and this is what I do for a living?*

On Saturday, she was thrilled to see Josh's pickup truck in the parking lot. But when she hustled inside, she found him talking to Taylor at the front desk. Taylor was giggling like Josh had just said something hilarious.

"Hi, K. K.," he said when he saw her. "How was the lake?"

She couldn't tell if he was being genuine or passive-aggressive. "It was fine, thanks," she said. She wanted to apologize for leaving him high and dry, but she couldn't exactly do that in front of Taylor without offending the girl. She stood there awkwardly for a minute, feeling like a third wheel, while Taylor scrolled through Google images of monkey-looking creatures to show Josh. "Well, I'd better go fill up the pool like Beth asked. It's supposed to be ninety today."

"Okay," Josh and Taylor said at the same time.

Dejected, Kelsey hauled the blue hard-plastic pool out of the storage area all by herself. She dragged it to the backyard, unwound

the hose, and turned on the water. Usually pool days were her favorite days at the pet lodge because she loved watching the dogs
splash around. But that morning a sludge of guilt, sadness, and jealousy had settled in the pit of her stomach, and even the sight of
Cookie—the timid little spaniel who had been staying with them
for a week and seemed to miss her owners like crazy—dropping her
tennis ball joyfully in the pool and fishing it out again and again
couldn't cheer Kelsey up.

"Fine, thanks?" Josh had come out into the yard without her
noticing. "I slave away for ten hours on Sunday so that you can
go catch some rays at your family's lake house—nice tan, by the
way—and that's all you're going to tell me?"

She was so happy he wasn't really mad at her that she almost
hugged him. "No, that's not all. But I thought you might want to tell
me about your adventures first."

He picked up the hose and ran his hands under the stream. "My
adventures? Hmm. Well, how much time do you have?"

"I'm so sorry," she said, making a face. "I felt so bad bailing out
on you like that at the last minute, but I was just so burned out. Then
my sister invited me to this cookout on the beach..."

"You can tell me all about it at Tony's," he said, dropping the
hose back into the pool with a small splash. The icy droplets tickled
Kelsey's leg. "When are we going? I'm free tonight."

Kelsey tried not to look as stunned as she felt. The text—she had
meant she would order pizza sometime when they were both working, not go to the restaurant together after work some night, not like
a date. *Does he think I was propositioning him?*

He was smiling at Cookie, tossing her waterlogged ball for her,
seemingly oblivious to the delay in Kelsey's response. It seemed like
minutes but was probably only seconds. Josh was tall and loose-
limbed, comfortable in his own skin. In their two years of working
together at Green Valley Pet Lodge, she had talked to him about

everything under the sun—when she first got Sprocket, her family, ex-boyfriends, recipes she was dying to try—and Josh did the same, telling her about his tabby cat, Tumnus, his woodworking projects, and the obnoxious antics of his three older brothers, all with their J names—John, Jason, Jordan, and Josh.

"Tonight works for me too," she said, and the weight of sadness that had been burdening her for days suddenly became lighter.

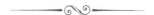

TONY'S PIZZA WAS MOSTLY a delivery and carryout place, but they had a small seating area with rickety bistro-style tables and a lot of dusty fake plants. Kelsey and Josh had gone home after work to feed and take care of their respective pets and agreed to meet at the restaurant an hour later. Kelsey had changed out of her Green Valley T-shirt and shorts and into her jersey-knit dress and gladiator sandals. She'd eyed herself in the mirror then whipped the dress over her head and opted for a white lacy tank top and the same shorts she'd worn to work. Sprocket watched all of it with grave interest.

"Sorry, buddy," she said as she threw him a treat and locked the front door behind her.

She was reassured to see that Josh hadn't dressed up either. He had changed out of his work T-shirt into a different T-shirt, and his wet hair suggested he had showered, but he looked like the same old Josh, and she could see that the green dress would have been a mistake.

They found a table among the families with young children and teenagers hanging out with their friends.

"You said any toppings I want, right?" Josh asked, tapping the large laminated menu with his pointer finger. "How would you feel about basil, artichokes, sundried tomatoes, kalamata olives, and goat cheese?"

"That sounds delicious," she said. She walked over to the register to put in their order, and when she came back, Josh was sitting ramrod straight in his chair with his hands folded on the table. She wanted to tease him for his schoolboy posture, to say something to defuse the tension that had suddenly snuck up on them, but was, for the first time in his presence, at a total loss for words.

"I'm so glad Cookie had a good day," she said lamely, grasping at the first topic that came to her mind. "Her owners are coming for her tomorrow, aren't they? She's going to be over the moon."

Josh eagerly clung to the conversational life raft she had thrown him, and for several minutes, they rehashed work and talked dogs and vented and complained. Then Josh gave her the real scoop on how things had gone down on Sunday with Taylor filling in.

"So I explained to her the order that we should let the dogs out in the yard," he said. "But not the reason, I guess, so it was kind of all my fault. I was out there with these two males, when all of sudden, here comes Taylor with Starlight, and she lets the poodle off her leash. And Starlight tears across the yard to the beagle, practically thrusting her butt in his face. So then I sprint across the yard just in time to scoop her up before he could mount her! I mean, I'm pretty sure he's neutered, but you never know. Could you imagine Jeannette's reaction if her dog got knocked up while she was staying with us?"

Kelsey was laughing so hard, her sides hurt. "Those high schoolers behind you are staring at you like you're nuts," she whispered. "Probably your references to 'mounting' and 'neutering.'"

He laughed his nice, normal, non-Ernie-sounding laugh. "Eh. All in a day's work, I guess."

She pulled out her phone to show him the house listing, and as he flipped through the photos, his eyes got wider and wider. "Holy cats! I didn't know you were an heir to the Kennedy fortune. Why are you still driving that old junker?"

Their pizza arrived, and it was so good, and they were so hungry, that it wasn't long before they were haggling over the last piece.

"I think I should get it because I'm the girl, and after all, I did pay," Kelsey said.

"Well, I think I should get it because I had to deal with humping dogs because of you."

Giggles erupted behind them, and Kelsey and Josh joined in.

"Fair enough," she said, but he cut the last piece in half with a knife and handed her one of the slivers.

The teenagers were scraping their chairs against the floor and teasingly pushing each other as they left the dining area. An employee in a black apron came in with a broom, scowled at them, and stalked back out. Kelsey was startled to see that she and Josh were the only ones left.

Behind Josh's retro glasses, his eyes were a kaleidoscope of colors. Kelsey had always thought he had green eyes, but she could see that was just the outer rim of his irises. Radiating from each pupil like a golden sunburst was a yellowish-brownish-orangey inner ring. Once she noticed it, it was hard for her to look anywhere else. It was so unusual, so striking.

"I think that's our cue," he said and took one last swig of his root beer before hopping up.

Kelsey got up reluctantly. She wasn't ready to say goodbye to him just yet, but she didn't know what the alternative was. Asking him to get a drink at The Blue Lounge seemed wrong, but even worse would be suggesting they go back to her place to hang out. She followed him past the surly waitress out into the parking lot. Josh stood with his hands in his pockets, as if he were unwilling to part ways too.

"It's such a beautiful night," he said. When the sun had gone down, it had taken a lot of the heat and humidity of the day along with it. "You wouldn't want to walk to Gosling Park with me, would you? It's only about three blocks from here."

"Sure," she said. "We can burn some of those calories off."

The sky was thick and textured with clouds, and the moon peeked out like a white button nestled in a pillowy quilt. Kelsey tried to match her strides to Josh's longer ones.

"Do you want me to come to your open house next weekend and stand around saying things like, 'They're not asking *nearly* enough for this place,' and 'Are these original 1900s oak floors? Why, I never!'"

"That's quite all right," Kelsey said, smiling at the thought. "Actually I think I'd prefer if you went around pointing out flaws instead. Maybe that way no one would put in an offer."

Josh scratched his cheek and glanced at her sideways. "Still having second thoughts about selling?"

"Only every hour of every day," she said dismally. "Melanie makes a compelling argument, and my brain is totally on board. But my heart is a different story." Her heart felt like the sale of the house would encompass not only the physical structure and the land but also the summers of her childhood, a hundred years' worth of history, and the last living link she had to her mom.

"Have you guys talked about alternatives? Maybe continuing to rent it out year-round? Or hiring a property manager to rent it for short-term stays in the summer? Or you could even turn it into a B and B."

"A bed-and-breakfast?" Kelsey snorted. "Who would run it? Melanie's not going to leave Kinsley College to do it. And everyone knows I'm a total flake. It would be like Amelia Bedelia trying to run a bed-and-breakfast."

They had reached the park, which was little more than some plastic playground equipment, a small grove of trees, and two benches.

"I'm not sure who Amelia Bedelia is, but you're *not* a flake," Josh said with conviction. "You're smart and dedicated and a hard worker. If you wanted to make it happen, I bet you could."

A ready retort was on her lips—*Thanks, Dad*—but she suppressed it. He was being so earnest. He had worked alongside her for two years, and he thought she was smart, dedicated, and hardworking. It was nice to know that someone did.

"Thanks," she said.

Instead of sitting down on one of the benches, Josh headed for the row of swings. Kelsey hesitated a second then followed suit.

"I could handle the breakfast part of it." She sat down and started to pump her legs. "Muffins and scones. Quiches and frittatas." She envisioned a snowy-white tablecloth spread over the table on the wraparound porch, and a middle-aged couple drinking mimosas out of champagne glasses. They would love her strawberry pineapple bread so much, they would ask for seconds.

In the moon-dappled park, flying high on her swing, Kelsey felt like a little girl again—like anything was possible, like entire aisles of possibilities stretched out in front of her like goods in a grocery store. She just needed to stretch out her fingers and choose one. *Turning the lake house into a bed-and-breakfast? Sure, why not? Convincing Melanie to go along with it? Easy peasy. Falling in love with someone who's kind and good and won't break my heart?*

She turned her head to study Josh. The swing's momentum was blowing his floppy brown hair back, out of his eyes and off his forehead.

He must have felt her eyes on him, because he turned, too, to beam at her—a little dopey, a little self-conscious but full of glee. "What are you thinking?" he asked.

"I can't believe you've never read the Amelia Bedelia books," she replied.

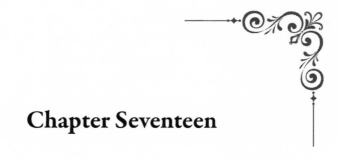

Chapter Seventeen

"It's supposed to be in the eighties and nineties all week," Melanie said into the phone. She had caught Kelsey on her lunch break. "When are you coming out for a swim?" She stopped herself just in time from adding, *It might be our last chance, you know.*

"Is Everett finished with the basement?" Kelsey asked, surprising Melanie. Since Melanie had revealed the information about their mom's message and how she'd seen her pregnant, Melanie had thought that Kelsey would be leaping at the chance to return to the lake house and the world behind the tapestry. But apparently Everett was a strong enough deterrent to make her think twice.

"Today's his last day," Melanie said. The afternoon sun was hot on her neck. "Just installing the drainage pipe outdoors and testing the sump pump."

A door banged shut—the Fletchers' house. She ducked out of sight behind a lilac bush. She really wasn't in the mood to make small talk with rude Nicholas or even his kind wife, Jess, with her beautiful, enviable children.

"I have off tomorrow and Wednesday," Kelsey said. "Sprocket and I could come for an overnight."

"That would be great," Melanie said. "See you then." From her vantage point behind the sweet-smelling lilacs, she could see the mother-in-law, Marie, walking down the porch steps, carrying something. It was long and black, like a photographer's tripod.

"Why are you whispering?" Kelsey asked.

"I'm not whispering," Melanie hissed. "Got to go."

Marie was loading the tripod into the truck bed. Her blond hair was up in a bun, and an orange scarf was tied around her head like a headband.

"All right, weirdo. See you tomorrow. Probably sometime mid-morning."

"Okay. Bye." Melanie put the phone in her pocket, hoping Marie was going to drive away soon. It would be embarrassing to pop out at that point.

The door slammed shut again. "Are you sure you don't want me to come along?" someone called from the porch.

"Heavens, no," Marie replied, putting her hands on her hips with a smile. "All you do is mope around and ask me if I'm nearly finished."

"I do not," the woman replied. "I love watching you paint."

Melanie couldn't see who the speaker was from behind the lilacs.

"You love the *idea* of watching me paint. You are bored stiff by the actual act," Marie said. "What you really want to do this afternoon is go for a swim then take a nap in the hammock. And you have my blessing."

Melanie's knees were starting to ache from her crouched position. She straightened her legs and bent at the waist instead. *This is getting ridiculous.* Maybe she should run around the back of the house and go through that door. If they spotted her, she could just pretend she had come back up from the lake. She was worried Everett was going to come outside looking for her and blow her cover. *Oh, why did I go the antisocial route?* She could have just waved at Marie and headed back inside to start making up the bed for Kelsey.

"Would you bring me my tote, love? It's right there by the door."

A woman with long silver hair, parted down the middle, descended the steps, lugging a heavy-looking canvas bag. Melanie's breath caught in her throat. She ducked down even lower. The woman heaved the bag into the truck bed then came around to the driver's side window. Melanie couldn't hear what the two women were saying with their voices lowered, but she didn't need to.

It was Vinnie, older than Melanie had last seen her in real life—when Vinnie had been in her midforties—and definitely older than Melanie had last seen her in the time portal as a high schooler. She was probably fifty-nine, the same age Christine would have been, and was still slim and regal looking in her emerald caftan.

Lavinia Birdwell Fletcher, in the flesh, living right next door to Melanie—not Nicholas and Jess's landlord but Marie's partner.

THEIR LAST SUMMER AT the lake house, when Melanie was fourteen and Kelsey was twelve, they had spent on the dock. Previous summers, they had rowed across the lake with their dad, tossed a Frisbee with the Fletcher kids, played board games, or read on the wraparound porch with their mom. But that summer had been the summer of the dock. Spread out on two striped towels, sometimes listening to their Discmans, sometimes doing their summer reading for ninth and seventh grades—*To Kill a Mockingbird* and *The Secret Garden*, respectively—they rarely moved except to dive into the lake to cool off or reapply sunscreen. "Teenagers," their dad said, shaking his head every time he asked them if they wanted to pick raspberries or go for a pontoon boat ride. Their mom would bring out fresh lemonade and call them in for lunch. By the end of the summer, both Melanie and Kelsey had been the color of warm gingerbread.

Melanie blamed that summer for the sprinkling of light-brown spots on her shoulders and the one on her temple that she could mostly hide with her hair. Now she wore SPF 50 and a sunhat that made her feel like Audrey Hepburn. She slathered some more sunscreen on her legs and kicked off her sandals.

"Are you going to come in or what?" Kelsey called from the water.

"In a minute." She positioned the cooler closer to the bench so that Sprocket's water dish was in the shade and he had somewhere to lie if he got too hot.

"I wish we had some Vertical Horizon. I always associate that CD with the lake because I must have listened to it a million times here!" Kelsey floated on her back, her arms undulating, her hair spread out on the water and even more mermaid-like than usual.

"I think I have some of their songs on my phone. I could go get the outdoor speaker."

"Thanks, but no thanks. Just get in here already!"

Melanie sat at the dock's edge, submerging her feet and calves. She had already shared with Kelsey what she had seen and overheard in the Fletchers' yard the day before, but Kelsey was adamant that she didn't want to see Lavinia, much less talk to her. "Good. Let her be some other woman's problem," was what she had said when Melanie told her she thought Vinnie and Marie were a couple. Though Kelsey had zero interest in talking with the living, breathing link to their mom's past right next door, she was all about replying to their mom's note as soon as possible and claimed to have a draft underway. The thought of what Kelsey's draft contained made Melanie feel slightly queasy, so she was hoping to put her sister off for as long as possible. She wanted to keep things light and fun between them and not bring up the sale of the house, the time portal, and what they would be losing.

"So I want to hear about this date with your coworker," Melanie said. "Josh." She remembered him from her visit to Green Valley Pet Lodge—tall and polite, with hipster glasses and eyes only for Kelsey. She wholeheartedly approved of him if only for the fact that he was breaking Kelsey's "type" and he had shaken her hand when they met.

She liked old-school manners—firm handshakes and holding doors open for strangers.

"I already told you—we ate pizza at Tony's and walked to a nearby park."

Melanie took off her wide-brimmed hat and lowered herself into the lake. It felt like a warm, wet embrace. "What did you guys talk about?"

Kelsey paddled away from her. "Oh, you know, work stuff. And... um... books." She clearly was hiding something. Kelsey was a miserable liar.

"Do you think you guys will go out again?" Melanie asked.

Kelsey was swimming for the wooden raft, the place where Jilly had almost died. Melanie swam after her.

"Maybe," Kelsey called over her shoulder. "I don't know."

"Why not?" Melanie pressed.

Kelsey reached for the metal ladder and pulled herself toward the raft. "He's my coworker and my friend. I just don't want to screw anything up."

They clambered onto the raft, and Melanie could practically feel the ghost of slippery elbows jostling her ribs, the rocking under her feet as other children jumped up and down. Around them, the lake was silently rising and falling.

"I totally get it," she said. "There are higher stakes with him. But at the risk of sounding cliché, nothing ventured, nothing gained."

"It's not just that," Kelsey said. She splashed some water onto the sunbaked wood and sat down. "I also don't know if I feel that way about him. I mean, we've been working together for two years. Shouldn't I have felt a pull toward him before now? And it was almost by accident that we even went on a date. I texted him that I owed him pizza, and he misinterpreted it as us going to the restaurant together."

He didn't misinterpret it, Melanie thought. "I think you're talking about love at first sight, which doesn't happen for most people. More often than not, that spark—that click that happens when you just *know* someone is right for you—doesn't come right away." She sat down cross-legged next to Kelsey. "You know how Ben and I met, right?"

"Yeah," Kelsey said dismissively. "You were both panelists at a science career day at some high school. And he and the med student were acting all superior to you and the chemistry major because you would be 'working in a lab all day, pipetting things,' while he and the med student would be out there helping sick people. When he asked you for your number at the end of the day, you told him he could stick his pipette where the sun don't shine."

Melanie laughed. "Not exactly." Although she liked Kelsey's more colorful version. "I think I just said, 'No, I'd rather not.' But then we crossed paths a month later at a graduation party for a mutual friend. I hardly recognized him because he had a full beard then—it was awful, like he was some mountain man. And I told my friend to save me from the most arrogant guy on the planet, but she abandoned me because they were cutting the cake. I really only gave him my number that time to get him to leave me alone. And he called about five times before we finally set up a date. Thank God, he'd shaved by then, and I started to understand his sense of humor and that he didn't really think pharmacists were better than anybody else. But the point is that I didn't feel that click right away. It took months. And it caught me off guard when it finally happened because Ben wasn't the type of person I had ever pictured myself marrying. He's so disorganized and spontaneous and athletic, so different from me in so many ways. But somehow he was just what I needed."

Talking about Ben made her miss him even more than usual. She yearned for those silly, carefree first years of dating and the beginning of their marriage when being just the two of them had been enough.

"I used to be scared I would never find that with anyone. That 'click.'" Kelsey put air quotes around it. "But I'm not so sure I even believe in it anymore. Or if I do, it's something you could find with multiple people, not just one. And definitely not something permanent. Maybe only five or ten years max until the drudgery sets in."

Melanie stood up. The raft felt hot under her bare feet, and the sun beat down on her poor shoulders. "You're not being serious, are you? Is this about Mom and Dad?"

"No. Yes. Maybe a little."

On the dock, Melanie's cell phone started ringing. Maybe it was Ben. Sometimes she swore he had a sixth sense.

"Mom and Dad were happily married for twenty-nine years. Do you not remember how sweet they could be together? Dad would rub her shoulders and leave those little Shakespearean sonnet Post-it notes all over, and Mom would bake him Black Forest cake and knit those slipper socks that he loved. And every anniversary, they would put Rod Stewart on the stereo and dance around the kitchen."

"Okay, so maybe at some point in time, they had 'the click.' But now Dad is happily remarried to Laila, and as it turns out, Mom was probably seeing the neighbor lady on the side."

They both turned to stare at the Fletchers' bungalow, which was mostly hidden by the trees. It looked squat and secretive next to the white Victorian, all red-shingled roof and no façade. For all they knew, Lavinia could be watching them from its dormers at that very moment.

The phone stopped ringing.

"Dad chose to remarry because he was lonely, and I'm pretty sure Mom would have given him her blessing. He was so helpless without a wife to take care of him." She paused, choosing her next words carefully. "And we don't know for sure that Mom was unfaithful to Dad. And either way, all the complexities of Mom and Dad's marriage shouldn't dictate what you believe in or how you choose to live your life, Kels. Falling in love with one person, staying faithful, those are still worthy goals—"

The high-pitched ringing of her phone interrupted her again.

"Maybe you should get that," Kelsey said. "It might be important."

As Melanie stood immobile, contemplating all the gut-wrenching scenarios that would require someone trying to reach her in back-to-back phone calls—Ben in an accident or her dad in the hospital—Kelsey positioned her toes on the raft's edge, bent forward, threw her arms up into a perfect point overhead, and dove in. Something about seeing her sister's graceful entry into the water and reemergence unstuck Melanie. She dove in, too, sloppily, like the amateur she was, and swam after her sister for the dock.

Kelsey toweled her hands off before picking up the phone. "Whoever it was left a voicemail," she said and squinted at the screen. "Oh. Charlene Hallbeck."

"Thanks," Melanie said, snatching the phone away. In her overpowering sense of relief—it wasn't Ben or his parents, thank God, or Laila or her dad calling—she felt whiplashed and a tad peeved with her sister, peeved at the drama and sense of unnecessary urgency she had instilled. "I'll just go call her back by the side of the house, okay? It's where we get the best reception."

"Oookaaay," Kelsey said, drawing the two syllables out so that she sounded skeptical. "But maybe before you do that, we could talk about something."

The phone gave a frantic little buzz in Melanie's hand. It was a text from Charlene. *Please call me at your earliest convenience. Good news!* "Of course we can keep talking about this, Kels. But just give me five minutes to talk to Charlene first, okay? Before she decides I've gone missing and sends out a S.W.A.T. team to break down the door."

"It's not about this. It's about something else." Kelsey's cheeks were pink, and Melanie couldn't tell if they were flushed from sunburn or nervous energy.

"Our response to Mom's note?" She sighed heavily. "Fine. But it needs to wait just a bit longer. I'll be right back." She cut Kelsey off before she could say anything else and jogged up the hill.

What good news will Charlene have for us? An ad for the house in Midwest Living? *A ton of phone calls to try to schedule showings?* Melanie imagined the smug smile on the realtor's face as she politely told buyers' agents that they'd have to wait until Sunday's open house.

"Hi, Charlene. It's Melanie Kingstad-Keyes." She paced the side of the house, not sure why she suddenly felt so scared.

"Melanie! Thanks for getting back to me so quickly! Did you get my message?"

"I didn't listen to it yet. I wanted to call you right back. It seemed urgent."

"Well, as you probably know, we have been getting *lots* of interest in your house—several requests from multiple buyers and agents trying to get a looksee before the open house. And until now, I've turned them all down." She paused for so long that Melanie thought the call had been dropped.

"Hello?"

"Until now," Charlene repeated. "A *very* wealthy buyer has expressed interest. He's a client of an agent I've worked with many times before. He paid *cash* for his first lake house, and they closed in less than thirty days."

She paused again, and that time, Melanie realized she was waiting for her to say something. "Okay?" she said.

"He and his wife want to see the house tonight," Charlene continued. "They're flexible about the time. Anytime between four and eight. Whatever works best for you."

Melanie turned to look at the lake, which was the color of mulberry wine and sparkling in the sunlight. Kelsey was throwing a tennis ball for Sprocket off the dock. "But I thought you said no exceptions. No showings before the open house."

"This is the *only* exception we will make. And even if they put an offer in, which I suspect they might, we'll add in a clause that we need until at least Monday to accept or reject their offer instead of the typical twenty-four-hour period. We won't want to limit ourselves until we know the outcome of the open house. Sound good?"

Melanie heard a vehicle approaching, probably one of the neighbors—hopefully not Vinnie—returning home. But the tires crunched up *her* gravel driveway, not the neighbors'. She peeked around the side of the house to see a battered van with Flood Repair Pros in bold typeface on the side. Everett. *What the heck is he doing here?* He'd finished the job the previous afternoon, and she'd paid him in full.

"Okay," she said. "We can do tonight. Six o'clock."

She tried to rush Charlene off the phone so she could intercept Everett—there was no way she wanted him bumping into her sister in her little red bikini—but the realtor wasn't having it. Charlene wanted to explain that she'd be sending someone right over to install the lockbox on their front door, then she wanted to make sure Melanie would have the house in shipshape condition. Melanie felt insulted by the implication that the house would be anything less than perfect in her hands.

But by the time she had disconnected the phone, Everett was stooped down, petting Sprocket, and Kelsey was making her way up from the lake. Her body language was closed off and tense as she hugged a towel around herself.

Give him a piece of your mind, Melanie encouraged her sister. *Send him packing.* But instead, Kelsey uncrossed her arms, letting them fall to her sides, and the pair kept talking.

Annoyed, Melanie decided not to return to the backyard. Let Kelsey deal with Everett on her own, then. Melanie had other more important things to do, like scrubbing away any residual toothpaste and soap scum out of the upstairs bathroom sinks. And the master bedroom was probably a catastrophe. Whenever Kelsey stayed over, she draped her clothes, both clean and dirty, over every surface. Since Sprocket was in total shedding mode, Melanie would also have to vacuum and sweep one more time. She had no idea where she, Kelsey, and Sprocket would go during the showing. More importantly, she had no idea how she was going to tell her sister that a very interested, very wealthy buyer was all lined up to see the place in only a few hours.

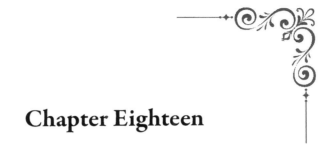

Chapter Eighteen

W hen Kelsey had finally found Melanie in the master bathroom, Melanie had been on her hands and knees, scrubbing the tile grout with an old toothbrush. She had informed Kelsey that the realtor had scheduled their first showing for six that evening. "Would you mind putting all your clothes on hangers in the closet?" she had asked. "Then maybe you could run to Dern's to pick up a bouquet for the mantel. Maybe some lilies? Those pink stargazer ones would look really nice."

Kelsey had stared back at her, feeling like a cartoon character whose jaw had just dropped to the floor, accompanied by the sound of a clanging anvil. *Tonight? As in, this very evening?* As her sister relayed the details about the prospective buyers—*Just who the heck owns more than one lake house, anyway?*—Kelsey felt even more one-dimensional and cartoonish, immature and out of touch. This was reality, where money talked and some people apparently could pay for houses in cash. She wasn't sure how she had ever thought she could persuade Melanie to believe in a bed-and-breakfast fantasy, especially since a neat and tidy sale with a multimillionaire was just within reach. The mimosas, the strawberry-pineapple bread, the hand-tatted lace pillow shams, the mismatched china plates and teacups from thrift stores... all of it was a pie-in-the-sky, castle-in-the-air, Pollyanna pipe dream.

"Where are you going?" Melanie asked, sitting back on her heels. "To clean up first or the store?"

"Neither." Kelsey propelled herself out of the bathroom. Her fingers traced the top of the chair rail as she made her way down the hallway to her sister's bedroom.

"Kelsey, I could really use your help," Melanie called after her. "Kelsey?"

The tapestry was hanging slightly askew so that she could just make out the edge of the hidden door. She almost tripped over Sprocket in her hurry to reach it. He let out a small whine.

"What are you doing?" Melanie was behind her. "We really don't have time for this right now."

"Well, we certainly won't have time for it once you sell the house to Mr. and Mrs. Moneybags, will we?" she retorted, touching the border of the tapestry.

"That's not necessarily such a bad thing," Melanie said. She crossed the room cautiously, as if Kelsey were holding a loaded gun. "This can't be healthy for us. We're still grieving Mom, and we're here at the lake house with all of our old memories, and to be unearthing all this stuff about her on top of that—"

"I don't really care if it's healthy or not, you hypocrite. It's a freaking enchanted door into Mom's life, and since you seem hell-bent on making sure we don't have access to it for much longer, I'm going in while I still can. And I'm leaving her a response, whether it's 'Melanie approved' or not." She made vigorous air quotes. "So there! Mom deserves an answer. On her end, I'm sure our lack of a response has been gnawing at her for years." She squatted down to stroke Sprocket's head. "It's okay," she told him. "I'll be back soon."

"If you've absolutely got to leave a note on the bench for her, fine," Melanie said, shocking Kelsey to the core with her sudden acquiescence. "But please come right back, and don't disappear into Mom's world right now. I'll even hold the door open for you, okay? The showing starts in less than two hours, and I can't have you popping out from behind the tapestry in the middle of it and scaring the bejeezus out of the buyers. We never know how long you'll be gone, for ten minutes or ten hours. Kelsey, just please... this isn't the right time. I need you to think like a responsible adult right now and do what's best for everyone."

Kelsey had been ready to comply with her sister and wait to go inside until after the showing, right up until that last little patronizing dig. "Oh, I need to act like a responsible adult, huh? Just like you're such a responsible adult who claims to know what's best for everyone, when really I think what you mean to say is that it's whatever's best for *you*, right at this moment? Since you keep changing your mind and breaking your own rules whenever it happens to suit you? Is running away from your problems and your husband and hiding out here how a real, responsible adult acts, Melanie? If so, then please don't sign me up."

She closed her eyes briefly, expecting another protest, horrified that she had really done it—she had gone way too far and battered her sister's already wounded feelings—but no protest came, and she couldn't back down after that outburst, so she pushed onward. Inside the closet, she was surprised to see that the cardigan was gone, and a blue plastic lighter lay beside the pack of cigarettes. But the novelty of that and its possible meaning didn't register for long because when she turned around, another surprise overtook her. Melanie had come into the portal with her after all, her nostrils flared in reproach. She was still clutching the frayed toothbrush.

A PARTY WAS IN FULL swing, the kind Kelsey remembered from her childhood. "I Want a New Drug" by Huey Lewis and the News was playing on the stereo, and adults were elbow to elbow in the living room and kitchen and even spilling out onto the wraparound porch and backyard. *What year is it? The mid-eighties?* Kelsey wondered if she and Melanie were upstairs sleeping in the tiny bed-room—but surely they couldn't be with all the racket.

She spotted Grandpa Jack immediately with his terrible orange tan and his white *Miami Vice* blazer. So clearly her grandparents still inhabited the lake house, at least occasionally, and hadn't handed over the full ownership to her mom yet. Uncle Bob hadn't wanted the place. He preferred to spend his time off far away from Wisconsin, in destinations like Tokyo or Singapore. A circle of men stood around Grandpa Jack, and her dad was among them, laughing it up, still broad shouldered and thick haired but with fuller cheeks and a slight paunch. He was probably younger than Kelsey but already the father of two and on his way to being partner at the firm.

Melanie stepped on Kelsey's heel. She was looking down to set the timer on her watch. "Thirty minutes," she said firmly.

Kelsey didn't acknowledge her. Her sister's attempt at control, even in the face of supernatural, uncontrollable forces, would have been laughable if it hadn't been so exasperating. She plunged into the crowd, which consisted of women with poofy perms and clothes in every shade of pastel and men with Burt Reynolds mustaches and loafers with no socks. She heard laughter and the clink of ice cubes in brandy old fashioneds. Her mom wasn't anywhere.

On the back porch, Lance Fletcher was rocking a loud-patterned shirt and telling an even louder story to a rapt audience. A pretty brunette was hanging on his every word, touching his arm. But Vinnie and her mom weren't among them. Kelsey was about to give up and head back upstairs to see if she could at least glimpse herself and Melanie as young children when a tall silhouette slipping across the dark lawn caught her eye. Her instinct told her to follow.

The figure was alone and headed toward the Fletchers' boathouse. Her heart flipped over in her chest. She glanced at Melanie, who looked grave. Her sister's shoulders and head were pointed downward, as if she were battling a strong wind, and Kelsey wished she hadn't made that last comment about Melanie running away from Ben and her problems.

The moonlight glinted off the lake's surface, and Kelsey could finally make out the silhouette. Christine was leaning against the side of the boathouse, palm cupping the end of a cigarette as she lit it. Apparently, stealing the packs of cigarettes hadn't been a strong enough hint to quit. She took a long drag, and her body sagged against the wooden wall. *Why is she out here? Is she just sneaking away for a quick smoke? Or is she meeting Vinnie?* Kelsey's heart gave another flip, like a goldfish in a too small bowl.

They watched Christine smoke three cigarettes in slow succession. She fluffed her hair out and straightened the red plastic belt on her dress. After disappearing into the boathouse for a second, she reappeared smelling like sandalwood, the scent Kelsey associated most with her mom—a perfume or body spray, she suddenly realized, to cover up the smoke. A feeling of betrayal crept over her.

"I thought you were quitting," Lavinia called from the other side of the boathouse, and Kelsey jumped.

But Christine seemed unfazed. "Still trying to cut back," she replied. "But you know how edgy these parties make me." She turned to appraise Vinnie, and Kelsey and Melanie did too.

In the darkness, Kelsey couldn't tell if the short, ruffled outfit Vinnie was wearing was a dress or a nightgown. Her red hair was long again, wildly curly and teased up high, like Julia Roberts's in *Pretty Woman*. It was a much better look for her than the seventies pageboy bob had been.

"How's Beau?" Christine asked.

"His fever broke." Vinnie leaned against the wall a few feet away from her. "I think I'm going to send the babysitter home, though, and call it a night. I doubt Lance will notice."

"He'll notice."

"Well, maybe he will," Vinnie said flatly. "But he won't mind. I feel lousy, anyway. Probably coming down with whatever Beau has." She made a face.

"That's too bad." Christine pulled herself upright. "I'd better go rejoin the party. Charlie will be wondering where I am."

"Nice of him to join you all this weekend. It's been a while, hasn't it?"

"Vinnie," Christine said warningly.

She held up her hands in a placating gesture. "I know, I know. Once he becomes partner, things will get easier. However, it's been my experience with lawyers—which, granted, is limited—that their responsibilities and time commitments only seem to increase the higher they climb up the ladder." She rolled her long ballerina's neck on her shoulders. "That spinach dip was delicious, by the way. I'll have to get your recipe."

"My mom made it. She made everything. All I did was buy the paper plates and brandy."

"Well, the brandy was excellent," Vinnie said, bumping her hip against Christine's. "This party wouldn't be a party without the brandy. And that's not *all* you did. You also took care of two little girls and kept up a gigantic house all week while living with your up-tight, overbearing parents. Well done, you!" She grinned at the hint of a smile that had appeared on Christine's face. "That's more than I can say for myself. Today I didn't wash my hair until three. And the boys have been wearing their pajamas all day long. Stephen's too little to care, and I've convinced Beau it's a game."

Christine's smile widened until it reached her eyes.

"Why don't you get out two more cigarettes?" Vinnie said. "I'll smoke one with you for old times' sake. Twist my arm, why don't you?" She grabbed the lighter. "You're such a bad influence on me."

Melanie was watching the boats tied up along the twin docks bob up and down with the waves, but Kelsey knew her ears were tuned in to their mom's conversation by the stiff way she held her head and the way the muscle in her jaw kept clenching and unclench-ing. Vinnie and Christine smoked, and the lake pushed the boats in-to the dock and one another with a *slap, slap, slap.*

"Do you think the ghost bride is still out there?" Christine asked. "You remember, right? From your supposed sunken ship?"

"Of course I remember," Vinnie said cheerfully, stubbing out her cigarette into a soda can. "And it just so happens that tonight is the anniversary of their wedding and the terrible storm that capsized the ship. July twentieth."

"It's July twenty-first."

"That's what I meant. July twenty-first." Vinnie's voice became the somber, rhythmic voice of a poet reading her work. "Tonight she swims up from the depths of the lake and walks the shore, keening and bemoaning her fate. In her hair are jewels that the merchant ves-sel was carrying and shells and water lilies." As if on perfect cue, a loon warbled out its haunted cry. "See? There she is, crying for her lost lover to come join her."

"I thought it was her husband she was crying for," Christine cor-rected. "The ship's captain."

"Sure," Vinnie obliged, pulling her hair to one side. "That's what I meant. I thought you were going back to the party."

"I am."

"I see." She came close to Christine, and Kelsey thought for sure Vinnie was going to kiss her, but she only squeezed her elbow. "Well, I'm going home to take a few aspirin, drink a hot toddy, and get in bed. I'll let Lance deal with the babysitter when he gets home."

"Good night. I hope you feel better."

"Good night," Vinnie echoed. Her porcelain-doll face looked both wistful and concerned. "I hope you do too."

Kelsey thought for sure her mom would return to the raucous party since Vinnie had left, but Christine lingered alone for several more minutes, staring down at her sandals and the makeshift soda-can ashtray on the ground, her shoulders stooped, her curls almost entirely covering her face.

Melanie tapped her watch. "There's five more minutes," she whispered. "But do you want to go now?"

"You can go," Kelsey hissed back, not wanting to leave her mom alone like that.

Melanie glowered at her but didn't move.

Kelsey wanted her dad to notice her mom's prolonged absence from the party and come find her and cajole her back into happiness, the way he'd done so many times. She wondered if her mom was hoping for the same thing. But their dad didn't come, and Kelsey was forced to watch the painful process of Christine slowly composing herself, piece by piece—another spritz of body spray, the straightened posture, and the polite smile. They followed her back up the lawn, into the glow and noise of the party, where she laughed at jokes and offered refills and kissed their dad on the cheek. He pulled her into his arms in a showy dip move and kissed her back. *Can't he see?* Kelsey wondered. *Can't anyone see?*

Melanie's watch beeped, and though Kelsey had had no intention of abiding by her sister's arbitrary time limit, she ascended the stairs with her willingly. She had seen all that she needed to see—*more* than she needed to see. It seemed that her mom and Lavinia had remained friends after marriage but tried to keep their distance. But her mom's unhappiness—that gray, slightly out-of-focus backdrop of her childhood—had sharpened into a crystalline resolution before her eyes.

Kels-Bels, all I wish is that you'd be happy, her mom had said the afternoon she died. *You need to find what makes you happy, no matter what that is. Believe me. I would be the last person on this earth to force you to be something you're not.*

Not a hypocrite but a mother who'd wanted so much more for her daughters than she'd had for herself.

At the top of the stairs, Kelsey saw Grandma Dot turning away from the smallest bedroom and tiptoeing down the hallway. *Checking on Melanie and me*, she thought affectionately, which wasn't a feeling she often had for her maternal grandmother. She turned toward the right instead of the left.

"You can't go in there," Melanie said. "I think we're sleeping in there."

"That's kind of the point."

"But what if we wake up and see ourselves? Isn't that like the number-one no-no of time traveling?"

"I won't wake us up," Kelsey said, rolling her eyes. "And even if I did, why would we be able to see ourselves when no one else can?"

Melanie looked unconvinced, but she held up her pointer finger. "One minute," she conceded. "Then we really need to head back to get the house ready for the showing."

"I'm not keeping you here. You can leave whenever you want."

"Well, I'm not leaving without you. God knows what would happen if we separated. Maybe you'd get stuck here forever."

The glow of a night-light met them when Kelsey slipped through the door. The room was stuffy, with only a box fan blowing from its one window, and it smelled like children, or at least the smell Kelsey always associated with children—sugar and milk, Johnson's baby lotion, clean sweat, and wet diapers. A twin bed was pushed against one wall, a white-spindled crib against the other. Kelsey's foot floated over something soft and fuzzy as she approached Melanie's bed. *A dog or cat?* But her parents and grandparents had never let them keep pets.

"Marvelous!" Melanie whispered joyfully.

"What?" Kelsey asked, confused by her sister's sudden change of heart.

"My stuffed dolphin, Marvelous. Do you remember him? Oh, I wish I could pick him up and put him back in bed with me. He must have fallen out."

Kelsey was less interested in the stuffed toy and more interested in the sleeping girl. Melanie looked about three or four. She was lying on her side with her knees bent, her mouth slightly open, and her caramel hair fanned out on the pillow. A pink floral sheet was twisted around her legs. She exuded peace, and Kelsey wished she could lie down beside Melanie and rest her cheek against her small sister's. She imagined it would feel like the velvety petal of a flower.

Inside the crib, a one- or two-year-old Kelsey looked less graceful in repose. Wearing only a cotton onesie, she slept with her flushed face pressed into the mattress and her diapered butt up in the air. Her blond curls were stuck to her head with sweat, and one of her chubby feet was dangling between the crib spindles. She turned her face slightly, so Kelsey could see the spiky shadows her eyelashes cast on her round cheeks. "Mama," she exhaled.

"Man, we were cute," Kelsey whispered to her sister, but Melanie was already exiting the room. Kelsey found her pacing in the hallway.

"Why was Mom down there smoking with Vinnie?" Melanie asked, not even trying to keep her voice down. "I just don't get it. How could she have been so miserable when she had us?" Her eyes flashed.

"I don't know," Kelsey answered honestly.

This was about her sister's struggles to have a baby, she knew, but also something much deeper than that. It was the same feeling Kelsey had been trying to push away—the child's longing to fill every nook and cranny in her mother's heart, to want to be the "only sunshine" her mother needed for complete and total happiness. That had been one of the songs she'd sung to them when they were little. It was quite the tall order, being somebody's *only* sunshine.

"I think it's just exhausting being a stay-at-home mom to little kids," Kelsey said. "Especially since Dad was gone at work so much. Mom probably needed to take a breather every now and then. Just to be herself. Not someone's wife or mother for a little while. But I know she loved us, and I know we made her very happy."

Melanie held the tapestry up for Kelsey so she could duck underneath. "You're probably right. It just hurts so much, seeing Mom like that. In all my life, I don't think I've ever seen her look so forlorn."

"That's because she was careful to conceal that side of herself from us." Kelsey pulled the string attached to the light bulb to illuminate the closet. "I brought my letter along. Do you want to read it?"

Melanie sat down cross-legged on the bench and nodded grudgingly. "Read it to me."

Kelsey pulled it out of her pocket. She'd forgone the butterfly stationery and written on a sheet of college-ruled notebook paper instead. "Dear C. A. K.," she started. "We're sorry it's taken us so long to respond. In our time period, one week is equivalent to a few of your years, so there's unfortunately going to be some lag time in any of our correspondence. We're so glad you liked the picture. The little girls are indeed your daughters, as you've already figured out. And as you've probably also guessed, because you're a very smart woman, your daughters are also the writers of this letter."

She sneaked a peek at Melanie, but her sister was staring straight ahead, expressionless, with her palms resting on her knees.

"We discovered the door behind the *Tree of Life* only a few weeks ago in our time, and it was quite the surprise, as you can imagine. Since then, we've gone inside the closet on a handful of occasions, and with every encounter, we've seen a different moment from your life—from your childhood, your teenage years, or your young married life. It's been amazing getting to witness your memories firsthand, especially since you told us so little about your past. We love seeing you so young and beautiful—you're still beautiful, of course, but wow, you were stunning as a teenager!—and getting to know more about you, but we don't want you to feel like we're intruding because we love and respect you so much.

"Please know that we aren't judging you as we view these memories, and we're not trying to interfere. We're only trying to understand you better because you mean the world to us. You always have, and you always will. Your daughters—Melanie Jane and Kelsey Ann." She set the note down on the bench next to Melanie and waited. After a minute of silence, she asked, "So what do you think?"

"I think it scares me to death—all the doors this opens, all the questions it might prompt her to ask about the future, all the things we can't admit to her. But otherwise... otherwise I think it's perfect." She scowled and stood up. "Now let's get out of here so we don't miss the showing. Hey, where did my toothbrush go?" She pointed to the bench where the cardigan was now neatly folded.

"I have no idea," Kelsey said. "But the cardigan's back. When we came in here, it was gone." They gaped at each other for a few seconds. "What could it mean?"

"Well, I don't think my toothbrush decided to time travel of its own volition." Melanie put her hand on the doorknob. "I think Mom probably took it. Just like we took her cigarettes. We must have just crossed paths with her time traveling."

"Oh my God. Really?" Kelsey surreptitiously kissed the letter for luck before following her sister out of the closet. "You think she was in this very same moment, reliving it with us? I wonder how old she was and what she was doing here. And why didn't we see her?"

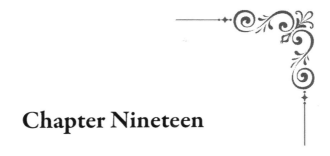

Chapter Nineteen

"Oh, F-U-C-K!" Melanie exclaimed, scrolling through all the missed calls, voicemails, and text messages from both Charlene and Mr. and Mrs. Moneybags' agent. According to her phone's display, it was 8:02 p.m. They had missed the scheduled showing by two hours. Though they had been inside the time portal for only forty minutes, they had disappeared for about four hours.

"Why didn't they just let themselves in?" Kelsey asked, leaning against the kitchen counter, not looking remotely remorseful or concerned. "Didn't Charlene say she was sending a guy over to put that keypad thingy on the front door?"

"Yes," Melanie groaned. "She did. But we weren't here to put a house key inside it for them, so it's kind of a moot point. Besides, both our cars were parked out front, and some of the lights were on, but no one was answering the door, so that kind of freaked them out." She pulled her phone away from her ear and deleted one more message from Charlene, who was icily asking where they were, and why they were choosing to stand up one of the most promising buyers around.

I am SO sorry, Charlene, she texted. *We were in the middle of a family crisis. Is there any way we can reschedule? For ANYTIME tomorrow or Thursday or any day this week, for that matter. Please let me know. I promise we'll be ready this time.*

If Kelsey's headstrong impulse to go into the time portal at the worst possible time had just cost them the sale of the lake house,

Melanie was going to strangle her. But even as Melanie articulated that thought, she knew she was just as responsible as Kelsey. She had recognized just how irregular the time flow was inside the portal, yet she had still gone inside with her sister, accepting the risks. Yes, primarily to make sure Kelsey didn't bungle anything up, but also, if she were being honest, because she didn't want to miss a single glimpse of her mom, no matter how painful it could be.

"Well, if they want to see the house that much, they can reschedule, right?" Kelsey poked her head inside the fridge, and Melanie stuck out her tongue at her turned back.

Of course Kelsey could be blasé about the missed showing because she didn't want the house to sell. She wanted to keep living in a fantasyland where they could forever keep the lake house for free and continue interacting with their deceased mother. *And she has the gall to accuse me of running from my real-life problems? What does she have to say for herself?*

No one else in the world could strike a nerve in Melanie quite like her sister. *Is running away from your problems and your husband and hiding out here how a real, responsible adult acts, Melanie?* Like a tuning fork banging against cold hard metal, Kelsey's words, even her glances, could send a sharp clang reverberating right through the center of Melanie's very being. *I'm not running away*, Melanie thought vehemently. Kelsey didn't understand the first thing about miscarriages or infertility or marriages, even. But maybe... just maybe... there was a germ of truth in her sister's rash diagnosis of the situation.

"Oh, sure, they can reschedule. Easy peasy," Melanie said, heavy on the sarcasm.

"Good," Kelsey said, intentionally ignoring her tone. "I'm starving since we apparently missed dinner. What are you going to feed me?"

"I think the better question would be: What are *you* going to feed *me*?"

Twenty minutes later, they were sitting in Kelsey's car, eating sloppy cheeseburgers over paper wrappers spread across their laps. In the back seat, Sprocket wedged his snout between their seats, sniffing hopefully. Melanie watched the bustling activity of the hamburger stand's crowded outdoor seating as she chewed a french fry and tried not to think about the fact that Charlene still hadn't called or texted her back. *Should I try her again? Did the first message not go through?* She didn't want to exacerbate the situation by having Charlene think she was ignoring her.

"Why did Everett come by today?" she asked. "What did he say to you?"

"He forgot his tubing cutter," Kelsey said. "It was behind the sump pump, I guess, so you wouldn't have noticed it."

"Oh, is that all?" Melanie raised her eyebrows.

"No. He also wanted to know why I hadn't responded to his texts or calls. I thought about being polite at first and just telling him I'd been busy with work, which isn't even a lie, but then I realized I didn't have anything to lose by telling him the truth. So I told him that as a rule, I don't date guys who already have girlfriends, and I explained how I had figured it out. He was completely taken aback. He said he was living with someone but a female roommate, not a girlfriend. Then he asked me if I'd consider going out on another date with him—a real date this time—now that I knew he was legitimately unattached."

"And what did you say?" Melanie asked, sneaking a french fry to Sprocket.

"I said sure," Kelsey said, a tad shamefaced. "But I told him he'd have to come to Bartlett for it."

"But what about Josh?"

"If he asks me out again, I'll go, and I'll see if the click develops. And if not, we'll just go back to being friends. Hey, that's my malt! If you wanted some, you should have bought your own."

Melanie smiled and wiped her mouth on a napkin. "I just wanted a sip."

In the past, she'd enjoyed listening to her sister talk about her dating exploits. Melanie hadn't dated much before Ben, and sometimes she wondered if she had missed out on some important rite of passage—the awkward approaches in bars, the flirtations, and the walk home in yesterday's dress. Other times she suspected that if she hadn't met Ben, she would still be single, that no one else could possibly have made her so happy while also putting up with her particular brand of bossiness. It made no sense that her sister hadn't found someone yet. She was so much more low-key than Melanie. She was cute and spontaneous and huge hearted. She was an excellent cook, when she got around to buying groceries, and she even liked watching sports.

But listening to her talk about her dates on the phone three hundred miles away was a different experience from watching the dates unfold and meeting the guys up close and in person. Melanie suspected that Kelsey had edited the stories over the phone for her benefit—made them pithier, more upbeat, often ending with a kind of punch line. Seeing Kelsey in the raw—the aftermath of her night with Everett, the way she'd looked when she declared she didn't believe in the concept of soul mates anymore—was hard for Melanie to watch.

"Well, my vote is for Josh," she said. "And don't blame me if I slip up and accidentally call Everett 'Ernie' the next time I see him." She watched as one of the hamburger stand employees—a gawky yet handsome boy in a white paper hat—delivered a tray of food to a table full of giggling adolescent girls.

"His laugh isn't that bad," Kelsey said, but she sounded dubious.

"It's pretty bad. Hey, was there something you wanted to talk to me about earlier?" Melanie glanced down at her cell phone again for the thousandth time, willing Charlene Hallbeck's name to pop up on her screen.

"No." Kelsey slurped loudly on her malt straw. "It was nothing important, anyway."

BEN WASN'T ANSWERING his phone. For the last two hours, Melanie had been alternately texting and calling him with no response, and she was starting to stress out. It was a Tuesday night. *Where could he be that he doesn't have access to his phone?* Even if he was at a Cleveland Indians game, he usually still sent her texts. Maybe something had happened to his phone. She typed an e-mail from her laptop. *Is everything okay? Call me ASAP please! I love you!* It was late, but he couldn't be sleeping already. He hadn't texted her good night, which was their custom.

She was trying not to let her imagination fly to the morbid place it had earlier that afternoon when Charlene kept calling. Unfortunately it was flying to other worrisome places instead. Maybe he was tired of her and her need for space. Maybe he'd decided to retaliate by taking his own break from her. It didn't sound like something Ben would do, but then again, their limits had never been so tested before.

She couldn't hear Kelsey moving around next door anymore, and Melanie wondered if she was asleep. She checked her phone again. No new calls, voicemails, texts, or e-mails from Ben—or Charlene, for that matter. Maybe something was wrong with *her* phone. She set it down on the nightstand with more force than she'd intended. It connected with the edge and fell to the floor with a clatter. When she bent to pick it up, she hit her head on the bedframe and dropped it again.

Dammit! She was just so frustrated—frustrated with Ben for making her worry, frustrated with Kelsey for giving Everett a second chance and guilting Melanie about selling the lake house and causing them to miss the showing and having the nerve to suggest *she* was the one being an irresponsible adult. But most of all, she was frustrated with her mom for smoking down by the lake and pitying herself when she had everything Melanie wanted—two beautiful, healthy children who adored her.

She rubbed the back of her head, which was throbbing, and reached for her phone. It had fallen pretty far under the bed, and as she grabbed for it, her fingers touched something flat and rectangular. It was the *Midwest Living* magazine that had started her off on the whole demented, down-the-rabbit-hole journey. It must have slipped out of her suitcase when she first arrived. She stared down at its glossy cover and headlines—*The 10 Most Romantic Lake Retreats*, *The Year's Hottest Gardening Trends*, *7 Sensational Summer Salads*—before throwing it in the trash can with a satisfying *thump*. But no—it wasn't the magazine landing in the trash can doing the thumping, because there was that noise again. *Thump, thump.* It was coming from downstairs. Kelsey must have gone down for a glass of water.

Melanie poked her head out into the hallway and was surprised to see Kelsey's door still closed. From the hallway, the thumping was louder, like someone knocking on the back door. *At one o'clock in the morning?* She tiptoed to the turret room to look outside, but the roof precluded seeing straight down to the porch, and all she could see was a truck she didn't recognize parked next to Kelsey's car. *Oh my God. Who could it be?*

Maybe someone needed help—a neighbor or a passing motorist. But on the off chance that it was a rapist or serial killer, maybe she should grab a knife from the kitchen. Or maybe she should get Kelsey and Sprocket up—there was strength in numbers. Man, she watched way too many home invasion stories and murder mysteries on *Dateline.*

Melanie stood at the top of the stairs, gripping the newel post, and took a deep breath. The thumping had stopped. Oh, good. She wouldn't have to pretend to be brave. But the thought of going back to bed without knowing if the person was still lurking outside seemed futile. She wouldn't be able to sleep a wink. Descending the stairs as quietly as possible, she was trying to decide which window had the best vantage of the back porch, when she thought she heard her name being called, not coming from upstairs but from outside the door—a male voice. Every inch of her skin prickled, and her heart rocketed toward her throat.

"Melanie?"

It wasn't. It couldn't be.

"Mel? Are you up? It's me!"

She threw the door open, nearly hitting the man on the other side. "Ben?" Her husband was standing on the porch, looking rumpled and tired and even more handsome than she remembered him. She let out a shaky laugh and collapsed into his arms. "Thank God it's you! You scared me half to death. What are you doing here?"

"I was trying to surprise you, but the drive took a lot longer than I expected. I thought I'd get here around eleven and you'd still be up. Then my cell phone died, so I couldn't even call you. I thought for sure you'd call the cops when you saw the unfamiliar truck or come out here wielding a knife when I knocked. But I didn't know how else to alert you I was here. I was this close to sleeping in the truck tonight."

"You were this close to having a knife wielded at you," Melanie admitted, resting her face against his neck. His skin smelled clean and spicy, like shaving cream.

"I figured. I'm so sorry I scared you. Maybe we should have a secret knock in the future." He clucked out a rhythm with his tongue.

"Hmm... something to consider. But in the meantime, why don't you tell me whose truck that is and why you drove nine hours instead of flying? I would've happily picked you up from the airport, you know. And why are you here in the middle of the week, anyway? I thought we agreed—"

Ben lowered his head for a kiss, and suddenly, she forgot all about her unanswered questions and her earlier scare, with his hands wrapped around her waist and his mouth pressed against hers. It had been over two weeks since they'd last kissed like that—longer, truth be told, since they hadn't been doing much kissing before she left either—and it made Melanie wonder how she'd survived so many days without access to his lips and tongue. *We should do this more often. Every day. All day.* Kissing had become a chore probably around the same time that sex had, but it suddenly felt like something they had just invented.

"I've missed you," Ben murmured into her hair. "No one steals the sheets from me at night or demands I buy low-sodium turkey bacon, and I can set the AC to whatever I like." He maneuvered them inside the house and shut the door. "It's been awful."

"At least you're still shaving," she teased back.

He rubbed his chin and smiled. "Did this just for you, darling, right before I left." He scoped out his surroundings and let out a low whistle. "The pictures really didn't do this place justice. It's stunning. Hey, is your sister staying overnight? I thought I saw her car. I hope I didn't wake her."

"I doubt it. She'd be down here right now if you had." They headed into the kitchen, where Melanie switched on the lights and poured him a glass of water. Ben stretched out his long arms and legs and explained how he had borrowed his brother Shaun's truck so that he could drive the outdoor table that Melanie had sanded and stained to their house in Ohio. And any other furniture she wanted to keep, he added.

"I told my boss not to expect me back until next week sometime," he said. "So you can have me for as long or as little as you like." His brown eyes were gauging her reaction.

"Oh, good!" she said, sidling up to kiss him on the cheek. "That means I can put you to work." But the truth was there really wasn't that much more work to be done on the house. Her ruthless efficiency over the past two weeks and Everett's completion of the basement had ticked the majority of the boxes on her to-do list. And though Ben was a hard worker, he was also the kind of person who tended to inadvertently create a lot of work. Melanie envisioned bath towels left on the floor, dishes piled next to the sink, and gardening tools abandoned in the dirt. Ben and Kelsey were two peas in a pod when it came to their tidying-up habits.

"Please do," he said, letting out a lion-sized yawn. "But first thing tomorrow. My body is still on East Coast time. Where are we sleeping?"

"I don't know," Melanie whispered as they mounted the stairs. "Kelsey's got the only room with a queen-size bed. The others have twins, and they're both super narrow." She showed him her room then the small room that Kelsey should have been sleeping in. "We could try to squish into one just for the night, or we could attempt to move the beds and push them together."

"Nah. I'll be fine in here for the night." Ben stooped down to plug his cell phone charger into an outlet.

"I'm afraid you're going to have a lot of panicked texts and voicemails from me."

"I wondered about that. Sorry for freaking you out." He sat down on the bed and slid off his khaki shorts, revealing a pair of blue plaid boxers. "It's warm in here. I was going to ask you to tuck me in, but now I'm thinking I might sleep on top of the covers."

Melanie glanced over her shoulder to make sure the door was shut. She wished it had a lock. "Are you *sure* you don't want me to tuck you in?" She lifted her camisole over her head and let it drop to the floor.

"Well, when you put it that way," Ben said. "Come over here, you."

She straddled his lap to kiss him, and he lightly massaged her shoulders and breasts. Her neurons were firing with his every touch—happy little fireworks exploding just beneath her skin. She pulled his T-shirt off and was taken aback by how wiry and thin he looked, as though all the running he'd been doing had pared him down to something gravely fundamental. He had no soft flesh around his belly anymore. Instead his chest and abdomen seemed almost hollowed out. *Oh, Ben*, she thought and pressed herself against him, wanting to absorb all the unspoken sadness and pain in his body. *We're both trying to run from our grief, aren't we?*

That was the click she had been trying and failing to explain to Kelsey—not just the physical intimacy, which was awfully nice, of course, but the fact that Ben had shown up uninvited, on the spur of the moment, because he knew her better than she knew herself. He had asked her over and over if she wanted him to come visit, and each time, she had said, "No, I'm fine, thanks," when what she should have been saying was, *Yes, yes, yes, I need you*. She needed his strong hands and his boyish sense of humor and his hopeful, panoramic worldview to break her out of her horse-in-blinders approach.

Nibbling on his earlobe, she tugged at the waistband of his boxer shorts. He seemed a little slow to oblige her, though. Instead of raising his hips to immediately remove them, he held her tighter, his lips against the hollow of her throat.

"Are you done bleeding?" he asked so quietly, she hoped that she had misheard him.

She stiffened involuntarily as her thoughts returned to the bloody water and the tight clench of her abdomen. "Yes, of course," she said. "It's been a month."

"And have you... did you have a period since then?" His words were still so quiet, as if by speaking them softly, their impact would land more gently.

She pulled away so she could look him in the eye. "Ben. I'm not bleeding. What's going on?"

He was gauging her again. It was annoying to be watched like that, like she was a tiger he suspected might pounce on him. Then she understood. It wasn't just the recovery of her body after the miscarriage he was asking about. He was trying to find out where she was in her cycle to determine if there was even a miniscule chance of their conceiving—so he could *avoid* it.

"Melanie." He touched her cheek, but she barely felt it. "I told you I wanted to take a short break."

"I didn't know you meant six months of abstinence!" She twisted off his lap and stood up. He didn't try to stop her.

"You know that's not what I mean. But you remember how Dr. Maroney said it might be a good idea to wait for a cycle or two for emotional reasons? Since it's still so early, I just wondered if we should maybe use something."

"Use something? Like a condom? You've got to be kidding me." She snatched her pajama top off the floor. "I'm not taking the drugs right now, and we both know there's no hope of me getting pregnant without them. When you advocated taking this break, I thought you meant you didn't want to *actively* try, with the Letrozole and the ovulation calendar and the scheduled sex and all of the pressure. I didn't know you meant you wanted to actively try to prevent us from getting pregnant."

"Of course I don't. I'm sorry I said anything. Can you just come back here and sit by me?" He smoothed the rumpled pink-and-purple quilt. "You're right. I was breaking my own rules by bringing all this stuff back up. I should've just let it happen naturally for once. But I wanted to make sure we were on the same page."

She sat down beside him. "I think we're in totally different books."

"Maybe so." He reached across the empty space between them and held her hand. "But we won't always be. Now about that tucking in. Are you going to take your top off for me again?"

"I think that ship has sailed." She was pretty sure he wasn't being serious, anyway, and was only trying to help her save face.

She kissed him good night and headed back to her room, thinking how strange and utterly symbolic it was for her husband to be there with her at last but sleeping in another bed. She tried to regain the feeling she had had as their bare skin touched and their lips met, that he was her better half, her truer half, that he intuitively understood things deep down inside of her that even she couldn't fully fathom. But mostly she just felt rejected.

Stop being so sensitive, she scolded herself. *He drove nine hours to be here with you. He brought a truck so he could haul the table that you mentioned you really wanted to keep.*

She slid her hands under the pillow into the cool spot. The problem wasn't with him. He was the same unfailingly thoughtful man she had married. Even if his efforts were misguided, a part of her realized that he was doing his best to support her and try to keep their marriage afloat. She was the one who had changed, or more accurately, she was the one who was broken.

She kicked off the sheets and stood up. Inside the closet, the books, the lighter, the cigarettes, and the cardigan were all still positioned just as she had left them. But a plain white envelope was lying there, too, and her heart skipped a beat at the sight of it. She plucked it off the bench and saw it was sealed. Pressing it to her chest, she carried it back out to the bedroom.

Why are there no names on it? Is it not intended for us, and is this some kind of test to see how trustworthy we are? Or did Mom simply assume we would know it was for us because, really, who else is she corre-

sponding with inside the time portal? Melanie wondered if she should wait to read it until Kelsey was awake. She lay back down, set the envelope against her pillow, and tapped it a few times against her cheek.

She slipped her nail under the envelope's flap and tore along the edge.

Dear Girls,

I would be lying if I said I had hoped you would one day discover the room behind the tapestry. I have been sincerely praying you never would. I just want so much to protect you, and I can't help being worried about what consequences your visits might have on your lives. Also, truth be told, I am unnerved by the thought of what you might witness and how it might alter your opinion of me. But I understand how strong the temptation to dabble in the past is because, as you can see, I have succumbed to it too.

Just remember, the past is unchangeable, and the future is always just out of your reach. Only the present is truly worth giving your full time and attention to. Take it from someone who knows. Right now, in my present, Melanie, you are eight and love helping me weed and water the flower beds, and Kelsey, you are six and keep begging us to let you wear Dad's headlamp to bed so you can stay up reading Berenstain Bears *books.*

Love,

Mom

P.S. You don't have to answer this, but I can't help wondering why you wrote me a letter instead of talking to me about this in the present. Exactly how far in the future are you two?

She refolded the yellow paper and stuffed it back into the envelope. Her mom had finally asked the question Melanie had been most dreading. To locate themselves in time and age would be to acknowledge that Christine was no longer alive and well. *Does she already suspect her fate?* Something about her careful wording and the way she'd cautioned them that they didn't have to answer made Melanie wonder. The slim envelope sat like a stone on her chest.

Would it be better for Mom to know the truth, even if there's no certain way to prevent her death? A pulmonary embolism was not an easy thing to fix—who knew when the errant blood clot had formed, and why? Knowing might lead her to live her life more fully, treating each day as a precious gift, or it might have the opposite effect on her and cast a pall over the rest of her time with her friends and family. Melanie wasn't sure which would happen, and she desperately didn't want to play God and be the one to make such a dicey call. *There is no way we can tell Mom the truth*, she thought adamantly. *Absolutely no way.*

Chapter Twenty

"I can't believe he's still going strong," Kelsey said, pulling Sprocket's leash taut as a car passed them. "This has got to be the longest jog I've ever taken him on." She and Ben were almost halfway around the lake, approaching Harris Beach.

"It must be those turkey sausage links Melanie fed him," Ben said.

"You know, she thinks she's being so sneaky, but I see her every time she slips him something. I should probably tell her I don't care if she gives him table scraps occasionally, but I think she gets a bigger kick out of it this way."

Ben nodded, laughing. "To be fair, I can't believe that *you're* still going strong," he teased. "I thought you were more of a swimmer than a runner."

"I am," she said. "But I've been working so much lately, I take my exercise where I can get it. Just don't let me hold you back, okay? You won't hurt my feelings if you want to run ahead. I know I'm slower than a three-legged turtle."

"No, you're not. And even if you were, I wouldn't mind. I like the company. Melanie never wants to come on runs with me." He mopped at the beads of sweat trickling down his face with his sleeve.

When Melanie had left for the grocery store that afternoon, insisting she'd be faster on her own, Kelsey and Ben had been at a loss for how to occupy themselves. Feeling like a third wheel since her brother-in-law had arrived, Kelsey had considered heading home early, but then Ben had asked if she'd be willing to show him around. So she'd given him the "official" tour of the house, the yard, and the dock, then he'd asked if she wanted to join him for a short run. Ben loved hearing stories about their childhood summers, especially the ones that involved Melanie doing something embarrassing, like the time she flipped out of her inner tube and got a thong-like wedgie for everyone to see while tubing with the Fletchers. Kelsey was all too happy to comply, although she was starting to get breathless from all the talking while running.

The houses along Lake Indigo were an eclectic jumble: Craftsman bungalows, Tudors, Cape Cods, a smattering of contemporary-style homes, and a few Victorians similar to theirs. Most had immaculately kept lawns and landscaping, but it looked like some of them hadn't gotten the memo.

Every so often they caught glimpses of the lake between the houses, little slices of a wider vista, and it was like a breathtaking surprise each time. *Yes, well, hello there, lovely lake. There you are again.* It was as purple as the skin of an eggplant, as alive and shiny as the wings of a butterfly. *I love it here so much*, Kelsey thought. Her soul felt happier at the lake than it felt anywhere else. *How did I not realize this for the last fifteen years? Or is this something entirely new?*

As they rounded a corner, a particularly cheerful bungalow came into view. Yellow with blue porch steps and a red front door, the house was one Kelsey had never noticed before. Because of its high position nestled among the trees, she doubted it was visible from the lake. As they ran closer, she spotted a small sign posted on the front lawn—Namaste Yoga Studio.

"Hey, look at this," she said, pointing.

"I'm not really that flexible," Ben said. "I can't even touch my toes. You and Melanie could check it out, though."

"That's not what I meant," she said, swatting at his shoulder. "It's a home studio. Do you think it's legit? Like they applied for a business license and got permission from the city? Or do you think they're operating under the radar?"

"I don't know." He lifted his sunglasses to better inspect the house then cocked his head to study her. "Why?"

"Just wondering how these houses are zoned, if they're considered strictly residential or if they're open to small businesses like, say, for example, a bed-and-breakfast."

"Just wondering, huh?" Ben grinned. "Well, if I were you, I'd start doing some serious reconnaissance like *yesterday*. Especially since the open house is only a few days away and you guys already have one potential buyer. You'd need to totally change course. Have you talked to Mel about this?"

Kelsey swallowed. *Oh no.* For a minute there, she'd forgotten she was talking to the husband of the enemy. But he was right. Mr. and Mrs. Moneybags' showing had been rescheduled for later that week. *Why am I even still toying with this idea? It's a lost cause.*

"No, huh? I can see why. She can be such a steamroller when she gets her mind set on something, can't she?"

They turned onto the county road, which was busier with a speed limit of fifty-five, and Ben maneuvered to the outside so she and Sprocket could jog on the shoulder.

"A bed-and-breakfast, you say? So what would you call it?"

"The Montclare Inn," Kelsey replied without hesitation. She had been up brainstorming in bed a few nights ago—the Tapestry House, the Victorian Bed-and-Breakfast, the Inn at Lake Indigo—but when the Montclare Inn popped into her brain, she knew it was the one. "After my mom's family."

"Oh, I like that. I would totally stay at the Montclare Inn."

A car beeped at them, and they scooted over farther onto the side of the road. Sprocket gave a put-upon bark.

"Hey, guys!" Melanie called out the passenger-side window. She slowed to a crawl and waved. "Fancy seeing you here! Want a lift?"

Speak of the devil. It was like she had a sixth sense for rooting out topics Kelsey really didn't want to broach with her.

Sprocket barked again, that time in recognition. His tail thumped back and forth excitedly. He still seemed to have energy, so Kelsey thought he was okay to finish their run, but she didn't want to speak for Ben. Model husband that he was, he probably wanted to help unload the groceries. Kelsey was hopeful he would turn Melanie down, though, because she had planned to extract a promise of secrecy from him first.

"We've run nearly around the entire lake, so I'd feel like a cheat if we quit now," Ben said. "What do you think, Kelsey?"

"I think we should keep going too," she said. "Thanks, though. We'll be home soon."

Melanie's face fell, but she recovered quickly with a bright smile. "Sure thing. See you guys soon!" She signaled and pulled away.

They were on the stretch of road that Kelsey was most familiar with. The trees arced over the road, forming a dense canopy and cool, lovely shade, and the houses were set back far, close to the lake, down long, winding drives. As a child, she had imagined the road was a magical tunnel leading to a secret world of fairies. If they just kept going and reached the opening at the very end, she knew they would meet the fairies, but they never did, because her parents always turned the station wagon into their driveway before that. Now she knew the tunnel of trees was indeed magical, but it led to something better than fairies.

"Please don't tell Melanie about the B and B," Kelsey said. "Just forget I even said anything. It's a stupid idea, and I'm sure I could never make it work, anyway. I don't want to get her all riled up for no reason."

"I won't say anything if you don't want me to. But I think *you* should. This is just as much your house as hers. If you have other ideas for what to do with it, you need to speak up. Mel might not like it at first, because she's so focused on selling as the only way to go, but she would at least want to hear it. And personally, I think it's a kickass plan. A bed-and-breakfast here would really clean up."

They were almost home.

"Ben..." Kelsey said as they started up the long gravel driveway. "I wanted to tell you how sorry I am about the loss of your baby." She wanted to convey oceans more to him, but she didn't know how to express it. "For what it's worth, I think you're going to make a great dad one day."

"Thanks, Kelsey," he said with a ghost of a smile. His eyes were inscrutable behind his reflective sunglasses, but his posture suddenly looked defeated, his arms dangling at his sides, his back stooped—exhausted. "I hope you're right."

RAINY DAYS AT GREEN Valley were the worst. Both the pets and the humans were restless from being cooped up, and everything smelled like wet dog. The forecast called for a forty percent chance of thunderstorms, which Kelsey hoped would miss their area because she didn't want to think of poor Sprocket whimpering and cowering alone at home. She wished she were home with him instead, drafting a reply to her mom's newest letter. It would likely be the last one she would ever have the opportunity to write.

Her mom was already in her early thirties and had stopped coming to the lake house in her forties. Time moved so rapidly inside the portal. A whole decade could slip away in a week. *And what will happen when we reach the end of Mom's memories? Whose memories will the time portal move on to—the house's next inhabitants, the Holloways, perhaps? Or will it start replaying Mom's memories over again in a loop? Or will it simply... end... and go back to being a regular closet?* Kelsey had no idea. But it felt urgent to get in one more correspondence with her mom before their last summer at the lake happened, even though she knew she wasn't going to be able to say half of what she truly wanted to say.

Josh was working, but he and Kelsey had been orbiting each other at a shy, polite distance since their date. He hadn't felt the click, either, Kelsey suspected sadly. She wondered how long it would take their work relationship to go back to its normal mix of teasing banter and intimate confidences. Because in a week or so, the lake house would have an accepted offer on it, and Melanie and Ben would return to Ohio, then Kelsey would have only her work friends. Thank God for her sweet schnauzer and the cooking channel, but the thought of returning to her "normal life" made her unbearably sad. For a little while there, it had felt like her world was rapidly expanding in so many new directions, and now it felt like it was shrinking down and closing in on her again.

She had a date that night with Everett, and she was trying to get excited about it, but everything else was conspiring to get her down. Not knowing the area, he had suggested Sheehan's, the heavily advertised and overpriced Irish pub that all the locals knew to avoid because of its notoriously rude waitstaff. He'd also suggested going to the nearby botanical gardens, which they would probably have to take a literal rain check for. Lastly, with the effects of the rain and humidity on her hair, she was going to look like a fricking bichon frise on their date.

Beth walked by with a dreary expression and a purple cat carrier. "Did we remember to order more shampoo and ear rinse?" she asked.

No, Kelsey thought, we *didn't*. Methodical Beth had always been the one in charge of ordering supplies and keeping things well stocked. "Nope. But I can put in an order right away," she said. "Or if we're all out, I can run to the store if you prefer."

"Hmmm... yes, thanks," Beth said distractedly. "That would be helpful, Kelsey." The cat inside the carrier started wailing, and Beth hurried away before Kelsey could ask her what she had meant. *Order online or dash to the store? And which shampoo?* They used several kinds. Kelsey would have to do a thorough inventory of the supply closet to see what they were in need of.

If Beth's daughter had been standing there right then, Kelsey would have been tempted to smack her. The girl's antics were turning her normally upbeat, super-efficient boss into a scatterbrained, depressed zombie. And though Beth had been personally confiding in Kelsey less lately, she was professionally relying on Kelsey more than ever. Once, that would have made Kelsey feel valued, but now it just made her feel trapped. If a better opportunity came along, she wasn't sure how she could ever leave in good conscience.

On her way to the supply closet, she passed Josh in Pooch Place. He was in one of the kennels, playing on his hands and knees with a Pomeranian. "Why, thank you for the kisses, Miss Cinnamon," he said. "Okay, that's enough, sweetie. No kisses on the mouth, please. Yes, yes, who's a good girl? Now be a lady and keep your tongue to yourself." Kelsey smiled in spite of herself.

EVERETT WAS TEN MINUTES late picking her up, but Kelsey didn't mind because she was also running ten minutes behind, and he had shown her the courtesy of texting her to let her know. He came to her front door with an umbrella high overhead, walked her to his car with his hand positioned gently on her lower back, and even opened and closed the door for her. He was wearing a pale-green Henley, so his hazel eyes looked even more hazel, and a shark-tooth necklace dangled between his collarbones. Generally, Kelsey found those necklaces kind of lame, but on Everett, it was down-right sexy. He probably could've made a kid's macaroni-strung necklace look sexy, though.

Because of the pouring rain, Sheehan's was quieter than usual, and their waitress was bubbly and attentive—due to Everett's charm and heart-stopping dimples, Kelsey suspected, and she couldn't really blame the girl. If he had come in to Weber's Steakhouse when she was waiting tables, she would have brought him refills and ketchup all night long.

"So there I was, wading through three feet of water, when all of a sudden, I run into something huge and solid." Everett slapped his palm on the tabletop for emphasis. "It was a pool table! Totally submerged! Can you believe it? I have no idea how much damage that frozen pipe cost these people. I mean, I'm sure their insurance covered most of it, but it was just insane. Probably the worst basement flood I've ever seen."

Kelsey tried to look interested, but an uncomfortable pressure was growing in her bladder from all the refills she'd drunk. She glanced over Everett's shoulder to see if she could spot a restroom sign, when a familiar coppery mane caught her eye. But it wasn't Lavinia Fletcher, of course, whose trademark red hair had become a tarnished silver, at least according to Melanie. Still, the thought of Vinnie felt like a splash of cold water in her face. Her mom had clearly cared deeply for her. Vinnie was "the one that got away," or probably more accurately, the one she had pushed away.

Kelsey wished she knew if that was because her mom had fallen in love with her dad or if her mom was simply worried about making waves in her conservative family by coming out as gay or bisexual. Certainly, being in a same-sex relationship in the seventies and eighties in small-town Wisconsin would have been faced with more discrimination than it was today. But it made Kelsey doubly sad to think of her mom choosing Vinnie over her dad in her heart but not being brave enough to act on it.

"I'll be right back," she said to Everett, who was in the middle of another basement flood story.

After relieving herself and washing her hands, she texted Melanie from the ladies' room. *Everett talks about his work a lot.*

He-he-he! Melanie replied immediately. *That was an Ernie laugh in case you couldn't tell. I'm sorry. That sounds boring.*

Not as boring as my work stories are, I'm sure.

Your stories are full of wit and verve, Melanie texted back.

And lots of dog poop.

True.

You haven't gone back in the portal without me, have you? Kelsey asked.

Of course not.

So you don't know what year it is?

No, but I'm sure we still have time, Melanie replied, anticipating Kelsey's worries. *Why don't you come over Sunday after the open house for dinner?*

When Kelsey returned to the table, the waitress was hanging around, talking to Everett, and Kelsey had the perfect view of the girl's spectacularly toned butt in her black leggings.

"Did you want a box?" Everett asked as she sat down, flashing her his dimples, and Kelsey's jealousy dissipated. It wasn't Everett's fault the waitress was being a flirt.

"No, thanks," she said.

The waitress sashayed off, and they decided to go to Kelsey's apartment for dessert and a nightcap: dark chocolate soufflé cupcakes she had hurriedly baked before he picked her up and a bottle of Shiraz. The rain was coming down in sheets, and the first rumbles of thunder were starting, so Kelsey was all too happy to return home to Sprocket. Everett opened the passenger door for her again and walked her to her front stoop with the umbrella, holding her a little closer than last time. Anticipation coursed through her—being nice and dry and tucked away inside, savoring the chocolate and wine, kissing Everett again.

They stepped inside together, giggling as they removed their soaked shoes, gripping each other's shoulders and trying not to slip as the umbrella dripped water all over her tile entryway.

"I like your TV," Everett said, pointing at the sixty-inch flat screen her dad and Laila had had shipped for her birthday the previous year and which Kelsey frankly found to be a little too big and ostentatious for the size of her living room.

"Thanks," she said. "It was a gift. I don't really watch much TV. Mostly cooking shows." *Where is Sprocket?* It was unlike him not to run out and greet her. She wondered if he was cowering under her bed because of the thunderstorm. "Sprocket!"

"It would be awesome to play Call of Duty on that thing. You don't have a PS4, do you?"

"A what?" She peeked between the couch and the end table, another favorite place of Sprocket's to hide when he was stressed out.

"A PlayStation," Everett clarified.

"No, sorry. Why don't you make yourself at home? I'm going to go check on my dog. It's really weird that he's not coming out to greet us."

As she approached the bedroom, a repulsive stench met her—dog feces or vomit, maybe both. *Oh, Sprocket. Did the thunderstorm really scare you that badly?* Several piles stained the beige carpet, and she gagged so severely, she thought she might throw up. "Sprocket?" She stepped carefully across the room and lifted her bed skirt to peer underneath. Sure enough, her little dog was huddled against the far leg of the headboard and the wall, as far back as he could possibly get.

"Come here, sweetie," she said, crouching down, but he didn't twitch to his feet and crawl toward her. In fact, he didn't even raise his head. "Sprocket?" She whistled, a sound he absolutely couldn't resist, but he continued to lie there motionless, and her heart plummeted. She squeezed the top half of her body as best she could under the bed to reach him. When her fingers touched his shaggy fur, it felt warm, thank God. He opened his eyes and tried to lick her, and a grateful little sob escaped her lips. "Sprocket, are you okay? What's wrong, sweetie?" She gripped his lower back and his front legs and gently pulled him out from under the bed with absolutely no resistance on his part. He felt like a rag doll in her arms.

"My dog's really sick," she told Everett, who had indeed made himself comfortable in her absence. He was sitting on her parents' sectional with one leg propped up across his knee and one arm draped along the back of the sofa. "He had an accident—actually several accidents—in my bedroom."

"Oh no!" Everett stood up. "He didn't get into the chocolate cupcakes, did he? One time Bailey ate a Twix, and he had diarrhea for twenty-four hours straight. It was horrible."

With Sprocket still as docile as a newborn lamb in her arms, Kelsey turned to survey the dark chocolate soufflé cupcakes, which she had left to cool on the counter. No telltale crumbs or chewed-up wrappers littered the floor, but she had accidently left a kitchen chair nearby, which Sprocket might have used to jump up. She counted the cupcakes to see if any were missing—twenty-one were there—although she didn't think the recipe had made the full two dozen to begin with, so it was hard to say. But chocolate was incredibly toxic to dogs, and if he had eaten one... or two... or three... he was such a small dog, not a big, hearty retriever like Everett's dogs.

"Do you think I should take him to the vet?" she asked.

"Nowhere will be open at this time of night, and those after-hours emergency places charge an arm and a leg. Just take him in tomorrow morning if he gets worse. With any luck, it will be out of his system by then. You have a garage, right? You should probably just spread out some towels for him in there so he doesn't make too much of a mess."

Locking my helpless, miserable dog in the garage? On the night of a thunderstorm, to boot? She lightly squeezed Sprocket against her chest, and he let out a tiny half whimper.

"These cupcakes look amazing," Everett said, and Kelsey decided then that she would pack up a half dozen cupcakes in disposable Tupperware and say good night to him.

Once he was gone, she pulled out her grubbiest bath towels from the linen closet and made a little nest for Sprocket on the living room floor. He collapsed into it, and she hurried to bring his water bowl over, but he didn't seem interested in drinking. She sat down on the floor beside him, petting him with one hand and using her phone with the other. First, she googled "chocolate toxicity in dogs" and got even more freaked out. Then she called her veterinary clinic and was greeted by their out-of-office recording, which encouraged her to visit the twenty-four hour animal hospital if she was having a pet emergency. Next, she googled the animal hospital and found that they were a forty-five-minute drive away.

She didn't know what to do. She wondered if she was overreacting, as Everett had seemed to think. But even when Sprocket had eaten her phone charger that time, he hadn't been so sick. She had never seen him so lethargic, so unlike himself. She considered calling Melanie for her advice or even Beth, but somehow they both seemed all wrong. She scrolled through her contact list until she found the number she wanted.

"Josh," she said into the phone, "Sprocket's sick." Then she gave in to the tears she had been holding back since she had found her beloved dog's unmoving body under the bed.

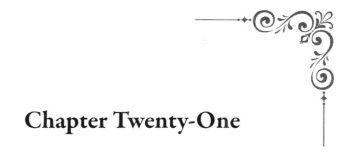

Chapter Twenty-One

"He's going to be okay," Josh said for probably the hundredth time. They were sitting in the waiting room of the Pet Health Center across from a saltwater fish tank. It was another, closer emergency vet clinic that Josh had recommended once he had deciphered what Kelsey was trying to convey through her tears. In less than half an hour, he had driven to her house, loaded them up, then chauffeured them to the clinic so she could sit in the back seat with Sprocket wrapped up in a towel in her arms. The poor dog had started throwing up by then: a watery, foul-smelling substance that Kelsey tried to catch with the towel.

The vet tech had taken one look at Sprocket and rushed them to an exam room, which made Kelsey feel validated in her decision to bring him but even more deathly afraid. Both the tech and the veterinarian seemed to take it very seriously that Sprocket might have ingested chocolate. They wanted to hook him up to an IV, give him fluids and medicines that would help get the toxin out of his system quickly, and keep a close eye on him.

"I would never forgive myself if..." Kelsey couldn't finish her sentence. She put her head in her hands. "I just can't believe how careless I was, leaving that chair out. I had to stand on it to reach the baker's chocolate, then I was in such a rush, I guess, I must have forgotten it was there." She didn't tell Josh why she was in such a rush. She hadn't mentioned Everett at all to him, choosing instead to say she had gone out to dinner with a "friend." She didn't want to hurt his feelings.

"You are being way too hard on yourself," Josh said, leaning over to squeeze her shoulder. "Chair or no chair, dogs can be quite resourceful when they want something badly enough. Only a couple of hours have passed, tops, and Sprocket is in good hands. He's going to be back to his old self in no time."

The vet came into the waiting room a few minutes later with a frown on his face, and Kelsey leapt up. "We think there might be something more to this than chocolate toxicity," he said. "Maybe some other foreign ingestion? Has he gotten into anything around the house lately?"

Kelsey didn't know whether to be hopeful or more worried by that turn of events. She racked her brain but couldn't think of anything—no ripped pillows or chewed-up toilet paper rolls for the last couple of weeks, and at the lake house, he'd been a perfect angel. "Not that I know of, but my sister has been feeding him a lot of table scraps."

"Hmm. Well, I'd like to do an ultrasound to take a look at his intestines and belly. I'm worried there might be an obstruction. If so, it just might be early enough that we could remove it with an endoscopy instead of surgery."

Kelsey numbly signed forms as the vet did his best to explain the procedures and the inherent risks. *Endoscopy? Surgery?* She gripped Josh's hand as she sat back down. She knew she should call Melanie, who had taken to calling Sprocket "my little jellybean," but Kelsey didn't want to worry her. It was almost eleven o'clock, and her sister would probably insist on driving the seventy-five minutes to be with her. Kelsey decided she would call Melanie in the morning instead, as soon as she had some news to share—*good* news to share. She was trying not to picture Sprocket limp and sedated on a metal table with an IV in his paw and a tube down his throat.

"You didn't get Sprocket as a puppy, right?" Josh asked. "He was a shelter dog? I think I remember the week that you adopted him and showed us all pictures."

"Yeah, the shelter thought he was at least two or three, judging by his teeth. Some kind soul had found him wandering around on the hottest day of the summer, dehydrated and emaciated, with matted fur and scrapes all over his body, and brought him in. By the time I met him, though, he was doing much better and almost back to a normal weight but so shy, and rightfully so."

"I didn't know that," Josh said, shaking his head. "That's horrible."

"I don't tell many people because it makes me so angry to think about it, and someone always says something like, 'Wow, Kelsey, you saved him.' But I didn't. The stranger who brought him in did. The vet at the shelter did. I only adopted him and brought him home. And I know it's cliché, but when I adopted him, he was the one who saved me." *From my loneliness*, she thought but didn't add, *and my lack of purpose in life*. Sprocket was her constant companion, her shadow, her cuddle buddy, and her reason to take a leisurely walk at dusk every evening.

"It may be cliché, but it's true." Josh stretched out his long legs. "I feel the same way about Tumnus. He was from a litter of farm kittens someone had dropped off at the shelter. But when I saw him, I thought, 'Oh, it's you.' Like somehow this little orange ball of fur was the one thing my life was missing at the time."

He was describing "the click," Kelsey realized, but between pets and owners, not lovers, and it was, quite frankly, adorable. She glanced down at the floor and noticed for the first time he was wearing two different flip-flops: one brown leather, one navy-blue plastic.

"I like your shoes," she said, trying not to smile. Something about those mismatched shoes, the indication they gave of how quickly he had rushed to her aid, made her want to hug him.

It was another hour until they heard news from the vet that he had performed the endoscopy and successfully removed an entire washcloth from Sprocket's bowels. Sprocket was coming out of his sedation well and resting comfortably. They wanted to keep giving him IV fluids and watch him overnight, however, so they suggested Kelsey go home and get some sleep and return to pick him up in the morning.

"An entire washcloth?" Josh kept saying, his shoulders shaking with silent mirth as he drove her home.

"I wonder if it was a kitchen washcloth," Kelsey said, twisting her hair into a giant bun on top of her head. She was so giddy with relief that she couldn't stop talking. "Like there were some crumbs on it? I can't imagine what else would possess him to want to eat a washcloth. Although this is the same dog who ate my phone charger, so who the heck knows? Do you think the vet kept the washcloth? I should've asked to see it. Maybe I should frame it for posterity."

"I saw this news story once about a vet who found forty-some socks in a dog's stomach. Can you imagine?"

"It must have been a big dog if one little washcloth wreaked this much havoc on Sprocket."

"It was a Great Dane, I think," Josh said, and they both erupted into uncontrollable laughter for no other reason than it felt good after such a stressful incident and it was late at night and they were glad to be in each other's company.

They were only a block away from her apartment, and just like after their dinner at Tony's, Kelsey didn't want to say good night. She wanted to tell Josh how grateful she was that he had come to her rescue and sat with her until the literal and metaphoric storm had passed. She wanted to convey to him why he had been the first one she had called, but she couldn't even explain it to herself.

"Josh," she started, and he turned, fixing those greenish-gold eyes on her, making it impossible for her to remember exactly what she'd meant to say. "Thank you so much."

"Anytime, K. K.," he said with his lopsided smile.

It was so cute that Kelsey kind of wanted to nibble on him, and before she could question what she was doing, she was leaning forward to press her lips against his. His smile relaxed into a kiss that felt just as warm and inviting. They sat like that for a long time, kissing but not otherwise touching, until Kelsey thought that if he didn't touch her soon, she would burst. She gripped his knee with one hand and his shoulder with the other, pulling herself closer to him, and that seemed to give him the permission he needed. He cupped his hand around the back of her neck, caressed her shoulders, and stroked her face. *This is Josh I'm kissing*, she kept telling herself. *This is Josh touching me.* But instead of seeming weird or daunting, it seemed only good—crazy good, in fact. She liked how unhurried each of his caresses felt, like he was simply enjoying acquainting himself with her skin. Then a terrible thought occurred to her.

She abruptly pulled away. "Oh my God. I don't smell like dog vomit, do I?"

"No," Josh said, laughing. "You actually smell kind of like mashed potatoes. Which just so happens to be one of my favorite foods."

The shepherd's pie, she thought and tamped down a guilty pang. *Starting the night with one guy and ending it with another?* But it was clear whom she should have started the night with in the first place.

I didn't feel that click right away, Melanie had confided to her about Ben. *And it caught me off guard when it finally happened because Ben wasn't the type of person I had ever pictured myself marrying. But somehow he was just what I needed.* Kelsey had written off her sister's comments as irrelevant because she hadn't believed that such chemistry existed between Josh and her. But now she understood that it did exist and that it had been there all along, a little spark waiting to burst into a flame. She just hadn't recognized it as such because it felt so comfortable and easy compared to the manic, tortured relationships she had sought out during the rest of her twenties. Instead, being with Josh felt like reading a really good book she didn't want to put down. It felt like diving into a lake for a luxurious, lazy swim on a hot afternoon or eating the ooey-gooey center of a pan of warm brownies.

"I'd invite you inside," she said, suddenly feeling shy, "but I'm worried about all the doggy land mines that Sprocket left on the carpet."

"Do you want me to help you clean up?" Josh asked, turning off the ignition and pocketing his keys.

"That's really sweet of you to offer, but no thanks," she said. "I'd rather you kept kissing me."

"NO LIFEGUARD ON DUTY. Swim at your own risk." Ben was reading the sign staked in the sand of Harris Beach. "That always sounds so sinister." He helped Melanie spread out the old quilt they'd brought. "Swim at your own risk," he repeated menacingly, punctuating it with a maniacal laugh. It would've been more humorous to her if she hadn't known someone had actually died here.

"They used to have lifeguards. My mom was one," she said. "I guess there's not as much of a demand now." She gestured to the handful of families who were building sandcastles and splashing on boogie boards. It was so different from the bustling beach of her mom's youth. Instead of coming together as a community to enjoy the lake and sun, it seemed like most of her current neighbors preferred to stick to their own little piece of lakefront.

"Why am I having such a hard time picturing your mom as a lifeguard? I thought she hated the water." Ben peeled off his T-shirt, kicked off his sandals, and flopped down onto the blanket. After eight years together, Melanie had thought she had every detail of his body memorized. But his new, rawboned runner's physique made him look and feel like a stranger to her.

"She was a much more complicated woman than we gave her credit for."

"I guess so. The diary?" Ben asked knowingly. Her hypothetical question and all the new information Melanie had about her parents had convinced Ben that she had actually found her mom's journal and was reading it. She hadn't corrected him. A diary was a much more practical explanation than the real one.

Melanie settled next to him and began rubbing sunscreen on her forearms. Ben squirted some into his hands and started slathering it on her back and shoulders. He never wore sunscreen but never seemed to burn or freckle. Instead, the more sun exposure he got, the younger and healthier he looked. It was kind of irritating.

"Are you nervous about tomorrow?" He worked the lotion under the halter tie of her bikini top.

"No." She closed her eyes and leaned against him. "I feel pretty confident that I've done everything I can. And Charlene Hallbeck is good at what she does. I think it will go really well."

The only thing she hadn't decided on for the open house was if she should remove the *Tree of Life* tapestry from her bedroom beforehand. Obviously, the room looked more beautiful with it, and it hid the weird closet that wasn't a closet, which might raise some questions, especially since Charlene didn't even know about the door's existence, but it scared Melanie to think what might happen if someone peeked behind the tapestry and wandered into the closet on their own, bumbling into her mom's past. If her experiment had been accurate, removing the tapestry would prevent that from happening and close off the portal temporarily.

On one hand, it had taken her thirty years to discover the time portal, so the odds that someone touring the house would do so immediately were small. On the other hand, prospective home buyers, especially at open houses, were notorious snoops, and Charlene had offhandedly divulged that rich people were the absolute nosiest. *Don't be surprised if your medicine cabinet is rearranged*, she'd warned.

Ben scooted around to sit cross-legged in front of her. "I'm sure it will be great." He handed back the bottle of sunscreen. "Do you think you'll be sad to say goodbye to this place?"

Melanie reached for her black sunhat. "Of course. But I came to terms with my dad selling our house in Elm Grove, and I'll come to terms with this, too, because it makes the most sense. Logistically, geographically, financially." *Emotionally.* Her last few trips into the time portal had persuaded her that her mom had felt almost chained to the lake house—bound by her parents and their expectations of her, bound by her secret relationship with Lavinia, and bound by the shame she felt over the little boy's death. If she were alive today, Melanie felt certain that her mom would support her decision to sell. It would give her mom the closure she had never achieved in her too-short life. Of course, Melanie could simply ask her, but that, she worried, would be giving too much away about the future.

Ben lay back on the quilt. "It all makes sense to you, Miss Left Brain," he said. "Are you sure it makes the most sense to your sister?"

"As much as it can, I think, with someone like Kelsey, but honestly, we've talked it to death. She just keeps clinging to this fantasy that we'll both have daughters one day and bring them here in the summers, I guess. Which you and I both know won't happen."

Ben didn't respond, and Melanie wondered if she'd finally succeeded in striking a nerve. A perverse thrill raced through her. But after a while, he draped his arm over his eyes and said only mildly, "And why is that?"

"I'm not talking about this here, Ben."

"Fine. But I happen to think it's a very nice fantasy, and I don't blame Kelsey for holding on to it one bit. You two should definitely talk before anything with this house sale gets too serious, though. You know, just to make sure you're both on the same page."

"What's with you and pages lately? You need to get a new metaphor." Melanie frowned and stuck her toes into the sand. "Besides, what do you mean by 'too serious'? How much more serious can it get? The house is listed. Showings and an open house are happening imminently. I'd say that's pretty damn serious."

"Yes, well, you should still talk to her some more about it." He dug into their beach bag and tossed her a *People* magazine. "Here are some pages for you. No decoy this time, though."

"Thanks." Unfortunately, the magazine seemed like the unofficial baby issue. One TV actress was pregnant with twins. Another was smiling with her newborn son in her arms. A Hollywood power couple was adopting a baby from Haiti. She glanced up to see that Ben was watching her. "What?"

"Do I need a reason to look at my wife?" The crinkles around his eyes were deeper than she remembered them.

"You do if you keep looking at me like I'm some kind of chemical compound you're trying to puzzle out." She tossed the magazine onto the beach blanket in frustration.

Ben looked away.

"Kelsey put you up to this, didn't she? She asked you to intervene on her behalf, right? Try to get me to see reason and not sell the house? And because I'm such a tyrannical Wicked Witch of the West, she had to go through my better half, huh? My... my *keeper*." She had stood up without realizing it and was towering over him where he was still lying on the quilt.

"For Pete's sake, Mel, your sister didn't put me up to anything." He shielded his eyes from the sun and squinted up at her. "It's not a secret that she doesn't want to sell, all right? Will you just sit down and relax, please?"

"No. I'm tired of you and everyone else acting like I'm so difficult and unreasonable all of the time. This is who I am. This, unfortunately, is who you married, and I'm sorry if you're starting to regret that." As soon as she spat the words out, she instantly wished she could swallow them because they were so close to the truth she most feared.

"No, this isn't who I married," Ben countered, sitting upright. "I married a girl who could be a little OCD at times and as stubborn as hell but who was stubborn about the good things, the *important* things in life. The kind of stubborn you wanted fighting in your corner. But you're not fighting in my corner anymore. You're trying to fight this battle all by yourself, and even worse, you're trying to make me the enemy, but for the love of God, Mel, I am *not* the enemy."

"I know you're not. It's been clear to me for a while now that *I'm* the enemy. My body especially." A hot gush of tears flooded her eyes, and she was suddenly grateful for her sunglasses and Audrey Hepburn sunhat. She glanced over her shoulder at two preteen boys, but they were too intent on bonking each other with their boogie boards to care about her hysterics.

"Will you please just stop?" Ben draped his angular elbows over his even more angular knees. His calmness was provoking. "Yes, you might just be your own worst enemy right now with how you're trying to shut everyone out and shoulder all the blame, but your body is not the enemy." He lowered his voice. "Your body is fricking amazing, whether or not it's capable of conceiving and carrying a baby to term."

"Well, you can say that because it's not *you* that's the problem. It's me." She snatched her cover-up tunic from their beach bag and, with it, tried to discreetly wipe away the tears that had dripped down her cheeks.

"But that's where you're wrong. It is me, too, Melanie, because we're a couple. For better or worse, remember?"

She sat back down, hugging the tunic to her chest. "Yeah, but that was before you knew this about me, right? So I'm sure it won't be long now before you decide that you would rather be with someone else. Someone who isn't so stubborn and difficult. Someone who can easily give you your own biological child."

Ben didn't respond, and Melanie's world froze. *Is this where he admits that he agrees with me? That he's through with me and wants a different, better wife?* But when she turned to look at him, she saw that he was yanking his T-shirt over his head and clasping his Ironman watch on his wrist. She had finally done it. He was leaving.

"Where are you going?" she asked.

"For a run," he said, turning his back on her as he bent down to jam his feet into his sandals. "Don't expect me back until late."

"The showing is at seven thirty," she offered feebly.

"That's fine. I'll stay away until after." He stalked away from their blanket before she could even fathom what words she could say to make him stay. But he stopped midstride and returned to her. "You say you're tired of everyone treating you like you're difficult?" He squatted down so he was close to her but without actually touching. "Well, I'm tired of you acting like you're the only person who feels things deeply. Other people are hurting too. Other people are *shattered*. It's not just you." Then he was ducking under a game of Frisbee between a middle-aged couple and their daughter, and then he was simply gone.

She sat very still for a long time, goose bumps rising on her arms and legs despite the warmth of the day. A text message pinged on her phone. It was Kelsey. *Have I got a story to tell you about dog poop!* it read. *Are we still on for dinner Sunday night? Can I invite someone?*

Melanie hurled the phone away from her. It landed facedown in the sand.

A blond woman in a blue tankini was sitting in the shallow water, playfully splashing a little boy in water wings. Melanie squinted to see if it was Jess and Noah. But the woman looked too young, the child too freckled. Melanie hadn't seen any sign of her neighbors since the day of her spying on Marie and Lavinia in their driveway. She was starting to wonder if they were the type who only came up for holiday weekends.

She trained her eyes on the young mother and son, who were tossing a tennis ball into the lake and watching it bob back to them on the current. The little boy giggled and reached for the ball.

After Melanie's initial visits with Dr. Maroney, at which point her chart had read "You Were Diagnosed With: Infertility, Female, Primary," she had seriously tried out the idea of never having children. As a biologist, she knew not reproducing was the more responsible thing to do in terms of the environment, anyway: not contributing to overpopulation and excessive consumption and carbon emissions. But the negotiator within her knew that she would agree to forsake disposable diapers in favor of cloth and bike everywhere or drive an electric car and garden and compost for the rest of her life if she could only have a baby.

Several of her friends, like her coworker Aimee, were forgoing parenthood in favor of more dynamic lifestyles. Aimee and her husband had recently gone on a three-month-long rainforest ecology field expedition in Ecuador, and she'd suggested Melanie apply for the same program. However, the application process was long and arduous and booked out eighteen months in advance, and Melanie had thought hopefully, *I can't. I might be too pregnant to travel or even have a newborn by then.* But nothing was holding her back now. She thought of Ben and his obsessive running regimen and all the ways they could fill their life together without children. *But would it ever be enough for me? Would it ever be enough for him, despite what he claims? Or would the cold, hard seeds of blame and resentment grow into something large and thorny between us, cleaving us permanently?*

The prospect of rowing back to the other side of the lake on her own exhausted her almost as much as the prospect of attempting to repair things with Ben, so she lay down, closed her eyes, and tried to focus on anything except his angry exit. The memory of the night before her mom's death inadvertently came to her. She and Ben had come to visit for the weekend, and her mom had insisted on cooking a big dinner—homemade garlic bread, lasagna, and tiramisu—to celebrate the competitive Agatha P. Jacobson graduate award Melanie had just received for her research project. "I am so proud of you, honey," her mom had said as she embraced Melanie with more vigor than usual. It was a memory she clung to whenever she was particularly missing her mom, but now she couldn't help seeing it with new eyes.

Her mom had always nurtured Melanie's love of science and eschewed toys and activities that she deemed too girly. So instead of a baby doll and a pretend kitchen, Melanie had had a stuffed dolphin and a real microscope. Instead of taking gymnastics like all of the other girls in their neighborhood, she had spent three weeks of every summer backpacking, canoeing, and classifying rocks, plants, and bugs at nature camp. She had always viewed that encouragement as a selfless act of love, but now she couldn't help wondering if her mom hadn't also been living vicariously through her, bestowing on Melanie the kind of support she had never received from her own parents in her interests in marine archeology and limnology.

Am I living the life Mom would have preferred for herself? Researching and teaching in academia, unencumbered by children? She pictured her mom leaning up against the boathouse, smoking and wallowing, while a party unfolded in the lake house and her daughters slept upstairs. Melanie knew she shouldn't read too much into it—it was, after all, only one moment in her mom's fifty-five years of life—but it was hard not to let that particular moment fill in so many other blanks, from her mom's refusal to join them for dessert on the dock to the way she immersed herself in books about lighthouses and the Great Lakes. Clearly she had wanted so much more, and she had denied herself. For better or for worse, she had chosen them instead.

Melanie stood up and dusted the grains of sand off her legs. She walked into the lake and dove in when the water came up to her ribcage. She swam a ways, dove under again, and opened her eyes to see only a hazy blue with tall seaweed rippling beneath her. *Maybe this is the life I'm supposed to have. Maybe I'd be a terrible mom: over-protective, uptight, too nagging. Or maybe, like Mom, I'd simply find myself bored and unfulfilled. Maybe I'm better off devoting myself to my career.* She came up for a breath and turned in a slow circle as she treaded water. Once she and Kelsey had said their final goodbyes to their mom and sealed off the time portal for good, once the keys and the mortgage title of the lake house were transferred and she and Ben were back home in Ohio, then she would finally close the chapter on her dreams of motherhood and move on with her life.

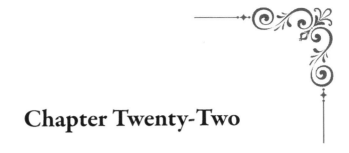

Chapter Twenty-Two

The showing came and went. Charlene reported from Mr. and Mrs. Moneybags' agent that though the couple had loved the property, they hadn't been too thrilled by the lack of updates in the kitchen and the size of the master bedroom, so she didn't know if they were serious buyers anymore. Though Melanie knew it was childish, she couldn't help feeling indignant that they would find any faults with her beloved family home. But she tried not to let it bother her too much, because it was finally the day of the open house.

Half an hour before the start time, Charlene showed up with two signs to stake into the ground—one on the main road and one at the end of the driveway—two bouquets of delphiniums and zinnias with mason-jar vases, and a tray of pastel-colored French macarons, which she positioned on the kitchen table next to the huge fruit basket Melanie's dad, true to his word, had sent. She smiled reassuringly at Melanie and Ben then shooed them out of the house. "Feel free to come back at three thirty," she said. "We should be all wrapped up by then."

It was a funny feeling, getting into the truck that Ben had borrowed and simply driving away. It was like planning to host a bridal shower or holiday get-together then not even being invited to stay. Melanie wouldn't get to see the fruits of her labor. She wouldn't get to see prospective buyers' faces light up as they admired the immaculately clean claw-foot tub or hear their oohs and ahs as they stepped onto the wraparound porch and laid eyes on the lake. That being said, she also wouldn't have to put up with any snarky remarks made about the house, either, so that was a plus.

Days ago, she and Ben had made a plan to grab a quick bite to eat at a chili place in Arbor Creek then catch a matinee, and even though things still hadn't fully thawed between them, they stuck to their plan as if in tacit agreement to pretend everything was just fine. Melanie let Ben pick the movie as part of her penance—and because she didn't particularly care to see any of them—and he chose a comedy about inept CIA agents that she found hard to follow. She didn't know if it was because the plot was poorly conceived or if it was because she kept zoning out to study Ben's profile and try to guess what he was thinking. She also couldn't help wondering how the open house was going, if it was well attended, and if anyone had peeked behind the tapestry, which she had decided to leave in place at the last minute. It had seemed like the less risky of the two options.

After the movie, which Ben didn't seem to have enjoyed all that much, either, they stopped at the grocery store to buy some New York strip steaks and a few bottles of wine. Kelsey had related her "dog poop" story over the phone the previous night, and Melanie was pleased to hear that her sister and Josh were dating. Thank God the "someone" Kelsey wanted to invite over for dinner wasn't Everett. Though Melanie was genuinely happy for her sister's news, she was also seriously kicking herself for suggesting the post-open-house dinner in the first place.

How did it ever seem like a good idea to invite the very person who is most dead set against selling the house to celebrate the impending sale? The conversation would be tense, if not downright hostile, and she couldn't even count on Ben to help defuse the situation. Besides, Melanie knew the dinner was mostly an excuse to Kelsey, anyway, to get back into the portal and leave their mom one final letter—one final letter that could cause major ripples through time, if Kelsey had her way.

Charlene met them at the door, bursting with enthusiasm. She showed them the sign-in sheet with over twenty names listed and described one family in particular who seemed to be head over heels for the house. The elementary-school-aged son and daughter had adored the turret room and porch swing, and the husband and wife were already talking about what kind of boat to buy. "I wouldn't be surprised at all to hear good news from their agent tomorrow or even tonight." She held up her houndstooth-pattern-encased cell phone and gave it a shake. "Keep your phones close."

Ben helped Charlene carry a few boxes out to her car, while Melanie considered whether to eat the last pear in the fruit basket or nibble on a leftover pink macaron. She went with the macaron.

She felt that strange sensation of being unexpectedly let down when something she'd been anticipating for quite a while had finally gone off without a hitch. She peered out the back window and couldn't help visualizing an unfamiliar boy and girl rocking on the porch swing, the same porch swing that her family had been sitting on for the last one hundred years—all those sunrises, sunsets, and late-night talks, all those glasses of lemonade and cups of coffee and tea, all those books read, and all those Montclare and Kingstad butts. She reached for a lime-green macaron as well.

THIS *is the way I want to remember my family's lake house—gathered around the candlelit porch table with Ben, Kelsey, and Josh, drinking a glass of cabernet as a lone owl hoots and the clouds and lake turn jewel-bright shades of yellow, pink, and purple.* It was just too bad that the picturesque tableau didn't match the reality. Ben had gone for yet another long run after the open house, barely returning in time to shower and get the charcoal briquettes heating, and certainly not enough time to talk to Melanie about what had happened between them on Harris Beach. He was barely speaking to her unless he had a practical question for her—"Do you want me to grill the potatoes, or should we bake them instead?" And ever since Kelsey had arrived, she had a wild, nervous energy about her, like the crackling atmosphere before a thunderstorm.

A few minutes before dinner, Melanie had found Kelsey interrogating Ben about blood thinners as he flipped steaks.

"Do you think if my mom had gotten on Warfarin before she had her PE, she would have survived?" Melanie had heard her ask as she came up to them, carrying glasses of wine. She'd nearly spilled the cabernet all over herself and the porch. Ben and Kelsey had both looked up at her, as if bothered by her sudden intrusion.

"It's entirely possible," he had said and accepted his wine without comment. "But a doctor would've needed to have prescribed it, and from what it sounds like, she wasn't having any symptoms, right? No shortness of breath, chest pain, cough, leg pain, or swelling? She wouldn't have known to go to a doctor, unfortunately."

"At least no symptoms that she told us about," Kelsey had replied somberly, avoiding meeting Melanie's eyes.

Only Josh was acting like a normal, sociable, non-secretive human being. Melanie liked the crisp button-down shirt he was wearing, the bottle of wine he'd brought—probably much more expensive than the stuff they'd picked up that afternoon—and the way he listened to Kelsey as if she were the smartest, most fascinating person he'd ever come across. Melanie could tell Ben approved, too, as they'd quickly found out they were both die-hard Packers fans and from families of all boys, although Josh was the youngest of four, and Ben was the oldest of three.

Josh was in the middle of a story about how his brothers had superglued all the flaps on his boxer shorts shut when Melanie's cell phone vibrated—Charlene. She met Ben's questioning eyes across the table—he had heard the telltale buzz—and nodded at him in confirmation. Kelsey was the only one still picking at her steak—she had barely eaten three bites of food the whole night—and she didn't even look up as Melanie pushed her chair back.

"I'll be right back," Melanie said, stepping into the kitchen.

"Sorry to call so late," Charlene said, "but as I'm sure you probably already know, I'm calling with good news!" The family of four's agent had just faxed in an offer, only ten thousand dollars less than asking price. They wanted to close quickly, by the end of July, so they could still enjoy the remaining days of summer. "Oh, and they're asking if they can purchase some of the furnishings. Let's see here." Melanie heard a furious flipping of pages. "The four-poster bed in the master and the tree wall hanging in the second bedroom."

"No." Melanie dug her fingernails into the loose cork on the counter. "Absolutely not."

"Okay." Charlene sounded caught off guard by Melanie's brusqueness. "No problem. I don't think it's a deal breaker. They were just quite taken with both pieces. But I'm sure they'll understand once I explain how long they've been in your family. So how do you feel about the offer? Do you want to talk with your father and sister about it? We have until this time tomorrow night to accept, counter, or decline."

When Melanie returned to the porch, they all stopped talking and watched her. Ben looked grave, Kelsey pale and panicky, and Josh totally clueless. It was like they were waiting to hear the results of some major medical test, not good news about a nearly million-dollar sale.

Melanie's blood whooshed in her ears. "That was our realtor." She took a shaky breath and held up her wine glass. "We have our first offer, and it's a pretty damn good one."

She didn't exactly expect cheers or applause, but she also didn't expect a thick, volatile silence. Kelsey was the first to break it. "Yay," she said sarcastically, holding up her nearly empty wine glass. "Let's hear it for Melanie. For selling our family, our mom especially, down the river. Good for you."

Josh's eyes widened, and he swiveled his head back and forth to take in both sisters. Ben drained his glass in one quick slug.

"Kelsey." Melanie wanted to sit back down and hear the rest of Josh's silly story as the lake swallowed the sun. She wanted to serve the berry parfait and bask briefly in her achievement—even if no one else apparently viewed it that way—that she had fulfilled her goal and could strive to find a new normal. She wanted to touch Ben's knee under the table and have him squeeze her hand and for everything to be magically all right between them again.

But a jagged crack that had existed between her and her sister for a long time was bursting open and widening, threatening to obliterate what was left of the thin pretense that they were still having a nice dinner party. She tried desperately to plaster over it, to salvage the night, at least for Josh's sake. "Don't be so melodramatic," she said, trying to keep her tone light and teasing. "You know I'm trying to do what Mom would have wanted but also what's most sensible for you and me. But I haven't agreed to anything yet. We have twenty-four hours to decide what we want to do. So let's just talk about this together later, okay?"

The whites of Kelsey's eyes flashed as if she were a horse about to bolt. "You keep saying that, but whenever we talk about it, you're the only one who seems to do the talking."

Melanie silently appealed to Ben to intervene, to crack a joke to lighten the mood or say anything, really, but he was cutting a fatty strip of steak into teeny-tiny pieces, refusing to look up at her. He probably thought she was getting what she deserved. He had warned her after all.

"I'm sorry you feel that way," she said, slipping into her conciliatory-professor mode. She'd learned a thing or two over the years, dealing with confrontational undergrads trying to dispute their grades. "Should we go inside and talk about it? Or rather, you can talk, and I'll just listen?"

"We can go inside," Josh offered, the legs of his chair scraping the floor.

"No, you guys stay out here and enjoy the night," Kelsey said. "We'll go inside." She sounded vaguely threatening. Sprocket seemed torn between the men at the table with the food and his two favorite women. Kelsey whistled for him, and his choice was made. He dashed inside, clearly feeling more like his old self, the shaved front paw where the IV had been the only indication he'd been sick at all.

"We won't be gone long," Melanie called over her shoulder, hoping it was the truth. "Feel free to dig into the berry parfait." She was surprised to see that Kelsey was striding right through the kitchen and heading for the stairs. Melanie hurried to follow her. She and Ben had since taken over her parents' bedroom with its larger bed, and since Kelsey had planned to sleep overnight, Melanie had made up her own old bed with fresh sheets. She wondered if Kelsey would still stay after all of this was said and done.

But Kelsey didn't head for either of the bedrooms. She stomped to the turret room and thrust her arm out in the direction of the window seat like a pissed-off tour guide. "This is where I had my first kiss."

"Really?" That was news to Melanie. "With whom?"

Kelsey let a small smirk crack her otherwise stony face. "Stephen. We were eight, and he told me he wanted to marry me. I said sure, as long as he let me have his Creepy Crawlers."

"I always thought he had a thing for you," Melanie mused.

The smirk faded, and Kelsey turned on her heel and marched to the shared bathroom. "This is where I lost my first tooth. Do you remember? I was brushing my teeth, and it popped right out and got rinsed down the drain. I sobbed that the tooth fairy wasn't going to bring me anything until Dad practically took the sink apart to look for it. No luck, of course. Poor Dad. Then Mom had the brilliant idea of writing a letter explaining what had happened and putting that under my pillow instead. And it worked. The tooth fairy brought me a crisp five-dollar bill."

"I get what you're doing, Kels," Melanie said. "And believe it or not, I have a lot of good memories of this place too. Do you remember the night Mom brought out her old record player and albums and the three of us sang along to 'I Got You Babe'? But just because we sell the house doesn't mean we lose the memories."

"I know that. But it's not just *our* memories, Melanie, and it's like the house *remembers* them all. Otherwise, how can you explain the time portal?" She held up her palm quickly as if she didn't really want Melanie to answer. "This house is our legacy. It's the one thing we have left of our family."

Melanie realized she had her arms folded tightly across her chest, so she tried to relax her posture. "That's not true. We have a lot more keepsakes than most people do—quilts and furniture and photo albums. Grandma Dot's wedding china." If anything, they had too many keepsakes. When their grandma had passed away two years ago, she had bequeathed four large boxes of mementos to Melanie and Kelsey, but Melanie was the one holding on to them because she and Ben had more storage space in their house.

"I don't care about the quilts and teacups." Kelsey stormed into Melanie's old bedroom and smoothed her hand over the pinwheel quilt as if to prove her point. She frowned. "Okay, so maybe I do. They're beautiful. But they don't compare to this." She motioned to the hidden door. "Mom is in there. Do you really want to leave her?"

Melanie almost couldn't speak. She remembered the way she and her sister had lain on the couch together, side by side, head to feet, under the same blanket, the day after their mom's death. Kelsey had kept repeating, "I shouldn't have left her. Why did I leave her?" and Melanie had tried to persuade her that it was such a freak occurrence, there was no way Kelsey could have known what was going to happen, and nothing would have been different even if she hadn't left for her hair appointment, even though Melanie wasn't sure she believed that. Of course it wasn't Kelsey's fault, by any means, but if someone had been there sooner, heard her fall, called 911 immediately...

"That's not really Mom in there," Melanie said. "You understand that, right? It's just a shadow of her, like the negatives of a movie reel. She's not alive, Kels. It's just the memories she left behind."

"Of course I know she's not really alive. But she's not just a shadow either. How can you even say that after interacting with her? She's still capable of thinking and feeling, reading and writing, and most importantly, *changing*." Kelsey furiously pushed a loose curl out of her eyes. "You're just trying to distance yourself and put an end to all of this because you don't like what you've seen in there. You'd rather hold on to *your* version of Mom because it's easier and safer. I think that's what's making you so relentless about selling the house. I know you came here specifically to put it on the market, and I went along with you blindly, like I do with everything, but when we found the time portal, I thought things would change. They did for me, anyway. But you only seemed to become even more obsessed with selling it."

"That's not true," Melanie said automatically, but her sister's words seemed to embed themselves in her skin like fishing hooks. "I have loved seeing Mom. Yes, it's been hard witnessing some of those moments and learning things about her that caught me off guard. But we've gone in there enough. I don't think we should keep this up indefinitely. Even Mom has expressed her fears about how the portal might corrupt us. And I'm still not convinced it's one hundred percent safe."

"Believe me, I get that this is well outside your comfort zone. It's outside of mine too. But I'm done with easy and safe. I want the *real* Mom." Kelsey threw her arms up in the air. "And I *don't* want to sell

this house." She laced her fingers behind her head, her elbows pointed out aggressively, and stared at Melanie, ready for a standoff.

"I kind of gathered that." Melanie slid slowly down the wall.
*Dammit, Kelsey. Where was your loud, assertive opinion one month
ago?* "So what do you want to do?" she asked tiredly. "You want to
move out here and live here year-round? Spend your summers here?
What?"

"No." Kelsey unlaced her fingers and let her arms fall to her sides.
"I'd like to turn it into a bed-and-breakfast."

Melanie couldn't have been more surprised if Kelsey had announced she was pregnant. Every cell in her body immediately recoiled against the idea of a B and B. *Perfect strangers coming and going
in the house that my family has inhabited for a century? Lounging in
the living room with their shoes on and showering in the bathrooms,
their unfamiliar hair getting caught in the drains?* The thought made
her slightly queasy. *Dummy*, she admonished herself. *Isn't that exactly
what you're agreeing to, anyway, by selling the house? Isn't that exactly
what you allowed the Holloways to do for the past fifteen years?* "A bed-
and-breakfast?" she repeated, her face as neutral as she could make it.
Melanie had told Kelsey she would hear her out, and she was going
to even if it nearly killed her.

"Yeah." Kelsey wouldn't look at her. "I've already done some preliminary research. Since Lake Indigo is unincorporated, they're a
part of Fairfield Township, and their zoning laws consider homes-
tays and small bed-and-breakfasts, like this one would be, to be a residential business, so it would be allowed. I could use the rest of my
inheritance as the start-up cash I would need for any renovations,
new linens, advertising costs, and whatnot. And Josh's oldest brother,
John, is an accountant. Josh said he'd be happy to help me set up the
lodging and sales taxes account and federal and state tax ID. There's
a lot more to consider, I know, but that's as far as I've gotten at this
point."

Incredulous, Melanie stared at her little sister. Kelsey was speaking a foreign language—residential businesses, start-up cash, and tax IDs. Flighty Kelsey—the girl who still had their dad do her taxes, the girl who notoriously shrank every nice article of clothing she had ever owned because she forgot to read the label before tossing it in the wash—had done all of that. Melanie would have been downright impressed by Kelsey's out-of-the-blue gumption had she not felt so profoundly hurt. While she'd been roller-painting the walls and strategizing with their realtor, Kelsey had been looking up zoning ordinances behind her back. And it was clear that Josh knew. She wondered if Ben had too. His not-so-subtle comments about making sure she was on the same page as Kelsey made her suspect as much. She was the only one left out in the cold.

She twisted her hands into the fabric of her skirt. "Oh, well, that's good that you did preliminary research since, you know, you kept this a huge secret from me, and the house is practically sold, and we have an agent who's been busting her butt for us and really looking forward to her five-figure commission. Do you have any idea what kind of assholes we're going to look like if we back out now?" She pulled her skirt taut over her lap. "I'll give you a hint. Big ones."

"I know," Kelsey said, and she sounded almost tearful. She sank down onto the floor, too, but across the room from Melanie, near the tapestry. "I should have said something sooner. I tried to. But you have to admit that you didn't really leave me any openings. Any time I got up the nerve to talk to you about it, Charlene would call or something else would happen to push us that much closer to the house sale. And anyway, I haven't had the idea for very long, and it seemed so intimidating at first, like something totally out of my league. But the more I've looked into it and thought about it, the more I think that this is exactly what I need. Exactly what I should be doing with my life." She raised her eyes hopefully. "You know me.

I love talking to people, I love cooking and baking, and I love this house."

Melanie didn't know what was wrong with her, but the more vulnerable her sister made herself, the more she wanted to shut Kelsey down. "Sure, but you don't love doing laundry or scrubbing toilets or dusting. You hate anything involving finances or computers, and you can't show up anywhere on time to save your life. You can't exactly keep your guests waiting around all the time. There's no way you could make this work on your own." She felt mean and hollow as soon as the words left her mouth.

"I thought you might say something like that." Kelsey gave her a pained smile, her eyes glistening. "But just because I'm not as anal-retentive as you doesn't mean I'm not a smart, capable person. Just because I'm not as rigid and as sterile—" She stopped talking and covered her mouth with her hand. "I'm sorry. You know that's not what I meant."

Melanie shook her head, suppressing tears of her own. "It's fine. It's true, isn't it? Everything you've said about me is true." She leaned her head back against the wall, picturing her home office in Ohio, the oak bookcase with the biology textbooks, the binders with hard copies of all her lesson plans, and the empty desk and chair just waiting for her to sit down and update her curriculum and syllabus for the fall semester. She would retreat there and let Kelsey do whatever she wanted with the house. It would be another failure, another defeat that she would have to chalk up, but maybe something good would come out of it for Kelsey. Melanie needed to go somewhere she was needed and wanted, somewhere she could make herself useful, and clearly that wasn't here anymore.

"It's hard to believe we share the same DNA sometimes," Kelsey said. Her raw, fiery emotion seemed to have been tamped down to embers. She was absentmindedly tracing the bottom border of the tapestry. "You got Mom's intelligence and Dad's work ethic, and all I got was her out-of-control curls and his honker of a nose."

Melanie knew that was Kelsey's one great hang-up: her belief that their parents had been prouder of Melanie because of her academic achievements. But it wasn't true, at least not in the way Kelsey supposed. While Melanie had made her parents proud in the traditional way of the driven first-born child, Kelsey had made them proud in the head over heels, totally smitten way of the youngest. They were charmed by her free spirit, amused by her diverse hobbies and interests, and downright delighted by the very surprise of her, the fact that they never quite knew what the wild, mermaid-haired girl would do or say next. Melanie was a relief, the daughter they could count on to do what they expected, but Kelsey—Kelsey was a joy.

But Melanie didn't know how to say that to her sister, especially since she was still smarting from the shock of the bed-and-breakfast and the other insults.

"Stop fishing for compliments," she snapped. "You know you've always been the prettier of the two of us, Dad's nose and all. And you hogged up all the athletic genes too."

As Melanie and Kelsey had grown up, everyone had always compared Kelsey to their mom because of their curly hair and blue eyes, but Melanie knew that she was Christine's true double—in mannerisms, in interests, in obsessive-compulsive cleaning, and in holding back their feelings, too, and trying to project the perfect image of themselves while they were really crumbling inside. *Is it any wonder, then*, Melanie pondered, *that I'm so disillusioned with her because I can see these character flaws in myself?*

"I'm not fishing," Kelsey said, furrowing her brow. "And I know you're only trying to be nice, but I'm kind of tired of being called pretty. Why does no one ever say, 'Wow, Kelsey, you're so resourceful,' or 'Thanks, Kelsey. That was a clever idea.'?"

"Now you really *are* fishing."

"I'm not. I'm just sick of you and everyone else thinking I'm this birdbrain who has no business hiring someone to do basement repairs, let alone trying to run my own bed-and-breakfast."

"It's hardly fair for you to say that I *assumed* that. I only learned about your plan five minutes ago." Melanie rocked forward, gripping her knees. "And for the record, I don't think you're a birdbrain. I think this would be a huge undertaking for anyone, Mensa member or otherwise."

Kelsey squinted at her. "I don't believe you. I doubt you think this would be a huge undertaking for you. If *you* were the one starting your own B and B, everyone would probably be slapping you on the back and lining up to make reservations."

Melanie squinted back at her, trying hard not to smile. "Well, it's not like you asked me for my help."

"I don't want your help!" Kelsey pushed off the floor, her face reddening. "I know you have your own job, a job that you love, in a different state. I'm not asking you to leave it. I'm just asking you to give me a chance."

Melanie stood up too. "We should head back downstairs. Ben and Josh are probably starting to wonder if we're having a cage match up here."

"You're not answering me."

"I'm still thinking about it. I have at least twenty-four hours. Twenty-three. Don't rush me." She turned to exit the room, but Kelsey didn't follow her. "Aren't you coming?"

"I'll be down soon."

Melanie knew in an instant what her sister was up to. The pull of the tapestry was like a magnet. She felt it too. *What year is it inside the time portal right now? Somewhere in the nineties?* She and Kelsey were probably tubing with the Fletcher kids without a care in the world. How nice it would be to slip into that, far away from the headache of her adult concerns. *Just what the heck am I going to do about this pending offer on the house?* Either choice she made, she was doomed.

"Kelsey..."

"Will you just mind your own business? I'm just going to drop in for a minute."

"It's never just one minute. You know that. What do you want me to tell poor Josh?"

"That I'm crying in the bathroom after an out-and-out brawl with my overbearing sister, but I'll be right down after I pull myself together."

Melanie glared at her. Kelsey's earlier inquiry about the blood thinners was still setting off a slowly pulsing alarm deep in Melanie's brain. Kelsey had expressed to her several times over the last week that she thought she might only be able to get in one last correspondence with their mom. *Just what is she planning to do, especially in a moment of desperation?* Melanie felt like letting out a loud, guttural growl of frustration but settled for a deeply exasperated sigh instead.

For pity's sake, it was a lot of work to be the big sister. Sometimes she wished she could just throw caution to the wind and be like Kelsey, not caring about the two men waiting for them downstairs or the berry parfait, which was undoubtedly melted by now, or Charlene, who was probably wondering why they hadn't called her back already, or the state of her hormones and ovaries. *Screw it*, she thought. *All of it.*

"Fine," she said. "One minute. Let's go."

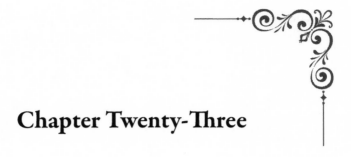

Chapter Twenty-Three

Kelsey could feel the energy coursing on the other side of the door even before they'd opened it. It reminded her of the crazy rattling that shook her tiny apartment whenever her washer was on the spin cycle. Maybe it was just her and her adrenaline. She was so revved up, it wouldn't surprise her, but Melanie was looking antsy too.

The energy was soundless, but it felt like she was physically colliding with someone and had just had the wind knocked out of her. She had gone there looking for a sign from her mom, to see if she should give the bed-and-breakfast thing a shot or step aside and let Melanie have her way. Kelsey also wondered if she should try to warn her mom of her untimely death or leave fate to its cold mechanisms. She hoped her mom wouldn't let her down, because she was severely conflicted. After taking a deep breath, she shoved open the door.

She and Melanie had scarcely tumbled out of the closet, letting the tapestry flap against the door, when a person rushed past them and hefted the tapestry back upward—their mom, in her mid- to late thirties, her hair tied back with a black ribbon.

Oh God, this is it. Mom is time traveling! Where is she going? She was turning the silver latch, and Kelsey lurched forward, ready to slip in behind her as soon as the door opened. But Melanie put her hand on her shoulder, slowing her down, yanking her backward, and Kelsey nearly fell. The door was open, and their mom was stepping inside sideways, shoulder first, so she wouldn't have to pull it open far. Kelsey thrust her hand out, hoping to prevent the door from closing, but she was too far away. All she caught was the edge of the tapestry as it tauntingly slid back into place.

"What the hell?" she shouted at Melanie. She felt like throwing something at her and would have gladly, had anything been in reach.

"What did you think you were doing?" Melanie shouted back. "Jumping into a memory of a memory? What if you never found your way back out?"

"I wanted to know where Mom was going!"

Melanie laughed bitterly, shaking her head. "Come on. Honestly? Like you don't know? The house is probably sending her back to her first kiss with Vinnie."

"You don't know that." Kelsey gathered the tapestry in her arms and pushed it to the side. She hooked her finger around the crescent-moon latch.

"Stop that," Melanie said. "You've got to give her a second to get where she's going."

"It's not opening."

"It's probably because Mom's still in there. Just wait a minute. Be patient."

Kelsey counted to sixty in her head before attempting to twist the latch again. It wouldn't budge. "Melanie, I'm not joking. I think it's locked."

Melanie pushed Kelsey out of the way. *Miss Know-it-All.* Her complexion turned ashen when she couldn't open the door either. She blew out a heavy sigh. "I wonder if the time portal only allows one set of travelers at a time," she said. "If it's 'occupied' right now, so to speak, we have to wait our turn."

"Meaning?" Kelsey prodded.

"That we can't return to our time until Mom gets back to hers."

"Oh crap. That could be hours."

"Or even longer." But for once, Melanie didn't seem as flustered as Kelsey. She was calmly looking around the room. A yellow-and-red starburst quilt covered the bed. Teardrop prisms and a dragonfly suncatcher dangled in the window, and a Discman and a stack of CDs were on the desk. It was the way Kelsey most clearly remembered the room, the way it had been in their last summers at the lake house, so she guessed they were in their early adolescence.

"The Spice Girls, awesome. I'd forgotten about them," Melanie said, reading the CD spines. She lay on her stomach on the bed, kicking her legs up behind her.

"Are you not bothered by this?" Kelsey asked. "We're essentially trapped here for God knows how long. Ben and Josh will have no idea what happened to us."

"Sure, I'm bothered. But it's out of my control. It's all out of my control." She sounded like someone who had just attended a new age self-help seminar and memorized its mantra.

"Who are you, and what have you done with my sister?" Kelsey joked. She sat down on the bed next to Melanie, remembering how her sister had always kept her bedroom door closed from age thirteen on and how she would have to knock and wait for permission to enter. She would find Melanie on the bed in just that position, listening to music and reading a magazine. Melanie would seem so grown-up, so cool and untouchable, that Kelsey would swallow back her invitation to row to Dern's together for a Popsicle and back out of the room.

"I think these rooms are way too small for a bed-and-breakfast," Melanie said. "Especially your dinky room."

"I think so too. That's why I was planning to knock down the wall between them to make one big room and the shared bathroom a private en suite."

"Oh, you were, were you?" Melanie rolled over onto her side. "And what are you going to do about that?" She gestured to the tapestry with her foot.

"Leave it there for decoration. Buy a padlock for the door whenever a guest is staying in here."

"You really have thought this out, haven't you?" Melanie was scrutinizing her in such a way that Kelsey had to wonder if her sister was starting to come around.

"Yes," Kelsey lied. She had no idea what knocking down a wall entailed or how much it cost, but people on HGTV seemed to do it all the time, so it couldn't be *that* complicated. And she'd never considered locking the time portal before until Melanie had just asked about it. In fact, Kelsey had had the romantic notion that she could stay in this room with the tapestry, but now she realized that made no sense, that it would have to be one of the guest suites, and she would have to live downstairs in the fourth bedroom. She was doing all of it on the fly, but if Melanie wanted to believe she had it more planned out than she actually did, so much the better.

Melanie sat up. "Should we go downstairs and see what we're up to?"

Her sister had surprised her again. "You don't want to stay up here and wait for Mom to get back?" Kelsey asked, a nervous little quiver running through her. *What if Melanie's theory is wrong?* Maybe the rush of energy Kelsey had felt was a sign that it was on its last leg, like a car with a grinding transmission. What if the time portal was just flat-out broken?

"What's the use? We'll know when she's back, and if not, we can always come up in a little bit and check if the door is unstuck." Melanie walked to the hallway, not bothering to look back over her shoulder. "But feel free to stay up here and keep watch if you'd like."

In the twilit backyard, their dad was pulling the tarp off their firewood rack. Kelsey, age eleven, judging by her braces, coltish limbs, and orange ruffled two-piece she had practically lived in that summer, was standing by him eagerly, ready to help. Melanie was artfully arranging lawn chairs around the campfire and giving everyone a wood-handled skewer. Her hazelnut hair was practically down to her butt, and she was wearing a chunky cable-knit sweater despite the heat. She looked like a wannabe cast member of *Dawson's Creek*, Kelsey thought.

"Why isn't Mom roasting s'mores with us?" eleven-year-old Kelsey asked her dad.

"Oh no!" he said as he revealed that the woodpile had been severely depleted. Only a few sticks of wood were left. "Because your dad is an idiot, and she's ticked off at me for neglecting to do things like chop more firewood and take care of that wasp's nest like she asked."

"Really?" Kelsey asked. "I thought it was because Melanie was being such a jerk to her. All because Mom wouldn't take her to the Arbor Creek mall."

"Don't be a tattletale, Kelsey Ann, and don't be a jerk to your mother, either, Melanie Jane. We're here to relax and enjoy the scenery, not to shop."

Behind his back, Melanie pretended to threaten to stab her sister with the roasting skewer.

"Now who wants to go next door and ask Mr. and Mrs. Fletcher if we can borrow a few logs for our bonfire? You can tell them we'll repay them tomorrow once I've chopped some wood."

All of a sudden, Kelsey realized what evening they had stumbled upon, and her stomach lurched. She had been the one to volunteer to go next door, and the encounter with Mr. Fletcher had been such a surreal one that it had seared itself onto her childish brain, then she'd promptly buried it under the dust of all her other memories.

At first, she'd almost given up knocking because the house was dark and she couldn't hear any movement inside. But then Mr.

Fletcher had flung the door open. Of the two Fletcher adults, Mr. Fletcher was definitely her favorite. He was much more even-keeled than Mrs. Fletcher and unfailingly kind to all of the kids—furnishing them with an endless supply of water balloons and ice cream sandwiches. He talked like a TV weatherman—cheerful with lots of arm movements. But that night had been a different story.

"What do you want?" he'd barked at Kelsey as if she were a strange salesperson. He looked sweaty and jaundiced, unsteady on his feet. Probably totally blitzed, she realized as an adult.

"Just... uh..." Kelsey was so intimidated by his demeanor, she could hardly form her request. "My dad sent me over here to ask—"

"Oh yeah? What else can I get for your dad?" Mr. Fletcher spat. "Haven't I already shared enough with him?" He gripped the doorframe as if he might topple over.

Kelsey took several steps backward. "Okay. Um... sorry to bother you." She scurried down the porch stairs, and Mr. Fletcher had slammed the door without another word. Standing empty-handed in the gathering darkness, she didn't know what to do. She couldn't return to her dad without the firewood. Then she'd have to explain what had happened with Mr. Fletcher and what he'd said. She was worried her dad would get upset and storm over to confront their neighbor. It hadn't occurred to her then just to lie and say no one had been home. So she simply stepped around the side of the house, where she knew the Fletchers kept their firewood in an unlocked shed, and grabbed as much as her thin arms could carry. Guilt and fear consumed her as she darted back across the lawn, hoping Mr. Fletcher wouldn't see her out the window.

She related her memory to Melanie as they stood around the fire pit, watching their dad aimlessly try to start a fire with his limited supply of wood and teenage Melanie unwrap a Hershey's bar. They waited for young Kelsey to return.

"That's really creepy," Melanie said. "Why did you never tell me that?"

"I don't know," Kelsey said, claiming one of the empty lawn chairs. "Probably because you were too busy listening to the Spice Girls on your Discman. I tried to tell Stephen about it once, and he acted really huffy. Said I had probably woken his dad up and that he's always in a bad mood when his sleep is interrupted."

"Sleeping? It's probably only seven or eight at night!" Melanie said. "More like drinking." She leaned on the back of her younger self's chair. "I wonder if he thought Dad and Lavinia were having an affair. I mean, 'What else can I get your dad? Haven't I *shared* enough with him?'"

"Boy, was he barking up the wrong tree," Kelsey said then regretted it. Poor Mr. Fletcher. Maybe he'd suspected the wrong Kingstad, but clearly, he'd known something was wrong with his marriage. Drinking alone in the dark—he was just as much a victim of Mom and Vinnie's lingering relationship as Dad was, perhaps more so, since Dad had never seemed to suspect it. She thought of both couples and how precariously entwined their lives had once been and how disconnected and adrift they all became. Lance and Lavinia were probably divorced and in different, happier relationships. Her dad had remarried and was living in the sunny southwest. But only her mom was truly separate and permanently alone, her ashes buried in a cemetery plot in Elm Grove, where no one even lived anymore. It was so devastatingly unfair.

"Melanie," she started. "I'm worried this might be our last chance to get a note to Mom. It's coming up on our last summer here, and we have no idea what's going to happen to her memories inside the portal once we reach that. If there's anything we want to tell her for sure, we should probably do that before we go."

Melanie paced slowly around the circle of chairs. "You mean like the blood clot in Mom's lung that killed her?"

Kelsey inhaled sharply, astounded by Melanie's bluntness. "Yes!" she agreed. She had thought she was going to have to ease into the subject cautiously, tiptoeing around her intentions.

They were quiet for a little while as young Kelsey, pink-faced and hefting a bundle of firewood, returned to their yard.

"I've done some research online, Kels," Melanie said, astonishing Kelsey even further, "and I don't know what we could even say to help Mom prevent it. Even if we told her to go see her primary care doctor a week before the date of her death, it still might not be enough. We could advise her to tell them she's having leg pain and swelling, and they'll probably do an ultrasound to look for a deep vein thrombosis, but if there isn't one there, they'll probably just send her home and have her check back in a week, which would obviously be too late. And if we just instruct her to ask to be put on anticoagulants, for no other reason than time travelers from the future told her to, they're not going to take her seriously. They'll probably do a psych workup instead."

"But what if they do find a DVT?" Kelsey asked, practically breathless at the possibility. "Oh, Melanie, at least it's something. How can we have this opportunity to prevent a horrible, tragic fate for Mom and do absolutely nothing?" Her heart was pounding at the prospect of rewriting the worst day of her entire life, her single biggest regret—the day she had let her mom die all alone with no hope of any medical interventions or even a kind face and a gentle touch to let her know she was loved in her last minutes on earth.

Melanie stared out at the lake. "I don't know," she said at last. "But this is major ripping-holes-in-the-fabric-of-time stuff, and I don't think it should be taken lightly. Just think about the extent of the impact this would have on all of our lives."

"Yes, but think of the impact it would have on Mom's life! She would get to have one!" Kelsey cried, standing up from her lawn chair. If they'd been back in their own time, it would've toppled backward from the force. "I don't understand why you're so hell-bent on not disrupting the present. What's so freaking great about the present? Our mom is dead, our dad is remarried and off living his own life, and you and Ben just lost your..." She drifted off. "I just mean that things could only get better, right? Just think how much better our lives would be with Mom still alive."

She imagined family dinners and board game nights at her parents' house in Elm Grove. She imagined getting her mom's blessing to open the Montclare Inn and the pride her mom would have that Kelsey had finally found her ambition and a calling; taking Sprocket for long walks with her mom and introducing her to Josh; no more Christmases in Arizona; no more Laila, Ezra, and Joni, period; and maybe even going shopping with her mom one day to pick out a wedding dress.

"Please don't get too far ahead of yourself," Melanie begged. "It probably won't even work. Mom might be too stubborn to listen to us, or her death might be somehow destined regardless of what we do. Or we could resurrect her, and it could all go very differently from how we want it to."

"What do you mean by that?" Kelsey asked warily.

But Melanie only shook her head. She looked drawn and washed-out, like the insubstantial ghosts they were in that place. Something caught her attention behind Kelsey's head, and when Kelsey turned to follow her gaze, she saw that their mom had appeared on the wraparound porch.

"Did you guys save me any marshmallows?" she called down to them. With her brown curls tied back in a ribbon, she looked pretty, and her smile was wide and relaxed looking—authentic. *Where did she just go inside the time portal?* Obviously she had seen something that had rejuvenated her—a romantic moment with Vinnie, like Melanie suspected, or maybe something happy from her childhood.

"We haven't even started toasting them!" teenage Melanie called back, waving a skewer. Apparently her mom's heinous crime of not taking her to the mall was forgiven.

"We should go," Kelsey said, eager, for the first time perhaps, to head back to the closet. "Check and see if the door will open for us now. Write Mom that note." She wondered how much time had passed in their reality and what Josh would think if they had gone missing for hours. *Would he be worried about me or just irked that I invited him over for dinner just to get into a fight with my sister then disappear on him?*

"Sure," Melanie said, but she continued watching their mom and didn't make any motions to leave.

Their mom gave their dad a small peck on the cheek then settled into a chair, pulling leggy Kelsey onto her lap. She tugged a lightweight sweatshirt over the girl's head then whispered something into her ear, and young Kelsey laughed, and suddenly adult Kelsey understood why she had forgotten all about Mr. Fletcher's unusual behavior. Her mom's lavish display of affection had nearly erased it.

Kelsey and Melanie watched as their mom reached across the short distance to where Melanie was sitting and stroked her long, straight hair. They watched as their dad got a roaring fire going and passed out marshmallows. They watched as Melanie toasted hers a golden brown and Kelsey thrust hers too close to the flame and promptly lit it on fire.

"I'm going back upstairs," Kelsey said, but what she was thinking was: *this is my sign*. Her family huddled around a bonfire, toasting marshmallows, her mom's arms tight around her, the lake a glassy backdrop—she was meant to do everything in her power to reunite them, to bring their mom back, mysterious forces of destiny and the butterfly effect be damned. She was meant to hold onto that place, where they had been so happy together once upon a time and where maybe even one day not too far in the future they could be happy together again.

"All right," Melanie agreed.

With her sister behind her as they climbed the stairs, Kelsey asked, "What do you think of the name the Montclare Inn?"

"It's nice," Melanie said noncommittally.

When her fingers touched the latch and it turned easily, Kelsey let out a deep sigh of relief. "Thank goodness," she said. "It must be working again." They ducked under the tapestry together and closed the door. The rattling energy was gone, and its absence made the closet feel eerily still. "Holy moly! Is that what I think it is?" She bent down to pick up a toothbrush from the bench.

"One and the same," Melanie said. "Orange with splayed bristles. So now we know where Mom just went. She must have picked it up and brought it here from the night of the party we saw."

Kelsey studied the toothbrush as if it could reveal all the answers she was looking for. "But why would the time portal want her to go and relive the night of that awful party? That's so random." She tried not to evoke the image of her mom smoking behind the boathouse and staring down at her shoes, a stranger in her own life.

"I don't know," Melanie said. "Maybe Mom guided herself there. Maybe she wished she had done things differently."

"You think Mom can control where she goes and what she sees?"

"Who knows? They are *her* memories, after all. We've certainly considered much crazier ideas in the past twenty-four hours."

That still didn't explain why their mom had looked so happy and relaxed when she had rejoined them in the backyard. *What about that depressing party in the late eighties managed to boost her spirits?* Kelsey would have to meditate more on that later. Their most pressing order of business was the letter. She handed Melanie a sheet of paper and a pen that she'd had tucked in her back pocket.

"Can you write this one? I'll help."

After several minutes, numerous cross-outs, three new sheets of paper—thank goodness she'd brought extra—and two major disagreements, they came up with:

Dear Mom,

We are both adults now, but Melanie still loves gardening, thanks to you, and Kelsey is still an avid reader—although she doesn't use a headlamp in bed anymore.

In a few years your time, our family is going to stop coming to the lake house, so sadly, this might be one of the last communications we can send to you through the closet. We have a very important request for you, however, and we'd like you to strongly consider it.

Can you please make an appointment with your doctor for May 1, 2015, regardless of whether you are feeling sick? Tell him or her that you are having leg swelling and pain and request that you be put on a blood thinner like Warfarin. Don't take no for an answer.

We're not trying to frighten you or take away your agency, but maybe the future doesn't always have to be out of our reach.

With love now and forever,

Your daughters

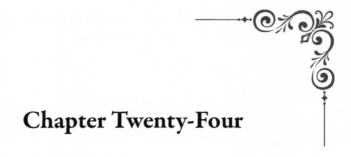

Chapter Twenty-Four

The bedroom was dark and silent when they returned. Melanie rushed to read the time on the nightstand's alarm clock: 2:47 a.m. "We've been gone for over seven hours!" she hissed. "Just how are we going to explain this? Ben is probably sick to death right now, thinking we were kidnapped or maybe even murdered each other."

Kelsey gently sealed the closet door behind her. "We can say we went to a bar to umm... drink our differences away."

"Kind of hard to believe when the nearest bar is six miles from here and our cars didn't move the whole time we were gone. Besides, they would've heard us leave and come back, right? Unless we climbed out a window."

"Sure, we can climb out a window," Kelsey said gamely. "Stephen and I used to do that for fun. From the turret room, it's actually not that far of a drop to the porch roof, then you can scale the columns fairly easily. At least I could when I was nine. I might be a little out of practice now, though."

Melanie shot daggers at her. "I am *not* scaling a roof out a second-story window. I just don't know how the heck to explain our prolonged sudden disappearance to my husband!"

"How about the truth?"

"The truth is batshit bonkers!"

"Well, yeah, it is. But it's still the truth." She took a step toward Melanie and tripped over her duffel bag, which was lying between them in the darkness.

In an instant, Melanie knew that Ben had heard them. They heard an abrupt scraping noise downstairs then the sound of feet clambering on the stairs. He was coming up to investigate, and Melanie still didn't know what to tell him. She didn't even know what conclusion she and Kelsey had reached about the pending offer on the house.

"Listen," she whispered hurriedly. "I'm really not sure how this is going to work, but you own fifty percent of the house, and I'm not going to stand in your way if you feel that strongly about turning it into a bed-and-breakfast. But if Charlene decides to take legal action against us for pulling the house off the market and defaulting on our contract, then I'll just let you handle that, okay?"

"Oh, Melanie," Kelsey said, gratefully throwing her arms around Melanie's shoulders. "You don't think she would actually try to sue us, do you?"

And that was how Ben found them after giving a perfunctory knock on the door before flinging it open—hugging like two desperate and delirious people who'd been shipwrecked on the same island.

"YOU KNOW, THAT'S QUITE the story to swallow," Ben said, stretching his arms over his head. They were lying on top of the covers of the four-poster bed in the master bedroom. "You probably should have just told me that you two jumped out a second-floor window, walked six miles to a bar to get drunk, walked six miles back, and scaled the side of the house Spiderman-style." He smiled sleepily, which turned into a yawn. "That would have been less far-fetched."

"Believe me, I know," Melanie said. She had just spent the past hour rehashing, in great detail, everything that had happened at the lake house since the moment she had arrived and uncovered the door behind the tapestry. She hadn't left anything out—the first time she'd seen her mom and grandma in the kitchen, the conversation between two friends about her mom's hopes and dreams, the drowning at Harris Beach, the forbidden kiss with Vinnie, her pregnant mom, the party, the bonfire, the frequent sparring matches with Kelsey, the stolen cigarettes, the time-traveling toothbrush, the contents of their notes to and from their mom, even including the latest one that might or might not bring their mom back from the dead. *Everything.*

"Why are you first telling me this now?" Ben asked, rolling over onto his side to face her. "Because your back was against a wall?"

"I didn't tell you right away because it's so far-fetched," she said. "I didn't think there was any way you would believe me. I barely believed it, and I experienced it firsthand. So I tried to share what I could with you by pretending I had found my mom's diary."

He closed his eyes thoughtfully, or maybe he was just drifting off to sleep. Melanie was so bone weary that if the bucket of adrenaline from the past several hours hadn't still been coursing through her veins, she would have been out like a light in a minute.

"Maybe you should review our marriage vows," he said softly, his eyelids fluttering. "For better or for worse, for richer, for poorer, in sickness and in health, in far-fetched time-traveling scenarios or really any of life's struggles, until death do us part."

She couldn't help laughing. "I don't remember that last part about far-fetched time-traveling scenarios."

He opened his brown eyes. They had a roguish twinkle in them she hadn't seen in a long time. "It was in there. I remember. It's probably even in the Bible. Go look it up if you don't believe me."

"I'll believe you if you'll believe me," she whispered.

He scooted off to the side so he could pull the quilt up over them. "Do you think your mom will read that note and really take your advice?" he asked. "Will we wake up tomorrow morning and find out she's stopping over for a visit and nothing was ever amiss?

And if so, will we remember what life was like when she died? Or will our memories just totally be revised to reflect the new reality?"

"I have no idea," Melanie replied. "But *if* it happens, which I think is really unlikely, I don't think it will happen tomorrow already. It might take a few days because of the way time moves so differently inside of the portal."

Ben yawned again. "I can't believe you're not selling the house, Kelsey's turning it into a B and B, and your mom might be miraculously alive again in a few days because of a letter you sent her through a time portal."

"Me either." She inched closer to him as she curled the quilt around her legs, daring herself to take a risk and say what she wanted to say next. "And to add on to that list of incredible things, I can't believe you still love me." She said it like a definitive statement, desperately trying to conceal the terrified question embedded within it.

"Who said anything about still loving you?" He adjusted the pillow under his head and inched closer to her too. "I'm still very much hurt and pissed off at you, you know."

"Yes, I can tell. But you're still here, aren't you?"

"I am, Mel, but I honestly don't know how much more of this I can take." He had dropped the sleepy, lighthearted tone and sounded wide-awake and deadly serious. "When you said that you thought I was going to leave you for another woman just so I could have a biological child, that was probably one of the most hurtful things you could have ever said to me. Do you honestly think that? Have I ever given you any indication that I would leave you because of this, or anything else, for that matter? Do you honestly have that low of an opinion of me? Because if you do, I don't see how there's a way out of this seemingly bottomless hole we've found ourselves in."

"No, I don't really think that." She moved her face until it was only inches from his and he could see how earnest she was. "I just have so much self-loathing right now that I can't help projecting some of it onto you. It's hard for me to imagine that you wouldn't want to leave me."

"Well, I don't." He pressed the tip of his nose against hers. "But this self-loathing has got to stop. You didn't do anything to cause the difficulty of getting pregnant. You didn't cause the miscarriage. It is not something you did wrong or something you chose. It is something that just happened, Mel, and not just to you but to both of us. Every single day, my heart breaks but not just for our baby. It breaks because I feel like I've lost you, too, and I don't know how to get you back."

One fat tear escaped her eye and dampened her pillow. "I'm trying to come back to you," she whispered. "I promise."

WHEN MELANIE AWOKE, she was alone in the queen-size bed, and her alarm clock read four thirty. *I slept for nearly twelve hours? Why didn't anyone wake me?* She needed to talk to Charlene as soon as possible. In fact, she had a missed text message from her, sent around noon. *Have you guys made a decision about the offer? Let me know if you have any questions. I'll need you to sign some papers, and I'm happy to come out there to do it. We need to give them an answer by 7:00 p.m. at the very latest, but sooner is always better.*

"Ben?" she called as she padded barefoot down the stairs. In her still-groggy state, she half expected her mom to glide out into the living room. All the windows were open, and the curtains were dancing in the cross breeze. "Ben?"

"Out here!" She found him in the gravel driveway, unloading a bag of mulch from the back of his truck.

"Why did you let me sleep so long?" she asked. "I need to call Charlene before our twenty-four hours are up."

"Clearly your body needed the rest." He wiped sweat off his forehead, causing his already messy hair to stand straight up in the front. "Besides, Kelsey told me she was going to take care of it."

"Kelsey?" Melanie leaned against the tailgate. "Take care of the call to our realtor?" She widened her eyes at him. *What if she broke things off with Charlene too indelicately, making it seem like we'd been planning the bed-and-breakfast for ages and only using her?*

"Yeah," Ben said. "She said she didn't want you to have to worry about it, and since she's the one responsible, she thought she could best explain it."

They stopped talking as a silver SUV drove slowly up the Fletchers' driveway. Maybe Jess and Nicholas were back with the kids, or maybe it was Marie and Lavinia. Melanie tried to hide behind the truck because she was still wearing her pajamas at four thirty in the afternoon, but Ben waved cheerfully at the driver. Melanie couldn't make out who was inside or if they even waved back because of the glare on the windows.

"Why don't you give Kelsey a quick call and see how things went?" he suggested. "Then come back out here because I want to show you something."

She'd discovered another pocket of cell phone reception in her parents' bathroom, and she headed there. As the phone rang, she took off her pajama top and pulled a clean shirt over her head.

"Hey," Kelsey answered. "Don't worry about calling Charlene, okay? I just got back from her office."

She went to see Charlene in person? Melanie hadn't known that her sister even knew where the realtor's office was located. "Ben told me," she said. "So how did it go?" Though she knew Kelsey's intentions were good, it was driving her nuts that something of this magnitude had been taken out of her control.

"Really well, I think." Kelsey paused. "I'm sorry I kind of did this without you. But it made me feel so bad when you brought up all of

Charlene's hard work last night, and I wanted to try to make things right. And I didn't want this to fall only on your shoulders since it was really the mess I had made."

Melanie caught a glimpse of her face in the mirror. Despite the twelve hours of sleep, she still looked careworn and tired. But she also looked relieved. Kelsey had shown initiative and handled a sticky situation so Melanie wouldn't have to, and the house would stay in the family after all, under Kelsey's direction, as a new, reimagined incarnation—and a new incarnation for her sister too. Melanie was the only one still struggling to adapt.

"I explained to her how the idea of holding on to the house by turning it into a bed-and-breakfast had only just recently come to me," Kelsey continued. "And that I'd hesitated to share it with you and take the house off the market right away because I wasn't sure at first about the zoning ordinances and other issues. Then I told her how incredibly grateful we are for all the time and energy she put into our house, that we would be highly recommending her to all of our neighbors and friends, and we wanted to make it up to her in some way. I asked if she'd be interested in staying at the Montclare Inn, all expenses paid, for a romantic weekend with her husband as soon as we open. She seemed a lot more forgiving after that."

"Wow, Kels." Melanie grinned at her reflection. "That was really clever of you. Very resourceful."

Kelsey burst into laughter. "Thanks, sis." She suddenly clapped her hands. "Sprocket! Drop it. No, no! No more washcloth-eating for you." Her volume lowered as she returned to the phone. "Can you believe that little stinker? Sorry about that. So you haven't gone back inside the closet yet to see if Mom replied, have you?"

"No." She hadn't planned on it either. She figured she and Kelsey had done enough tampering with fate to last a lifetime. What was done was done, and all they could do was hope and pray for the best. But try as she might, she couldn't fathom an ending where it worked out with their mom happily restored to them, an ending where they all simply returned to living the lives that had been upended four years ago. A miracle of that magnitude could exact a terrible, terrible price.

"I wonder how long it will take," Kelsey mused, sounding almost giddy. "And how will we know?"

BEN HAD MOVED INTO the backyard. He was digging a basketball-sized hole near the porch footings with a hand trowel, probably because a shovel wasn't among the random assortment of tools Melanie had accumulated at the lake house. He sat back on his heels and smiled at her. "Everything squared away with your sister and the realtor?"

"I think so," she said and relayed what Kelsey had told her. "What are you planting?"

"That's what I wanted to show you," he said, reaching for two lime-green buckets he'd tucked out of view. "I hope you like them."

They were young rose bushes—one the same pale pink as a ballet slipper and the other the cheery color of a ripe peach. "They're beautiful," she said. "But why did you buy me rose bushes to plant here?"

"I thought they could be a kind of memorial." Ben touched the petals of a pink rose. "This pink one in memory of your mom." So just like her, he wasn't counting on her mom's escape from a pulmonary embolism as a foregone conclusion either. He cupped his hand around one of the peach blooms but didn't say anything for a few beats. When he spoke again, his voice sounded hoarse. "And this peach one for our baby."

Melanie knelt down on the ground beside him. Her eyes stung, and her chest constricted. She placed her hand over his and squeezed.

"I feel like we never got to properly mourn him or her," Ben said. "No funeral or ceremony. So I thought it might help us to have somewhere physical to visit. And I couldn't think of a more beautiful place to remember our baby than right here with this view, especially now that this house will be staying in your family."

She nudged her head into the space between his neck and shoulder, and he turned to kiss her cheek. He smelled like soil and sweat and, underneath it, the quintessential smell of the man she had loved for the past eight years and would continue to love for as many more years as she had left on the earth. It would take that long to love him as well and as deeply as he deserved.

"I love the roses," she said, "and I love you even more."

"I love you, too, Mel." He kissed her other cheek. "I've been thinking about it a lot, and we can start trying again once we get back home if you'd like. The Letrozole, the ovulation calendar, the whole nine yards. If you're ready, that is."

"Thanks," she said, and she surprised herself by the words that were on the tip of her tongue. "But I think you were right to want to take a break, to just be *us* for a little while without all the pressure."

It didn't feel like the white flag of surrender she had imagined. Instead it felt like making a conscious choice to focus on her marriage. A child would come—she and Ben simply had too much love to give not to become parents one day. How that child would arrive was the only question—whether it was fertility treatments or IVF or adoption. She would have to learn to give up her control and be more patient and open-minded about the possibilities, which would, admittedly, be a huge struggle for her. But it would happen if they could continue to be a team and love one another. Leaning against her devoted, optimistic husband, she felt sure of that.

"Just to be clear, I don't want to give up sex, though," she added, and he grinned.

They took turns digging the second hole, then Ben wiggled the plants out of their containers, and Melanie loosened the soil around the roots the way her mom had shown her a long time ago. He filled the holes while she held the roses upright. While he went to fetch the margarita pitcher that had become their substitute watering can, Melanie spread the bags of mulch he had bought and admired the flowers.

They were so gorgeous that it almost hurt to look at them. There was definitely a reason why poets used roses as a comparison for a beautiful woman's lips or a baby's downy cheek. The exquisite color, the silky petals, the delicate unfurling—everything about a rose seemed lush and ephemeral.

Ben's voice rang out in the distance, but it didn't sound like he was calling for her. "That's really kind of you. Thanks so much," he said. "She's back here." Before Melanie had time to leap up from her undignified squat in the dirt, Ben and a silver-haired woman were rounding the wraparound porch.

"Melanie Kingstad, all grown up!" Lavinia said, walking toward her with both arms outstretched.

Melanie tried not to stiffen as the older woman hugged her, but she felt like her emotions were raw and prickling just at the surface of her skin. She didn't want Lavinia standing there where she and Ben had just planted the rose bushes for her mom and their baby, while the soil was still crumbly and her eyes were still red. She didn't want to make small talk with her mom's "other woman" while she and Ben should have been sharing a private moment.

"Mrs. Fletcher," she said, trying to sound warm. "It's been so long!"

"Oh, please call me Vinnie." Lavinia swatted Melanie's etiquette away.

"Vinnie spotted our ridiculous pitcher and brought this over for us to borrow," Ben said, holding up a large galvanized metal watering can. His face looked apologetic. *Please forgive me for bringing her back here*, it said. *I couldn't be rude, and I didn't know what else to do.* People were always going out of their way to be kind and helpful to Ben. Grocery store checkers, librarians, waiters—they all took a shine to him. Melanie thought it was his mussed-up hair and quick smile, like a grown-up Dennis the Menace. She suspected that she could have been outside watering the flowers with an eyedropper and Lavinia and the rest of her family wouldn't have lifted a finger to offer Melanie a watering can.

But maybe not. Maybe Lavinia was actually over there to talk to Melanie. *Why else would Vinnie ask Ben about me? And how else was she at the ready with the watering can at just the right moment? Unless she was watching us.*

"We have a spare hose we could loan you, too, if that would be easier," Vinnie said. She was wearing gray yoga pants and a pink tunic. Her long hair was tied back in a low ponytail, and though initially Melanie had been shocked by the fact that the once-proud redhead had let her hair go gray, she realized why Vinnie had made the decision. Somehow the silver hair made her still-delicate, youthful-looking features even lovelier because Melanie was expecting an older, more weathered face. She looked like the poster child for the health benefits of yoga.

"That's really nice of you, thanks, but the watering can should be just fine," Melanie said. She knew further conversation was expected of her, but she was coming up empty. *Should I mention I met Marie, or would that seem too prying?* "So how are your kids?" she asked, settling on what was usually a safe topic. "What are they up to these days?"

"They're all terrible disappointments," Vinnie said, but her almond eyes were twinkling as if she were telling a really good joke. "Living miles and miles away and not giving me any grandkids yet. Beau is an anesthesiologist, and Stephen is our writer in the family.

He just had a short story published in *The Paris Review*. And Jillian—she insists we call her by her full name now—just joined Teach for America."

Ben's college roommate had also done Teach for America, so—God bless him—he jumped into the conversation. Melanie was left to let their words wash over her and silently stew. She hated the whole "not giving me any grandkids yet" shtick. It drove her nuts, and she was grateful that her mother had never participated in it. *Besides, doesn't Vinnie consider Noah and Gracie her grandkids?* But maybe her relationship with Marie wasn't as serious and established as Melanie had assumed. Or maybe Vinnie simply didn't want to get into an awkward conversation about her divorce, sexual orientation, and relationship status.

"I heard you and your sister are thinking of converting this old place into a bed-and-breakfast," Vinnie said, toying with the tassel at the end of her necklace.

Aha! So *that* was why she had come over for a "neighborly chat." She was pissed off that a stream of tourists and out-of-towners was going to be lodging right next door. *But how did she even hear about it?* The ink on the listing cancelation was practically still wet. Ben raised his eyebrows at Melanie, clearly on the same wavelength.

"I'm on the Lake Indigo Neighbors Association," Vinnie quickly offered, reading both of their minds. "I have been for years. Someone from Fairfield Township contacted us about it last week."

"Yeah, we decided not to sell after all," Melanie said as levelly as she could, but inside, she was spoiling for a fight. "Kelsey thought a B and B would be a great way to keep it in the family and honor the history of the house."

Vinnie leaned forward confidentially, and her ponytail fell over her shoulder. "Some of the members aren't too keen on the idea, but frankly, I think it's genius. It'll revitalize the community and generate more business for Lamson's Market and Tom's Marine Supply.

And what a great investment for you girls. Your mom would be so pleased."

"Thank you." She didn't want Vinnie's compliments to mean anything to her, but they did. Too many summers had passed with Mrs. Fletcher as her second mom for Melanie to totally distance herself from her. She couldn't help remembering the way Mrs. Fletcher had always wanted to braid Melanie's hair when she was a little girl, when Mrs. Fletcher had had only boys and was pining for a daughter. She had especially loved doing something she called a fishtail braid then tucking daisies between the sections of Melanie's hair. Melanie had always felt like a wood nymph afterward.

"I am so, so sorry for your loss," Vinnie said, touching Melanie's shoulder. "I know it's been a few years, but I haven't seen you since..." She drifted off, clearly uncomfortable. "I was just heartsick when I heard the news." She *looked* heartsick—her complexion had suddenly lost its healthy yoga glow. *The Fletchers sent a flower arrangement*, her dad had said. *Something big and expensive. They didn't make it to the funeral, though.* For the first time, Melanie wondered why Lavinia hadn't made it to Christine's funeral. *What kept Vinnie from saying goodbye to her one-time lover and best friend?*

"Thank you," Melanie repeated. "We were all heartsick too. We miss her terribly." It hadn't gotten any easier accepting people's condolences. "I know how much you meant to each other," she added experimentally, lifting her eyes to see what Vinnie would make of that last comment.

Vinnie squinted at Melanie for a few seconds, pursing her glossy pink lips as if trying to decide how best to reply. *Did I ruffle her otherwise-poised demeanor?* She touched her tassel necklace again as if it were a talisman.

"Hey, Mel," Ben said, setting the watering can down on the porch step with a clunk. "Did you still want to get Chinese food like we were talking about? I know you said you were starving."

He was throwing her a lifeline, a get-out-of-the-awkward-conversation-free card. Even though his timing was positively awful, she loved him so much right then that she wanted to kiss him. But awkwardness notwithstanding, she needed to have the conversation. She wanted to face the woman who was somehow so ordinary and familiar but also a total stranger. Lavinia Birdwell Fletcher was her mom's biggest secret, and Melanie wanted to learn absolutely anything and everything she could from her.

"That sounds great," she told Ben, trying to convey her understanding and gratitude with her eyes. "You wouldn't mind picking it up, though, would you?" She didn't even know where the nearest Chinese restaurant was, but she knew he would find out or figure out an alternative. She hadn't eaten since dinner the previous night, but surprisingly, she wasn't very hungry.

Vinnie was standing in the shade of their maple tree, looking upward. "I heard your dad is remarried and living in Albuquerque." Before Melanie could respond, she added, "The woman who was renting this place, Lucinda, was a major gossip."

"Tucson, actually," Melanie corrected. "They've been married a little over a year now." She considered adding, *They're good for each other*, or *They're very happy together* but was worried either would be taken as the evidence that Vinnie seemed to be looking for, that their dad hadn't loved their mom enough to remain a widower. "So you guys have still been coming up here every summer?"

"Almost every summer. It's been hard to get the whole gang together the last few years. It's been pretty scattered—Beau and his wife one week, Jillian and her girlfriends another. Stephen has been coming up in the winters to get some writing done. This summer it's been mostly me and Marie—my partner's—family. I think you met them at the Memorial Day cookout." Her voice was all studied nonchalance, as if daring Melanie to be shocked. But Melanie wasn't shocked, of course, because she had already known that and so much more about Vinnie.

"I did," she said, sitting on the bottom porch step. "They're very nice."

"Except for Marie's son, you mean." Vinnie fluidly sank onto the grass and sat cross-legged across from Melanie. "Nicholas is a bit of an ass. He doesn't really like to acknowledge that his mom and I are more than friends."

"Well, he certainly doesn't mind using your lake house, though, does he?" Melanie said, and Vinnie snorted with laughter. Her eyes widened in mischievous delight, and she looked like she was reappraising Melanie, finding something there that she hadn't before, something that she liked.

"When your mom and I were little girls, we used to imagine our futures. I was going to be a supermodel, the next Twiggy, and have eight kids—don't ask me how I planned to do both—and your mom was going to be a deep-sea diver and discover all these shipwrecks and hidden treasures."

"I wish she'd stuck with it." Melanie forced a small smile. "It would've been cool to have a treasure-hunting mom."

"Kind of hard to be a diver when you refuse to swim, though," Vinnie said matter-of-factly. "I understand why she gave it up, but I still wish she had found a way to come to terms with it. I knew she probably wouldn't ever be able to forgive me, but I wanted her to at least forgive herself."

Melanie sat very still, almost afraid to speak. *Is Vinnie hinting at the rift that had ended their friendship? But didn't Mom stop swimming as a result of the boy's drowning?* "Forgive herself for what?" she asked with her own studied nonchalance, but inside, her empty stomach was a jittery mess.

Vinnie trained her catlike eyes on Melanie as if she were trying to parse out how much Melanie already knew and how much she should tell her. Melanie tried to look calm and impartial—a trust-worthy confidante.

"My daughter's near drowning," Vinnie said finally.

"But why would my mom blame herself for that?" Melanie asked as she remembered the statue-like way her mom had watched as Jilly had been pulled out of the lake, the way her fist had been pressed against her mouth as if holding back a scream.

Vinnie's shoulders were curling upward toward her ears, her arms hugging her chest. She looked like a little girl—like the version of Jilly Melanie remembered—rather than a middle-aged woman. "Because she wasn't there."

Melanie frowned. No, her mom hadn't been there. She had arrived well after Mr. Fletcher. But none of the adults had been. It wasn't like they had needed a babysitter or lifeguard. "But we were good swimmers," she said, "and mostly teenagers. We didn't need to be watched all the time."

"But she did watch you." Vinnie fingered the embroidered neck-line of her tunic. "Didn't you know that? There was an accident when we were teenagers, a drowning when Christine was a lifeguard on duty. So whenever you girls went swimming, she watched you like a hawk. You were never out of her sight. I think she would have been happiest if she could have convinced you to wear life jackets the whole summer. As much as she and I meant to each other," she said, eyeing Melanie suddenly as if challenging her, "you girls meant even more."

Melanie scanned her memory for an overprotective mom hovering on the dock as they splashed on their wakeboards, biting her nails as they carelessly pushed each other off the raft. But her brain couldn't dredge up the image. All she could picture were her mom's athletic legs and khaki shorts as she bent over Melanie to hand her a glass of lemonade, condensation dripping down the sides. Often she would sit in a lawn chair on the shore, immersed in a thick book. *Was she only pretending to read behind her sunglasses? Was she really sur-veying us the whole time, making sure another child didn't drown on her watch?*

So why wasn't my mom watching us that afternoon? she wanted to ask Vinnie. *Where was she?* But she was scared she already knew the answer.

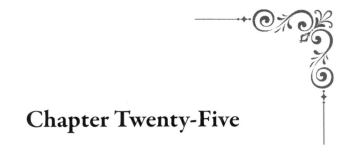

Chapter Twenty-Five

Kelsey watched her boss's face turn from enthusiastic to concerned to despairing. "Part-time?" Beth echoed. "Only two to three days a week?"

"Until at least February," Kelsey said. "That way I can still help you train my replacement before I need to go." She had done the math and decided an April opening would be manageable for the Montclare Inn. But that meant she'd need significantly more time during regular business hours to meet with contractors and Josh's brother, the accountant. She thought if she tightened her belt a little—no more coffee and doughnuts or lunches from Soup, Sandwiches, and Such, no more expensive cuts of meat or exotic vegetables from the grocery store—she and Sprocket could get by on her part-time salary and savings until the bed-and-breakfast started making a profit. Which, hopefully—oh God, she didn't like thinking about what would happen if the B and B was a total flop—she would never be able to face Melanie again—it would.

"I am going to miss you so much," Beth said, shuffling around her desk to wrap Kelsey in a hug.

"I'm not leaving yet!" Kelsey said, laughing, but secretly, she was pleased by Beth's reaction. Her boss's hug felt warm and maternal, and Kelsey let herself relax into it, resting her chin on Beth's shoulder.

"At least it's for a good reason. Your own bed-and-breakfast? I always knew you were going places."

ANDREA LOCHEN

When she left Beth's office, she could hear Taylor up front, arguing with someone—at least as argumentative as sweet Taylor ever sounded. "She's in a meeting right now," Taylor said helplessly.

"Can't you just let her know I'm here? I've only got five minutes, and she's going to be pissed if she thinks I blew her off."

Leona. The teenager's black hair was streaked with blue, and she was wearing a maroon ruffled skirt with dangling garters that looked like something a dominatrix would don. Kelsey stood in the hallway, watching her for several moments. Her urge to slap the girl hadn't gone away.

"Leona?" She marched toward the reception desk. "Do you have a second to talk? Great." Before the teenager could protest, Kelsey was ushering her outside. It was a beautiful day, the sky the same aquamarine as a swimming pool, and her future felt just as blindingly bright and clear with the prospect of the bed-and-breakfast and her mom being restored to her. She had all but given her resignation, and besides, it wasn't as if Beth would fire her. She needed her. So Kelsey had nothing to lose by speaking her mind.

"Your mom is one of the kindest women I know," she started. "And you are making her life a living hell."

Leona's eyeliner-enhanced eyes bugged out at her. "Really? Little Miss Employee of the Month is going to give me a lecture? Why don't you just stay the hell out of it? Go and be the model employee, the daughter my mom wishes she had, somewhere else."

Kelsey swallowed hard. Leona's retort sounded eerily familiar, like something Kelsey would have said to her mom or sister in her teenage years and early twenties. "I am far from perfect," she said softly. "I am always screwing up and letting people down. And when I was your age, I was a total bitch to my mom, then she died unexpectedly, and I never got to apologize and let her know how much I loved her." It was less painful to admit when she knew that the opportunity to put things right was just around the corner.

Leona scuffed her knee-high combat boots against the sidewalk as if she were bored. "Well, I'm sorry, but I don't see how your sob story relates to me and my mom."

"You've got to grow up, Leona. Learn from my mistakes. Your mom doesn't want *me* as her daughter. She wants *you*. She loves you despite all your attention-seeking crazy-ass behavior." Unexpectedly, a stinging pressure built behind Kelsey's eyes, like she was going to cry, because it was true, not just for Beth and Leona but for Kelsey and her mom too. Her mom hadn't wanted her to be a clone of Melanie after all. She had loved Kelsey for herself. She had only wanted Kelsey to be safe, healthy, and happy.

"So stop with the self-destruction," Kelsey said. "Stop running amok just to get your mom's attention. You already have it. But if you keep wearing her down, you might lose it one day. Then you'll miss out on the adult mother-daughter relationship that I would give any-thing to have right now." *Please, please, please*, she thought. *Please let me have that with my mom. Give her back to me.*

Leona blew her long bangs out of her eyes and scowled. "Gee. Thanks a bunch, Dr. Phil." She walked back inside, but Kelsey thought that maybe, just maybe, she had gotten through to Leona.

Climbing into her car, she noticed Josh's pick-up truck parked at the end of the row. *He's working right now? Why didn't he come by to say hello when I stopped in to talk to Beth?* Worry nagged at her as she suddenly realized she hadn't talked to him for almost two days, not since the night of the disastrous dinner at the lake house when she'd gone missing for hours, leaving him to finally give up on her and drive himself home alone. She had texted him a brief apology the next day, and he'd replied, *That's okay*, but their exchange had ended there. She had been so busy squaring everything away with Charlene and making logistical plans for the bed-and-breakfast, so distracted by the contemplation of her mom's possible return, that she hadn't even spared a moment's notice for the boy she thought she just might be falling in love with. She was a hideous excuse for a human being.

She marched back into Green Valley Pet Lodge, right past Taylor, Leona, Beth, and a couple of customers who were dropping off their dogs, and straight to Pooch Place, where Josh wasn't hard to find. He was in the back kitchen, measuring out cups of dry kibble into carefully labeled bowls.

"Hey," she said, hoping that he would look up at her with his lovable, lopsided grin and all would instantly be forgiven.

But he barely lifted his eyes from the twenty-five-pound bag of dog food he was pouring. "Hey."

"I just wanted to tell you again how sorry I am about Sunday night." She took a few hesitant steps into the room. "Melanie and I really got into it, and we lost track of time. When I realized how late it was and that you had already left, I felt awful," she said. "But the good news is that I persuaded her not to sell the house. She's going to let me have a shot at this whole bed-and-breakfast thing." She paused for his reaction, for a smile, for a congratulations, for *anything*, but none came. "So because of that, yesterday and today have been such a whirlwind with canceling the listing with our realtor and telling Beth I'd like to cut back to working part-time while I prepare for the B and B's opening—" Still no reaction. "That I didn't even realize I had never called you to properly explain. I know there's no excuse for my rudeness, but please forgive me and know how sorry I am. I didn't intend to make you feel like you didn't matter to me, if that's how you felt."

"It's okay," Josh said flatly. He returned the large bag of dog food to a cubby and reached for a small pink bag for dogs with food allergies.

"Are you sure?" she asked, advancing to the kitchen island where he stood. "Because you don't seem... okay with it." His indifference was starting to alarm her. *Did I simply imagine the click between us?*

No, she couldn't have—it was the sweetest, most earnest thing she had felt with a man in years. There had to be more to his reaction that she didn't understand. "Is there something I can do to make it up to you?"

He finally looked up, his sunburst eyes unreadable behind his glasses. "Not really. In fact, it's probably good Sunday night happened. It opened my eyes to how we both feel about each other."

"What do you mean?" she asked warily.

He turned his back to open a tin of cat food with the electric can opener. When the mechanical whirring stopped, he said at last, "I guess I hadn't realized quite to what extent, but I'd fallen for you ages ago, and it was always clear to me that you didn't feel the same way. So the last few weeks have been great and all, but I couldn't help wondering, why now? What changed? Why were you suddenly seeing me in this new light? But now I know it wasn't the same for you. That you weren't really seeing me in the same light I see you. I'm just a guy you work with. I'm just someone to occasionally have fun with, not serious-boyfriend material."

His mask of indifference had slipped and revealed how dejected he really was. His long-limbed body looked large and out of place in the tiny, fluorescent-lit kitchen. She wanted to step around the butcher-block island and embrace him, but she felt too unsure of herself and unsure of what his reaction would be. Instead, she leaned against the counter so that they were directly across from each other. Their eyes met.

"I don't just see you as occasional fun, Josh," she started. "I mean, it's been a lot of fun—don't get me wrong—but it's more than that. The light, the click, whatever you want to call it, it's real for me too. And I'm sorry it's taken me so fricking long, but I've been having some help from my sister lately, if you can believe it, in recognizing what I should have seen a long time ago."

"And what is that?" Josh asked, a skeptical tilt to his head, a reluctant hopefulness in his eyes.

Heart racing, she skirted around the island and put her hands on his arms. They felt strong and reliable under her fingertips, like the kind of arms she could fall asleep in at night. "You are serious-boyfriend material," she said. "And we're perfect for each other."

The reluctance in his eyes melted into understanding. In one swift motion, he had scooped her up and set her down on the kitchen island, right next to the open bag of dog kibble and a bowl of slimy cat food. He stood gravely in front of her, so intensely serious that she felt a little weak in the knees, so she wrapped her legs around his waist to steady them.

"I'm so glad to hear you say that, K. K.," he said and bent down to kiss her.

She felt like dissolving at the touch of his warm body pressed against hers, his large hands on her back, and the gentle graze of his mouth against hers. She was just starting to wonder if they could lie down on the kitchen island without anyone walking in and noticing them making out, or getting any of the cat food in her hair, for that matter, when Josh pulled away.

"And I'm so, so happy to hear about you and Melanie agreeing not to sell the lake house. You're going to be your own boss. A small-business owner. Congrats. That's so wonderful."

"Thanks," she said, pulling him back to her and squeezing her legs more tightly around him. "And what do you think about this other idea I've been toying with? What if I made the Montclare Inn a pet-friendly B and B?" She planted a quick kiss on his lips, inadvertently preventing his reply. "That way, I can merge my love of animals with my dream for the lake house. Guests could bring their dog or cat with them." She interrupted herself again to give him another kiss, longer and more lingering. "We can have an infinite supply of tennis balls on the dock and a jar of special homemade treats in the living room, watering stations everywhere and cushions and pet beds in front of the fireplace..." She drifted off as Josh took the reins and kissed her so deeply that she totally gave up on her train of thought and gave in to the moment instead.

Chapter Twenty-Six

Kelsey couldn't believe her sister and brother-in-law were leaving in the morning. She understood that Ben needed to get back to the pharmacy and Melanie needed to start prepping for the fall semester, and really, since they weren't selling the house, they had no real reason to be here. But a small part of her had hoped they might stick around and help her with the initial legwork for the bed-and-breakfast, although she had repeatedly insisted that she didn't need Melanie's help. Their driving back to Ohio to return to their own lives while she grappled with the giant project of the lake house made her feel shaky and entirely out of her depth. And a large part of her couldn't comprehend how they could just up and leave Wisconsin when any day, maybe even minute, their mom could come walking through the front door.

It was because they didn't believe the time-traveling note would work its magic, that Melanie and Kelsey's vague, veiled medical recommendations wouldn't save their mom from her sealed fate. And Kelsey couldn't blame them too much, either, because she was starting to lose heart as well. It had been five days since they had left the letter in the closet, and so far, they'd received no reply from Christine and seen no other discernable changes. *How long is it going to take? And how would we know when and if anything happened?* She tried to busy herself with her shifts at the pet lodge, the complicated paperwork she needed to file for her business license, and Harry Potter movie marathons with Josh, his cat, Tumnus, and Sprocket—who amazingly tolerated each other—but it was all she could really think about.

Melanie had suggested Kelsey, Josh, and Sprocket come over for "the mother of all bonfires," as she put it, which sounded like the perfect distraction and a fitting farewell. They would have hot dogs, s'mores, Nutella pudgy pies, and bacon wrapped around a stick. But Josh was taking a woodworking class that he couldn't miss, and the weather wasn't cooperating—it was raining sideways and pinging off the windows—so it was just the three of them sitting around the kitchen table, eating frozen pizza, and playing B. S. instead. Sprocket was lying hopefully under the table. Kelsey suspected that Melanie had already slipped him a few slices of pepperoni.

"Two jacks," Kelsey said, slapping two facedown cards onto the discard pile.

"Bullshit!" Melanie crowed, turning them over, and she was right, of course, as she had been right the last three times. Kelsey liked to think she was a perfectly adequate liar until she was around Melanie, who could read her like an open book.

"You suck," Kelsey said, scooping up the entire pile and adding it to her hand. She already had over half of the deck and was struggling to organize it. Soon she wouldn't have to lie, because she'd have multiples of everything.

Ben made a sympathetic face at her. He was a terrible liar too. "Maybe we should play crazy eights," he said.

"I think you need at least four players for that." Melanie wiped the pizza grease off her fingers and solemnly laid down a card. "One queen."

"Are you sure you guys don't want to take the patio table with you?" Kelsey asked for probably the fourth time that evening. "Melanie, you were the one to refinish it, after all. I can easily buy a new table."

"Thanks, Kels, but I think it belongs on the porch with that view. Consider it my housewarming gift."

It was hard not to think of those other rainy days when they had chowed down on popcorn and played seventies board games with their mom. A wave of nostalgia and sadness swept over Kelsey. Though she was tremendously glad they weren't selling the house, and that even her dad was reluctantly on board with the B and B, she couldn't help wondering if it was more the people and memories inside it that she cherished and wanted to preserve rather than the house itself. *When all of the people are gone, when I'm alone and caring for overnight guests, will it still be as special to me?*

She could almost hear her mom's voice as the rain buffeted the house and Melanie and Ben teased each other. *Kels-Bels, you need to find what makes you happy, no matter what that is.*

I'm trying, Mom, she thought. *I'm so scared I won't be any good at this and I'll fail, and I don't know for sure if it will make me happy, but at least I'm trying.*

Did you try? she couldn't help wondering. *Or did you just resign yourself to what you thought was your fate?*

She was surprised when Melanie and Ben turned in early for the night, only ten thirty, explaining they were planning to pack up and leave at five in the morning for the nine-hour drive. Melanie insisted Kelsey didn't need to get up to see them off, but the thought of waking up alone in the large house was too much for Kelsey, so she said she wouldn't dream of sleeping in. She took Sprocket out to go potty one more time then retreated to Melanie's old bedroom. She wasn't even remotely tired, though, so she grabbed her iPad and started scrolling through pictures of bed-and-breakfast interiors, bookmarking her favorites and steadfastly ignoring the door behind the tapestry, which she had already checked for a note two hours ago—still empty—while Sprocket dozed at her feet.

A quiet knock on her door came at midnight.

"Come in," Kelsey called softly.

"You're still up?" Melanie rubbed her eyes against the bright light. She was wearing a pink camisole and gray cotton shorts.

"Apparently. Here, let me show you these lampshades. Don't you think something like these would look perfect in the living room?"

Melanie sat down on the edge of the bed and looked over Kelsey's shoulder. "So you're going for a Victorian-era look? If so, I think they're perfect."

"Yeah, I wanted it to look reminiscent of when the house was first built."

"You should hit some rummage sales and flea markets. I know there isn't much around here, but Cleveland and Toledo have some great antique malls. You should totally come visit me sometime, and we'll go antiquing."

Kelsey set the iPad down, trying not to think about how much more fun it would be to hunt for vintage lampshades with a companion, even one as exasperating as Melanie. Maybe Josh would go with her. He'd already offered to build a pedestal-foot end table for the living room, and she couldn't wait to see how it would turn out. The headboard he was making for his niece was stunning.

"Yeah, that would be fun," she said, but she was already calculating the cost of her plane ticket and any shipping costs for antiques she purchased to send back to Wisconsin. Sprocket let out a loud, rumbling snore worthy of an old man.

"Aw, I'm going to miss my little jellybean," Melanie said, stroking his side. She laughed when Kelsey shot her a look. "And you, too, of course! I thought that was implied. These last few weeks have been the most fun I've had with you since we were in elementary school, riding bikes around our cul-de-sac. When I didn't feel like killing you, that is."

"The feeling's mutual." Kelsey folded the sheet down. Though she hated to admit it, she would also miss her aggravating perfectionist of a sister. "I like to think that Mom had something to do with that, that she was using the house to bring us closer together."

"I think you're right." Melanie leaned over to rest her cheek on Sprocket's fur. He stirred a little and let out another snore. "I'm sorry we haven't heard back from Mom yet. I know you had your hopes pinned on that letter, but remember, it probably caught her off guard. It's a lot to digest, you know, the implication that you're going to die unexpectedly in your fifties. She might still be considering how to reply to us. I don't think it's quite over yet."

"Maybe." Or maybe the letter hadn't reached her in time. Or maybe she hadn't taken them seriously. Maybe she had planned to follow their advice but had forgotten the date because it was so far in the future.

Melanie gave Kelsey a sisterly shove so she could occupy more space on the bed. "I talked to Mrs. Fletcher the other day."

"Really?" Kelsey still hadn't seen their old neighbor, but in her mind's eye, Mrs. Fletcher looked the same as she had in her early forties, sporting a strapless sundress, a turquoise necklace, and matching earrings, only with a shocking head of platinum hair.

"Yeah, she came over to lend us her watering can. I guess she's on the Lake Indigo Neighbors Association, and she's in favor of the bed-and-breakfast, although some of the other members aren't."

"Huh. I had no idea there even *was* a neighborhood association. Hopefully they won't cause any trouble for me." A row of additional hurdles materialized before Kelsey's eyes.

"I wouldn't worry about it. Vinnie's on your side, and she seems like she can be pretty persuasive." Melanie gave Sprocket one last pat and sat up. "She said something else that I just can't get out of my head, though. About Mom and the day Jilly almost drowned."

As Melanie described the conversation to her, Kelsey lay back against her pillow and tried to remember that day in as much detail as possible. But what she remembered most was the elaborate game of Sharks they'd all been playing, and when she noticed Jilly was no longer there, Kelsey had simply assumed someone had tagged the younger girl out and she was being a baby about it as usual and had swum back to shore. But then Beau had started diving under the water, and it wasn't even his turn to be a shark. Whenever he surfaced, he screamed, "Jilly!" in one breath, then "Mom! Dad! Help!" in the next, and Kelsey had plunged under the water to help too. It was the first time she had ever dove under with her eyes wide open. Everything was a fuzzy blue green. Tiny fish and their shadows darted around her, but she saw no sign of Jilly.

"We should go inside the time portal," she suggested. "Maybe it will take us back to that day and we can find out why Mom blamed herself."

Melanie rolled her eyes. "What are the odds that it's the correct year right now, let alone the correct day and exact moment? One in a thousand? A hundred thousand? A million?"

Kelsey pushed her sister off the bed so she could stand up, and Melanie groaned in annoyance. "I don't know. Maybe pretty good. The house has been showing us important moments all along, hasn't it? And this seems pretty major. It's worth a try, at least."

"I just don't know if I even want to relive that again."

"But it seems like you're reliving it, anyway," Kelsey pointed out. "You just admitted you can't stop thinking about it. Maybe this will put it to rest. Besides, this is most likely your last chance to go in. Our last chance, for that matter, if it is the last summer and Mom's memories end like we think they might." She was laying it on thick, but as soon as she'd mentioned the possibility of going into the closet, she knew somehow that it was the right thing to do. It was like the house wanted them to, like the tapestry was calling to them. The deep-blue background looked even richer than usual, and the four birds' beady eyes were shiny and bright, as if they were watching them.

Melanie threw up her hands. "All right. But I'm only going inside so that we can say goodbye."

Kelsey tried to swallow her disappointment as she confirmed, for what felt like the hundredth time, that the bench was still empty of any correspondence from their mom.

TWO SETS OF FEET WERE pounding up the stairs, and the sound of giggles reached them. *Young Melanie and me?*

"This is definitely our last summer here," Melanie said, pointing to a worn copy of *To Kill a Mockingbird* on her desk.

Kelsey peered into the hallway. A coppery head of hair emerged over the newel post, inch by inch, like a mermaid breaking the water's surface. Her mom's curly head wasn't far behind. Vinnie was wearing a floral-patterned skirt, and Christine's hand was tucked into the back of the waistband. *Oh crap*, Kelsey thought, turning to watch her sister's equally dismayed expression. *What are we walking in on?*

"The kids," their mom said breathlessly as they reached the doorway of the master bedroom.

"We'll lock the door," Vinnie said, and the next second, they were both inside and the door was closing. A lock clicked.

Kelsey turned to find her sister heading resolutely for the closet. "Where are you going?"

"Not sticking around to watch Mom have an affair."

Kelsey ducked her head to look out the window. "But, Melanie, I think this is it! Look!" Outside, kids were splashing around the swimming raft. She could just make out Melanie in her green Hawaiian-print bikini standing on the raft next to Stephen, the afternoon sun illuminating them. "We're playing Sharks!"

"It doesn't matter anymore. We already know the one missing piece of the puzzle—that Mom wasn't there because she was with Vinnie. I'd already suspected as much, but if I'd had any doubt..."

Melanie tugged her fallen camisole strap back up on her shoulder, looking forlorn. "We already know the rest of the story. What else is there to see? Let's just stop while we're ahead and go."

"But we're *not* ahead."

Jilly's hot-pink swimsuit was as visible as a red flag. Kelsey tried to follow her every movement, but it was like watching ants scurrying at a picnic. She observed herself shoving Stephen off the raft and triumphantly pumping her arms into the air. And at just that moment, she saw something that none of them had seen the first time.

Jilly's head, as small and shiny as a penny from where Kelsey was standing, was in the water, at the edge of the raft. As Stephen fell off and Beau attempted to climb on the opposite side, the raft rocked violently upward then crashed over Jilly, shoving her down with all its wooden weight.

"Oh God! I saw it! Jilly just went under!"

Melanie's hands were suddenly on the windowsill, too, pushing Kelsey to the side.

"It wasn't a rock like we all thought. It was the raft!" She wanted to run downstairs and dive into the lake, but she knew it would be useless. She would glide over the surface, ghostlike, unable to penetrate the depths, unable to grab Jilly and heave her upward. Still, her muscles twitched with potential energy. She knew it would all work out in the end—Beau would notice and call for help any second, and Mr. Fletcher would save his daughter—but it was still unbearable to watch, thinking of the slim seven-year-old sinking to the lake's bottom like a stone.

"Why is it taking us so long to notice?" Melanie asked anxiously. "It's got to have been minutes already!"

"Jilly?" Beau called uncertainly, and Kelsey felt the tension in her neck and shoulders loosen a little. She watched herself join Beau as he plunged below the surface. Stephen and Melanie caught on eventually, too, and all four of them were disappearing and popping up like a group of seal pups. "Help!" Beau screamed as he thrashed toward the shore. "Help! Mom! Dad! It's Jilly!"

In the room next door, something made a loud thump. There were muffled noises and heavy, hurried footsteps, then the door burst open, hitting the wall with such force that it bounced back. Kelsey ran to watch her mom and Vinnie leave the room. They were both fully clothed, but their faces were flushed, their hair messy. Christine hurtled down first, the fastest Kelsey had ever seen her move.

In her haste, Vinnie nearly stumbled and fell. "Shit," she said, catching herself on the banister, and the curse seemed to open a floodgate. "Shit, shit, fuck!"

Kelsey ran down the steps behind them. They all reached the bottom of the stairs and snaked through the hallway to the kitchen.

"We did this!" Christine said, her eyes wild and frantic. "*You* did!"

"No." Vinnie shook her head and groped for the kitchen doorframe to pull herself through.

"You distracted me, just like at Harris Beach. You make me selfish and reckless, and I hate myself. I already have blood on my hands, Vinnie. If Jilly—"

"Shut up. Shut up." Vinnie grabbed Christine roughly by the shoulders as they stumbled out onto the wraparound porch together. "She's going to be okay."

Kelsey followed them to the sandy shoreline, where a knot of solemn kids, she and Melanie among them, was watching Mr. Fletcher perform CPR. Melanie fell into step beside her, her jaw set.

"My baby," Vinnie cried as she fell to her knees beside Jilly's abnormally pale body, but it was Christine who took over for Lance, showing him how to properly compress the center of his daughter's chest with the heel of her hand.

"Like this," she said. "Has anyone called 911?" When Lance answered in the affirmative, she switched places with him again and felt

Jilly's pulse. "The breaths are really important right now because we don't know how long she's been without oxygen."

Kelsey didn't remember her mom being such an active part of Jilly's resuscitation. In her mind, Mr. Fletcher had been the hero, the one who'd fished his daughter out of the lake, the one who'd done mouth-to-mouth and kept the oxygen circulating to her cells. But she could see that her mom's lifeguard training and the CPR certification she kept current every year for her elementary school job had probably saved Jilly from dying or being brain damaged. The ambulance bounced up the gravel driveway. Thank God it was the nineties and nearby Concord now had a fire department and ambulance service.

"Why don't I remember Mom helping with the CPR?" Kelsey whispered to her sister, who was fidgeting beside her.

"I didn't either," Melanie admitted. "So weird."

"Over here! Over here!" Mr. Fletcher boomed in his TV weatherman voice. He even stopped the compressions to wave both his hands at them, and while he did, Christine immediately took over.

Maybe that was why. Lance looked the part of the hero, with his sodden clothes and hysterics, while their mom, composed and ordinary in a middle-aged mom way, blended in until she was nearly invisible. She stepped back as the paramedics assessed Jilly and started ventilating her, but she stayed there, hovering on the periphery, watching and listening with her hands clasped as if in prayer, until they had loaded the girl on an orange backboard, a C-collar in place, and wheeled the cot up to their ambulance. Vinnie hurried alongside them, her hand on Jilly's cheek, quietly sobbing.

With the paramedics and cot gone, Kelsey had a clear view of her mom. She raised her eyes from the grass where Jilly had been lying and seemed to stare directly at her.

"Is Mom looking at us?" Kelsey asked, her breath catching in her throat.

"She is," Melanie said. She motioned over her shoulder, where their fourteen- and twelve-year-old selves were standing directly behind them.

Their mom's pale-blue eyes were windows into all the guilt and anguish she was feeling, and Kelsey understood why. But she also had tremendous love in her eyes. It was a look that told Kelsey that their mom would swim across the lake and back as many times as needed to save their lives, that she would sooner stop breathing than let one of them die. She was choosing them.

"Is Jilly going to be okay?" twelve-year-old Kelsey asked with a trembling lip, and their mom stepped across the distance to pull them both against her body. She held them and swayed as if they were much younger children. And when she glanced up to notice Beau and Stephen standing alone and in shock, their father distracted and adrift in his grief, she pulled them into the embrace too.

A SHEET OF YELLOW PAPER was lying on the floor under the bench when they got back to the closet. *Did it appear out of thin air while we were gone? Or was it there all along, and we simply missed it?* It was folded in half, and just by looking at it, Kelsey could tell it was probably not the response she had been hoping for.

Dear Girls,

So now you know my deepest regret and why we needed to leave Lake Indigo. My unfaithfulness to your father was so selfish and negligent that a child almost died as a result. For once, I am grateful for the gap in years between us so that I don't have to face the immediacy of my sweet daughters learning this horrible truth. That will have to wait until another day in my future, when you are older and more experienced in all the ways people can hurt each other and let each other down. You are more experienced now, I assume? I'm sorry that I had to be the one to teach you this lesson.

I'm sorry also that I didn't have the nerve to tell you this in person. It's somehow easier for me to express myself in pen and paper, when you are nothing more than figments of my imagination. Strong, independent women, no doubt, who like to garden and read and maybe won't be such harsh judges of my infidelity as the real versions of you I would have to sit down with one day and look in the eye. But no matter how harshly you judge me, rest assured you won't be able to condemn me as much as I have already condemned myself.

There is no possible excuse for the hurtful choice I made. Loneliness? Too many years of self-denial? Fear of the days of drudgery blurring into each other and waking up one day to find I had taken no risks and left no tangible mark? I once might have claimed love as an excuse, but it seems like the paltry defense of a teenager, not a middle-aged woman who should know better.

Thank God Jilly is going to make a full recovery, I hear. But in my darkest moments, I think about how it could've gone so differently. It could have been either one of you. My recklessness could have endangered you, and that is the one thing I will never be able to forgive myself for.

I know you told me this might be our last communication inside this room, and you probably want me to give you some reassurance that I will follow the advice of your last letter. Although at this point, I can't see myself deserving the divine intervention of angels from the future when I have been so careless with the lives of others, I want you to know that I will see my doctor and try to express the concerns you have for me on May 1, 2015. Not because I think I merit any special help after all of the mistakes I've made in my life so far, but because I love you girls so, and I'm hoping you will have the chance to forgive me one day.

Love,
Mom

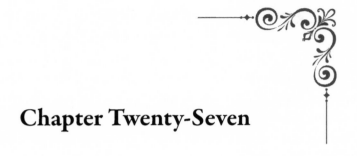

Chapter Twenty-Seven

"Did Mom drive Beau and Stephen to the hospital that night, or did Dad?" Kelsey asked, pushing her feet off the floor to rock the porch swing.

Melanie closed her eyes briefly and tried to remember. "Dad did, I think. He had just arrived for the weekend and hadn't eaten any dinner yet, but when he mentioned that to Mom, she just gave him a look. She'd been keeping us busy baking chocolate chip cookies that afternoon, remember? Until we heard news that Jilly was breathing on her own again and had woken up."

"Mom didn't want to see Vinnie," Kelsey said. "That's why she had Dad drive them." She broke a square of Hershey's chocolate in half and popped it in her mouth.

They had raided the bonfire supplies and had the bag of marshmallows, the jar of Nutella, the box of graham crackers, and the chocolate bars between them on the swing. Like soldiers recovering from the shock of the battlefield, they needed something sugary to fortify them. It was three in the morning, and the lake was the color of grape jelly. The rain had stopped, but the sky was still a thick canopy of clouds.

"You're probably right." Melanie rubbed her forehead, thinking of Lavinia's admission. *I knew she probably wouldn't ever be able to forgive me, but I wanted her to at least forgive herself.* She felt cold, even though the night air was humid and in the seventies. The purple afghan had slipped off her bare shoulders, so she picked it back up and rearranged it across her lap. "I wonder if they ever talked again. I think we left the next week. It was almost the end of the season, anyway."

She had cycled through all the negative emotions she was capable of and now felt mostly deadened. Yes, her mom might have been sleeping with Vinnie while her dad was away, but that wasn't much of a surprise given what she and Kelsey had seen on their other trips into the time portal. Yes, her mom had probably been dissatisfied and bored with her role of wife and mother and reading specialist. Yes, her mom had a whole other existence separate from them that they had never been privy to. But what surprised her the most, what cut her to the quick, was the blame and loathing her mom had carried with her, probably up until her death.

You distracted me, just like at Harris Beach. You make me selfish and reckless, and I hate myself. I already have blood on my hands, her mom had practically shouted at Vinnie.

The two drowning incidences were a horrible, horrible coincidence that her mom had read meaning into that hadn't been there. Harris Beach had been overcrowded, and the little boy's death had been a tragic accident. It hadn't been her fault. It hadn't been Vinnie's fault either. And Jilly's near drowning also had nothing to do with them. Jilly was an excellent swimmer and had blown through all the swimming levels at the Fletchers' country club, where she had taken private lessons. As much as it upset her to think where her mom and Vinnie had been at the time, Melanie didn't find them negligent for stepping away. And she honestly didn't think her mom sitting in her lawn chair, watching and hovering, would've changed Jilly's outcome, anyway.

But her mom had seen herself and her entanglement with Vinnie as responsible for the accidents. Maybe she saw them as her punishment for her attraction to Vinnie or her punishment for her infidelity. *But no matter how harshly you judge me, rest assured you won't be able to condemn me as much as I have already condemned myself.* She had carried that culpability with her like Atlas with the weight of the world on her back and never set it down. It made Melanie want to cry, thinking of her good-hearted mom, continually censuring herself.

The weight of culpability was one she was all too familiar with. It was sitting on her shoulders right at that moment, no matter how hard she tried to shake it, the way she blamed herself for her inability to conceive and for not being able to keep her baby alive. She knew she needed to set it down and have mercy on herself the way her mom hadn't been able to.

She leaned against the porch swing, and the rose bushes she and Ben had planted caught her eye. Speckled by raindrops, the blooms looked like they were covered in tiny diamonds. The orangey-peach of their baby's roses made her think of something else orange, something that was nagging at her, but her exhausted brain couldn't quite place it.

"Do you think we should try to write Mom a reply quickly?" Kelsey asked hopefully. She handed Melanie the rest of her chocolate bar. "I mean, she didn't cause Jilly to drown. She saved her life. She deserves to know that, don't you think? Aren't you glad we went inside the portal and saw that?"

Melanie nodded, her weariness making it difficult to move, let alone eat any more chocolate. "I really am. But something tells me that Mom won't be back in the closet to get any more of our notes."

"Maybe she won't need to." Kelsey raised her eyebrows, and her blue eyes were as wide and trusting as an infant's. "What year do you think it is right now in her parallel time? Maybe it's approaching the date of her doctor's appointment, and we'll be able to tell her *in person* that we forgive her and she should forgive herself."

"Yes, maybe," Melanie agreed reluctantly and patted her sister on the leg. "But we just might have to content ourselves with the idea

that the time portal was Mom's one last gift to us and she isn't coming back. But even if our warning doesn't prevent her death, at least
we still had the chance to try. And she knows we tried. That we did
everything in our power to help her."

"Not *everything* in our power." Kelsey's brow creased as she
stared into her lap. "If only there was some way for me to leave a note
for *my* younger self. I could warn myself to cancel my fricking hair
appointment and not leave Mom's side for a second that day."

"Oh, Kelsey." Melanie reached out, grabbed her sister's hand, and
squeezed. Perhaps it was a trait that all the Montclare women inherited: intense self-blame for things that were wildly out of their control. "You are not responsible for Mom's death. Do you understand
me? It was a massive blood clot. It killed her within minutes. There
was nothing you could have done. Can you repeat that after me? 'I
am not responsible.'"

"I am not responsible," Kelsey repeated, but her expression still
looked so doleful that Melanie gave her hand another harder
squeeze.

"Well, that's a start. But now you need to work on believing it."
She closed her eyes as Kelsey continued to rock the porch swing. It
was only about an hour away from the time that she and Ben had
planned to get up to leave for Ohio. *Should I even bother trying to get
some sleep?* She thought about her mom, standing there on the wraparound porch, looking down at them and smiling broadly as they
built the bonfire, her curls tied back and tamed with a pretty black
ribbon. Suddenly, she jolted upright as if she were falling, startling
Kelsey beside her.

"Oh my God, Kels! The orange toothbrush! The cardigan! The
black ribbon! It was Mom." The details were winging into place before her eyes.

"What are you talking about? Of course it was Mom who moved
the toothbrush. I thought we had already decided that."

Melanie leaned toward her sister. "Do you remember the night we saw ourselves as little kids in the nursery? The night of the party? Just as we came upstairs, someone was leaving our room. I assumed it was Grandma Dot because she was older, and we had just seen Mom downstairs. But even then, I thought it was kind of out of character that she was checking on us because she was never an affectionate grandma. And I was right. It wasn't Grandma Dot. It was an older version of Mom. Time traveling. She was wearing the cream-colored cardigan from the closet, but I didn't recognize it at first. And her hair was tied back in a black ribbon."

Kelsey froze. "So that was the night your toothbrush got snatched? Then it reappeared—"

"The night we had our family bonfire. When you and I got locked out of the time portal because Mom was time traveling. She was going back in time to watch us sleep, Kelsey!"

Her head was filled with the memories of them fast asleep—with rosy cheeks, open mouths, and messy hair. Of all the places their mom could have been in that moment—at the boathouse, watching herself smoke with Vinnie, shadowing her husband or other party guests, even spending a little time with her deceased dad, she had chosen to sit with them in the stuffy, darkened room, to watch them peacefully inhaling and exhaling. And when she had returned to her present—Melanie remembered how content her mom had looked to be rejoining her family, even if her daughters were both ungrateful, moody adolescents instead of sweet, angelic babies. *Did you guys save me any marshmallows?* she had asked with a grin.

Oh, Mom, she thought, grinning as well. The clouds were thinning to reveal the sky was lightening into dawn. *You considered us a moment worth reliving.*

THE MONTCLARE INN WAS opening in two weeks, and Kelsey had invited everyone to stay at the bed-and-breakfast for the weekend to celebrate. Melanie and Ben's flight had just come in that morning, and her dad, stepmom, and stepsiblings would be arriving in a few hours. It was May, a full month later than Kelsey had hoped, but unexpected electrical wiring problems in the new suites upstairs had delayed her. With her website up and running, a steady stream of online reservations had started coming in. She was proud to announce she was already booked for the rest of May, all of June, and even one week in July.

"Oh no! You went with the strawberry pineapple bread?" Josh asked, carrying a stack of china plates into the living room. He set them down on the coffee table. "I guess I'll have to squeeze in a trip to the gym tonight." He'd been happily doing a lot of the taste testing of Kelsey's recipes but kept joking that he'd gained five pounds since they started dating. After one particularly delicious, postcoital breakfast in bed, he'd teased, "If you married me, K. K., I'd be the happiest, fattest man alive."

"I see what you mean," Ben said, reaching for a second piece. "It's awesome, Kelsey. Is this homemade butter too? It's so creamy."

"It sure is," she joked. "I milked the cows and churned it myself this morning. Just kidding. It's from a farm over in Concord. They're one of my main food vendors."

"I don't think so, Sprocket." Josh pushed the plate away from the coffee table's edge and away from the dog's curious nose. "Sorry, buddy."

Melanie hadn't touched her slice of bread yet and had also declined a mimosa, which Kelsey had never known her sister to turn down. *Is Melanie avoiding alcohol because she's pregnant?* The thought made Kelsey giddy. She scrutinized her sister for any other signs—a paunchy stomach, a tired-looking face, or larger breasts, but Melanie looked like her usual crisp, slim, pulled-together self. The only difference Kelsey could detect was a slightly more lovey-dovey behavior between her sister and Ben. They kept smiling and squeezing each other's hands when they thought no one was looking. *Will they be making an announcement later when Dad arrives?* She could hardly wait.

Everything was almost as perfect as she'd imagined it, except for one glaring absence among them. In the days and weeks after their last trip into the time portal, Kelsey had remained cautiously optimistic about the past rewriting itself in her mom's favor. Every phone call, every text, every unexpected knock on her door had made her heart pound with anticipation. But as the weeks turned into months, her anticipation had dulled, especially when she discovered one depressing morning that the time portal was no longer operational. Even the books and cardigan had disappeared from the bench. It was just an empty, useless closet, no matter how many times she stepped into and out of it. Just as Melanie had suspected, fate had had other plans for their mom.

Still, Kelsey couldn't help wondering where it had all gone wrong. Her memory didn't seem to have changed at all to accommodate a different version of her mom's death—as far as she could remember, and her dad and sister remembered, her mom had still died of a massive pulmonary embolism on May 8, 2015. *Why weren't the early ultrasound and blood thinners, assuming she went through with them as she promised, enough to save her?* It seemed it was going to be an unexplained mystery that Kelsey was going to have to somehow learn to live with.

She sipped her mimosa and watched Melanie appraise everything in the living room, from the art nouveau etched glass lamps she'd found at an estate sale to the dried lavender wreath over the mantel to the plaid pet bed and basket of dog toys in front of the fireplace to the wooden sign that read "Every Family Has a Story... Welcome to Ours." Beneath the sign were silver-framed wedding photographs of her great-grandparents, grandparents, parents, and even her sister and Ben—each a unique marriage with their own love story. She wondered if one day her wedding photo with Josh would hang beside the others on the wall.

Kelsey felt her stomach clench and reluctantly admitted to herself how much she wanted her older sister's approval. She loved the bed-and-breakfast, loved it more than she had ever loved anything else she had ever created or accomplished. She wanted Melanie to love it too.

"Your guests are going to adore this place, Kels-Bels," Melanie said at last, her eyes and cheeks luminous. "It is *so* beautiful, and I love how you incorporated little details from our family. I think they'd all be so proud. I know I am." She was biting her lower lip as if to prevent herself from crying. "And I know Mom would be too."

When Josh and Ben stepped outside to cut down a loose tree branch that had been worrying Kelsey, Melanie reached inside her carry-on bag and pulled out a beautifully wrapped rectangular present. "Just a little something to commemorate this special day," she said as she handed it to Kelsey.

Inside was a gorgeous mahogany box with a silver-plated square on its lid. Engraved in the silver square was a miniature rendering of the *Tree of Life*, birds and all. The box's interior was lined with a deep-blue velvet.

"I thought you could use it for special keepsakes," Melanie explained. "Photos. Little notes and letters. Maybe all the important things you wish you could share with Mom if she were still alive. Or if the time portal were still open to our communication with her."

"Oh, Mel," she said, leaning forward for a hug. "I absolutely love it. And I know just where I'm going to keep it."

Melanie's old bedroom looked very different since the wall between the girls' rooms had been torn down, but the tapestry was still hanging in its place of honor. Since Kelsey figured no harm could come to it now, she had had it professionally cleaned, and the wall hanging glowed with the brilliance of its original, freshly woven colors.

Melanie held the tapestry off to the side for her, and Kelsey unlocked the thin padlock she'd installed two months ago—unnecessary now, but it made her feel more secure about letting guests stay in the room. She hadn't looked inside the closet since she'd padlocked it. However, as she tried to pull the door forward, it seemed to catch on something. She tugged on the door again and still felt a slight resistance.

"What's that?" Melanie asked, pointing down. "Is something caught under the door?"

It was a faded wad of yellow paper. They goggled at each other. Kelsey stooped down to snatch it up. Her hands were shaking so badly she nearly dropped it. She unfurled the paper and smoothed it out as best she could. Unlike all the other letters their mom had written, it was dated, and surprisingly, it was only a few days before her death. She and Melanie bent their heads together and began to read.

Dear Girls,

I can only pray that this letter will make its way into your hands one day. I can't help believing that this shared time portal of ours will somehow find a means to reconnect us one final time. Ned and Lucinda were surprised to see me, but after I explained I was here to check their smoke detectors, they didn't bat an eye. (I know—smoke detectors? What a terrible lie!) But it gave me a chance to drop off this note.

By now, you know that I have passed away, and I hope you aren't missing me as much as I anticipate missing you. But what you don't know is that I did take your advice about seeing a doctor. In fact, I went to the doctor a few weeks earlier than you recommended because even though I hadn't felt the leg pain that you were worried about, I had been experiencing some headaches and nausea. So I went in.

Just as I'm sure you suspected, the ultrasound picked up a DVT in my left calf, and they wanted to put me on an anticoagulant medication. But that still didn't explain what had caused my blood clot or where my headaches and nausea were coming from, so my doctor ran some more tests. She even wanted to get an MRI of my brain, which I thought was unnecessary, but as I found out, I was wrong.

The MRI revealed I had pretty advanced brain cancer. Apparently cancer makes you more susceptible to blood clots, which had caused my DVT.

I know I've had to ask your forgiveness a lot in these last two letters, but please indulge me one more time. Please try to understand why I flushed the Warfarin the doctor prescribed for me down the toilet. Please understand why I never let on to any of you that I had just found out I was so sick.

It was all because of love, you see. Not the destructive, foolhardy love of teenagers but the genuine, heart-bursting, I-would-sooner-die-than-cause-you-a-moment's-pain-in-this-life-if-I-could-prevent-it love. But I know I can't prevent it. Because I'm pretty sure your letter meant that my days are now numbered, and it's only a matter of time until I cause you a great deal of pain.

One day, I hope your pain won't be so intense. It gives me great solace to know you two have each other, even if you don't quite know yet what a remarkable blessing that is.

Melanie, you are so thoughtful and sensitive, and you are always taking care of others. Don't forget to let yourself be taken care of sometimes too.

And, Kelsey, you are so warm and huge hearted, and you have the gift of making everyone else feel like they're the most special person in the room. Just don't forget that you are more extraordinary than you know.

Be good to yourselves and each other. Find what brings you joy, and hold on to it with both hands. You girls brought me so much joy.

Love always,

Mom

It was several minutes before Kelsey could claw her way back up to the surface from under the oppressive waves of shock and sorrow. But when she did, she felt her sister beside her, kneeling on the floor—*how did we get on the floor?*—bracing her, even as Melanie braced herself against Kelsey.

Their mom was there too. Although she wouldn't be coming back to them physically, as Kelsey had fervently prayed, she realized that her mom had never truly left them either. She was there in the words of her letter, in the worn wood floor beneath their knees, in the scarlet-breasted birds of the tapestry, and in the spring sunlight streaming through the window. She was in their hair follicles, deep in their blood, and rooted in their bones, and she always would be.

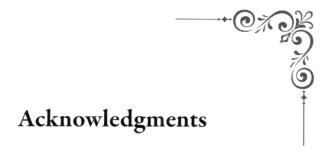

Acknowledgments

First and foremost, thank you to my readers, especially the ones who kept asking me, "When is your third book coming out?" in increasingly impatient tones. Your kind, persistent encouragement helped make this book possible, so thank you! You are some of my very favorite people.

Thank you to all of the talented folks who helped this book make its way into the world and into the hands of readers: my agent, Stephany Evans, and the wonderful team at Red Adept Publishing: Lynn McNamee, Jessica Anderegg, Susie Driver, and my fellow RAP author and mentor, Traci Borum. Your expertise all made *Versions of Her* a better novel. Thank you also to Streetlight Graphics for the gorgeous cover design.

To my dear friends and writers-in-arms who read early drafts of *Versions of Her* and gave me excellent constructive feedback—Rebecca Adams Wright, Kodi Scheer, and Kate Blakinger—thank you, thank you, thank you. You ladies rock as both writers and readers, and I honestly don't know what I would do without your insightful comments and enthusiastic support.

A whole bucket of thanks to my family, who supports me in innumerable ways. Special thanks to my dad, who gave me some pointers with seventies slang and also helped me out in all things Victorian houses. Thanks to my older sister, Steph, who is not Melanie (or Kelsey, for that matter!) but without whom I would never have been able to write about the deep, complex love between sisters. And thanks so much to my mom, who is one of my biggest fans and has hand-sold my books to every single person she has met in a grocery store check-out line since my first novel, *The Repeat Year*, came out in 2013. I love you guys so much.

And last but certainly not least, thank you to my husband, Matt. Your contributions to *Versions of Her* were integral, and your patient brainstorming with me made this a stronger, more heartfelt book. In the midst of our busy, wonderfully chaotic lives, thank you for helping me carve out the time to bring this book to life. To paraphrase Melanie (it's not cheating since I *did* write her, after all): I will love you for as many years as I have left on this earth. It would take me that long to love you as well and as deeply as you deserve.

About the Author

Andrea Lochen dreamed of being an author since the third grade, but she didn't realize creative writing was an "actual thing" until she stumbled on the program as a college freshman. After graduating from college, she earned her Master of Fine Arts in creative writing from the University of Michigan and later achieved her dream of becoming a published author.

Andrea teaches creative writing, encouraging young writers to learn the craft and pursue their own writing dreams. She lives in Wisconsin with her husband, two small children, and their adorably fluffy dog, Maddy. In her free time, she likes to bake cupcakes and cakes, see musicals and plays, and read as much as humanly possible.

Read more at andrealochen.com.

About the Publisher

Dear Reader,

We hope you enjoyed this book. Please consider leaving a review on your favorite book site.

Visit https://RedAdeptPublishing.com to see our entire catalogue.

Don't forget to subscribe to our monthly newsletter to be notified of future releases and special sales.